THE BURNT CHILD

F.V. GEORGHIOU

THE BURNT CHILD

© Francesca Georghiou 2020
F.V Georghiou has asserted her rights under the Copyright, Design and Patents Act, 1988 to be identified as the author of this work.

THE BURNT CHILD

*For Peggy Georghiou,
the woman who believed I had a book in me.*

THE BURNT CHILD

A burnt child loves the fire
~Oscar Wilde~

ALEXANDRA

ISLAMABAD

We storm through the compound, heavily armed with a shoot to kill protocol. The sound of a helicopter whirs outside, the repetitive chuff of metal blades acting as our own personal timer. Our senses are isolated, closed to the outside world, our brains fine-tuned to the frequency of the operation ahead.

Simon Haines is at the front. I'm in the middle. Charles McGuire and Wayne Gibbs are on each side. We stalk ahead, carrying HK-53s, standard SAS rifles. Our fingers guard our triggers, ready to react. Haines and McGuire burst into another room, shouting instructions as we encounter multiple women pleading in Arabic. It bothered me at first, but you get used to it after countless ops. After shadowing an explosives technician in Damascus, I've seen what a desperate, pleading woman is capable of. We call out to each other as we assess the threat level and secure the nooks of the large living area, moving around the kneeling women. Haines instructs them to put their hands above their heads. They do as they're told, their suspicious eyes following our movements.

McGuire drops his rifle. 'No sign of target.' He chatters into the radio. 'Room at the end of the hall is the last one.'

We follow him in single file down the hallway, our boots creating synchronised treading sounds against the stone floor. He reaches the door and turns to Haines; Haines nods his head. McGuire uses the tip of the HK-53 to push the door slightly, taking a step forward. We brace to follow his lead, ready to secure the last room with distant shrieks and wailing protests from MI6 detained occupants.

McGuire throws up a fist: he wants us to wait. The target should be somewhere in this compound. We've searched every room and found nothing. This is the last. If he wants us to wait, it means he's seen something unexpected. If it's not the target, then MI6 has bogus intel. Adrenaline pumps through me, my pulse beating to the dull ticking of the helicopter as we stand obediently still, waiting, watching. McGuire peers through the small crack in the door, his body finally exhaling tension as he drops his gun and beckons us forward. Charging through the doorway, he begins the standard process, yelling in Arabic, shouting instructions. But something's off. I can hear it in his voice. This time, it's different. This time, his words aren't the same.

'Step away. Listen to me and step away. We are here now. You don't have to do this.'

I look to Gibbs, who shrugs. McGuire is repeating it. There's no sign of the usual, abrasive tone in his commands. He's trying to appear calm and controlled. He's attempting to reassure someone. I watch Gibbs file in after Haines. I'm the last to go, and finally, as I step through the doorway, I understand. Three young boys are in the middle of the room; not a single one wears any clothes. Their small, trembling bodies are kneeling in front of rows upon rows of dismantled IED equipment. They can't be more than eight years old; bare-skinned, dirty, their hair covered in dust, their lips dried and cracked, they stare up at us, confused and skittish. I drop the rifle, letting it hang across my shoulder, and take out the SIG strapped to the holster around my waist. I train my eyes down at scattered heaps of battery parts, wires, and metal scraps in front of the boys as McGuire describes our findings over comms. Evidence support needs to confirm, but we're all aware of what an explosive kit looks like. Haines crouches down, picking up bits of equipment as he starts questioning the tallest of the three. He asks his name. The boy tells him it's Abeer staring back with wide, startled eyes. Haines shifts position suddenly, and Abeer's hand twitches towards the machete at his bare feet. I step in and point my gun at him, instructing him to stay still, kicking the machete out the way. That's when I'm close enough to get a good look. That is when I finally take stock of the boy's appearance. Every limb: every arm, every leg, each side of his face is covered with burns; some old, some scarred and healed, others bold and standing out, red and blistered. He has one working eye; the other has been so badly burnt it has healed shut, and the skin around his eye socket fused in strange patterns. As we wait for the evidence team to arrive, I turn to the others, running my eyes over the smallest boy. He is missing his left ear and most of the hair on his left side. My eyes flit from one child to the next, each one showing more injuries than the last. Haines steps in; he's asking Abeer if he knows Abu Ahmed. That's the target. Abeer looks at me, his working eye quivering with fear as he starts shaking his head. He doesn't know, he says. He repeats this in broken English as the other two boys tremble beside him, their gaze fixed on Gibbs' weapon. Abeer begins to mumble in Arabic as he rocks on his feet. Haines repeats the question about Abu Ahmed. Abeer continues, and I tell Haines to back off and give him a moment; he's praying.

He scowls and steps back; he thinks I'm soft. We've seen our fair share of death out here, but this feels worse; this is indoctrination, abuse, and even torture. I could never admit that it bothers me; Haines would berate me and take great pleasure in it. He would say that we're soldiers; he'd tell me that death and tragedy are our currency. Honestly, I'm more than aware of what we've done. I've loaded enough bullets into bodies to understand what I am. But those targets understood the concept of consequence; these boys are children with no detailed understanding of what they're being asked to do.

Tired of waiting for the support team, McGuire stalks off to the back of the room. With a sudden urgency in his voice, he beckons me over. I look to Haines, who nods and steps in to take my place, shouting at the explosives team to get a move on. When I reach McGuire, I look up at the surrounding walls, noticing crumpled maps of Islamabad pinned up, with scribbled annotations and coordinates pencilled across them. McGuire's eyebrows shoot up to his hairline as he scans each one. Judging by this evidence, Imran Almasi might not be here now, but he was, and it appears he was planning a highly coordinated attack. Moving to the south side of the room, McGuire begins reading the blueprints of a hotel in Islamabad. It looks like the Marriott. Something catches his eye, and he hurriedly disappears behind a pile of dirty rugs as I hear him mumbling to comms, asking for urgent support. I swing the rifle into my hand as I move to join him, noting the concern in his voice as he repeats the request. I swallow past my instinctive fear, training the HK-53 in front of me, moving towards him cautiously until I reach the rugs and follow his eye line.

At first, it looks like a pile of washing in a neat row, a few clothes harmlessly put out to dry. And then my brain processes the full image. Vests. Three child-size vests have been laid out in an organised line, each of them rigged with countless explosives. Both of us take a synchronised step back before looking at each other.

Three vests, three children. They aren't making the bomb. They are one.

GABRIEL

CHAPTER ONE

My ears shudder from the shrill whining that fills the tiny room; I look around, disoriented as the previous night's memories flood in, assisted by the presence of the body splayed out next to me. I lean over the twentysomething, seemingly unfazed by the piercing sound as I hover over her, fumbling for the off button.

Who has an alarm clock anymore? Are millennials going backwards in time? The redhead, another nameless one-night stand with little significance, stirs next to me, shifting herself further up the bed before mumbling in her sleep. I freeze in the dark, barely allowing myself to blink as I will her to stay asleep. Hopefully, the previous night's exertions should be enough to keep her in a deep slumber, helping me avoid an unwanted conversation. My job usually provides a sure-fire excuse to make a quick exit if not. I could mumble the words casefile, operation, or emergency, as a speedy, no-questions-asked getaway. It was during Fresher's Year that I learned it's easier to get myself out of someone else's bedroom than it is to get them out of mine. Hence why sleepovers are prohibited at my place. I'd rather be the one escaping than spend the whole morning wishing they would fuck off.

I yawn, acknowledging how small this bed is for my six-foot-three frame, and suppress a groan as I swing my legs out, feeling a dull ache in my lower back. This is the downside of sleeping with strangers in your thirties; I don't know how I even did it in my twenties. Maybe I should start determining sleeping arrangements before making a committed decision, but probably a bit of a mood killer.

Having successfully dressed in near silence, despite stepping on Helen or Harriet's dreamcatcher twice, I make towards the door, destined for freedom.

'Don't fancy giving me a lift to the station, then Guv?' a small voice croaks behind me.

I freeze, mouthing a few *fucks*, grateful to the darkness of winter mornings for hiding my disappointment. 'Heading for a meeting. Didn't want to wake you,' I respond, barely trying to sound genuine.

'Bye then,' she turns away, pulling the covers over her naked body.

I don't bother replying as it takes me two strides to reach the front door. I start the trek back to my place, hoping to catch a twenty-minute power nap and a shower before I have to be at HQ. I call Julian to let him know I'll be a little later than expected, owing to unforeseen circumstances. Technically, the sexual advances from Hannah or Heather were moderately unforeseen, so it's not too far from the truth. After freshening up, I throw on jeans, a long-sleeve T-shirt, and boots before leaving the apartment and jumping in the car. Pulling out of the mews onto Upper Street, I make the journey to the National Crime Agency's HQ in Westminster. Tired of listening to a string of inane pop songs on Capital, I switch off the radio and continue the drive in silence. Anxiously tapping the steering wheel, I start to align the tasks for the day with nervous anticipation, acknowledging the sense that even my plates are spinning plates.

A thought that is all the more prevalent when I pull into the car park, instantly noticing Alison Collins, the NCA Director of Investigations, stood pacing. She catches sight of my car, and the disapproving expression etched in the tired lines of her gaunt face tells me all I need to know. It's going to be one hell of a day.

'Don't look so pleased to see me,' she says, pursing her thin lips.

'I'm just surprised you're greeting me at the front door.'

'I was looking for you.'

'Well, you found me.'

'We've got a meeting in five minutes.'

'I'm busy.'

'Ma'am.' She stops, raising her eyebrows like a disappointed headmistress. 'It's… I'm busy, Ma'am.'

I return her gaze with a blank stare.

'Meeting first. Then you can run off and do whatever you need to do.' She tries to pat me on the shoulder but on realising she can't reach, extends an arm to my lower back instead.

'Well, that wasn't patronising,' I mumble.

'Don't be late!' she calls out, the assertive stomp of her boots marching across the floor before disappearing into her office.

I sink into my chair and look around. Everyone seems to be engrossed in their own tasks. *Good news for me* – it reduces the likelihood of people approaching my desk with stupid questions before I've had caffeine.

Julian catches my eye with an expression of eagerness. 'You alright, Guv?'

'What have you got?' I nod to the files in his hands.

'Urm…' He looks down. 'An Albanian kid in custody is willing to flip on the Hellbanianz.' He licks the pad of his index finger before flicking through the pages.

'Where'd we pick him up?'

'Gascoigne Estate.'

Prime Albanian territory. 'Release him with a warning.'

'Really?' he looks puzzled.

'Aldyn Wolfe will kill him if we flip him.'

Julian nods and looks down at the next file. 'Border police have intercepted a shipment for the Turks in Harwich. Looks like a hell of a lot of cocaine.'

I pause, considering this. The Turkish mafia is a hot priority; any lead on their organised activity would be helpful. 'I'll take that one.'

'Speaking of the Turks, Nicky Black is in protective custody. I'm just waiting on some paperwork.'

'He's here now?'

'Yes, Guv.'

'Let's talk to him then…' I stand up, walking to the coffee machine.

'Collins said—'

'I know what she said, Jules, but it's taken weeks to get him in.'

He nods, suddenly reassured by my insistence. 'No, 'course, Guv. There's one more thing…' He lowers his voice as he steps closer. 'Your father was here this morning, talking to Collins.'

'Edward?'

'Yes, Guv.'

'Do you know why?'

'He was here in an official capacity.'

I nod and clear my throat, looking over his shoulder and into Collins' office. 'Cheers for the heads up.' I take the freshly filled coffee cup from the machine and take a sip. Julian stares at me with a questioning look. 'What?'

'I don't know how you drink that. It's like gravy.'

'I've had worse.' I flash a smirk, grateful he's decided not to push me further on my father's visit.

He chuckles and wanders back to his desk, shaking his head.

'James!' Collins bellows from the doorway of a meeting room, and I roll my eyes before turning and walking towards her.

As I enter, I notice the usual crowd of nerds and Junior Investigators are missing, save for Amber, a Senior Analyst, sitting between Collins and Julian.

'Where is everyone?'

Collins sighs before parting her hands and holding her palms out. 'This is it for the time being.'

'What are you talking about?'

'Well, if you sit down, I can give you an update.'

I huff, planting myself in the nearest chair.

'We've got to be sensible, Gabriel. You did a stellar job with the Christofi organisation, but we can't fund the same resources when the matter is largely dealt with.'

'Operation Sandbank is an ongoing case to tackle the big three. Toff was about to give us details on the Turkish operations.'

'That may be, but he's gone now, and until we have concrete evidence that there's ongoing activity, we need to scale back.'

'So, this is it? Amber and Julian? I get two people.'

'Gabriel, you've tackled one of the biggest crime families in the world. Take the win, have some downtime.'

'Ma'am, I don't think you're understanding—'

She takes a long calming breath, breaking into a condescending smile. 'For now, the Board is saying congratulations; you did well. And of course, all three of you, keep up the good work.'

'Funny timing, that's all.'

'Well, take some time to recuperate.'

I almost bite through my tongue, attempting to stay quiet while she continues to reel off bullshit textbook responses before swiftly leaving the room.

Julian exhales excessively like he'd been holding his breath for the entire meeting. 'What do we do now, Guv?'

'We interview Nicky Black.'

Amber's eyes light up. 'So, we're not giving this up?'

'No fucking way,' I say, standing. 'But whatever we get from Nicky, it stays between us three.'

'Understood.' She nods.

'Julian let's go. You're with me.'

CHAPTER TWO

Nicky Black, a short, plump man, sits in the bland, colourless interview room with his hands behind his head, his body shaking from the repetitive, tedious jerking of his knee under the table. I take a seat opposite him, ignoring the amusement stirring in his eyes.

'Did anyone ever tell you that you look like that actor Gabe?' He grins at Julian. 'You know the one I mean, don't you? The pretty boy?'

Julian affords Nicky a disapproving look before slapping the file down on the table and fiddling with the tape. '07.36 am, October 21st, for the benefit of the tape: officers present are Senior Investigating Officer and acting Team Lead Gabriel James and Investigating Officer Julian Sleet. Nicholas Black is here as a material witness. The purpose of today is for Nicholas Black to voluntarily supply the NCA with relevant information on illegal activity within Organised Crime Groups.'

Sweat begins to form over Nicky's brow as he nervously picks the skin on his fingers, waiting for Julian to finish. I lean over the table, inches from his pockmarked face and gesture towards the recorder. 'Make sure you speak up for the tape, Nicky boy.'

He clears his throat, aggressively hurling phlegm from his chest before speaking. 'What guarantee do I have?' he pauses before his tongue darts out and licks the sweat from his upper lip. '...that I won't get killed doing this?'

I sit back, observing him with puzzled curiosity. 'Haven't you been snitching for years?'

'The Turks are paranoid; Paytak could have had me followed.'

'It's entirely possible.'

His eyes widen, 'I'm not saying anything today. You just said I had to sign something.'

'Surely Paytak's nowhere near as paranoid as Toff.'
'He's the Head of the Turkish mafia; what do you think?'
'So, tell us…' Julian interjects.
'Do you know how much shit I'd be in?' His knee starts up again.
'It's alright,' I interrupt. 'He doesn't have to give us anything.'
Relief floods Nicky's face, and his posture sags, his shoulders rounding over his round stomach.
'Be sure to let us know whether you want to be cremated or buried...'
He snaps his head up, confused by the abrupt gear switch.
'Without helping us, without our protection, that's the only way you're getting out of any of this, isn't it?'
His eyes dart between us. 'I'm going to end up like Toff either way, so it doesn't fucking matter, does it?'
Julian opens the file, showing his eagerness to press on. 'Tell us what you know, and we'll see what we can do.'
Ignoring Julian's instructions, Nicky stares ahead for a moment, weighing up his options, the cogs grinding slowly in his vacant brain.
'I don't know much.' He scratches the back of his head. 'Paytak is using this online chat. Something on the dark web. The Turks are stepping into new territory. Stuff that Toff would never allow.'
'Be more specific.'
He sniffs a long drawn out grunt, making me wonder if his earnings have gone full circle and straight up his nose. 'The Turks have taken over the Ports; they're working with someone new; someone that gave them access to the chat and all other kinds of resources.'
'Hellbanianz?'
'Nah, Aldyn was loyal to Toff; he wouldn't help them.'
'A new cartel?'

'This is different. It's not mafia or cartels.'
'What is it?' Julian presses.
He shrugs. 'It's like an organisation.'
'Who's in it, Nicky?'
'Paytak won't say, but they're nothing like Toff. They're not working the system or making deals.'

Toff, otherwise known as Mario Christofi, had been the most successful gangster in London for many years. He was ruthless but a brilliant businessman; he worked out people's pain points, exploited their weaknesses and turned it to his advantage. He was the only gangster to forge strong working relationships with criminals and law enforcement in the same breath. Nobody fucked with him, he was merciless, but he had a code.

'Why would this new group choose the Turks? Everyone knows the Greeks have the best connections,' Julian asks, making notes.

'The Greeks are finished. And like I said, Mario Christofi would never have agreed to any of this.'

'Tell us about the organisation.'

'Only a heard a couple of things,' he flashes an ugly smile, smug that he's holding all the cards.

'Go on…'

He shrugs. 'And I can't guarantee it's real.'

'Just give us what you know,' I bark.

'Higgs.' He raises his eyebrows. 'Some bloke called Higgs who heads up a new group… like I said, it all sounds a bit made up.'

'The group…' Julian presses.

'The Singularity. That's what Paytak calls them.' He scoffs. 'I know it's a fucking stupid name.'

'What are they doing with the Turks?' Julian taps his pen on the folder, his own patience wearing thin.

Nicky closes his mouth in a sharp line.

'What does Higgs want the Turks to do Nicky?' I push, sensing he's shutting down.

'I don't know.'

'Don't bullshit me—'

'Where do you fit into all of this Nicky?' Julian asks. 'You used to roll with Toff, but now you're with the Turks? Isn't that a bit risky?'

His beady eyes slide from side to side. 'Paytak wants followers; he doesn't give a fuck.'

'You still haven't told us what he's doing,' Julian pushes.

He looks down at the tabletop. 'They got me as a runner, helping out here and there.'

'Nicky, if you don't start talking, this deal is off.'

His nostrils flare under the heat of my stare, his wild eyes search the room, glancing towards the blacked-out windowpane. 'It's trafficking. They're trafficking in and out of the country.'

'Drug trafficking?'

'Human.'

The word is inserted into the air quickly, causing my body to tense. I recall memories of trafficking cases throughout my time at the NCA. Human trafficking, for whatever purpose, is, hands down, one of the most hateful, cruel, and despicable acts one person could inflict on another. I've witnessed first-hand the evil, animalistic exploitation of under-privileged, vulnerable men, women, children; of all ages, of all nationalities, and unfortunately, it goes hand-in-hand with organised crime. The thought of a new group injecting resources into this specifically pricks at my senses. I'm reminded of the endless missing-child cases that land on my desk with evidence that points to abduction for modern-day slavery and forced prostitution. It's part of the sick, twisted underbelly of crime in this country, and if it were up to me, every single person involved would suffer an excruciating end.

'What are they doing with the victims?'

'I don't know.'

'Could you venture a fucking guess?' I move my hands off the table, removing the temptation to throttle him.

'Probably for sex, but it's not just women, it's men too… and they're all young.'

Julian's body stiffens.

I sit back in my chair, my eyes scorching into Nicky's, afraid to open my mouth for fear of what might come out.

'Where does this happen, Nicky?' Julian asks.

He shakes his head.

'When did this start?'

He looks down, unable to bear the disdain emanating from our side of the room.

'You're a fucking disgrace,' I spit.

'So, this Higgs bloke comes along, the Turks join his organisation, and they're trafficking for him, is that it?' Julian asks.

'Paytak dabbled a bit before. The Singularity has paid him to step it up.'

'Have you met any other members of this new group?'

He shakes his head.

'Have you had any contact with Higgs?'

He continues shaking his head.

'For the benefit of the tape, Mr Black is shaking his head,' I shout over him, making a point.

'Do you have any evidence Higgs exists?' Julian questions.

'Paytak does.'

I sigh and close my eyes, becoming bored with his relentless stupidity. 'Find out which ports they're using, and I want evidence of this new group.'

He nods slowly before hanging his head down, this time having the decency to look ashamed.

'Right…' Julian takes a heavy breath and shuffles some paper before continuing. 'Details of an undisclosed location will be sent via text. You'll convene with an NCA Investigating Officer at a given date and time where you will be required to share relevant intel. Do you understand?'

He continues looking down, bringing his thick, grubby fingers back towards the corners of his mouth, once again plucking at the loose skin. I grimace at the sight of him, noticing beads of sweat collecting in his hairline, indicating that he's overly stressed from merely having to use his brain.

I allow a minute to pass before my patience cracks. 'Do you understand Nicholas?' I raise my voice, repeating Julian's words.

Julian leans forward and speaks in a low tone, 'You're a criminal, Nicky. We have all the evidence we need to put you away, and it won't be a jolly old trip to Center Parcs. If the information you give us checks out, we can protect you.'

Nicky fidgets before he eventually nods.

'For the benefit of the tape… Mr Black is nodding his head.' Julian announces.

'Well, we're getting somewhere now, aren't we?' I flash him a wide grin, watching his face turn an unhealthy grey.

A muffled knock on the door interrupts us. Julian pauses the tape, calling out for the person to enter. Nicky instantly panics at our willingness to let a third party see his presence.

Amber pokes her head in the door and clears her throat, her eyes flitting to Nicky before offering an apologetic look. 'Sorry Guv, I have an urgent message from a DI Stanley?'

'Who?' I stare up at her before looking back to Julian, who curls his bottom lip and twitches one shoulder to his ear.

Amber's eyes shift back to Nicky nervously before settling on me again.

'Can you tell them I'll call back?'

She pauses for a moment, her eyes weighing up the consequences of pressing me further. 'Of course,' she nods and politely closes the door.

Nicky frowns, disbelieving. 'You really just going to let people see me like that?'

'Not everything is about you, Nicholas,' I goad, placing my hands in my pockets and leaning back in the chair. 'Where were we?'

CHAPTER THREE

The pub is loud, bulging with irritating, hedonistic murmurings, even for a Thursday lunchtime. I thank the barmaid and turn, holding a drink above my head, trying to shift through the assembled groups of suits before finding Julian sitting at the table by the fireplace. He takes slow, measured sips from his pint of Guinness, staring out at the Thames, his face displeased as if he's drinking the river water.

'Can you believe they found a whale out there once?'

'I presume it choked to death on all the used condoms,' I say as I look over my shoulder, feeling on edge with the thought of having my back to a crowded room.

It's become a habit over the years, the need to face the source of noise and activity in a social situation. Most people assume it's because I find them uninteresting, and it's got me in a lot of trouble before. One of the main problems, when I'm with Julian, is that he suffers the same subsequent need to have an exit in his eye line, which means we have one of two options: either we sit next to each other like we're on a panel of judges, or one of us draws the short straw. I take a gulp of my soda and lime, blocking out the drunken enthusiasm behind me.

'How long has it been?' he gestures towards my non-alcoholic beverage.

'About a year now.'

He smiles. 'Do you miss it?'

'Like a limb, but I guess it's easier to manage when you don't have a personal life.'

'It doesn't seem like you're lonely Guv, let's put it that way.'

'Yeah, well, I've had to tone that down recently...'

He arches a questioning brow.

'Women tend to make me want to drink,' I clarify.

He blows air through his cheeks. 'Tell me about it.' He takes another sip of his drink before frowning. 'What about Heather, though, Guv?'

'Casual,' I reply, slightly uncomfortable that we're taking a leap down this rabbit hole.

'Good luck telling that to her.' He smiles, his eyes lighting up with humour. 'Remember she nearly tasered that bloke for kissing someone else at Amber's engagement party.'

'Yeah, she's... excitable.' I answer back, smirking.

His eyes widen. 'Yeah, alright, I don't need details.'

'She's alright,' I add, trying not to admit that I find her useful for blowing off steam, and that's as far as it will ever go.

'When do you think you'll settle down then, Guv? You're pushing on quite a bit...'

I laugh and shake my head. 'You know you're older than me, don't you?'

'Only by a few years.'

'I don't know... relationships aren't my thing.'

'You've never had a long-term relationship?'

I exhale, wanting to move past this topic quickly. 'I did once, it didn't work out, and I realised it wasn't for me. Being on my own is... simpler.'

'Well yeah, I don't blame you. If Amelie is anything to go by.'

The mention of her name nearly causes me to choke on my drink, making me wish it were eighty per cent vodka as I recall the Amelie rollercoaster. Being twenty-five, unstable, and possibly the most attractive woman I've ever met, I allowed her to cross boundaries in and out of the bedroom, all the while knowing I didn't want anything long-term; mixing that with her erratic personality resulted in the need to transfer her to a separate department altogether.

'When was the last time you did something that didn't involve the case?' I ask, changing the subject.

'I call my wife daily to tell her I'm going to be late for dinner.'

I laugh. 'Ah shit, sorry, that's my fault…'

'She's a nurse, so she gets it.'

I mumble something in agreement, and Julian looks away, pensive. 'Do you ever feel like you're just shovelling shit up a hill, Guv?'

'How'd you mean?'

'First Toff, now we're onto this new group.'

'That's the job, I guess.'

'It bugs me that we cut off one head for an uglier fucker to grow back in its place.'

'We're not going to change the world, Jules. We're just trying to plug the holes.'

'You reckon Nicky is right?'

I look up, waiting for him to clarify.

'Are the Turks in bed with some nasty people?'

'Probably yeah.'

'Poor Toff.'

'Look, it happens,' I shrug. 'We lose people.'

'It's just too convenient, you know?' he leans in, dipping his head. 'He's about to tell us everything, give us the inside scoop to how it all works and then he's murdered.'

'From now on, mate, anything relating to Sandbank stays between you, Amber and me until we have the evidence to take it further.'

'How long do you think they'll let us investigate this for?'

'Not long; they're already phasing it out. This is what happens; they lose interest. We'll be back to hassling Aldyn Wolfe next.'

He nods, seemingly satisfied. 'Do you ever think about him?'

'Toff? He was a sixty-year-old Gangster... not really my type.'
We both laugh, but there's an unease in the air.

'I just mean, you know.' He continues. 'He was a likeable guy.' His eyes search my face with an energy that sets me on edge. 'He did his bit in the end.'

'The Christofis are a crime family. He knew he was on borrowed time,' I shrug, avoiding eye contact as the barmaid comes over to collect Julian's empty pint glass.

I stand and down the last of my drink, taking that as my cue to leave. Julian throws me a questioning look. I hesitate and tell him I've got somewhere to be. He thinks about this for a second and nods, used to my ambiguous routine.

'You know, Guv, it's alright to admit he was a friend...'

I stop, my movements slowing.

'He was a slippery son of a bitch, but he wasn't all bad.'

He waits for a response, but I mumble a quick goodbye before turning for the door and stepping into the crisp autumn air, finally breathing a burdened sigh of relief. I don't want to transfer Julian to a different team, but a cocktail of suspicion and paranoia is forming like a fog in my head. I storm across the road to my car, my breath coming out in sharp spurts. I respect him, he's great at his job, not to mention a good person, but that is precisely why he can never be involved. *It was a decision I made. It's my burden to bear.* I sit behind the wheel, rubbing my hands through my hair, weighing up his reaction to the truth and the consequences to his life.

Just as I'm about to pull out onto the High Street, my phone buzzes and I groan as Julian's name appears on the hands-free.

'What is it?'

'We need you back at HQ.' His voice sounds unsteady.

'What's happened?'

'You won't believe it, Guv.'

'What?' I snap.
'We were just—' he sighs, stopping himself. 'His daughter…'
'What?'
'Toff's eldest. You know his daughter… the soldier.'
My blood runs cold. 'What about her?'
'She's missing.'
'Be there in five.' I say urgently before hanging up.

I storm through the NCA's thrum of activity, a busy tapping of keyboards amongst a vast sea of noise and chatter. Julian waits at the entrance to the board room, beckoning me over.
'What do we know?' I ask.
'Apparently, she didn't show for a family meal last night.'
'She's only been missing a few hours?'
'She was last seen by a family friend yesterday afternoon, so it could be that she's been gone twenty-four hours.'
'What is it?' I snap, noticing his hesitation.
'She's ex-military, Guv. She was in the army for two years and got recruited straight into the Special Forces.'
'I'm aware of her record, Jules. We checked her out during the Sandbank preliminary.'
'Well, maybe she's on leave again?'
'Her contract is up,' I murmur, fiddling with an iPad, trying to find her new home address.
'Oh, right.'
'Have we spoken to the family direct?'
'Uniform visited them this morning.' He takes a seat opposite me. 'There was also something else I wanted to ask—'
'We need to interview them,' I say, cutting him off. Taking the pencil out from behind my ear, I note down Alexandra's address, pausing when I realise how close it is to my own.

Julian watches me with a troubled expression.

'Reach out to Nicky, set up a meet. Let's find out what he knows,' I ask, avoiding his gaze. 'Let's check out her place. This could be panic over nothing.'

'Guv...'

'Get Amber to do a full background check on Alexandra.' Julian nods, urgently taking notes. 'The Turks and The Singularity are our main line of enquiry until we know otherwise, understood?'

He shifts uncomfortably in his seat. 'Guv, don't you—'

'What?' I look up impatiently.

'Well, it's just... Should you be on this?'

'What are you talking about?' I glare at him.

'I checked her background. Don't you know her?'

'Because we went to the same Uni?' I throw out the words casually, feigning disinterest. *It's the truth and a well-practised admission.*

'Oh.' His gaze darts from left to right. 'I won't mention it to Collins.'

'Jules... hundreds of people went to Uni together. There's nothing to tell.'

'Understood.'

I turn away, trying to conceal the strain of concern on my face. When I was assigned lead SIO of Operation Sandbank, I made an informed decision to withhold my history with Mario Christofi's daughter, citing it as irrelevant. My involvement with her was nothing more than a young, meaningless fling nearly a decade ago. I've sacrificed a lot to get to where I am, family, friends, relationships. I've earned this position through hours of blood, sweat and tears. A minor complication wasn't going to stop me from taking on such a high-profile case, the NCA's biggest one in years. And since it started, I've worked tirelessly to put my background with Alexandra Christofi to one side, forcing myself to focus on the bigger picture. *Our past needn't get in the way of our future.* But as I sit here with my mind racing, my heart rate kicking up several gears, the sweat on my palms seeming to draw all moisture from my mouth. It finally dawns on me; how fucking stupid I've been.

CHAPTER FOUR

Julian pulls up outside Alexandra's first floor flat on Essex Road. I step out of the car, taking in the sudden influx of juice bars, vegan cafes, and organic supermarkets. Islington's gentrification has been coming for a long time, but only in the last few years has this extended beyond my Upper Street neighbourhood. The Old Queen's Head catches my eye, and I think of the countless times I've been in there over the years or, more appropriately, been thrown out. I can see why she'd want to live here; it's on the main road, well-lit, there are bars and pubs everywhere, and it's busy. Always someone around.

Olivia Christofi is standing by the gates of a small mews; she's taller than I imagined, with long, sleek limbs. She watches us cross the road, analysing our movements with sharp intensity. She looks so much like Mario that I almost stop in my tracks; the same thick dark hair, tanned complexion, and pronounced cheekbones. As we near, I note the dark circles twinned with the deep red of her eyelids. Seems like distress initially; understandably upset that her sister is missing. But it's her pupils; they're the true giveaway. And I've seen enough addicts in my time to know what withdrawal looks like.

'Ms. Christofi, I'm Investigating Officer Julian Sleet. This is Senior Investigating Officer Gabriel James.'

She looks me up and down, her mind processing the information before she mutters for us to follow her inside. Being in Alexandra's world again is a strange, unexplainable feeling. I feel I'm in close proximity to her without the effects of having her physically present. One way or another, she's ever present. Olivia observes us as we survey the space, trailing our eyes up to the high ceilings, listening to the buzz of activity beyond the large open windows. The flat has a warmth about it, and I wonder how much effort went into making it look lived-in, given that she only moved to London a few days ago.

'So, if you're here, Detective James…' Olivia says, wandering over to the sofa and switching off the TV above the fireplace. 'You must think her disappearance is connected to Mario?'

Julian hesitates. 'There could be a connection, Olivia. We would need to rule that out.'

'I think finding her is the main priority, don't you?'

'We know the background here. We know the family history, but make no mistake, we're here to find your sister.' I interject, wanting to cut through her superior tone.

'But her surname means she doesn't get a proper investigator – one that knows how to find missing people.'

'I know how to find all kinds of people.' I retort.

Julian frowns at me before continuing, 'Olivia, it's very likely that this is connected to an ongoing investigation.'

'Or someone just wants your family to pay for all the unspeakable things they did over the years…' I murmur, scanning the room.

Julian turns to me again, not bothering to hide his disapproval. 'Either way, we're concerned for her safety, we're highly experienced in these matters, and we want to find her.'

She scoffs. 'Well, your willingness is most appreciated.'

'Do you live here too, Olivia?' I ask.

'I live with our grandmother in Mario's house.'

'This is a nice place.'

'Yeah, I guess.'

'Why don't I go and put the kettle on?' Julian suggests warmly. 'We can sit around the table and go through a few things.'

She pauses for a time before nodding and gesturing to the kitchen; Julian smiles politely before disappearing through the door in the corner. Without another word, Olivia slowly ambles over to the oak dining table and sits down on one of the leather chairs, crossing her legs. She remains silent as I slowly wander around the living room, looking at books and novels piled into neat lines. Alexandra studied History and Modern languages, to which, if I didn't know already, her bookshelf is a dead giveaway. I stop at the end, noticing a stack of leather journals piled on top of the last few spines.

'I should tell you not to touch those.'

I turn over my shoulder. 'She keeps a diary?'

'It's a therapy thing,' she dismisses, waving her hand in the air. 'Something to help with the PTSD.'

'Does she suffer badly?'

'Yep.'

'What makes you say that?'

'Since Lexy came back from her last tour, she's had a hard time sleeping.'

'How so?'

'Hallucinations, sleepwalking, screaming in the middle of the night.'

'Have you met some of the people she served with?'

'No.' she replies quickly.

Julian carefully pushes through the door with three steaming-hot mugs. He treads cautiously towards the dining-room table before setting them down. I reach the table and join them, feeling Olivia's eyes burn into me.

'What made your sister join the army?'

'She's always wanted to be different, I guess.'

'How do you mean?'

'She's the golden child…. Cambridge, Sandhurst, the Army, the S.A.S. Hardly the CV of a gangster's daughter.' She smiles.

'When was the last time you saw your sister?'

'Yesterday. She popped round to my grandmother's, and then she left to see someone.' She fidgets on the chair before clarifying: 'Paul Theo. He was Mario's business partner.'

'How did she seem?'

'A bit quiet, I guess.'

'Has she been seeing anyone since she got back?'

'You mean like a therapist?'

I nod.

'Not anymore.'

I lean over to Julian. 'Check which therapists she saw. I'm sure the Army provides a list.' He nods quickly before we both look back to Olivia. 'Do you think it's possible something happened during her visit with Paul?'

'Well, she wouldn't have just left London.'

I look down at the file in front of me, pretending to read something. 'You were kidnapped once, correct?'

She clears her throat. 'Yes.'

'By a rival mafia gang?'

'That's what the police thought, but there was never any evidence. I was too small to know who exactly.'

I look down at the file. 'You were fourteen?'

'Mhmm...I blocked a lot of it from memory.'

'Your father never discussed it with you?'

She shakes her head.

'He paid a considerable sum of money to get you back.'

She stares at me blankly. 'A child should never discover their monetary value.'

'Do you think it's possible they took your sister?'

'I couldn't say, but there doesn't appear to have been a struggle.'

'No, there doesn't,' I say, observing her closely, waiting for a sign that indicates she knows more than she's letting on. 'Does the name Higgs mean anything to you?'

She begins shaking her head. 'No.'

'How about The Singularity?'

'Nope.'

'Heard anything from a man named Diren Paytak?'

'What is the point in all these questions?'

'Did Alexandra mention coming back to London to take over from your father?'

'Well, she was kicked out of the Army, wasn't she? We all just assumed…'

'Do you think it's possible somebody took her to prevent her from that?'

'From what?'

'Taking over.'

'I couldn't say.'

'Going back to Sandhurst,' Julian cuts in, reading from a file. 'Your sister only recently started her new job there, correct?'

Olivia nods.

'Why did she leave?'

'I don't know, but I doubt she'd go back.'

'Why not?' I sit forward. 'Why wouldn't she go back to Sandhurst, Olivia?'

There's a pause as she thinks about her next words.

'She wanted out of military life.'

'Did she mention any specific concerns?' Julian asks.

'Look, we're not that close. She doesn't tell me anything.'

'Is it possible she's gone to stay with friends?'

She scoffs as if the mere notion is ridiculous.

'A boyfriend?'

'Not anymore.'

I raise my eyebrows and note *boyfriend* in block capitals with a question mark. 'Since your father's death, have you heard from the people that worked for him?'

Her shoulders visibly tense. 'Why would I?'

'Have you received any threats?'

'No.'

'Olivia, I'm going to be straight with you now.'

'Ok…'

'You've been taken and used as leverage before, so you know how this works…I take it your father had someone who used to watch over you and your sister?'

She hesitates, gauging my motive.

'You might want to reach out to them.' I look at Julian, who seems flustered. 'I think we're done here.' I say, standing up.

'So, that's it?' she asks as we walk towards the door.

Julian turns, looking at me for reassurance.

'Yeah—' I freeze suddenly, looking back into the apartment. 'Can I take a look in her room?'

'Erm…' she wavers. 'I guess?'

'Guv, shall I…?' Julian hesitates.

'I'll just be a minute.'

I squint as the sun beams through the bedroom window, bouncing off Alexandra's white bedsheets. Her double bed sits in the centre of the room, with two small tables on either side. I wasn't sure how much she might have changed over the years, but it's almost the same as her room in Cambridge. Even the fresh smell of laundry elicits memories of us propped against her postered wall, talking for hours on end. The only dark object in the room catches my eye, and I reach down to pick up the leather journal tucked between two pillows. I briefly fan the pages of her scribbled reflections, checking it's what I think it is before slipping it into the inside of my jacket. I glance around, struggling to curate an accurate profile of her life: an ex-soldier living in an expensive Central London flat decorated with thousands of pounds worth of furnishings. It's not your typical situation. I stoop to look at a few framed pictures positioned on either side of the mirror. In the first, Toff looks back at me, grinning from ear-to-ear, his arm wrapped around his daughter's shoulders. They stand in front of a helicopter at an army base somewhere. Alexandra is in military attire; a khaki T-Shirt tucked into cargo trousers. I pick up the frame, taken in by her striking face. Her wide hazel eyes stare back at me, framed by a mane of wild, fair hair. She still has that same gaze with the same soulful glint. A face I've worked hard to erase from memory. A smile I've looked for in every woman since. Suddenly realising my mind is drifting, I straighten, scanning the bedroom once more before swiftly heading back to the living room. Julian is standing alone, shaking his head.

I look around. 'Where'd she go?'

'She got a call and left; said we could see ourselves out.'

'Strange...' I mutter, following him out.

'I think she's trying to keep a brave face.'

'No, I think it's strange she lied.'

'How do you mean?'

'Toff made sure those girls knew who his enemies were. I'm certain she knows exactly who took her back in the day.' I reflect as we descend the stairs and step outside. 'Not to mention...' I turn whilst we wait to cross the road. 'We explained that her sister might have been targeted by someone who wants to stop another Christofi from taking over.'

'Yeah...' Julian nods his head slowly, looking at the pavement.

'And she didn't once ask if they might also come for her.'

CHAPTER FIVE

The following day, I call Julian just before he reaches Paul Theo's office. He tells me Nicky Black is conveniently AWOL, and he's still waiting for Amber to run further background checks on all Christofi associates. I patiently listen, desperate to ask what the fuck they've been doing all this time, but it doesn't stop me from calling Amber directly.

'Sorry, Guv, I was off this morning… I had to take Graham to the hospital. I'm running checks on Paul. As soon as I have something, I'll let you know.'

'Everything alright?' I ask, pacing the hallway.

She hesitates on the line. 'Yeah, all good… it's nothing really.'

'Great.' I move on, not really listening. 'Can you put out an alert for Diren Paytak, please? No arrest, just want to know where he is.'

'Yep… Oh, and Guv?! That DI Stanley is still looking for you.'

'Ah shit.'

'I told her to leave you another voicemail, but she's pretty pushy.'

'Alright, thanks, I'll speak to her.'

I hang up the phone and look down at the journal in my left hand. All thoughts of DI Stanley instantly pushed to the back of my mind. I started reading last night to better understand who she is today, but it's only served to muddy the waters. There are glimpses of the girl I used to know, but mainly, it documents her experiences in the forces. There's no way she was allowed to write this down at the time. These are the experiences that have stuck with her since.

In the trucker, before bed, even when sitting next to his sniper rifle, Gibbs always had a Dr Pepper. It's his drink, and I'll never be able to look at one of those bloody cans without thinking of him. Rhiannon, too. I know I will never escape the guilt. I know we should have stayed and gone back for them. Simon says we were just following orders, but, in my eyes, we betrayed them. That decision will haunt me for the rest of my life.

I stare at the words, wondering what she did. *What orders did she follow?* I turn the pages back, looking for an indication as to where she was at the time, but there's no mention of location or even the operation's name. She briefly mentions receiving medals for bravery but never once references what they were for. She describes her tour in a very matter-of-fact, detached way. Clearly, death became a large part of her life, and she treats it as such. She writes about roadblocks, artillery attacks, and ambushes as if describing a train's persistent late arrival. And then there are words written by the old Lex, where she describes the loss of her father. I try to skim them, but my mind lingers, rereading every sentence, her pain etched into my brain. I can't help but feel responsible - she isn't healing, not even close. My phone rings suddenly, and my attention jerks from the page. Grateful for the interruption, I close the journal.

'Yep...'

'Paul's story is the same,' Julian informs. 'She left his office at three-thirty.'

'Is he telling the truth?'

'He's a flash, arrogant prick, but he seemed genuine.'

'Has he heard of The Singularity?'

'It's never come up before.'

'So he says...' I mutter under my breath. 'And no threats to him or the family recently?'

'He says it's been understandably quiet since Toff died.'

I mumble something in agreement, searching for my car keys. 'I'll catch up with you later.'

'Won't I see you at the station?'

'Going to see a man about a dog.' I reply quickly before hanging up the phone, trying to avoid any more prying questions.

CHAPTER SIX

I step out of the car and turn over my shoulder, checking the area before striding down the narrow road that travels through the village of Clifton Hampden. It's quiet, the very antithesis of London, but I've always liked it here. With tiny thatches cottages set back from the banks of the Thames, it holds a peacefulness that's often hard to come by. I reach a long set of crooked steps and crane my neck at the gothic church on the hill. Taking a breath, I begin to climb, ascending them two at a time, gathering the right words in my head, rehearsing my delivery. Finally, I cross a patch of uneven grass and weave between a collection of neglected headstones. *Clearly, nobody visits.* I stop at the entrance, giving myself a minute to summon the energy. My surroundings darken, clouds move in above, creating a thick heaviness in the air. It's fitting, the weather mirroring the turmoil in my head. I take a long, deep inhale. *Let's just get this over with*

After sitting in a pew staring at a sad-looking Jesus for what feels like hours, I finally hear the slow whine of the church door grinding against stone, followed by determined footsteps filling the abandoned space. I stare ahead until the sound halts, and Mario Christofi sits down next to me. Undoing his expensive jacket, he rests back on the wooden bench.

I lean forward, turning so my eyes meet his. He shakes his head before a smile threatens the corner of his lips. He looks younger somehow, his peppered grey hair slightly shorter, appearing more striking against his Greek complexion. Despite retiring with no legitimate source of income, he's expensively dressed. His clothes are thrown together with an overwhelming amount of cologne – a smell I have never been able to disassociate from him.

'Gabe…'
'How are you doing, Toff? It's been a while.'

There's a warmth in his eyes before he slaps me on the back affectionately. The exchange almost resembles that of a father and son, which somehow makes this all the more difficult.

'This is a surprise,' he adds, eyeing me carefully.

I look down at my intertwined hands. 'Yeah, this isn't a social call, I'm afraid.'

'I guessed.'

I stare ahead, mentally pleading with him to hold it together before I've even said the words. 'Alexandra is missing.'

Blood drains from his face. His mouth parts in shock; he stares at me for a minute before his brain kicks into life. Toff is a very intelligent man, but sometimes it's a hindrance. Instead of believing me immediately, he's searching my face for a *tell* trying to deduce my motive for manufacturing a lie. His face tenses, his mind working to assess the agenda, trying to formulate any possible reasons as to why I'd use his daughter against him. It's a habit of being in the game for so long. He's so far gone that when something is given to him straight, he can't take it at face value. Here is a man ruined by his trade. But despite having the ruthless, brutal mentality of a gangster, I know he loves Alexandra more than anything in the world.

'Did you hear me?' I ask, lowering my voice.

He shakes his head. 'She can't be fucking missing. She's away… she's away all the time.'

'She moved back to London a few days ago.'

He stands abruptly, beginning to pace. 'She's always in and out of the country, Gabe. It's her job.'

'Her passport is at the apartment.'

'Who would dare!?'

'Nicky Black mentioned something to me yesterday… Something about the Turks working with an organisation called The Singularity.'

'I've heard rumours.' He waves a dismissive hand.

'They supplied the Turks with someone to take you out. Ever heard of a man named Higgs?'

'Higgs…Is he IRA? Who the fuck is he?' Echoes of his frustration rebound off the walls.

'Well, according to Nicky, the Turks have moved in on the Borders; they're manipulating the entire system.'

He stares at me blankly.

'If they hired someone to get rid of you, then it's possible they took Alexandra for the same reason.'

'I'll kill Paytak if he's laid a finger on her.'

'I've got people looking for him.'

'I knew one day it would be that bastard.' He huffs.

I stand. 'Where are you going?'

'What if Paytak knows I'm alive?' He stops, his expression frantic. 'What if he's taken her as leverage?'

'If he knew you were alive, he would come for you straight away.' I meet his stare, trying my best to believe my own logic.

He looks at the floor.

'Why would Paytak see Alexandra as a threat? Is it possible he thought she would take over?'

'I pushed her towards the S.A.S because I wanted her to be the best.'

'Could it be Paul?' I ask, keen to keep him on track, distracting him from falling into a pit of his own wrath.

'He wouldn't dream of it.'

'We're looking into him anyway.'

Moments pass, and I can almost hear the whirring of his mind, crossing enemies off the list, running through lists of associates.

'How long has she been gone?'

'Nearly forty-eight hours,' I admit cautiously.

'She's been missing all that fucking time, and you're only here now?' he storms towards me with an accusing finger.

'I can't just come running off to the countryside whenever I feel like it.'

'If there was ever a reason for me to come back...'

'Out of the fucking question.' Now it's my turn to raise my voice. 'We would both be sent to prison, and no one else has a chance of finding her.'

He snaps his head around, taken off guard by the confrontation.

'I know the history.'

He nods his head slowly, absorbing the legitimacy of my words. 'After Olivia, I told them both...' he sighs. 'I made sure they could never be caught off guard again. I wanted Lexy to be ready for anything, knowing she might have to endure the worst consequences of my choices.'

'... you were protecting her.'

'I was preparing her,' he clarifies. 'What about Olivia? Is she safe?'

'Uniform are keeping an eye on her.'

He mulls a thought. 'It wouldn't have been easy to take Lexy, Gabe.'

'I know...'

'I should never have let you talk me into running.'

'It was either that or let you die,' I state bluntly. 'Mario, I've got my best people on this.'

He exhales sharply before looking up to the ceiling. He knows I will find her by any means, and he knows he can't go back. The Turks will hunt him the minute they find out, and I need him alive. His knowledge of this world is seemingly endless. He's helped us get the inside track on organised crime for months; how to find multiple distributors, locations of drug drops, contacts of others willing to give up intel in exchange for leniency on their crimes. But admittedly, there's something else. Over the years of going after him, negotiating his surrender, and ultimately making him an ally, he's become a friend and more like a father to me than my own ever was. For that reason alone, I could never let him return to London.

He steps in, 'You've got twenty-four hours to come up with something. After that, I'm taking this shit into my own hands.'

I don't bother looking at his face, I'm certain his eyes are burning into mine. If I don't come up with something soon, he won't stay put. Without another word, I nod and turn towards the door, saying a silent prayer to *sad Jesus* that I'll swiftly be able to deliver answers.

CHAPTER SEVEN

Given that the Turkish Mafia were tipped for the attempt on Toff's life, I make it likely that they've taken Lex. Locating them is a different matter. I was reluctant to go into detail in the church for obvious reasons, but if Diren Paytak took her, it's not for leverage, especially if he thinks Toff is dead and buried. The prospect of finding her body in a ditch somewhere makes me feel sick to my stomach. *How have we ended up here?* This isn't how her life was meant to be. Part of me hopes this is a mistake, that she's been recruited for an operation, given a new identity with separate passports. But there's no evidence she even headed towards an airport. Amber checked her records; they're sealed, of course, but they do have to give an end date to contracts, and that clearly states that she left the S.A.S. I scroll through my phone, needing to run some of these theories by Julian, when an unknown number suddenly flashes across the screen. I curse as I try to operate the hands-free, accidentally clicking accept.

'James,' I murmur through gritted teeth, mouthing *fuck* at my own incompetence.

'SIO James. DI Stanley from Major Investigations.'

'Yeah?'

'I've been urgently trying to get hold of you.'

'What do you need?' I ask, pulling out onto the main road.

'I have information that might be of interest to your case.'

'Which one …?'

'Sandbank.'

I sit up straight in my seat, my interest piqued. 'Go on…'

'My department has been investigating the disappearance of Kristine Kingley.'

'Right...'

'The minister from the Home Office.'

'I'm familiar.' There's a long pause, and I look down at the dashboard to check she's still on the line. 'You there?'

She hesitates before continuing, 'We had to break into her house yesterday; she's got a young child, and we were worried for her safety.'

'Right.'

'Well, now they're both missing, and we found evidence that points to Kristine's detailed knowledge of organised crime groups.'

'Such as…?'

'She's been in contact with a man named Diren Paytak. An individual with strong links to the Turkish Mafia and other groups connected to the Christofi crime family.'

My head jerks at the mention of the name. I almost tail-end the car in front of me before abruptly slamming on the brakes. 'Where are you now?'

'Leaving the Kingley house. Forensics are here, but I've got pictures.'

'I've got a debrief in an hour at NCA HQ. Meet me there?'

I hang up and push my foot down on the accelerator, lighting the blues to quicken the journey time.

By the time I pull into the station, knots of anxiety have begun to creep in as the pressure of Toff's deadline looms. I park up, resting my head on the seat, trying to arrange my thoughts, working out what to prioritise and how to go about it. The only plausible connection with the Home Office and Diren Paytak is Border Control. Was Kristine manipulating the borders for Paytak's trafficking operation? Did he take her daughter as leverage? My brain swerves in a new direction suddenly when a familiar figure catches my eye across the car park. I freeze and slide down behind the steering wheel, watching my father walk determinedly out of HQ to a blacked-out 4x4. Typical

Edward. Being the Director of Counterterrorism, the job always comes first. It wouldn't occur to him to let me know. *Probably for the best.* I wait behind the wheel, watching the vehicle speed off. The prospect of Edward James working with my department for any reason fills me with dread. Hopefully, it's nothing.

Julian lingers by the door as I finally make my way to the reception of HQ. He fidgets on my approach, trying to appear casual as he fumbles with his phone.

'Did Collins tell you to wait for me here?'

'She said it's better if I'm the first person you see, then you're less likely to bite heads off.' He smirks.

'You have no idea.'

'As it also happens, I have something you should hear.' He holds out his screen. Taking the device, I click play on the voicemail recording.

Alex, it's Simon. You said not to call, and I've been respecting your request for time apart. We both know how this goes. I hope you will be back as we know that's best. Bye now.

I listen a few more times, paying close attention to the tone of his voice. 'He sounds like someone that just got dumped.'

Julian nods. 'I'll pay him a visit later.'

We head through the office to our department, and Julian catches me up to speed with the ongoing search for Nicky Black whilst I share a brief rundown of all my working theories, along with details of the call with DI Stanley.

Expectant faces greet us in the briefing room; a few excited Junior Officers stare at the image of Alexandra projected on a screen. Amber is sitting in front of several smart devices, flicking through her notes; she smiles quickly before returning to an iPad. A woman, who I presume is DI Stanley, is perched closest to the door. She stares at me with sure, determined eyes. I glance back with disinterest. Clearly, another of those twentysomething, power-hungry detectives who haven't yet been traumatised into resignation. The NCA, Scotland Yard, the Met Police are all the same – I wish they'd stop recruiting them. It's precisely these types who fall into the trap of closing a case with the wrong suspect because it fits their career goals. Stanley double-takes before seeming to turn a shade of red. *Whoops.* I wonder if Collins has met her yet. As if summoning her with the power of my mind, a sharp slam of the door resounds behind me.

'Right, listen up Team.' Her clear-cut matron's voice ceases the chatter immediately. 'This is the core group for this investigation, and as usual, everything here is strictly confidential. DI Stanley is present under the request of SIO James. There's information from the Kristine Kingley investigation that may be relevant.' She calls across the table before sitting down. 'James, over to you.'

I place my pencil behind my ear before addressing the room: 'Alexandra Christofi has been missing for forty-eight hours. The last-known location was at Paul Theo's office on the Cockfosters Road. We'll start with DI Stanley's findings during her investigation into Kristine Kingley and her daughter's disappearance. Amber will supply info from the analytics team, and we'll have questions and next steps after. It goes without saying, we all know who Alexandra is, not just to UK Organised Crime but to Operation Sandbank. Officer Sleet and I have been looking at known links to other OCGs, and we're tracking down a lead about a new group who may have had a motive to keep Alexandra out of London. Updates to follow shortly. DI Stanley.'

'Thank you, SIO James.' She nods over to me before clearing her throat and fumbling with the remote.

After a few moments, the screen flicks to an image of a large home office. The back wall is covered with pictures, scribblings, post-it notes, mafia names and known mafia businesses.

I lean forward in my chair, squinting at the mess. Silence fills the room.

'All of this was attached to the wall of Kristine Kingley's home study. It appears, so far, that she was working alone. We have no known connection between Kristine Kingley and any of these individuals.' Stanley stands suddenly and hands out printed copies of the wall around the table.

I scan the prints one by one. 'Was Kristine Kingley assisting an investigation we don't know about?'

'Not that we're aware. We're looking into local Personal Investigators as well.' Stanley responds.

I sift through the cluster of notes, skim reading descriptions of suspects and conspiracy theories. But one image, in particular, captures my attention. A grainy picture of a tall man. It's been taken at night, but it's undoubtedly Diren Paytak. He's standing on the street; his arm stretched out to hug the small, hooded figure opposite him. From the snapshot of their body language, they're familiar. Kristine has simply written one name under the image: *HIGGS?* I look down to cover my reaction. *What has Kristine Kingley got herself into?*

'It doesn't look like she had professional help,' I add. 'This picture is shit quality – a PI wouldn't make that mistake.'

'We surmise she was looking for information on Diren Paytak concerning her missing daughter.'

Collins appears unimpressed, shifting to face Stanley. 'And how did you come to that conclusion?'

'The school nursery said that Samantha Kingley has been absent for weeks... And none of Kristine's neighbours has seen the little girl for quite some time.'

'Is it possible she killed the girl and ran?' Julian interjects.

'It doesn't explain the research into the Christofi family,' Collins retorts.

'You think Diren Paytak has taken Samantha Kingley?' I ask.

'That is our current line of enquiry.'

'Have you located him?' Collins asks, holding up Diren Paytak's picture.

'We've been searching, Ma'am,' Stanley replies.

'Good luck with tha…' I abruptly cut my words, catching a warning glance from Collins.

'Well, Kristine clearly thought he was important. And it's worth looking into.' Collins responds, nodding at the screen as she fiddles with an expensive ballpoint pen. 'But as far as Operation Sandbank is concerned, until we have evidence that Kristine was involved with organised crime, I'm not sure what there's a strong enough connection for us to join forced.'

'That looks like a woman,' Julian announces, pointing at the small figure opposite Diren Paytak. 'Could that be Alexandra Christofi?'

'Well, yes…' Stanley hesitates. 'We've been looking into the possibility that it's Alexandra.'

'Highly unlikely she'd be hugging the head of the Turkish mafia,' I retort, discarding a copy of the image onto the table. 'She's Greek.'

Stanley stares at me blankly.

'Her father and Paytak notoriously hate each other,' I clarify bluntly. 'The Greeks and the Turks are sworn enemies.'

'Well, there's more…' She says before clicking the remote again. We all turn to the screen as the next slide reveals an enlarged passport picture of Paul Theo and Mario Christofi.

'We found these in Kristine's desk drawer.' She gestures to a collection of digits under each picture. 'We've traced these numbers. It's their mobiles, and she called them several times.'

'She must have noticed that Mario's is disconnected.' I point at Toff's picture. 'Considering he's dead.'

'She had two lengthy conversations with Paul, it seems.'

'How did Kingley get these?'

'We think they're from her work database.'

'She hacked into a database for information on the Christofis, and that didn't raise any red flags with anyone in the Home Office?' I ask with disbelief.

'Correct, but she's quite senior – she reports directly to the Home Secretary.'

'This is all fascinating, DI Stanley, but as it stands, we have no tangible connection linking the missing women, apart from they knew the same people.' Collins rebuts.

I smirk, unable to hide the smug look on my face – it's a pleasant change watching Collins hate on someone else.

'But the woman in the Paytak image?'

'It's not her,' I state plainly. 'We have intel that Paytak hired an assassin to target Mario Christofi. It's possible he did the same with Kristine. This woman could be anyone.'

'Or that is Alexandra, and she's working with Paytak.'

'She would never-' I begin raising my voice.

'That's enough!' Collins interjects.

'Ma'am, I think we need to go back to Paul Theo. He's been in contact with Kristine Kingley, and he was the last to see Alexandra. If there's a connection between the two women, then he'll know.'

'That's a priority, James. Write that down,' Collins instructs before she looks around the room expectantly. 'What else is there? I want everything on the table.'

'I'd like to join SIO James on that, Ma'am,' Stanley announces determinedly.

'SIO James will gather the intel and report back,' Collins snaps as she looks at her watch. 'Right, what's next?'

Amber looks startled and shuffles her notes, 'Ah urm... yes, sorry, Ma'am. I should have spoken up earlier, but...' she pauses, looking panicked before announcing in a shaking voice, 'I think I have the connection.'

I whip my head up, pondering how she sat through the earlier exchange without speaking up.

She notices my disapproval and quickly averts her gaze.

'Paul Theo said the last time he saw Alexandra was at his office, but we managed to track her vehicle, leaving Barnet, travelling to Southgate High Street. At about four fifteen PM, she parked at a BP Garage. Their cameras caught her walking out of the forecourt.'

I sit forward, now interested.

'So, I checked CCTV in the surrounding area...'

'And?' Collins presses. 'I take it you have something?'

Amber nods hesitantly.

'Can you connect your laptop to the screen and show us the footage?'

After a few moments, the media window pops up on the screen, and the video begins. It's jarring and slow but easy enough to make out. A snapshot of a laundrette emerges on Southgate High Street with a timestamp that reads five past four in the corner. The camera producing this footage is fixed to a high point opposite. At seven minutes past four, a small woman, roughly early thirties, with an angular face and thin brown hair, runs into the frame, beginning to bang her fists on the window of the laundrette aggressively. There's no sound, but it's easy to tell from her body language that she's upset. Paul Theo walks out. It appears he's trying to calm her down.

Eventually, he pulls her up to her feet, and they walk towards the entrance. He takes something out of his pockets – keys presumably – before unlocking the door and taking her inside. At sixteen minutes past four, a woman appears, walking to the front of the shop. Paul steps outside, and after a brief discussion, he gestures for her to follow him. She looks back over her shoulder before doing so. It's undoubtedly Alexandra. She follows Paul inside, and the footage is played forward again, skipping to when Alexandra reappears outside the laundrette, alone, at nine minutes past five. The screen goes dark, and the video disappears.

'What happened? Is that it?' I half rise from my chair.

'The tape just goes blank,' Amber informs nervously.

'And what about the CCTV from inside?'

'It was wiped, and the shop was closed at the time, so no witnesses inside.'

'The CCTV has been wiped inside and outside?' I ask, astonished.

'Convenient,' Stanley mutters without looking up from her notepad.

Collins stares at the blank screen before turning back to the table. 'Well, DI Stanley, there's the connection.'

'We need to speak to Paul Theo again, Ma'am.'

'Go now. Take Julian.'

'Amber, can you get me all the background you have on Paul? I need information on Hellbanianz as well, and I want to know what Aldyn Wolfe has been up to recently; if anything's happening, the Albanians will know. Share what you find with DI Stanley. Keep me updated.'

'Yes, Guv.' She nods before closing her laptop. 'I should have info on bank accounts and phone records for Paul, Alexandra, and Kristine soon.'

'Still waiting on background for Olivia, too.' I nod across to her before turning to Stanley. 'We'll reconvene after I've spoken to Paul.'

She stands, her expression smug before she follows Amber out of the room. I move towards the door, only to be stopped by the sound of Collins calling my name. I know what's coming, acknowledging the tense look on her face. She waits for everyone to shuffle out before gesturing for me to close the door.

'I didn't want Stanley involved in this, but I can't deny she's brought more to the table than you in the last forty-eight hours.' She holds a hand up as I attempt to protest. 'You realise she is making a play for this entire case, don't you?'

'I don't think-'

'You don't know Major Investigations, Gabriel,' she insists with a condescending tone. 'They send in someone like her to weed their way into a pre-existing case. Some unassuming, wide-eyed, pretty face...'

I bite my tongue to prevent from laughing.

'Someone knows your reputation; they're using her to get to you. Do you think it's an accident they sent someone that looks like her?'

'Can't say I noticed, Ma'am,' I lie, ignoring the insinuation.

'Bullshit. It's exactly why you rolled over and let her in before you knew what she had to offer.'

'I invited her to the briefing based on a telephone conversation, so unless I've got a sixth sense...' I smirk down at her. 'You know this conversation isn't very inclusive, Ma'am.'

'Don't give me that shit.' She spits, grinding her teeth. 'From now on, if you want her involved, you come to me first. Until you bring me something concrete, you've lost the right to call the shots.'

Now I'm fucked off. I breathe in a long breath, willing my mouth to follow my brain, not to lose my cool. 'Say what you want about my methods, but if these cases are connected, we need to use her to our advantage,' I respond calmly.

'You best make sure it stays that way. I'm not having another Amelie on our hands!'

Another low blow. It's like she's goading me, waiting for me to lose it.

'Amelie was a fantasist.' I remind her, my voice low.

'You got away with that because of your personal connections, but we can't go down the same road.'

'Speaking of my personal connections… Care to share why S015 was here today?'

She offers me a blank, no bullshit stare. 'Keep your focus on the case, Gabriel.'

'Yes, Ma'am,' I say, not even bothering to hide the disdain.

She stands in front of me, unafraid of the temper that's brewing, utterly unfazed by the look on my face. 'Don't be petulant. I mean it, don't fuck this up,' she offers as a final warning before turning on her heel.

I stand alone in the boardroom, fists clenched, listening to the furious repetitiveness of my own breath. Over my dead body will DI Stanley take this case. With that in mind, I stride out of the boardroom and over to Julian's desk, about to tell him to grab his coat, when Amber's panicked voice calls across the room.

'Guv!' She rushes over wild-eyed. 'Uniform found a body. It's female.'

'Where?'

She hesitates, her mouth moving, but no words are coming out.

'Amber. Talk!'

'Forty Hill, Enfield.'

I groan. 'Tell uniform I'll be there in twenty minutes.

CHAPTER EIGHT

I swallow down the sickening sense of unease as hordes of media swarm the entrance to Forty Hall. Recognising my face through the window, they begin shouting questions, knocking on the glass of the unmarked vehicle as I navigate the car through the crowd. Desperate enquiries are fired in my direction, and I put my head down, shoving through the bodies, ignoring their requests for comment. Eventually, I make my way onto the footpath towards the house, my shoulders deliberately knocking into my least favourite journalists.

'You going to do me a solid, Gabe!?'

I turn and acknowledge Thomas Young with a short nod. Youngy is one of the decent ones, and he knows that if he keeps me sweet, I'll always throw him a bone. Leaving the incessant noise behind me, I walk across the grass to Forty Hall Manor. It's a large regal property surrounded by walled gardens. It was one of my favourite places to go as a kid. Lily, my sister, and I used to come here during the school holidays. We'd build forts and dens by the stream. I haven't been here in years, but it hasn't changed much; the same outstretched fields, swans and geese still nest on a small island in the middle of a lake. My father used to tell me Forty Hall was haunted, and if you stayed on after dark, you'd be murdered by a headless horseman. I smile at the thought of Lily begging to leave just as the sun started to go down. Clever bastard, my father –getting us home without having to move.

Someone clears their throat, and I turn, catching the sight of DI Stanley, who stares back at me, her garishly red lips pursed.

'What are you doing here?'

'Collins said I should join.'

I know it's a lie, which instantly infuriates me. Stanley is the worst person to have around at a time like this, watching my every move, every reaction.

'Do you think it's Alexandra?' She hurries to match my pace as I head towards the crime scene.

'Left my crystal ball at home.'

'Are you always this rude?'

'Why are you here?' I stop, turning to her. 'I know Collins didn't send you.'

'I want to be involved.'

'You need to be less attached to this.'

I tread down the hill, approaching the Forensic team by the lake and duck under the police tape.

'You shouldn't disregard help, Gabriel. Major Investigations has….' She pauses at the white tent, the colour draining from her face.

'Have you seen a dead body before?'

She swallows. 'Not like this.'

I take a second to hide my amused judgement before walking on to collect gloves and shoe covers from the lead forensic. He introduces himself, running through the general procedure, ensuring no crime scene contamination takes place.

'You have seen a body before?' he asks, studying Stanley's apprehension.

She locks eyes with me.

'Sure have,' I respond quickly, saving her from embarrassment a second time.

'You just… You look fresh.' He looks back to her, concerned.

'Can we get on with this?' I demand impatiently.

He hesitates before nodding. 'It's not pretty; she was badly beaten. It's unlikely you'll be able to make out specific features.'

'Jesus Christ,' Stanley mumbles.

I hold my breath. This is known mafia dumping ground. Everyone here knows it, and I'm aware that I, too, must appear pale. I swallow the bile rising in my throat and nod to myself, preparing my brain to accept the truth before seeing the facts. I have to pre-empt my outward reaction when I see her body; I can't show a hint of attachment to this.

Stanley stops abruptly in front of me. I move to join her, willing myself to get a grip. We stare down at the discarded mound of skin in an almost comatose state. A ringing arrives in my ears. My eyes clamp to the charred, tortured flesh of what was once a woman's face, poking out from under a white sheet. I can hear the distant sounds of the forensic team listing areas of the body, but everything has become muffled and out of focus. Everything except the gruesome sight in front of me. *It's her. It has to be.* My brain continues to repeat the words, over and over again, coaching its way into acceptance. Stanley begins to ask questions, her face a pastel shade of green. But my focus cannot be torn away. My brain struggles to catch up. *Contusions, multiple blows, head injury.* There was no exaggeration when they said we wouldn't recognise her; it is impossible to make out a single facial feature. All I can see is one horrific mess of matted, tangled skin scrambled on swollen flesh. Two lumps have formed where eye sockets once were, displaying an angry red and purple discolouration. The area where her nose should be is collapsed. One of her cheeks is shredded to such an extent that I can see through to her back teeth. *How is this the girl I knew?* I screw my eyes shut. Memories flash across my brain, images of us by the river, cycling through narrow streets in Cambridge, laughing as we lay entangled in bed sheets for hours on end.

'Obviously, the hair would be a useful indication for the pathologist, but her head has been so badly burnt. I doubt there would be a single follicle.'

I run my hand over the top of my brow, knowing I will never lose this image from my mind. My brain won't accept it. *This isn't how Alexandra Christofi died. This wasn't the life she was meant to have.* Toff will never forgive himself for leaving. And I will never forgive myself for sending her father away.

'In your opinion, what is the significance of only burning her head?' Stanley asks.

'Destroying evidence?' he suggests, a little unsure.

'And the cause of death?' I ask, unable to tear my eyes away.

'Well, there's a deep laceration across her throat. I wouldn't be surprised if that's what killed her.'

I stare down at her again, closing my mouth to avoid tasting the metallic stench of death.

'Was she burned before or after she died?'

'Likely after.'

'Any signs of sexual assault?' Stanley asks, and my body tenses.

'Not on first inspection.'

I clear my throat, trying to keep the disturbance at bay—my brain glitches, seeing this scene through Toff's eyes. I try to move past the unavoidable sense of panic. Every part of me hopes that I'm wrong.

'James...'

I turn slowly to face Stanley, whose face appears ashen and sweaty, despite the cold temperature.

'I need to see the rest of her,' I state, turning back to the analyst. 'Pull the sheet back.'

Both he and Stanley stare at me, puzzled.

I exhale impatiently. 'I need to see all the evidence. Can you show me the body?'

He hesitates slightly before nodding and obliging, stepping forward and pulling the material back slowly, too slowly. I hold my breath, waiting for the end of dread and the arrival of bitter realisation, knowing the next few seconds will deliver everything. After what feels like an age, the sheet comes off, and I stare down at the pale body, crumpled into an undignified heap amongst grass and mud. Looking over every inch of skin, my eyes dart up and down, from toe to thigh, from hip to chest. More memories race into my head, flashes of tracing my fingers across the perfect lines of Lex's body, recalling the sculpt of her shoulders, the immaculate carve of her clavicles. I look down at the body before me, scrutinising every freckle, every jut of bone, every curve of flesh with erratic precision. And finally, I allow myself to breathe.

'I don't think it's her,' I say, trying to hide my relief.

Stanley frowns, looking confused. 'Don't think it's who?'

'Alexandra.'

'What do you mean?' She studies my face for a beat too long.

'It doesn't look like her.'

'How...?' her brow furrows, suspicion on her face. 'Because of that?' she asks, pointing at one of Jane Doe's hands, filled with grime, smeared with dried blood.

I follow the direction of her finger. This person has a tattoo. It's a small sketch of the sun, drawn onto the side of their wrist. She pulls out her phone and busies herself with something on her screen. I take another step forward and crouch down, using the pencil behind my ear to move the bruised and bloodied hand over, analysing the ironically joyful ink.

Standing up, I eye Stanley, noticing a sudden weight of resignation settled on her face. She exhales a long breath, holding her phone out towards me. I look down at her screen; a Facebook picture stares back at me. It's Kristine Kingley; she's beaming at the camera, her daughter by her side. Her chin is resting on her right hand, making her small sun tattoo visible.

CHAPTER NINE

Dropping my head and pushing against the tide of a media frenzy, I rush out of Forty Hall. Stanley calls my name over a cacophony of badgering from eager reporters, desperate to know where I'm going next. I slip into the car, start the engine, and accelerate, flashing blue lights to properly impart my urgency. A few of the crowd have to rapidly jump out of my way, which admittedly provides me with a sick sense of satisfaction. With one hand on the wheel, I dial for Julian. He picks up almost instantly.

'The body is Kristine Kingley.'

I'm met with silence on the other end of the line.

'Jules?'

'Yeah, Guv, I'm here. It's just…'

'None of this makes sense.'

'It's Paul Theo…'

'What?' I ask, wishing I didn't have to know the answer.

'He's missing.'

'How?' I bash my fist against the radio.

'Uniform found signs of a struggle at his office.'

'Someone is trying to cover their tracks.'

'Hmmm… it's not looking good for Alexandra.'

'What do you mean?'

'First Kristine, now Paul…'

'Jules, I need you to head to Sandhurst. We need to tick the ex-boyfriend off the list.'

'Got it, Guv. I'll head there now.'

I hang up and weave the car determinedly through the steady amble of traffic on Upper Street, turning the corner into the mews behind the Hope and Anchor pub. Letting myself into my apartment, I don't even bother to switch on the lights before flopping down on the sofa. Closing my eyes for ten minutes, I run through the last few days, a dark web of shit that replays over and over. I know that I'm missing something obvious. It's nagging at me, pulling like a tangled wire in my brain. I sit up, knowing I can no longer prevent the inevitable, and pull out the burner phone, knowing this is bound to be difficult.

Toff picks up immediately. 'This better be an explanation for whatever the fuck the press is on about because I'm about to fucking lose it.'

I look down at the phone. 'What are you talking about?'

'Turn on the fucking news.'

I fumble around in the dark for the remote and switch on the TV, pressing one for the BBC. A middle-aged woman is standing in front of the laundrette, talking to the camera. Leaked CCTV images of Alexandra and Kristine flash across the screen. Underneath reads: *BREAKING NEWS: Soldier suspected in Home Office murder.* For once, I'm stunned into silence.

'Tell me she isn't a suspect for the murder of this government minister?'

'Neither is an active line of enquiry.'

'Don't give me that detective bullshit, Gabriel. My daughter is still missing, and so far, you've done fuck all. Now she's being accused of murder.' He continues ranting.

I'm lost for words. I haven't even had the chance to speak to Youngy – I usually offer up a carefully collated list of information that keeps him from hassling me and other people at the NCA. This will ruin that beneficial relationship completely, not to mention a rat has leaked our most vital piece of evidence.

'I like you, Gabriel. I don't want your life to turn upside down over this, but she's my daughter. I don't give a fuck about my own life, let alone yours. I'm coming back.'

'Toff. No. Listen, Kingley is dead. We found her body. And we know Alexandra saw her the day she disappeared, but nobody in our team thinks she did this.'

He sighs, and I hear the rage begin to dissipate. 'I don't know why she would meet that woman, Gabe. Unless she knew her from the Forces?'

'I guess their paths could have crossed.'

'My daughter did not do this. Speak to Paul.'

'We've tried.'

He swears under his breath. 'He's gone, isn't he?'

'Yeah, he's gone.' I sigh, realising how much more complicated this has become.

'This reeks of Paytak, Gabe.'

'I think Kristine was helping Paytak traffic across the borders.'

'And her little girl?'

'He might have used her as leverage. But I need to figure out how Alexandra and Kristine are connected. And without Paul...' I trail off, losing the thread.

'Did Kristine look like a professional job?'

'What do you mean?'

'Was she killed by an assassin, in your opinion?'

I think back to the perfect slice of flesh across her neck. 'It's possible. But an assassin wouldn't have dumped her in a mafia burial ground.'

He's silent for a time, and I look down at the phone to check he's on the line. 'You need to find Nicky Black. Forty Hill is where Nicky used to bury people... for me.'

'I'll find him. But do not come to London. I am handling this.'

I hang up the phone before he can respond. I know I'd have to be insane to believe Mario Christofi will sit by the phone and twiddle his thumbs, which means I've got to move fast.

CHAPTER TEN

With the moonlight as the only guide for Julian and me, twigs, and leaves crunch under our heavy footsteps before finally, the abandoned barn comes into view, creaking eerily in the wind. The low groaning sound in the rafters adds to the thick feeling of unease in the air; the surrounding area is empty, save for disused pieces of farm equipment and a few old tractor wheels discarded around the outside. Julian eyes me suspiciously, clearly not satisfied with my explanation for getting him up in the middle of the night and dragging him out to a random forest in the suburbs. Without a word, he begins to pace around the space, surveying our surroundings for a sign of unwanted company. I sense his apprehension, and I take a moment to give the area a once-over before sitting on one of the large tractor wheels with my hands in my pockets. 'Jules, it's all good.'

He steps back out from a busy section of wild shrubs and bushes. 'We should have told Collins about this, Guv.'

'Amber knows we're here.'

'What the fuck is Amber going to do?'

'What would Collins?'

He knows my methods aren't orthodox. They never have been. But this case is exposing him to just how far over the line I'm willing to go, and I can see he's getting increasingly uncomfortable with it. On turning up at his house at one in the morning, I didn't need to be a detective to see that Sarah was pissed off when she answered the door. She resents me for pushing her husband to break boundaries that I bulldozed long ago, and I don't particularly blame her for it.

'Sit down. It's going to be fine.'

He laughs sarcastically. 'It sure seems that way right now. In the dark. With no backup.'

'Will you give it a rest?'

Just as I finish the end of that sentence, a rushed and violent rustling resounds in the woodland behind me, and I stand abruptly, pulling my gun and cocking it in one swift motion.

'Yeah, you seem really calm, Guv,' He comments. Despite keeping my eyes trained on the source of the noise, I know there's a slight smile playing on the corners of his lips.

Nicky Black stumbles through a narrow opening, looking wide-eyed and dazed. 'Not being funny, but it's the middle of the fucking night.' He suddenly registers the firearm trained on his chest and throws his hands in the air. 'What the!'

'I think you're a little past beauty sleep, mate.'

He raises his eyebrows and looks at Julian before eyeing the gun. 'Has he finally fucking cracked?'

'Sit down, Nicky.' Julian gestures towards the large wheel.

Nicky slowly creeps across the space; his hands stuck above his head.

'You came alone, didn't you, Nicholas? Because if you didn't, I will find out and shoot anyone hiding out there.'

'Have you lost your mind?'

'Shut up, Nicky.' Julian interjects. 'Answer the question.'

'I'm alone. Can you put that down, for fuck's sake?' He sits.

I lower the gun and approach him until I'm standing right above his chubby face with my arms crossed. 'You been busy?' I spy the mad helplessness in his eyes. 'We'll take that as a yes.'

He says nothing.

'You missed out some important details the other day, didn't you?'

'Did I!?'

'Who killed Kristine Kingley?'

'I don't know!' He protests but even in the dark, I see the lack of conviction.

'I knew this barn would come in handy,' I heave him up with one arm and begin to drag his wriggling body across the opening.

'Fucking hell. Stop!'

I halt and pull him in by the collar. 'Who killed Kristine Kingley?'

Sweat coats Nicky's upper lip, his eyes frantically dart around my face. 'Paytak hires people… as I said.'

'Who did he hire for this?'

'Some chick, ex-forces. I don't know who she is.'

'What's her name?'

He shakes his head.

'Is it Alexandra?' I ask.

'You think she'd ever work for the Turks?!'

'Then, who?'

'I don't know. They hired her through that Singularity group.'

'Why did they kill Kristine?'

'She was making a fuss about her daughter, causing trouble. Paytak said she had to go. She was a loose end.'

I turn to him as something drops into my head, slotting perfectly into place.

'You were the go-between. Between Paytak and Kristine?'

'Just the messenger.'

'Was she helping Paytak traffic kids in and out of the borders?'

He nods. 'I just had to deliver details of the next load.'

'How long did this go on for?'

'Months and months…' He stops, looking over my shoulder nervously.

'Don't get shy on me now.'

He takes a deep breath. 'She just stopped coming through. Paytak lost his shit – he needed a way to get her back on track.'

'So, he took Samantha…' Julian chimes in.

Nicky pulls away from me and holds his hands up. 'They told me it was just to scare her. To make her finish the job!'

'Wait! *You* fucking took her?' My eyes widen in disbelief, and I lurch towards him. 'You fucking took her kid, you sick bastard!' I grab him with a venomous force, barely able to see straight.

'Paytak said we'd give her back!'

'Where is she, Nicky?' I pull him tighter.

'They took her somewhere. I don't know.'

I throw him down to the floor and pace away, needing to put distance between us before I strangle him to death.

As a police officer, you spend years witnessing horrific acts, becoming privy to the most appalling, heart-breaking scenes. Naturally, you begin to build immunity, forging a resistance to the horror to help your mind cope with the brutality of life. But every detective will tell you that they have one trigger, one thing that they will never get past, no matter how many times they experience it. And for me, this is it. The mere thought of anyone harming a child sends my brain into an incomprehensible rage. Julian is aware of this fact, which is why he's rapidly stepped between Nicky and me, trying to stop me from doing something I'll later regret.

'You better find out where they took her, or I will tell him you're my fucking snitch, do you hear me?' I say, storming away.

Julian turns to Nicky. 'All of this, blackmailing Kristine, taking her daughter, it's a lot of effort to keep a trafficking ring going, Nicky.'

'The Singularity made it very clear that they would kill all of us if we ever made mistakes. Paytak has to tie up loose ends.'

'But why is the trafficking ring so important to them?'

'I don't know. Paytak doesn't tell me everything.'

'Is Paytak scared of them?'

'He fucking should be.'

'Did you ever see Kristine Kingley and Alexandra Christofi together?'

'Never! I swear I don't know anything about Alexandra. I would never fuck with Toff's Family.'

'You need to find out who else is involved in this. I want names.'

'Mate, there's people everywhere. You could be in it. He could be in it,' he says, pointing an accusing finger at Julian. 'The Singularity is full of bent coppers, politicians…'

This is the reason witness protection was never safe for Toff. It makes sense to me now; every safehouse, every contingency to keep him alive was compromised. *What if The Singularity were behind the existence of Operation Sandbank in the first place? What if they orchestrated the removal of Toff through means of the NCA?* And when it was clear that we weren't going to take him out of the equation, someone wanted him dead. I sit on the floor, my head between my legs. 'Why didn't you tell us any of this the other day?'

'I didn't even know Kristine was dead then!'

'But you'd been meeting her!' I yell.

'I was scared.'

'Fuck!' I stand and kick the tyre out of frustration, trying to piece together this chaotic mess. Nicky flinches, fearing the consequences of not having all the information.

'How many other bodies has Paytak asked you to dump?' Julian asks.

'A few? a handful? I'm not sure.'

'Where are they?'

'Long gone.'

'Who are they?'

He swallows hard with shame etched onto his face. 'They're orphans…refugees.'

Julian groans, throwing his hands on his head.

I take a deep calming breath, pull out my gun and point it at his head. 'You've buried children, Nicky?'

He throws his hands up, yelping with fear.

Julian yells across the space, willing me to calm down.

'If you want me to keep this fucking charade up, then I have to do what I'm told,' he squeals.

'Gabriel…' Julian warns with disapproval in his voice.

I point the weapon at Nicky's feet and pull the trigger. He falls back off the tractor wheel and onto the floor, quivering in the foetal position. I walk over to his body and kick his arms out of his face.

'I did what I had to do,' he cries, his knees pulled into his chest.

'Where are the children being kept?'

'There are different warehouses across the country. They move location every four or five days.'

'You seem to know a lot about this operation for someone who just speaks to Paytak.'

'Yeah, well, he's got a big fucking mouth,' he retorts. 'Anyway, it's obvious the way these kids died. Some of them have been over-injected with something. Drugs maybe.'

'Opioids?'

'I don't know?!'

I close my eyes, trying to dissolve the image from my mind, *fucking monsters*. 'Could Alexandra be amongst them, Nicky?'

'Not for trafficking. She's too old. I told you they like kids.'

'But Samantha could be there?'

He shrugs.

'Find out their next location, and I asked you to find out where Paytak is, which you still haven't done.'

'They'll kill me.'

I step towards him, inches from his face. 'If you do not do what I am asking you, Nicky, I'll kill you myself. And I will ensure it's a long, excruciating, insufferable experience.' I pull him up and launch his flailing body back towards the woods.

Nobody in the underworld is playing by the rules, so why should I?

CHAPTER ELEVEN

I close the door and step into the pitch-black apartment, leaning against the wall. Sensing the all-too-familiar twitch in my hand, craving the one remedy to temporarily numb the stress and exhaustion that's wound itself around my brain like thick barbed wire. Piercing and permanent. I clear my throat, trying to shift the urge, visualising the cool brown liquid flowing into a tumbler.

Addiction is a different hunger, a deep yearning in the pit of your throat, a twisted longing that sifts slyly through your body like an oppressive fog. I groan and bundle my fists, pulling my body forward and towards the bedroom. I haven't been to an AA meeting in weeks, and the rational part of my brain longs for stability, the circle of understanding faces, the recognition of abstinence. I'd have to wait until the morning, but for now, I need to figure out a way to dull the ticking of desire racing through me. *Should I call Heather?* I pull out my phone, motivated by the need to suppress this with the appetite for something else. She'd answer in an instant but is that what I want? *Do I really want to be trekking to hers in the middle of the night, committing myself to sleeping on that diabolical mattress?* I ponder the thought as I remove my shirt and move to switch on the shower when a shuffling sound from the living room makes my ears prick up. I freeze in the doorway, standing motionless in the dark space, waiting for a sign of movement. A muffled knocking causes me to swing around and grab the gun from beside the bed. I stride to the door with my left hand around the weapon, stooping my shoulders to look through the spy hole. Stanley is swaying on my doorstep, reaching her hand out again with every intention of knocking a second time. I quickly pull the door open, and she falls forward, startled, and shocked by the disappearance of the surface.

'Whoa… you ok?' she squints up at me, her eyes moving in different directions.

I breathe an exasperated sigh. 'How did you get my address?'

'Amber.'

'She's fired in the morning.'

'Stop.' She smirks, nudging into me. 'Can I come in?'

'Mmhmm…' I widen my eyes amidst her already rushing past me, heading straight to the sofa.

'Got any wine?'

'I don't drink,' I tuck the gun into my jeans.

'Are you an alcoholic?'

'Do you always ask such personal questions?'

'Not to everyone.'

'What do you want, Theresa?'

'Oh, my first name…'

I raise my eyebrows and cross my arms, admittedly taken off-guard by the flirtation.

She catches my look of utter bewilderment and smiles, laying back on the cushions. 'You left quickly… from the crime scene.'

I offer her a questioning look.

'Where did you go?'

'Would you like to add me on *Find My Friends*?'

'Is there something you're not telling me in relation to this case?'

'Not specifically.'

'How did you know it wasn't Alexandra?'

'Hmm?' I tilt my head, feigning ignorance.

'I think you're hiding something.'

'Let me know how that pans out.'

'Where did you go today?'

'I had stuff to handle.'

She sits up, propping herself on her elbows before locking her clumsy gaze with mine.

'Are you ok?'

She ignores the question. Instead, she stares around my apartment, doing her best to take in every furnishing. 'Are you rich?'

'What are you doing here, Stanley?'

'Can I at least have a drink?' she whines, standing up from the sofa, taking a slow step towards me.

'You plan on staying long?'

'You're not very friendly, are you, Gabriel?'

'You turned up at my apartment in the middle of the night...'

'I know you have a source. It's why you keep disappearing. Does he know who killed Kristine?'

I turn away from her and walk to the kitchen, grabbing a tumbler from the cupboard; I fill it with ice and water.

'I thought you said you didn't drink,' she calls out to me.

I return and place the glass on the coffee table in front of her.

She stares down at the clear liquid and juts her bottom lip out childishly. 'This is no fun. Why are you so serious all the time?' she stands, swirling the liquid around the glass with her right hand as her left hand slowly reaches out to stroke my arm.

'Don't you think you've had enough?'

'Maybe...' She drawls the word out slowly and looks up at me through thick, mascara-covered lashes.

'What do you want?'

'I think you know.'

'Get to the point.'

'Maybe I'm here because I want something else...'

I pause, thinking about my earlier musings, before looking back down at Stanley. *Jesus, what is wrong with me?* I can't believe I considered that for more than a second. She's attractive sure, there's something sexy about her, but she's too made up. More importantly, I can't sleep with Stanley because she's teetering on the edge of being paralytically drunk, and although I've been known to do some shitty things in the past, that is too far.

'I can't help you there, Theresa,' I reply.

Her eyes become skittish, absorbing the burn of my rejection. 'I'm hot, I'll have you know!'

'Stanley, if you wake up tomorrow and still want to fuck me, we'll talk...' I concede, wanting her out of my apartment.

She giggles before wrapping her fingers around my wrist and hauling herself up from the couch, stepping in so her ample chest is pressed against me.

Having had my fill of crazy for the day, I abruptly remove the empty glass from her hand.

'I know how you got to where you are,' she murmurs, following me to the kitchen.

I turn to hand her another glass of water, but she stumbles back, and I catch her quickly by the wrist, steadying her.

'I know who your father is.'

'I'll bear that in mind.'

'Why don't you just give me access to your source?'

'Stanley, when I take a statement from my source, officially, on the record, you will be the first to know. And you don't even have to bribe me with sex to get it.'

Her face changes, frustration shifting into her eyes. 'Let's see how forthcoming you are when we declare Alexandra Christofi the prime suspect for the murder of Kristine Kingley and the disappearance of her six-year-old daughter.'

'What makes you think you'll get the go-ahead?'

'Collins is looking at it.'

'Collins is playing you.'

Her eyes brighten, leaning against the counter, arching her back as she spreads herself over the surface. 'Must get lonely up here… on your own.'

I almost groan, struggling to keep up. Perhaps if I say exactly what I think about her, she'll leave. But she looks like she's downed at least two bottles of wine, so I can't guarantee she'd find the exit even if I did insult her enough to want to.

'Let me call you a cab,' I say, pulling my phone out of my pocket.

'Collins won't be able to ignore the evidence.' She straightens, hiccupping.

'Look, Theresa, I'll admit I've lost track of what you're saying because we've been dipping in and out of work amidst your attempts to sleep with me, but I think you should go.'

'We have the evidence we need.'

'You have evidence that Alexandra met Kristine at a laundrette.'

She slams her glass on the counter. 'I just want us to work together.'

'You wanted us to do more than that a minute ago.'

She rolls her eyes. 'I will get what I want, Gabriel.'

Choosing to believe she's referring to the case, I decide to lift the lid on the day's accumulated frustration. 'Stanley… You want a narrative that doesn't exist. You want to tie this up in a neat little bow so you can get a promotion, I get it. You want the fast track.' I take a step towards her, ensuring I'm uncomfortably close to her face. 'But this world is messy and toxic.' I take another step. 'If you take a wrong turn, if you continue to make things fit where they don't, it will eat you alive.'

'Is that a threat?'

'It's a heads-up.'

She looks up with a smug, knowing expression. 'That's how you're so good at catching the biggest, maddest criminals in London.'

'Enlighten me.'

'You're just like them.' She slurs those final words before stumbling backwards, grabbing her coat, and marching for the door.

I dial the number for Collins as I hear it slam.

'Gabriel…'

'Ma'am.'

'I'm hosting a dinner party.'

'This is urgent.'

'So are my mojitos.'

'Major Investigations are making a play to name Alexandra their prime suspect.'

She sighs, and I hear her making muffled apologies amongst cheering and whooping in the background. *Sounds like much more than a dinner party.*

'What evidence have they got to support that?'

'The CCTV.'

'That's it?'

'Yeah, but Stanley was here, trying to get more information. She knows I have a source.'

'What info could you possibly give her at this point?'

'It appears The Singularity is connected to Samantha and Kristine. But the source has no idea where Samantha is now.'

'That makes things complicated.' She breathes. 'Well, tell her to get fucked.' *The irony.* 'She can't make Alexandra a suspect without my sign-off anyway.'

'Thanks, Ma'am.'

'But if the evidence points to it, then my hands are tied.'

'The evidence is all I care about,' I lie.

'Ok, good, now go away, behave yourself and do your job,' she says, cutting the line dead.

I walk through the living room, determined to hit the sack, the weight of recent sleepless nights catching up with me. I finally lie down on the bed and reach to turn off the lamp when I catch Alexandra's journal sprawled open on the bedside table. I hesitate, knowing I shouldn't put myself in her head and her in mine – I'm already aware that her personal musings will disrupt the foundations of logic even more. *What if I had gone after her all those years ago? What if I had begged her to come back? What if I hadn't joined the NCA? Would their lives be any different?* I know I'm teetering close to the edge, the fragments of our past relationship pushing me to act in ways that I wouldn't normally. But no matter what choices I made in my life, whatever path I chose, somehow, I sense the Christofi's were an inevitable piece. I ponder this for a few moments until I realise I'm only prolonging the inevitable, and I grab the journal:

27th January

I went on a date tonight. He was nice but a little vanilla. I don't usually tell guys the intricate details of my job, but I got so bored with his blandness that I wanted to shock him. Maybe the story about pushing McGuire's intestines back into his body was a step too far, but I just wanted to leave.

1st October

I don't want to tell Simon; I can't be bothered with the fuss. I used to think that I was destined to either settle for someone that I could not possibly love back in the same way or choose that raw, agonising love. I've had the latter once before. I was infatuated with him and our relationship's turbulent, unforgiving nature. No balance. No equilibrium. There was just pain or euphoria. I miss that feeling.

THE BURNT CHILD

I read this excerpt again and again, for obvious reasons, but eventually, I have to stop, knowing I'm already in too deep. This isn't healthy. I need to get out of her mind. Just as I'm about to close the book, my eyes scan the last line:

At the very least, this baby has made me determined to find the middle ground.

I shut the journal and stand abruptly from the bed. She's pregnant. Lex is pregnant. *How the fuck did I miss this?* I flick through the next pages, all the way up to the eighteenth of October, the day she moved to London; there isn't a single other mention of it. I frantically scan through, page after page, looking for further evidence, and the only tenuous reference I find is on the seventeenth:

I think Grandma could hear me being sick this morning, and then this afternoon, she told me to be careful when moving furniture to my new place. Does she know? How could she possibly?

I storm into the living room, not knowing where I'm going or what to do. Questions fly in and out of my head, one impossible tangent after another. If someone has taken her, there would be a trail, a thread. And I just need to keep pulling on it. But my mind has struggled to formulate the correct steps. It feels like something is missing. It's within reach, but I can't grasp it; its absence creates fragmented pieces of a nonsensical puzzle.

I head back to the bedroom to retrieve the journal once again. Opening it at random pages, I stand in the middle of the room examining the words, looking for something, anything to make sense. Finding absolutely nothing, I yell and slam it to the floor, defeated. I angrily pace at the foot of the bed, willing myself to get a grip. Losing my temper won't achieve anything. Any moment now, I'm expecting a call from Toff, announcing his return to London and his intention to torture people left, right, and centre for answers. The thought gives me clarity; updating him and preventing that entire situation from unravelling should be my priority.

An urgent tapping resounds from across the living room, and I groan, expecting to hear Theresa Stanley announce her return from the other side of the door. I don't have the energy to deal with her again. Grabbing a pair of jogging-bottoms, I hop from one leg to the other as a third knock resounds, becoming increasingly impatient.

'Alright!' I shout, shoving my foot through the second leg.

Tired and bemused, I open the door without first checking who it is, and I find myself blinking down at an unexpected figure. Large eyes, the colour of smooth espresso, stare back at me, encased with long thick eyelashes. Her hand twitches, smoothing down a mane of unruly blonde hair, and it takes a few seconds to register. Fatigue has clearly slowed my brain, my thoughts appearing laboured. Until I see it. That's when it hits me. *The smile.* A smile I've looked for in every woman since.

ALEXANDRA

CHAPTER TWELVE

I'm not sure what reaction I was expecting, but the minute Gabriel James looked at me, I felt the full catastrophic force of him. It all suddenly makes sense that this was the man to bring down my father's criminal empire. I shift on my feet, acknowledging he hasn't said a word since he opened the door. Instead, he remains impassive, every striking feature set in a firm line. His disinterested glare slides up and down my body, taking in my dirty clothes and unbrushed hair. It goes without saying that Gabriel has always had an arrogant confidence to match outrageous good looks, but there's something different now, something more. Clearly, he neglected to put on a top in his haste, and I'm doing my best not to stare directly at his bare, broad chest. My mind hesitates clumsily as the speech I'd memorised skips like scratched vinyl in my brain. *Explain why you're here. Tell him what's happened, tell him everything.*

'Where have you been?' he finally asks in a low tone, as if he's already bored by the answer.

I don't know whether he means in the last twelve years or three days. I look around, feeling hot, and I take a deep breath to slow my flustered pulse. *How does he have this effect on me?* I've come across some of the most dangerous men in the world, but thirty seconds with Gabriel, and I'm back to that awkward, embarrassing university student who couldn't bear to look him in the eye. I watch him shove a hand through his cropped, messy brown hair before he exhales sharply.

Get a grip, Alexandra. 'Can I come in, please?'

He pauses, considering this before gesturing past him, his eyebrows raised. 'By all means…'

I make slow, apprehensive movements towards the door, hovering my hand over the weapon strapped around my waist just in case I've misread this. Seeking refuge with anyone is a risk, but if I'm right, Gabriel is the only person that can help me. He follows me inside, running his hand through his hair again. I turn around, ready to explain everything, but the back of him is already disappearing down a long hallway without a word.

I stand motionless, unsure what to do or say. *Does he live alone?* Having been stood outside, keeping watch on his apartment, I counted one visitor, and by the look on her face when she left, it wasn't a pleasant encounter. I keep my hand trained on my weapon, scanning my eyes over the vast open-plan space. I check every dark corner of the dimly lit room, braced for unknown threats in the shadows. I snap my gaze to the window as the sound of a distant helicopter triggers flashes of missions in the desert, memories of searching for targets in the dead of night. *Is there a light switch anywhere?* Taking a breath, I quell my unease. Conflict is admittedly harder without an intelligence team in my ear, guiding me to the next marker. I pace up and down, fighting the urge to kick through every door and ensure no one is hiding in the shadows. After a few minutes, I walk towards the sofa, trying to distract my overactive mind. As soon as I see the cushions, I desperately want to fall back and close my eyes. *Where did Gabriel go? Is he coming back?* I squint at his possessions, struggling to gather an accurate picture of his life when he marches back into the room. He stops, crossing his arms, watching me warily, his dark eyes loaded with questions.

'What is going on?'

'I want to tell you, but it's a long story.'

'Why are you here?'

'I need your help.'

He hesitates. 'Do you need water? Anything to eat?'

'Could I take a shower, please?'

He nods before looking at the floor, refusing to meet my eyes. 'Are you armed?'

I stand from the sofa, sliding my hand into the waist of my jeans and slowly pull up my T-shirt, flashing the pistol in the holster strapped around me. He holds his hand out, and I unload it before placing it in his palm.

'I still have to search you.' He takes a step forward.

I hold my hands up whilst he methodically rakes my body for more weapons. His neck brushes the side of my face as he crouches down and pats his palms around my back with meticulous movements. I can't help but inhale that smell... his smell, the distinctive scent of cool sandalwood mixed with fresh washing powder. After all these years, I remember it as if it were yesterday. I hold my breath to stop myself from inhaling intensely as he continues, feeling uncomfortable at his proximity. He reaches my legs, now completely crouched down, and I can't help but observe the defined flex of muscles in his shoulders and upper back. He straightens suddenly, saying nothing before turning to exit the room again.

Looking back to the front door, I consider bolting. *This is a huge risk.* My eyes trail to and from the exit. I've been in dangerous, life-threatening situations before, but there was an objective with a clear strategy in those instances. I always knew who the enemy was. This time, it's different. This is an unknown entity, and it's happening in my own country. Against my instincts imploring me to go this alone, begging me to run and never look back, I have to trust my father's judgement.

Gabriel returns to the room, his presence jolting me from my train of thought. 'You can use my bathroom. It has a shower.' He hands me a towel.

I nod slowly before shuffling my feet past him.

CHAPTER THIRTEEN

Finally feeling clean, I step into the bedroom and notice a neatly folded pile of clothes on the bed. Looking around for Gabriel, I bend to retrieve them and quickly slip them on. I don't know what I expected, but I want to burst into laughter when I look at the mirrored wardrobes. Gabriel's size L T-shirt practically covers eighty per cent of my body as it falls past my knees. I slip on what appears to be black running shorts and, finally, big white sports socks, rolling my eyes at my reflection. This outfit, coupled with my frizzy wet hair, makes me look a comical mess, but at least I'm clean. I take the opportunity to gaze around his bedroom, not yet ready to venture out. I sit on the edge of the large double bed, relishing the feel of bedsheets after spending so many days sleeping rough in McGuire's workshop. I drift my eyes around the room, trying to gauge anything that might help me level with the Gabriel James of today, the man who works for the National Crime Agency and not the Cambridge undergraduate.

Before my father died, he sent me a letter of instructions. It wasn't a will as such but a contingency plan. Almost as if he knew his hold on the criminal underworld was slipping. *If you need help, Alexandra, you go to Detective Gabriel James.* In the days that followed, I lost my place in the army, had to sever contact with my squadron and then suddenly Mario was gone, gone before I could ask the vital questions. *Why did Gabriel choose to tear my family apart? Was he aware of the connection? Did he understand that he would destroy my life in the process?* Initially, I rejected the advice. I didn't need anyone. I wasn't going to seek help from the person responsible for this chaos, the reason my life had turned on its head. *How could I trust my father's judgment anymore?* Putting his faith in a police officer goes against everything he ever taught me. Part of me thought I should have told him about our past and what the name Gabriel James once meant to me. Perhaps that would have ensured Mario saw him for what he really was. *A liar.*

And then I read the letter again. And again. And again. Then I looked him up. *Gabriel James, the youngest detective at his level, assigned lead investigator to the biggest case the NCA had ever encountered.* Mario had no malice for Gabriel. There was no resentment, just respect, admiration even. He understood that he and Gabriel were not too dissimilar. Instead, circumstance had merely placed them at opposite sides. He knew the traditions of the underworld were vanishing. New networks were on the rise, looking to shake things up, and the dark web became the forum for business deals that used to take place in the back of a restaurant with a handshake. It wasn't the world he once knew. And Gabriel realised that Mario's influence was waning, that there were much bigger, fatter fish to fry. Together, they concocted a deal. Mario offered exposure to the bigger catch, elevating Operation Sandbank to a new level of success. And in return, he was protected. *Until he wasn't.*

For that reason, I don't know if I can wholeheartedly trust my father's advice, but with no other options available to me right now, it has to count for something.

It's clear the last twelve years have reshaped him; he appears more hardened, less approachable. I guess he could say the same about me; we've both changed.

I look down at a few casefiles lying sprawled across the duvet. I recognise Gabriel's handwriting scribbled across a few sheets of paper in pencil with notes upon notes of theories and leads. I check the door before nudging a few documents to the side, spotting the corner of a picture buried amongst the pile. It's Aldyn Wolfe, one of my father's closest friends and Head of the Albanian mafia. *What does Gabriel want with him?* I make a mental note to ask before returning the image to its original place.

Other than telling me he's got a minimalist taste; his bedroom gives nothing away; it's decorated like a show home. There's only one personal possession: a framed picture on his bedside table, and I shuffle up to get a closer look. It's a little girl smiling a big, wide, gap-toothed grin at the camera – she's beautiful, and the innocence in her joyful face causes my hand to touch my stomach instinctively.

Knowing I've stalled for long enough and dreading the awkward conversation if he catches me lying on his bed, I take a deep breath, pick up my bundle of dirty clothes and slowly walk through to the living room. As soon as I see him, I sense the tension. He's pacing. His broad shoulders stooped over whilst twiddling a small phone between his thumb and finger. On seeing me, he closes his hand around the phone and slides it back into his pocket.

'I made this in case you were hungry.' He leans over the kitchen island and slides a plate of toast in my direction. For a second, there's a familiar softness and then he notices my hesitation. 'Don't worry, I'm not going to poison you,' he grumbles.

I mumble my gratitude, moving to sit at the kitchen counter.

'Ok…' He takes a careful step towards me, his remarkable eyes meeting mine for the first time since I arrived. 'Start from the beginning.'

GABRIEL

CHAPTER FOURTEEN

Alexandra sits on the stool, her expression laced with an unnerving distance. She appears healthy at least, a few bruises here and there but relatively unscathed. I admit it's a relief, especially when I think about relaying the news to her father. I can tell she's uncomfortable; her eyes keep darting around the room as if she might have to make a run for it at any second. It makes me wonder if that's a consequence of her training or just part and parcel of being on the run. I wonder how much she knows about Operation Sandbank and my involvement in the investigation. She takes a breath to speak, and in those few fleeting seconds, I get the feeling I'm about to find out.

'I'm sorry to just barge in here,' she offers, hesitation gleaming from her golden eyes.

'What is going on here, Lex?' I ask, realising I've instinctively fallen back into using her nickname as if the last twelve years never happened.

'Did my father know?'

She stops suddenly, cut off by the sound of someone piling multiple glass bottles into the Hope and Anchor's recycling outside. A loud bang succeeds the unwelcome noise, and I watch her jump out of her seat, swiftly grabbing the knife off the counter, gripping it tightly in her hand.

'That's the pub landlord taking out the bins,' I tell her, my tone coming across more irritated than intended before I hold out my hand.

She stares at me for a second before surrendering the cutlery.

'I never told your father anything. He didn't know.'

She nods, twisting her lips. 'You must have known I'd figure it out one day, that I'd realise who you were.'

'I had a job to do. It's not like our paths could have crossed. You were always away.'

'Do you feel guilty, for what you did?'

'What exactly did I do?' I rebut, becoming increasingly tired of being interrogated in my own home.

'Getting him killed.'

'I did everything in my power to save him.'

'Was it because of us? Is that why you targeted him?'

I scoff. 'Don't flatter yourself… I didn't know the connection until I'd been assigned the case.'

'And his death? Was that part of the plan?'

'Of course not.' I answer, honestly. 'It might be hard for you to believe, but I was extremely fond of your father.'

'Did you strong-arm him into helping you?'

'He knew that his time had come to an end, either by my hand or someone else's.'

'And that someone else being Diren Paytak?'

'Whom would you rather?' I challenge.

Her lips purse with an aggravating stubbornness.

'Has he reached out to you?' I finally ask, forming a prioritised queue of questions.

'Paytak?' she snaps. 'No. Why would I—' she tilts her head. 'You think I'd work with him?'

'It crossed my mind.'

'You seriously think I could do that?

'I don't know you anymore, Alexandra.'

'He's done—'

'I know what he's done.'

She pauses for a time, processing something. 'I would never do anything to disappoint my father. Not within life or death.'

I swallow past the guilt. 'I really am sorry… for what happened to him.'

'Are you?' she replies, her newfound perception of me abundantly clear. 'Or are you just sorry you can't use him anymore?' She pauses. 'He told me about the deal.'

'Admittedly, we didn't give much time to the potential fall out of that decision.'

'Yeah, well… there were endless consequences.'

I raise an eyebrow.

'Your investigation got me kicked out of the army.'

'I know… I'm sorry.'

'Can you see how it's hard to believe it wasn't intentional? That you didn't mean to tear my life apart?'

'It wasn't personal…'

'Tell me what happened.' She looks up at me with pleading eyes. 'How did it fail?' Her lip quivers. 'How did he die?'

I take a breath, feeling an immediate pang of guilt for the lie I'm about to tell.

'After everything he was doing for us, it wasn't safe for him to carry on living as normal. Eventually, I had to get him to enter Witness Protection.'

'Because of threats?'

'He was being followed; he thought someone was tapping his phone.'

'Paytak?'

'Perhaps…' I shrug. 'Anyway, we set a date. We were going to relocate him, change his name, everything.'

'And leave us behind?'

'That's how it works, I'm afraid.'

'And then?'

'We were keeping him in a safehouse in Finchley. But when we went to pick him up, he was gone.' I pause, adding a break so it doesn't sound like I've recited this hundreds of times. 'There'd been a struggle. There was so much blood… there's just no way…' I trail off, watching the pain in her expression. 'There is no way he could have survived it.'

'You had a deal.'

'I know,' I look down, ashamed.

'You failed. He came through as intended. Like he always did. With everything… you knew that. You knew he was a man of his word! He trusted you!' She yells. 'He believed in you.' She dives into her pocket, pulling out a crumpled piece of paper and holding it up. 'He wrote this… before he died.' She swallows hard, lowering her voice. 'He told me how brilliant he thought you were. And yet you failed him.'

I exhale, unable to meet her furious eyes. 'If I could go back…'

'You would have turned down the case, left him alone?'

'Perhaps.'

'Well, I'm not here to make amends.' She murmurs. 'What's done is done.'

'I've been trying to get Paytak ever since.' I admit. 'He's joined a new syndicate. Or working with them at least.'

'Who?' she frowns.

'A group that calls themselves The Singularity.'

'What are they?'

'A very dangerous group of people.'

'Mafia?'

'No, this is different.'

'How so?'

'I think I should be the one asking the questions.'

'Somebody is after me. I need to know who.'

'Why did you come back to London?'

She hesitates. 'Not much of a choice... I had to resign my position.'

'That was months ago.'

'I've been up at Sandhurst.' She shakes her head. 'Trying to figure out my next move. But things up there... they weren't working out. So I decided to come back, for a bit at least.'

'Tell me about Paul and the laundrette.'

Her eyes widen, shocked by how much I already know. 'I went to meet him. And whilst I was there, he got a call. It seemed urgent. He said he had to leave.'

'A call from Kristine Kingley...'

She nods. 'She was threatening him, trying to get him to help her with something.'

'Did you know what Kristine Kingley did for a living?'

'How would I? I've never met the woman in my life.'

'You sure about that?'

'Paul told me about her. She knew about our family. She thought we could help get Samantha back.'

'So, you went to the laundrette with Paul?' I watch her closely, waiting for something that would force me to doubt her word.

'I insisted I come along.'

'What did he say to Kristine when you arrived?'

'He was trying to calm her down, but she was practically tearing her hair out; she kept shoving a picture of Samantha into my hands.' She closes her eyes for a second as if trying to cut the feed of the memory.

'What did she want you to do?'

'She wanted to pay us to get Samantha back. Apparently, she'd been calling Paul for weeks...'

'Did she know who had taken Samantha?'

'She said it was Paytak.' She nods, remembering. 'She kept saying we needed to find a man named Higgs...'

I say nothing.

'...but when we told her we couldn't help, that the Christofis weren't what we used to be, she got aggressive, started yelling. I tried to calm her down, but Paul had to pull her off me.' She pauses. 'And then the police showed up...'

'What do you mean?' My head snaps up from the floor.

She looks off to the side as if I've spoken another language. 'I mean, the police took her away.'

'The police took her from where?'

'The laundrette...' she says, drawing the words out slowly.

'What kind of police?'

'Plainclothes, but they flashed badges.'

'How many?'

'Two?'

'You're sure?'

She rolls her eyes impatiently. 'I'm sure what?'

'Are you sure that two police officers came into the laundrette?'

'Yes! Ask Paul, for God's sake.'

'He's missing.'

Her eyes widen.

'We're still searching for him.' I clarify as she flops her head into her hands. 'Tell me more about the two officers...'

She shrugs. 'They said they'd been made aware of the situation and that they would deal with it from there.'

'You let them leave with her?'

'They had badges. They said they were on the case.'

'And then what?'

'I walked her out to the car with them, and they took her away.'

'Wait.' I pause, trying to order my thoughts. 'When you walked out of the laundrette, the two officers were with you?'

'Yes! What is the issue?'

I think back to the briefing room, to Amber's evidence on the CCTV as I pace between the fireplace and the coffee table. None of this is on there. *How did they manage that?* Nicky Black is right. They've got people everywhere.

'It seemed so normal, so professional. But when I watched them drive away with her, it hit me. They just turned up, didn't ask my name, no statement; I knew something was off.'

'Is that the last time you saw Kristine?'

Her large eyes regard me cautiously. 'Not technically.'

I raise my eyebrows.

'I decided to follow them.'

'Where?'

'I don't know the road, but they drove to an old hospital in Dalston.'

'The German Hospital?'

She shrugs. 'I managed to see Kristine for a few seconds as they dragged her inside. She was out cold. So, I waited until it got dark, and then I went in.'

'Unarmed?' I exclaim.

'Do you always interrupt people when they're speaking?' she sits up, and for the first time since she arrived, I see Mario Christofi in front of me.

'Go on.'

'Yes, I was unarmed, but this is what I'm trained to do!'

'And what did you find?'

'It's mostly derelict, but the rooms and hallways were just filled with hundreds of children.' She shakes her head, the horror of the memory on her face. 'All of them were crammed tightly together, drugged up, completely out of it. Some of them had multiple injuries, covered in cuts and bruises.' She sighs a weary breath. 'I've seen some terrible things in the past, but this, this was evil in its purest form.' I can tell she's fighting tears, but there's also a sense of frustration in her expression. 'They were all just lying there in this helpless daze, lined up like animals, discarded like they meant nothing.'

'What age?'

'Young. Very young.'

'Did you see where they took Kristine?'

'I looked for her, but I heard voices, so I had to get out of there. I'm no good to those children dead.'

'What about Samantha?'

She doesn't respond, but her haunted expression gives me the answer I need. I close my eyes, tempering the rage stirring inside me. *If I ever see Nicky Black again, I'll kill him myself.* Her lip trembles, and I watch tears rapidly escape her eyes, every suppressed emotion rising to the surface.

'I was too late.'

I approach, awkwardly sitting on the stool next to her. She takes a sudden, deep breath appearing uncomfortable and embarrassed by her outburst.

'Someone must have known I'd been there or at least met Kristine.'

'What makes you say that?'

'When I came home, my flat had been ransacked; someone had obviously been looking for me.' She looks up across the kitchen. 'Could I have some water, please?'

I nod, confused by the sudden switch, and stand to fetch some.

She takes a gulp and pushes her hair back off her face. 'I knew I couldn't stick around, so I called one of the guys I served with, Charles McGuire. I asked him to help me disappear.'

I shake my head, confused. 'Then why are you here?'

'Because I can't walk away, I can't forget what I saw.'

'Why?'

'Pardon?'

'You're telling me this is the worst thing you've seen in the world?' I pause. 'What aren't you saying?'

Her eyes burn into my face. She still doesn't like being challenged; that's clear. 'I have told you all the factual information.'

'But there's more…'

'I don't want to speculate.'

I scoff. 'You can either sit here and tell me everything, or you can choose not to speculate in an interrogation room.'

'With all due respect, you have no idea-'

'Try me.'

'They're just rumours.'

'If you want my help, you better start talking.'

She considers this for a moment. 'That night, I was meant to go to a family dinner, but I didn't want to put Olivia and my grandmother in danger. I knew that Kristine had got herself into something, and somehow, I'd been implicated. Why else would they turn up at my place?'

'Did they take anything?'

'My journals and some other personal things.'

'Like what?'

'Some pictures of my squadron. Whoever was in my flat has taken a keen interest in my past. I wanted to warn McGuire.'

'Did it ever occur to you that they took the pictures to force your hand?'

'I had to make sure he was safe.'
'And you went to him?'
'Yes.'
'How did you know he would help you?'
'We served together.' She looks up at me like that's the only explanation I could possibly need.
'And?'
'He's heard murmurings of an organisation bribing people of high status: policemen, politicians. He said it could have been connected to Kristine.'
'So, you had heard of them? The Singularity?'
'I didn't know what they were called.'
'And you went and told him everything?'
She catches the look on my face. 'He would never betray me.'
'What did he say?'
'He said a private security company were recruiting vets he knew. The job involves protecting all kinds of dodgy people. And the work… all of it is off the books.'
'Where did he learn this?'
'He was approached by an agent… McGuire said he was a spook.' She looks off to the side. 'I think he said his name was Roe. He said Roe asked him a lot of questions: whether he'd been approached by a security company called Freeman Powell or asked to work for any specific gang members.'
'And where is that man now?' I ask, crossing my arms.
'I don't know.'
'McGuire gets approached by a spook looking for information on a security company loaning out vets to gangsters…'
'Roe mentioned one name to McGuire, and it's the same name that keeps coming up again and again.'

'Higgs.' I blurt out as my thoughts fire over one another. 'I need to speak to McGuire.'

'He's underground.'

'And he doesn't know who's working with Paytak? Who Higgs is?'

'Roe just told McGuire that this group silences people. And if he heard anything, to go straight to him. That's why it's important we don't expose him, Gabriel.'

'He must know how to find this Roe bloke.'

'I think we should focus on Paytak and what he's doing with the children.'

'Is that really what this is all about?' I ask, suspicious.

'Huh?'

'Do you really care about those kids, or are you just throwing your weight around? Wanting to teach Paytak who's boss.'

'I'm sorry?'

'With all due respect, the NCA can't get caught up in a revenge mission.'

'Ever consider there would be nothing to avenge if it wasn't for you?' She snaps.

I stay silent, trying not to feel stung by the truth in her words.

'Do you think my father would have ignored all of this? Gabriel, I care about this city, and I care about what happens to those children. How can I walk away after what I saw? A woman begged for my help, and now she's dead.'

'Why come to me?' I ask her again, unsatisfied with her previous explanations. 'You clearly blame me for the way your life's panned out, so why come here?'

'You know what, this was a mistake. I shouldn't have.' She rushes out, jumping off the stool.

I race after her, slamming the door shut just as she begins pulling it open. 'You're not going anywhere.'

'Gabriel, I'm warning you…' she says through gritted teeth.

'I can't let you go now.'

'You think if I wanted to leave that I couldn't?'

'You can try…'

'I don't think you want me to do that.'

'Tell me why you're here.'

She turns slowly, her face mere inches from my body as she looks up at me with huge sparkling eyes. For a moment, I allow myself to fall into them, mesmerised by the generous flecks of gold amidst the hazel tinge. It's almost as if any second, they might rise into an all-consuming flame, destroying everything in their path. She shifts awkwardly, prompting me to lift my eyes from hers.

'Against his better judgement, he trusted you. I wish I had another option…'

'You were in the S.A.S.… what could I possibly do to help?'

She stands straighter, irritated at my proximity. 'They sent me on numerous missions to protect this country. The things I had to do… unofficial surveillance, preserving peace, foiling attacks on cities across the country, the people that served and died to make this world safe. We didn't go through all of that to come home to this… in our own borders. Whoever is doing this has to be stopped.'

'Why isn't McGuire helping you?'

'I no longer have the luxury of being expendable, and that is a concept even McGuire can't comprehend.'

'Why?'

'Sorry?!'

'Why do you suddenly care if you live or die?'

'I thought you were a detective.' She challenges with a flash of curiosity in her eyes, her back still firmly pressed against the door.

'Because of the baby.'

She looks away, uncomfortable. 'I don't even understand it. I can't expect them to.'

I cross my arms, wondering how she's at a point in her life where she has to justify her desire to live.

'You helped him; you understood him.' She drops her gaze. 'He cared for you… I think he saw you as some twisted version of a Guardian Angel. He understood that Paytak would one day destroy him, that he would ruin the city we love. He told me to trust you because, without knowing our history, he knew I would need someone. Someone that cared about this place just as much as him. Even if you were on different sides, he knew you wanted the same thing.' She pauses. 'So the question is… will you prove him right?'

CHAPTER FIFTEEN

Stepping into the apartment, I pull out my headphones before carefully closing the door. Runs at five in the morning have become a thing in the last few days after I spend most nights tossing and turning, trying to figure out what to do amongst the mounting pressure from all angles. Alexandra's presence has tilted the world even further off of its axis. I can barely look at her without wanting to say the words *Mario is alive*. Deceit eats away at me, the guilt of having the power to end her suffering and the lack of ability to do anything with the knowledge.

On top of that, Collins is on my back more than ever. Stanley is borderline harassing me with her constant phone calls. Julian's becoming increasingly suspicious, especially when I'm dismissive about looking for the same woman who's currently sitting in my apartment. All the while, Toff continues to send me a barrage of texts detailing theories, conspiracies, and speculative leads around The Singularity. So, I get up in the middle of the night, put on my training gear, and run. If I don't do something to clear my head, I'll lose the plot. I haven't said much to Lex since the first night. In truth, I don't know what to do. It would have been foolish of me to accept everything she's told me at face value, and as a result, I've spent the last few days trying to corroborate her story. I checked out the German Hospital in Dalston, and it looks like she was right; there are signs that it was recently inhabited. I also managed to track down fragments of CCTV footage of two large trucks leaving the area the day after she was there, both unregistered with stolen plates. I called in an anonymous tip so Stanley can at least get Forensics down there to start the proper search to recover Samantha Kingley's body.

Truthfully, there is no longer anything I can do to save that particular group of kids, and the thought tears me apart every time I allow my brain to go there – another reason for lack of sleep. Of course, it has crossed my mind more than a few times that Lex is part of The Singularity, and this is all a pretence to cover her back. I've considered the possibility she's been planted here to lead me off the scent, to keep me away from tracking them down, using our past as a way to blur my focus. Or that she merely wants revenge for her father. Equally, it's plausible she's telling the truth and really cares as much as she says, but it doesn't feel like I've got all the pieces of the puzzle. Believing everything she's told me would be naïve, but the ramifications of ignoring her completely could be worse. Not only does her account of events align with Nicky's, but it makes the most sense given the evidence. I need her to trust me enough to open up; she has to believe I've bought into everything she's told me, whether she's the real victim or not; she needs to think I'm one hundred per cent on her side because that is how I'm going to solve this. I step into the kitchen and turn on the kettle, suddenly feeling more confident about moving forward, knowing exactly what I need to do.

ALEXANDRA

CHAPTER SIXTEEN

Tossing and turning, the blur of three small faces stare back at me, their wide eyes the colour of demerara sugar following me around the room as I frantically search for Diren Paytak. Abeer steps forward. He tells me I'm too late, and I turn to see his little head pressing into the muzzle of the rifle. Simon's rifle. I take a sharp breath, trying to tell him to run, yelling at him to find safety. He reassures me that it will be ok. And then I hear the trigger.

I bolt upright, checking my surroundings, waiting for the pathological expectation of danger to subside as reality rushes in, and I realise where I am. Finally, laying back, I close my eyes, feeling the grip of exhaustion. Despite enjoying the feeling of sleeping in a bed again, I've never felt this tired in all my life. The thought that my body can be working both for and against me is an uneasy and alien concept. I instinctively place my hand on my stomach, something that's quickly become my good-morning ritual. Despite the chaos swirling around us, every time I place my hand here, I feel hope. For the first time, I am looking at the world through the eyes of a mother. A mother that would do anything to protect her child. I can't help the terror that grips me as my new perspective highlights the stirring madness of the world we live in. And amongst all of it, I can feel myself changing in incomprehensible ways, gradually losing grip of the person I worked so hard to become; the composed, measured woman who's always ten steps ahead, the methodical comprised soldier that Simon taught me to be.

My sleepy haze is suddenly interrupted by an unpleasant clanging noise coming from the other room, quickly followed by the low drawl of Gabriel's voice mumbling a few curse words. I smile a little, amused at the sound of his impatience, and make to get out of bed. I walk out of the guest room to find him standing at the kitchen island, a pan in one hand and a spatula in the other. He's dressed in running gear, his roguish brown hair falling messily over his forehead. I blink hard, trying not to linger my gaze. He throws me a guarded glance across the island, his eyes flickering up through long dark eyelashes, registering my presence before returning to the task at hand. I try to look elsewhere, feigning interest in the city beyond the huge windows of his apartment. Still, I persistently return to him, involuntarily breaking into a smile at the intense furrow of concentration on his brow as he stares down at the pan. He's still got the same magnetism that had me hooked all those years ago, his impressive, masculine presence usurping the space around him, constantly stealing my concentration.

'Morning.' He says without looking up.

'Hello,' I respond awkwardly. There's so much I want to say, so many questions about him, his life, his investigation, but nothing comes as I watch him scrape some scrambled eggs onto two plates.

'How's the sickness?' he asks in a low tone.

I consider my answer, walking over to a kitchen stool and plop myself down; the metal is cold on my thighs, alerting me to the fact I've just walked out of the bedroom in nothing but his grey T-shirt. Thankfully, he's tall enough that it falls just above my knees, but I'm acutely aware that all I'm wearing on my bottom half is knickers.

'Better, thank you.'

He nods before sliding over a plate of eggs and a mug of coffee.
'Oh, I can't…'

'It's decaf,' he clarifies flatly.

I look up from the plate, baffled by the unusual effort and consideration. Usually, he's long gone by the time I'm up. Before I can show him my gratitude, the bitter smell of egg hits my nostrils, and nausea erupts through me. Standing abruptly, I yell a rushed apology over my shoulder and run to the bathroom, certain I can hear him laughing behind me.

He must think this is a complete joke. I show up at his house, claiming I want to take on the Turkish mafia, but I can't even stomach breakfast. On returning to the kitchen, I notice a plate of toast in place of the eggs. Another show of kindness that I wasn't expecting. It's more than I deserve.

'I'm sorry, I am sure you make a great breakfast.'

The corners of his mouth twitch slightly.

'Thank you for looking after me.'

'It's nothing.' He looks up briefly, and the softness in his eyes swiftly melts away the memory of his cold, icy demeanour. 'I've got to head to the office.'

'Do you have any updates at all? Can I do anything to help? I need to talk to you about McGuire. I've had a few thoughts, and I really think...' I stop, my stomach scraping with anxiety at the look of exasperation on his face.

'I'll keep you in the loop.'

'We have to do something about the children,' I call after him as he heads for the bedroom. 'I can't just sit here, Gabriel.'

He stops, looking at the floor without turning back as if mulling something over. In the short time I've spent in his presence again, it's like watching a thick and heavy storm brewing. I've spent a lot of time with quiet, closed men in the military, too scared to show any vulnerability, and I respected that the army had tainted their psyche. But this wasn't always Gabriel, and I'm desperate to know what's behind it. Maybe it's because we don't know how to be friends – we've never tried. The fact his guard is thrown up the minute I enter the room is overwhelmingly frustrating. And I have a festering doubt that he could just be stalling for time until he eventually turns me in.

'I will do what I can,' he says, continuing down the hall.

'If you saw what I saw…' I rush after him, eager to make him understand.

'You're not the only one who's seen evil in the world.' He bites, swivelling to face me.

I hesitate, almost jumping back.

'I've spent years witnessing shit like that. The children you saw – drugged up, helpless, being used – there are hundreds of cases like that all over the world. Countless children are going through it.' His callous expression causes me to take a step away from him. He catches my shock and lowers his voice. 'You know how I'm going to help? By cutting off the head of the snake. You need to forget what you saw. It's too late for them now.' He locks his eyes to mine, his brutal glare burning into me. All I can do is offer a short nod in return, too surprised by the outburst to argue any further.

He marches away before doubling back suddenly. 'I'm getting in the shower. Can I trust you'll still be here when I get back?'

'Yes, sir.' I murmur at his back, watching him disappear into the bedroom.

GABRIEL

CHAPTER SEVENTEEN

As the briefing begins, I sit, half slumped in the chair, thinking about this morning and the disdainful glare in Alexandra's eyes. I've seen that look many times before, but things are different now. This time around, we're back in each other's company, navigating a world of issues whilst also stamping down every emotion, good or bad, that we've ever felt for each other. It's a fucking minefield. We've got to find a way to make this civilised. She'd retreated into her room by the time I left. I'll have to apologise later, perhaps make conversation, or at least make a bit more effort to be around. If I'm going to figure this out, I'll need her onside.

Julian continues to carefully explain the intel we collected from our source, confirming that Kristine Kingley was being used to manipulate border control for Diren Paytak and The Singularity. I tap my fingers impatiently on the table as he speaks, hoping he doesn't slip up and reveal the intel we agreed to hold back: our source snatching Samantha Kingley himself for one but also the potential issue of internal corruption to contend with. *I should have done the update myself.*

'James, if this source goes on record, then we need to inform Interpol.' Collins waves her hand in the air. 'If we have kids being trafficked with the help of the Home Office, this is huge.'

'I'm waiting on names of people Kingley used, Ma'am. Anti-Corruption has been informed and is investigating that independently. The best shot is finding out who Paytak hired through this encrypted chat. We know we hired someone to get rid of Toff. This same person could be after his daughter.'

'James, if this source says Paytak hired a woman who also happened to be in the Forces, is it not entirely possible Paytak is working with Alexandra Christofi?' DI Stanley chimes in.

'Careful…there's more than one woman in S.A.S. Stanley.'

'It's all very convenient.' She scoffs. 'Alexandra comes back to London; she's the last to see Kingley, who's now dead, her father's right-hand man is missing…'

I turn to Collins, ignoring her. 'Ma'am, I wanted to suggest that we continue to pursue The Singularity line of enquiry. We need to find out how they're helping Paytak. And they're the key to locating Alexandra Christofi. Perhaps DI Stanley and Major Investigations can stay focused on the Kingleys? With each of us designated to a specific area, we're likely to be more efficient in uncovering a connection.'

Collins' eyebrows rise in surprise as she looks between us.

'You are aware I'm in the room James?' Stanley's face begins to turn crimson. 'Ma'am, we know Kristine was in contact with Paytak; we know she was looking into a man named Higgs. Based on this source, Higgs and Paytak are now part of The Singularity. Christofi could be too. I need direct access to all findings around this group.'

Collins holds her hand out to Stanley, silencing her in seconds. 'I'm inclined to agree with James. The NCA will pursue all leads to do with OCG activity, and as Alexandra is a Christofi, it sits with us. We'll make the call on her involvement. Stanley, you liaise with Major Investigations and keep your focus on Kristine's killer. We'll regularly share intel and meet somewhere in the middle.'

'You really think that's wise?' she stands with indignation. 'Splitting the taskforce?'

I take a breath to reply.

Collins shoots me a warning glance across the table, telling me to keep quiet. 'We'll see better results this way. James will organise regular updates with you.'

Stanley looks down and furiously rearranges papers in front of her. 'Well, we best be getting on with the task at hand.' She looks at me. 'I do hope you will be forthcoming with your information, Detective.'

'I will if you will.'

She rolls her eyes before storming out of the room, gesturing for a few analysts to follow her.

I wait for the group to shuffle out before turning to Collins, Amber, and Julian. 'Listen...' I lower my voice, leaning against the door. 'What I'm about to tell you stays between us.'

Collins nods, waiting for me to continue.

'Like I said, we had a chat with our source. And he's suggesting that with the CCTV leak and all the challenges we've faced during Op Sandbank - The Singularity might have an inside man.'

Julian's head nods frantically in support of my statement as Collins and Amber consider this.

'We know Kristine Kingley was manipulating people at the borders somehow. The laundrette's CCTV was partially deleted at some point, then leaked to the press. We need to consider that there's something bigger at play.'

'This is why you wanted rid of Stanley.' Collins muses, sitting on the edge of the table.

'Stanley has a fixation on Alexandra being a suspect in the Kingley case with only circumstantial evidence. We need to step back from that. I don't think we should launch a witch hunt just because she was the last to see Kristine Kingley. It's too easy to write Alexandra off like that.'

'What are you suggesting?' Amber asks quietly.

'We need to figure out how far this goes with The Singularity. Our sources confirmed that Samantha Kingley was taken as leverage so Kristine would help them on the borders. He also said there was more help from higher-ups.'

'Gabriel, it's one thing claiming there's a new crime ring in London; it's another to suggest that they're corrupting the police force.' Collins looks between Julian and me.

'Well, this is not without cause.'

'Go on.'

'I have another witness.'

Julian frowns, looking confused.

'This source saw two plainclothes officers take Kristine Kingley away from that laundrette on the day she disappeared. And as we know, that was not on the CCTV.'

'How the bloody hell would they know what plainclothes police officers looked like?' Julian asks, annoyed.

'They flashed badges.'

'Could have been fake?' Collins suggests.

'Do we want to take that chance?'

She shifts forward, looking at me intently. 'You're telling me someone in this office deleted evidence… Preventing us from seeing what really happened to Kristine Kingley?'

'Yes, Ma'am. Our Sandbank source told us that everyone in organised crime is terrified of this group, and for that reason, Paytak is meticulous about tying up loose ends. Perhaps he pulled a few strings, had someone leak the footage of Alexandra and Kristine to the press.'

Collins takes a deep breath. 'That's not enough to silence her.'

'No, but it increases the chances of her being found. Maybe he thought he could get to her inside.'

'This witness…' Amber starts, 'the person who saw the two officers, are they willing to go on record?'

'Maybe.'

'Well, either that or we need the full CCTV with proof that's how it happened.' Collins says, tapping her knuckles on the table before straightening. I lean out of the way as she opens the door, peering up at me before she leaves. 'Twenty-four hours, James. I need more.'

Julian turns to me. 'Guv, what the fuck is going on?'

Amber mumbles something about taking a call before rushing out of the room.

'This new witness…' Julian lowers his voice. 'I know there's a lot you can't say at times, and I trust you to make the right call. But you should have given me the heads up.'

I nod, looking down at the table. 'Think about it though Jules. It makes sense.'

He nods vigorously. 'I back you; I believe you but involve me.'

I meet his eyes. 'As long as it's safe, you have my word.'

CHAPTER EIGHTEEN

I sit behind the wheel of my car for over an hour, persistently watching the rain running off the windshield, eventually finding the soft pitter-patter of the water on the glass comforting as my brain accelerates into overdrive. Knowing what I do now, I should have left Mario Christofi where he was. But my arrogance led me to believe that with his help, I could put an end to the roots of organised crime in this city. Instead, Mario's absence merely created a vacuum of twisted possibilities, opening the floodgates to more greed and corruption. I look up at the window of my flat, shaking my head. *And I'm still paying the price.*

Popping the boot, I walk around to the back of the car and pull out the bag of clothes I took from my sister's house earlier today. I hope she won't notice, but if she does, I can easily explain that a one-night stand needed something to get home. Maybe this small gesture will be enough to appease Alexandra, and I won't need to paint a false smile on my face for the rest of the evening.

Letting myself into the flat, I look around the place, accepting I might have to apologise for my earlier behaviour and just grin and bear the onslaught of questions that will follow. Setting the bag down slowly, I sense something is off. Darting my eyes around the space, I wait to hear her voice, to catch a flicker of wild blonde hair from the corner of my eye. Nothing happens. *It's too tidy, too quiet.* Lex is a whirlwind, full of energy, her presence entirely unavoidable; if she were here, I would know. *Unless she's asleep.* I march across the living room and burst into the guest room. *Empty.* I leave and swiftly enter the guest bathroom. *Empty.*

My heart starts hammering against my ribcage as I head to the opposite end of the flat and walk into my bedroom. *Nothing.* I step in, instantly spotting the curtains flapping persistently in the cold wind as if they're warning me of something. I walk to the window and slam it shut with irritation. Standing stock-still, I look out to the darkness, my brain running through scenarios with intense speed. She's not here. So the question remains, did she leave, or was she taken?

ALEXANDRA

CHAPTER NINETEEN

Standing outside Aldyn's mansion, I peer through the narrow gaps in the wrought-iron gates, looking for any sign of patrolling security or CCTV. Once I'd scoured Gabriel's case files for Aldyn's last known address, I immediately left the flat, hoping he might have answers that Gabriel currently refuses to share. The mansion is set just off Wagon Road in Barnet, a quiet residential street but entirely accessible to anyone and everyone. Considering he's the leader of an Albanian gang, you'd expect surveillance or at least a few dogs, but so far, nothing. The prospect sets me on edge; something isn't right. Perhaps someone found him before I did. I'm certain he's wanted for a hefty list of dirty deeds. It's entirely possible I'm too late and leaving the safety of the apartment was a mistake. *But what choice do I have when he's all but shut me out?* Although I've come to better understand the context of my father's agreement with Gabriel, I still wonder where his true loyalty lies. A question that's becoming all the more prevalent the more he cuts me out, deliberately keeping me at a distance. *If I want progress, I have to make it myself.*

I scan the front of the house again, hearing nothing but the buzz of London traffic, coupled with my slow, steady breathing. I swallow past the dry lump in my throat, my hands becoming slippery with a cold sweat, making it hard to grip my gun. *The joys of pregnancy*. I take a breath, shoving down the flustered heat of anticipation, and wipe my palms on my trousers before cocking the weapon and hitching myself up and over the wall that circles the driveway, landing on a grass verge that runs towards the front garden. I wait, expecting alarm trips or a huge spotlight that might expose my presence, but again… nothing. There are four cars in the driveway, but that doesn't mean he's home. He loves cars. *I remember that about him.*

I tread down the small verge and decide to loop the entire property, needing to know for sure that there's absolutely no threat present. I look up at the windows. The house appears dark and empty, void of all life and activity. A motorbike zooms past on the road behind me, and my pulse lurches into sixth gear as the engine's sound triggers flashes of a past operation amongst heavy traffic in Mumbai. I screw my eyes and shake my head, redacting the memory. Pulling myself together, I silently creep through a small gate that leads to a walled garden, my head methodically turning from left to right, watching for an approach from either side. The Forces taught so many combative skills, but the one I always found the most useful was stealth, being able to spread your weight with such careful proportion that you could near travel over any terrain with silent, covert precision. It helps when an entire team of people just like me are deployed into high-risk areas, having to snake around debris, approaching poorly practised, ill-trained freedom fighters in the Middle East. But of course, that is merely one world of conflict, and I've since learned that I'm destined to come up against other enemies, people who are well-tuned to accuracy, often just like me.

Having checked the premises, I deduce that I'm either here alone or the threat is minimal. I decide to approach the back door and make my presence known. Shooting through the glass, I step into the kitchen, training my weapon out. I hate the dark, but it gives me an advantage. I'm used to it. Suburban gang members aren't. I wait for a beat, hearing nothing but the whirring of the dishwasher in the corner of the room; someone has been here this evening. I look around the kitchen. It's tidy. No sign of a struggle. In fact, aside from the dishwasher, there's no indication it's been used at all.

'Aldyn?' I yell out to the empty room. I grab a kitchen knife and tuck it into the waistband of my jeans. 'It's Alexandra Christofi. I'm not here to hurt you or anyone else. I need to speak to you, OK?' My voice feels alien, thrusting it out into the eery silence; having just spent the last few minutes trying to be as covert as possible; the sound of it travelling through the house makes me feel dangerously exposed. 'Aldyn?'

A creak of floorboards pulls my attention up to the ceiling. *Bingo.* I pace through the kitchen and out to the vast hallway, checking through open doors. My heart rate increases as I approach the sweeping staircase and glance up to the mezzanine level. Whoever is upstairs has the higher ground, and the minute I take the first step, I'm vulnerable. I can either sprint up them in the hopes of reaching the top, or I can force my assailant to come down to me. Deciding on the latter, I point my gun at Aldyn's extravagant chandelier and repeatedly pull the trigger, stepping to the side as it falls from the wall and crashes to the floor, shattered glass and crystal scattering everywhere. I turn back to the kitchen and take a seat at the head of the table, braced for whoever comes through the door.

CHAPTER TWENTY

Aldyn Wolfe stands in the doorway of his kitchen, his huge, mountainous figure filling the space, his sunken eyes watching me with wary apprehension. He was once a good friend of my father's, and I'm counting on his loyalty to my family to get the information I need. He stares at me intensely, his heavy hands gripping the shotgun trained out in front of him.

'Sit down, please, Aldyn.'

'You broke my light.'

'It was garish.'

'It's worse now!' He pauses. 'Are you here to kill me?'

'I would have done that already.'

'But they sent you, didn't they?'

'Who?' I look at him, puzzled. 'Can you put the gun down? I just need some information.'

He studies me warily.

'Something is happening... Something I can't explain.'

He sighs, whispering words in Albanian. 'The only reason I am putting this down is because I respect your family, and I trust your word. We have what Albanians call *Besa*...It means we have an oath, you know, a trust. So, don't let me down.' He wags a chubby index finger, setting the shotgun on the table.

'I'm here about Diren Paytak.'

'OK...'

'I know he was responsible for what happened to my father. He's after me, and I need to understand why.'

'Paytak is always up to something.'

'Please, Aldyn...' I request politely, knowing I have to appeal to his softer side. 'Do you know he's connected to the dead politician?'

'Why is this important to you?'

'Because we met with her… she came to Paul and me before she died. They already got to him. Paul is gone.'

He tilts his head to the side, curling his lip.

'I know someone took him, Aldyn, and that someone is after me. It's connected to Paytak and this new group. Whatever Kristine Kingley was doing, it's worth the risk of covering his tracks. He exposed me to the press and made me a suspect in Kristine's murder. I need your help.'

His brow furrows, the wrinkled lines on his forehead creasing together as he stares across at me, his blue eyes shining intensely in the darkness. 'You should leave this alone.'

'I don't have a choice.'

'Go to the Police. Explain yourself. Ask for their protection.'

'It's too late for that. Please just tell me what you know.'

'It's a long story.'

'I have time.'

'What is it in for me?'

I raise my eyebrows. *Unbelievable.* I've caught the man off guard, alone in the middle of the night, and he's trying to negotiate with me. 'Someone is helping me, a Detective… he might be able to help you, whatever you've got yourself into.' I gesture towards the shotgun. 'Clearly, there's a reason you're here on your own. Who were you waiting for?'

He waves a dismissive hand in the air, looking ashamed.

'You're informing, aren't you?'

He looks away.

'Are you?' I repeat.

He shrugs as if it's no big deal. 'It's survival, Alexandra.'

'And you know something.'

'Come to work for me, and I can consider helping you.'

'That'll paint a target on your back.'

'You are Mario Christofi's daughter. Just talking with you for five minutes has created the target, my dear.'

'Aldyn, I don't…' I stop, shaking my head. 'Why? Why are you informing?'

'I've made a deal in exchange for information… the Albanian monopoly of the drugs market is done. But when this is all over, we can start something new.'

I say nothing, with red flags, warning signals, and feelings of disloyalty to my family rushing around my brain. I take a deep breath, weighing up the options. I came back to London to partake in my family's business, so that isn't the issue. It's my father; all I can see at this moment is his face. *What would he think?* And then I look back at Aldyn, the man who holds all the cards. I don't like being backed into a corner; *I never have.*

'I'm not going to work with you.'

'Then we are done here.'

It takes me a second between the thought and the action, but in the brief moment Aldyn Wolfe draws his next breath, I've stood up, swinging my gun from my hip, and pointing it directly at his head. He reaches for his weapon, but I'm too fast, throwing it off the table to the other side of the room. 'I'm not playing games. Tell me what is happening, or I will put a bullet in your head…*Besa* or no *Besa*.'

He holds his shaking hands up before nodding to the corner of the room. 'I have CCTV; it's connected to my heart monitor. If I die, the police—'

'They're after me either way; this makes no difference.'

'Fine!' he shouts. 'Fine! Sit down, and I'll tell you.'

'Don't bother trying anything. I'm too quick for you,' I say, taking a seat, the gun still firmly in my hand.

He grits his teeth together with frustration; gangsters don't like feeling powerless, but maybe if he hit the gym now and again, he'd be more mobile. 'When Mario was alive, we dominated the cocaine industry, we cut out the middleman, went straight to the cartels. No need for brokers or fees. More profit for us.'

'Very smart. My father told me it was your idea.'

'It worked very well for many years. Yes, it was my idea, but your father built the relationship, and when he died, it all broke down. Without Mario's business nature, they didn't want to deal with us anymore.'

'Then what happened?'

'They opened up the business. Paytak stepped up. That was always his plan, you know, Alexandra. He wanted what your father had. Always has.'

'He had him killed.'

He nods. 'They've been enemies for a long time. Paytak was always waiting in the wings. But he stole that position; he hasn't earnt it.'

I stare at him with anticipation, desperate to have the golden ticket with all the answers.

'He tried to play some of the cartels off each other; they didn't like it. He has no honour, the man.' He shakes his head disapprovingly. 'He lost money. He was in a lot of danger... you don't fuck with the cartels, you know?'

'OK...'

'I thought he was finished. The cartels just take you in the night... nobody will ever know what happened.'

'But they didn't?'

He holds his hand up to stop me. 'He went quiet for a bit, obviously, but after a few months, he's back, more arrogant than ever. He says he's got an opportunity, a way to get the money back, pay the cartels, get rich and keep everyone happy.' He sits back in his chair and crosses his arms, resting them on his round stomach

'Trafficking.'

'Yes,' he shrugs, curling his bottom lip upward. 'For us, it is easy.' He points his hands to his chest. 'Hellbanianz is the best. We've been moving drugs across the borders for years.'

'Not just drugs Aldyn… this is children.'

He moves his head in a seesaw motion, looking up to the ceiling. 'We did other things too, but we've stopped. Never kids though. We would never touch children.'

'How is Paytak doing it?'

'Before your father died, he came to me. He wanted me to show him how it could be done. I told him no, I was loyal to Toff; I couldn't help. Anyway, it's not possible anymore. The government is much stricter, tougher on all this shit. But when Toff passed, he came back, he insisted on using my contacts.'

'You mean dirty border officers?'

'Yes, but I told him there's no business; we haven't paid them for a while. Who knows if they would take bribes anymore? I told him if that's what he wanted to do, then he's better off going to Spain, Portugal, and then using boats, taking them all to Marrakech.' He reels this off as if he's telling me an ordinary story about a completely legitimate business transaction, and I almost shiver from revulsion. Aldyn is so desensitised to this; he doesn't comprehend the reality of what he's saying. 'But he said it had to be London.'

'Why?' I snap. 'Why are the Turks suddenly so interested in this?'

'I don't know.'

'But Hellbanianz own most of the brothels in London. So, is he selling children into your brothels?'

'Not to me… and I don't deal with kids. It is the lowest of the low. Disgusting.' He shakes his head as if that's a boundary he'd never cross, despite breaking so many others.

'The people you moved across the borders. How did it work back in the day? How did you get them over?'

'It started in Serbia and Albania... people in my country were suffering, a lot of them needed asylum, but we know the governments in Europe wouldn't let them in – they'd rather let them sail on boats and watch them sink.'

'It started as a good deed?'

'We were paid very well by their families.'

'Then you took advantage of them...'

'Alexandra, we gave them livelihood here.'

'They were here illegally and had nobody.'

'We are going off on a tangent,' he yells, banging his palm on the table,

I twitch my hand around the gun.

He swallows, holding up his hands in apology before continuing. 'Anything was better than my country, trust me. If not for me, they'd be dead at the bottom of the English Channel. Can you imagine what drives a person to get into a small boat and sail across the ocean with nothing but the clothes on their back? We gave them jobs, helped them make money.'

'In brothels.'

'They were paid well. We looked after them.'

'But that isn't what Paytak is doing now, is it? I've seen those children. How is he rounding them up? There is nothing better about that, Aldyn.'

His eyes weigh heavy, guilt settling on his face. 'It's possible he is selling some of them to private sex rings, to people with big money and bad habits. But not all. Not on that scale.'

'Jesus Christ.' I close my eyes, trying to keep the image out of my head. 'And the rest?'

'I can't say, but we are not getting them.'

'It doesn't make sense – he must be doing something with the rest.' I pause, my mind throwing out possibility after possibility. 'You told him how it worked; you told him how to traffic them. Are they coming from Albania?'

'No, he isn't working from Albania. He is transporting them from elsewhere.'

'So what did you do for him? Because you helped him, somehow. I can see it in your eyes.'

He sighs. 'I gave him the warehouses and the contact of the lady we used to work with.'

'Kristine Kingley…'

'We paid her very well to keep her ear to the ground, to make sure there was no issue in the ports.'

'You're telling me that the Home Office… our government, who are so strict on immigration, are the same people being bribed for human trafficking?'

He nods.

That explains how Kristine knew how to contact my family; she's been dirty for a while. 'You gave Paytak Kristine's details, and then what?'

'He paid me a lot of money for the information. He offered me a role in the new trafficking operation. I said it wasn't for me; we're moving out of that.'

'Why did you help him, Aldyn?'

'It is just business,' he murmurs.

'And if it is just business, then why are you here, alone, waiting in the dark with a shotgun?'

He inhales a long breath, his gold chain straining against his thick neck. 'I moved my family out because Paytak has decided to tie up loose ends.'

'You guys have been working organised crime for years. If everyone decided to tie up loose ends in the criminal underworld, you'd all be dead.'

'Whoever he is working for, he is so scared... he will risk exposure to silence everyone.'

'Who is he working for?'

'There have been rumours... When he was trying to recruit me, he said how easy it would be; he said I would get instructions through a secret chat room. I had to carry out the job, then they'd wire me the money.' He stops suddenly.

'And?'

'Paytak has a big mouth... He said his new employer gave him anything he needed: guns, weapons, surveillance, assassins. Anyway, I told him I wouldn't do it, it's too risky, and there's no way he could guarantee protection. That is when he told me he had access to hire mercenaries. You know... ex-forces.'

'And you thought that was me?!'

'Well, when you broke into my house, it made sense. You came back to London. In the news, they said you killed Kristine. You're a soldier. So, yes.... I thought it was you.'

I look down at the floor, squinting at my blurred reflection in the polished tiles. 'Someone's putting pressure on him to get rid of all the evidence. It's perfect; nobody would question gangland violence. Paytak is the cleaner.'

'Exactly. And he is nothing like your father. He is more than happy getting paid to do what he's told with no reason to ask questions. And it's clear to me that whoever he is working with, they are very powerful.'

'The Singularity... that's what they're called, isn't it?'

Aldyn's head snaps up. 'Where did you hear that name?'

'It's been mentioned.'

'Don't say that to anyone else. You understand?'
'Who are they?'
'If this is true, then it's not good, Alexandra.'
'They can't do this in our city, Aldyn.'
'If they are involved, then you need to drop it.'
'What are they?'
'A myth.' He frowns, his eyes searching ahead for the words. 'It's a syndicate: not mafia, not cartels. It's a special network of people: businessmen, politicians, ambassadors, police officers, some even monarchy from across the world.'
'Like a club?'
'Yes, for all kinds of things. I heard some things; rumours but never anything solid. Nobody in our world has dealt with them before.'
'If it's so secretive, how do you know about them?'
He hesitates, shifting in his seat. 'I was approached by a gentleman. He knows about The Singularity, and he told me some things. He asked me for information on Paytak.' He exits a heavy breath. 'I told him about the trafficking operation, the hitmen and Kristine.'
'That's who you're informing to?'
He nods slowly. 'If Paytak finds out, I am dead.'
'Why don't you run?'
'That is not in my nature.'
I almost roll my eyes. 'Who is this gentleman?'
He hesitates, the whites of his eyes becoming more prominent in the darkness.
'Aldyn...'
'You should stop this, Alexandra.'
'I need to know his name...'
'You should leave this alone...'

'Aldyn!'

'Roe!' He yells. 'Roe... His name is Jacob Roe.'

I swallow past the constricting lump in my throat. 'And who does he work for?'

'I can't remember.'

I stand abruptly. 'I have to go.'

'Alexandra...' He calls after me.

I stop, facing the door.

'You have to know if you do this, if you go after them...you're not coming back. Nobody comes back.'

I stare at him for a beat, suddenly feeling an overwhelming urge to stay here, to stay with him. If we worked together, perhaps we could both be safe. And then I realise; no matter how ineffective Gabriel has been so far, I can't abandon him. That isn't the right path.

'Stay safe, Aldyn.'

I turn to leave, stamping down my concerns about his wellbeing, knowing I can't afford to save him as well. And then a thought occurs to me suddenly: 'Aldyn, the address...the location of the warehouses. Can you show me where they are?'

He nods.

'And I'll need a car.'

GABRIEL

CHAPTER TWENTY-ONE

There is no sign of forced entry, and you can't open that window from the outside. She couldn't have even let anyone in the flat through the front door. I literally locked her in, which means she left of her own accord. Either way, I know I have a short period in which to find her, and I'll admit, for the first time, I'm panicked. Not just for her safety and the fact her father will likely murder me if he finds out I found her and then lost her again, but the minute anyone discovers that I kept her hidden, everything with this case will go downhill. None of the evidence will be admissible, which means Paytak, and The Singularity will be able to continue doing whatever the hell it is they're doing. *We will never be able to stop them.* Based on the mess of the files on my bedside table, I've guessed that she's taken it upon herself to visit Aldyn Wolfe, the head of the Hellbanianz, which in itself takes extreme balls. Wolfe is one of the most dangerous men in the country, but if I'm right, then somehow Alexandra feels able to waltz into his house like they're old friends. *She's fucking unbelievable.*

I overtake another car, flashing blue and red lights, veering down the Cockfosters Road, when my phone rings, the handsfree on the car kicking in automatically.

'James.'

'Gabriel…'

As soon as I hear her voice, both relief and rage merge into one extreme emotion.

'Where the fuck are you?'

'I tried to help.'

'What?! Who?' I ask, still racing past cars, breaking every speed limit known to man.

'They're gone,' she whispers.

'Whose phone is this?' I look down at the unknown caller ID, already dreading the answer.

Silence.

'Alexandra, tell me where you are.'

'Unit six, Stephenson Street, Canning Town.'

'Stay there.' I yell, swinging the car around, speeding off in the other direction.

CHAPTER TWENTY-TWO

I park in the middle of the road, keeping the blue lights flashing as I race to the door of Unit six, a large industrial space on a grey, soulless plot of concrete. I look around before drawing my weapon and shoulder through the small, metal door. The hinges scrape loudly against the motion, swiftly announcing my presence with a low moan.

The first thing that hits me is the smell: the instantaneous odour of death. I know it immediately – a sweet, nauseating stench of rotting flesh drifting through the air with a poisonous effect. I opt to stop breathing through my nose, looking for the source. The whole unit appears empty, save for a few plastic chairs scattered around the place. Despite the bright lights, it has an eery feeling, an undisclosed emptiness. I step through pieces of torn clothing, cigarette butts, rubbish packets, and odd shoes littered in piles around the derelict space. I squint up to the ceiling, noticing a mezzanine level with two rooms at the top of the stairs. I start to head in that direction when a shuffling behind causes me to pull my weapon, swiftly turning over my right shoulder, pointing it towards the corner of the room. *There she is.* She's sitting with her head in her hands next to a pile of rags, her wild, wavy hair falling around her face. She must have seen me but hasn't said a word. I move towards her, ready to unleash hell for her stupidity, when I'm suddenly drawn to a halt. She's covered in blood. It's smeared like war paint over her usually flawless complexion, with prominent red hand marks around her neck, arms, and torso. Almost every inch of her is smothered with slurs and stains of red. She's holding her wrist, and I look down to see a deep gash sliced into the flesh across her forearm.

The anger dissolves instantly. 'What happened? Are you injured?' I ask, crouching down.

She raises her head slightly, her big golden eyes filled with anguish before she flits them away from my face and down to the rags next to her. I follow her gaze, scanning the lumps of dirty clothes, finally seeing the small, pale foot poking out from under a grimy white sheet.

'There are three,' she murmurs. 'They'd already taken the others.' She rubs her bloody hands over her face again, tormented by the near-miss. I stare down at the covered bodies piled next to each other. *Twice now, she's had to see this.* 'I just wanted to sit here with them for a while. I wanted them to have someone, at least in the end.'

'I understand,' I say, the image of what these children must have endured making my hands begin to tremble. I clench them into fists and quickly stand, walking a few paces away. *I have to get a hold of myself. One of us has to keep it together.* I screw my eyes shut as a past I've tried to forget weighs on my mind. I bide my time, waiting for the thoughts to pass, pushing them away like a child trying to unsummon a ghost and swallow hard, shoving every emotion deep down before I finally turn back to her. 'Is that your blood?'

Her brow furrows, and she blinks as if she's trying to ascertain the meaning of my words. She looks down at her body. 'I think I'm hurt, yeah.'

I walk towards her and gently take her arm, crouching down in front of her once more. 'You have a wound here; it will need stitches.'

'I can do it myself,' she mutters as if we're talking about opening a jar.

'I need to call this in,' I sigh.

Her head snaps up, her expression panicked.

'Anonymously...'

Her face doesn't change.

'We've got three dead bodies here, Alexandra. We can't just leave them. This place is full of evidence.'

'You've got five.'

'Sorry?'

'You've got five bodies,' she clarifies, her voice startlingly removed.

I look around the room, searching for the evidence, somewhat puzzled. She shifts, trying to stand up, and I move forward to help her.

'In there.' She nods towards a second door and then looks back at me. 'They were here when I got here. The men from the laundrette, the policemen. I had to defend myself.'

'Who are they?' I ask, my voice hoarse.

'Ex-military… they're wearing dog tags.'

'Is that their blood?' I nod towards her.

Her eyes widen before she looks down at her shaking hands, moving her gaze over the rest of her body. 'Yeah.' She nods. 'I think so.'

'You took them both on… yourself?'

She doesn't answer. Instead, she's staring back down at the rags. 'I caught them off-guard. And then they attacked me…' She trails off before slowly raising her head. It's like a switch has been flicked; there's nothing but a desolate distance in her eyes. 'I killed them.'

I clamp my jaw in a bid to control my reaction. So, this is what the forces does to a person: allows you to detach yourself from your actions to get the job done. I can see the complete disengagement in her face as we stand here, and I realise that in our current situation, the woman in front of me, the person that committed this act, is a stranger.

'Stay here,' I order. 'Don't bother running again because I will find you, so it's a waste of time for both of us.'

She rests against the wall, tearing off material from her T-shirt and tying it around her arm. I walk towards the second door, taking in the discarded objects littered around the warehouse. From the used needles, cigarette butts, and empty sandwich packets, it's clear a lot of people were hiding out here at one time. I reach the door, trying not to think what might be on the other side and just go for it - swinging it open, motion lights switch on in a smaller, carpeted room. There's nothing in it, save for the bodies of two men lying in conjoined pools of red, both dressed in blood-soaked black clothes. I take another step into the room and stand over their lifeless bodies. One of them had his throat slit. He might not have seen it coming. He has no other wounds on his body, no defence marks whatsoever. He did not attack first; *that was an execution.* The other is a different story. It's clear he put up a fight: he has multiple stab wounds in his legs, his abdomen, and most fatally, in the back of his neck. This would explain Lex's injury.

    I knew her record, of course, but it's not the same as seeing it first-hand. It was naïve of me to think that she wasn't capable of something like this, but here it is, right in front of me. When she has to, Alexandra can undoubtedly fend for herself. *So out of the two of us, who really needs protecting?*

ALEXANDRA

CHAPTER TWENTY-THREE

It's a little after midnight when we return to the flat. Gabriel circled Islington for almost an hour to ensure we weren't followed. At one point, I was sure he was going to drive me straight to the NCA and turn me in. But I think we both know it won't solve the bigger problem. I feel guilty that a car registered to Aldyn Wolfe will be found at the industrial unit, but as Gabriel wouldn't let me out of his sight, there's no way I could have returned it. He called in an anonymous tip, describing the warehouse from a phone booth in Star Lane. I watched him lean against the glass, his handsome face deep in concentration as he gave the tip, pretending to be a witness, describing a suspect that never existed, all so those poor children could be found. *All so he could protect me.* As soon as we get inside, I head straight for the bathroom. Gabriel walks off in the other direction, down the corridor to his bedroom, and I wonder if that's the last time I'll see him for a while. I wonder if he'll go back to ignoring me, return to shutting me out. I slide my clothes to the floor and come to stare in the bathroom mirror. *He was right.* I'm covered in blood; it's on my face, in my hair, smeared over me as a stark reminder of what I'm capable of. He hasn't brought it up again: the fact that I murdered two men tonight, but I know he was shocked. I could see it in his eyes: he went from understanding his part in all of this, accepting that I came here for assistance, to wondering who he let into his house. This is why vets are friends with other vets. We're aware we've all committed terrible acts and accept each other anyway. He might be a police officer, but I'm certain he doesn't come across this amount of chaos on a daily basis.

Just as I'm about to switch on the shower, there's a light knock on the door, and I pull it straight open without thinking. Gabriel stands in the doorway; he appears taken aback, quickly running his eyes down my body before trying to avert his gaze. I look down, realising my error: I have answered the door, in my underwear, with no towel. *Shit.* We didn't have time to be prudish on tour, but I forget things aren't the same in the real world. Still looking away, he leans past me and around the door, grabbing a towel and swiftly throwing it in my direction.

'Here,' he says, half frowning.

I take it and rush out a quick *thank you,* waiting patiently for him to say something.

He waves a medical kit in the air. 'I need to look at your arm.'

I shake my head before looking down at the deep slice across the flesh. 'Oh, yeah... thank you.'

I sit on the side of the bath, and Gabriel kneels in front of me, his long fingers carefully assessing the damage. Something about his touch, the fact he's so close that I can feel his breath on my skin, elicits a lightness I can't explain. I abruptly have to fight the urge to be comforted, for him to tell me everything is going to be ok. Maybe it's because I miss my father. Perhaps my hormones are just all over the place. But I'm desperate to crumple into his arms and never let go.

'We need to clean it up,' he says, grabbing a flannel, wetting it under the tap and dousing it with medical alcohol before carefully dabbing it around the wound.

'Fuck,' I hiss as he makes contact with my skin.

He raises his head, his chestnut-brown eyes laden with apology.

'Sorry...' he whispers, reaching for the stitches.

'I can do it,' I insist, leaning forward for the kit, desperate for him to leave. My emotions are all over the place. I don't know if I can trust myself around him right now. All I want is the boy from Cambridge. But that's pointless – he's long gone.

'You know, you don't always have to make helping you so hard,' he states bluntly.

I get the feeling he's not talking about the stitches. I present my arm to him again, conceding; my eyes becoming fixated on the slow, methodical way he pulls the needle up and through as if he's done this a thousand times.

'I needed to do something.' I comment.

His hand stills, his body tensing. 'I was doing everything I could.'

'You were keeping everything from me,' I reply softly. 'I told you I wanted your help. I told you I wanted to go up against them together.'

'The daughter of the gangster I investigated turns up here, claiming that she needs my help...' He looks up, meeting my eyes. 'Then she escapes my flat, breaks into the house of an Albanian drug lord, goes on the search for a trafficking ring with no backup and kills two men in the process. Forgive me if it's a little hard to trust you with information.'

'If you had worked with me in the first place, I wouldn't have had to take matters into my own hands now, would I?'

'You never needed my help, Lex: you wanted my permission. You needed someone on the inside to protect you, to make sure you didn't get arrested whilst you went on a vendetta.'

'You have no idea—'

'Then please enlighten me because you have unleashed fucking havoc tonight. You clearly don't need me, so why are you here?' His neck muscles strain with frustration, his eyes narrowing.

'Because I can't do this by myself. Because I need you.'

'Bullshit… Stop fucking lying.' He stands, throwing the needle into the bin. 'Let me know when you're ready to start telling the truth.' He adds before abruptly storming out of the bathroom.

GABRIEL

CHAPTER TWENTY-FOUR

I leave the apartment, pacing quickly down Upper Street, needing to create some distance. I know it's stupid to leave her alone again, but I need to think. And when she's there, I can't see past her. When you combine that with the fact that this case hits closer to home than I'd like to admit, it makes for an incomprehensible mess. And I don't have the luxury of failing. There isn't a choice to be made; I have to see this through. Darting and weaving between Islington's sprinkling of tourists, I take a deep breath and pull out the burner phone, calling the only number saved. It rings once before he answers.

'What do you have?'

'She's safe.'

'How?'

'Long story, but she came to me.' I decide to leave out the part where I lost her for six hours.

'Thank fuck. Thank fuck she's safe.' He breathes out a long sigh, causing a crackling down the line. 'Did she explain what's going on?'

'Yeah, and it's a shit show, Toff.'

'Tell me.'

'She got caught up helping Kristine Kingley when she went to see Paul. Kingley was on the Turks' payroll, helping them traffic through the borders. She told them she was done, and they took her daughter. She knew about your family, and she wanted help to get her daughter back, so she contacted Paul. Alexandra got in the middle somehow.'

'I fucking knew this had something to do with Paytak.'

'Apparently, Paytak has hired contract killers through The Singularity. It's how he got rid of Kristine. I think it's also the reason Paul is missing.'

'He's an evil motherfucker, Gabe. He has no morals. Are they coming after Lexy because she spoke to Kristine or because she's my daughter?'

'Both, it seems.'

'Shit...' He hisses.

'I'm handling it, but it's not easy, Toff. I know she's your daughter, but she's angry. She blames me for what happened to you, understandably. And it's making her a pain in the arse to keep an eye on.'

There's silence on the other end, and I sense he's working out his next move. 'She'll come around, Gabe. Deep down, she knows who's responsible.'

'It feels wrong not telling her the truth.'

'It's for her own good.'

I say nothing, unable to shake the guilt.

'You think anyone knows she's with you?'

'Not yet.'

'I'm glad you didn't take her in.'

'They've got men on the inside... we both know that.'

'She's not responsible for Kristine's death, Gabe.'

'I know,' I say in a low tone, looking across the street, examining the passing throng of locals, checking I'm not being watched. *Force of habit.* 'She wants to stop Paytak.'

'Typical,' he scoffs. 'I presume you've suggested she run and put all of this behind her?'

I remain silent, unsure how to respond. Selfishly, if everything she's told me is true, then I need her to stay put. It's one thing having Toff around to guide me, but with access to Lex, we might be able to stop them much quicker. Naturally, this isn't something I'm willing to share with Mario. Deep down, he knows she won't run.

'She's adamant she has to go up against them.'

'She's ok, though?' he asks, concerned, and I prevent myself from launching into a tirade, describing all the ways his daughter is decidedly not ok.

'She's alright…' I pause, weighing up the risks of my next question.

'What is it, Gabe?'

'Look, she's your daughter, and I know you don't want to hear this… but is it at all possible that she's part of this? That she's playing both sides?'

I immediately regret the question, but I can't shake the idea. I have to be able to say this aloud to someone else, someone that isn't me.

'Gabriel.' He pauses. 'My daughter would rather die than work for Diren Paytak. And she would never be involved in anything that harmed children. It's not her.'

'If they're after her because she's a loose end, imagine what will happen if they find out she's planning on going up against them?'

'Well, knowing her as I do, she won't give up.'

'I want to help her. I just need to be sure that we're on the same side.'

'Gabriel, Alexandra is stubborn and ruthless at times, but she's not a traitor. Loyalty is her foundation.'

I sigh, urging paranoia to accept what I'm hearing.

'Will you help her?'

'I don't have a choice, really…'

'Look, Gabe, thank you for everything. Being an ally to me isn't easy. I'll never be able to repay-'

'I'm just trying to do what's right.'

'Please don't tell her…not yet.'

I take a deep, tired breath. 'I won't tell her anything, but if shit gets worse here, then it's not safe keeping her locked away in my apartment. She'll have to know at some point.'

'I know,' he says, and I can almost hear the turmoil in his brain. 'I'll do everything in my power to protect your life, Gabriel. It shouldn't have to suffer for my family. I'm indebted to you.'

'All I want is to figure this out and be done with it.'

'I'll help you as much as I can, and then you never have to hear from any of us again.' He laughs jokily, but I know he means it. 'Stay safe and keep me updated.'

As I walk back, I remain deep in thought. Realistically this will end one way. Concealing a suspect, being complicit in the false death of an NCA witness, covering up the murder of two police officers; the odds are not in my favour. If I can prove that Alexandra didn't murder Kristine Kingley, expose Diren Paytak and, by proxy, the existence of The Singularity; that could soften the shit storm brewing on my horizon. I take a deep, long inhale and head back up to the apartment, wondering what life could have been like had the Christofi family never existed.

ALEXANDRA

CHAPTER TWENTY-FIVE

I stare up at the ceiling fan, thinking about the last few hours, watching the blades spin around and around, slicing through the air with precise repetition. I close my eyes as the motion resurfaces images of the desert and the countless Apaches landing and taking off for rescue missions, surveillance, covert operations. Some coming back intact, others not quite so lucky. More flashes of that time regurgitate, the compound, screaming women, abused children. I grumble, burying my face into the pillow as the simple motion of a ceiling fan can throw me right back.

I try to still my mind, but it replaces the desert with pictures of the last few hours. Haunting images, snapshots of the children, their beaten, discarded bodies in the warehouse. My inconsolable rage as I saw the two men sitting there, telling jokes like they were bouncers at the door of a nightclub, sharing old tales. Something clicked, and I couldn't stop it. I clutch my stomach, thinking of my own carelessness, the inconsideration of the little life inside me. *What sort of mother will I be?* The killing, the lying, the double-crossing, and constant second-guessing; it's the past, and that is where it should stay. What I've done, the things I've seen; it's my burden to bear. But it can't keep seeping into my present. *Not now.* I will never truly escape that version of myself, that I'm sure. But I have to be better. *For the baby. For Gabriel.*

Perhaps I should start by apologising to him; all he's tried to do is help, and I've done nothing but cause trouble since I arrived. My body jumps as the front door slams suddenly, and I stand from the bed, quickly reminding myself that it's likely to be the one person who actually lives here. I calm my panicked breathing and peer through the crack in the door, braced to grab the side table lamp, just in case.

I breathe out, observing Gabriel's tall, broad figure pacing the living room. I might claim I'm ready to freeze out my past, but today he saw what I'm truly capable of. If I were him, I'd turn me in, get rid of the problem. *Should I leave? Will it make his life easier?* Either way, I have to face up to it. I have to talk to him.

I walk into the living room, surprised to see his long body stretched out across the sofa, his shoes discarded on the floor, one arm flopped over his head, whilst the other dangles off the edge. He looks exhausted. I almost turn to head back into my bedroom when it dawns on me; this is my window to lay everything on the table, the chance to get everything out so we can work together. For a moment, I allow myself to study him. *Christ, he is strikingly handsome.* Despite his recent more sinister and intimidating persona, I'm grateful for a glimpse of the old him; the softness in his face, the curve of his mouth, his chest rising and falling steadily; the juxtaposition of his bulk strength blended with the show of vulnerability. My heart aches, recognising the boy I once knew: the man who made me laugh between lectures, the person who listened to me ramble on about my future and career choices with dedicated patience, the mind that pushed me to strive for greatness. *I miss that person.* Everything about him has always embodied alpha-male authority: every movement, every guarded look. Every word and mannerism an instinctive show of dominance, but watching him so relaxed at this moment sheds that image. His dark eyelashes begin to flutter, and I quickly continue walking towards him, pretending I haven't just stood here gawking. He lifts his body slightly as he wakes, leaning his weight on the arm closest to me. He turns, his warm brown eyes searching the room until they finally rest on me. For a second, they light up before he recovers, and the steely mask resumes.

'How long have I been out?'

'Just a few minutes.' I smile.

'You look…' he clears his throat. 'Do the clothes fit, ok?'

'A little tight, but it works. Your sister is clearly in excellent shape.'

'Yeah, she's a gym nut.'

'Well, I hope she won't be too pissed off to find them missing.'

He says nothing sitting up straight.

'Are you going to turn me in?' I blurt out, unable to hold it in.

He stares at me for a beat as he runs his hand through his hair. 'I can't protect or help you like this.'

'I came to you because of the letter.'

His brow twitches curiously.

'I found it difficult at first to accept what he was saying. I thought you'd targeted him deliberately. I wanted you to be the enemy. I wanted someone to blame. But since he died and the mess that followed, I realised he was right. In the end, you were just trying to save him, to preserve the future he had left.' I close my eyes, trying to gather my thoughts. 'I know that you crossed the line a few times for him. You sacrificed your career to keep him safe, convinced your superiors that he should be protected rather than imprisoned. You made him an asset. You saw the tide turning, and you told him to adapt. He respected you for that.' I look away from him, feeling uncomfortable. 'The letter told me to trust you, to believe in you as he did. He used to tell me that I was the most precious thing in his life. You knew him well, so you know what that means. And if he wrote your name, if he chose you as the person I should go to, without even knowing our history, then I thought that was worth paying attention to.' I exhale, only now just realising I've been holding my breath.

He stares at the floor, thinking hard on something. 'I never intended to put your father in harm's way. If anything, the connection to you...' He stops, suddenly appearing flustered.

'I want to believe his version of you because that's the person I knew too.' I trail off, feeling over exposed. 'That's why I came here.'

He gestures towards my arm. 'I can't have you behaving so erratically all the time. Not only is it endangering your life but also the life of your child.'

I nod, knowing he's right, despite the burning urge to defend myself, to shout and tell him that it's his fault that I had to do this alone, that he should have just kept me in the loop, helped me in the first place and neither of us would be in this position.

'Aldyn Wolfe had some important information to share,' I offer, slowly coming to sit on the coffee table opposite him.

His dark eyes regard me thoughtfully. 'Like what?'

'Paytak was in a lot of debt with some cartels. He agreed to work with The Singularity to pay those off. He approached Aldyn for help on the logistics of trafficking. Aldyn used to use Kristine Kingley too. He thinks the kids are being sold into private sex rings. Otherwise, he doesn't know. He hasn't seen them.'

'Aldyn Wolfe owns half the brothels in this country – where else is Paytak taking those children?'

'He said that Paytak gets instructions from an encrypted chat regarding the children, the trafficking... and he also uses the chat to hire mercenaries.'

'For what reason?'

'Apparently, whoever he's working for, they run a tight ship. Have contacts everywhere. He said Paytak hires mercenaries to carry out his hits. We should look into the men in the warehouse, find out who they really are. I think... I think they recognised me.'

'How do you mean?'

'When I entered, one of them looked at me and said: *Here she is*. Like they knew me? Not just from the laundrette, it was more familiar than that. Then I got closer, and they realised.'

He looks off to the side; his brain is working on something. 'Paytak has hired a woman.'

'Huh?' I ask, confused.

'Nothing.' He says, thinking to himself.

'There's something else...'

He meets my eyes, returning to the present.

'It seems Agent Roe also approached Aldyn. He told Aldyn he's investigating The Singularity and wanted details on Paytak.'

'What the fuck is this guy up to?'

'Clearly another agency is after The Singularity.'

'We need to speak to McGuire, find out what he knows about Roe.'

I eye him cautiously. 'That's going to be hard.'

'You know where he is, though, don't you?'

I stare ahead, unwilling to give McGuire up so easily.

'I'll take that as a yes,' He utters firmly.

'McGuire isn't your guy.'

His jaw tightens.

'We can't keep putting people's lives at risk. First Paul, now McGuire. I can't...' I make to stand from the coffee table.

'Interesting how you value the lives of some but not others,' he comments under his breath.

'I'm sorry for what happened today...' I reply, feeling ashamed. 'But McGuire is my most trusted friend. If he's in the wind, it's for a good reason, and he doesn't want to be found.'

'Wake up!' Gabriel stands, his tall frame looming over me. 'Do you want to stop The Singularity or not?'

'Of course I do!'

'Then we need to speak to McGuire!'

'I made a pact.'

'You were in the S.A.S, not fucking Brownie camp.'

'I won't betray him, Gabriel.'

He lets out a sharp disbelieving breath. 'I can't keep up with you. You're fine sneaking out of here, breaking into Aldyn Wolfe's house, threatening him, stealing his car, killing two men, and betraying me. But the minute I ask you to do something that might actually be useful-'

I turn away, needing to escape his glare. I move towards the guest room, but he grabs my wrist, pulling me back. My eyes narrow, entirely shocked by the intensity of his hold.

'You're going to want to let go of me,' I warn in a low tone.

We stare at each other, our ragged breathing the only sound that can be heard for what feels like minutes. His anger dissolves, his hand loosening, yet those blazing eyes still study me with penetrating speculation. His eyelashes flicker as he runs his gaze across every single one of my features. I try to move my wrist away, but he tightens his grip. I stand transfixed, unable to tear my eyes away. He remains impassive, his movements slow and controlled as he draws me in, his dark eyes fixed on mine. He knows exactly what I'm thinking. He can sense the cautious desire in my obedient response, the way my body gravitates towards him. My mind sparks as he commands me closer. I'm aching to touch him, to run my hands over his arms, his chest, to feel his hot, smooth skin under my fingers.

He drops my arm and takes a step back, fixing his glare over my shoulder, almost as if suddenly waiting for me to move. I jerk away, mentally chastising myself with embarrassment. I need to get away from him and the exhausting unpredictability of his moods.

'Lex... Alexandra, wait,' he calls after me.

'You have everything you wanted. I've told you the truth. But if you're going to cut me out or turn me in, then just do it already. I've laid my cards on the table.' I stare at him defiantly, trying to hide the fact that every encounter with him leaves me feeling hot and flustered. I'm usually stronger than this, but I know I'm losing control.

He stares at me, looking entirely disinterested. 'You're constantly allowing yourself to be led by emotion. You left here, put your life in danger because you were too impatient. You won't let me speak to a key witness, despite the fact it's the next logical step. How can you blame me for thinking you're deliberately trying to sabotage this case?'

I feel my body begin to heat. Now he's hit a nerve. I'm allowed to admit that part of creating this new life is forming cracks in the persona I worked so hard to adopt during my years in the military, the person that enabled me to be the perfect soldier, but I'm not about to accept it from him. Not when it's exactly the sort of thing Simon would say.

'And you're paranoid.' I snap back, responding with more fierce sparks of emotion, proving him right. He regards me blankly, which only pushes me further. Now I need a reaction, just something to tell me he's listening. 'I'm trying to protect a friend. But somehow, you've built this story in your head that it's about you. Because everyone is out to get you, nobody can be trusted. You're not special. You're by no means the centre of the universe,' I add, words regurgitating from my mouth without my permission. 'I'm holding back on McGuire for McGuire. It's got nothing to do with you.'

'Thanks for sharing your personal evaluation.'

'Do I have to die to prove that I'm on the right side of this?'

'You've done a good job of trying the last few hours! You think you have the right to stand here and rattle through my supposed issues because you knew me once. It wasn't your business then, and it sure as hell isn't now.' He stares me down, forcing me to look away. 'Have you ever given me a reason to trust you, Lex?' he asks, his voice softer. 'You're a smart woman. Has your behaviour expressed any evidence that I can count on you whatsoever? You left here and murdered two men... I'm a police officer; you do remember that don't you?'

I glare at him, unsure whether he actually wants me to answer all of those questions.

'If you want me to trust you, then earn it. Because I'm busy ignoring how painfully infuriating, reckless, and selfish you've been up until this point. I think that's enough for now, don't you?'

I sigh, jamming frustration down with every ounce of will I possess. 'If you can't trust me, please trust that we have the same goal in mind.'

He lets out a long, exasperated breath. 'I don't think we ever have, and we never will.'

His words silence me, a wave of sadness enveloping me as I catch the true meaning behind them. 'I'm asking you to at least give me the benefit of the doubt, the same as I've done for you.'

'You really trust me, Lex? Do you!?'

I say nothing.

'Didn't think so.' He turns.

'Where are you going?'

'To get some sleep,' he calls over his shoulder, storming down the long corridor to his room.

'We're not done talking!' I yell after him, taking two steps for his every stride. My mind begins glitching as the panic overwhelms me. *What if he shuts me out again? What if he refuses to help? Who will I go to?* 'Gabriel!' I shout again.

He stops in the doorway. 'Jesus, you're relentless.'

My mind becomes splintered by the spite in his tone. 'We have to work together; it's the only way we can win.'

He continues towards the bathroom, switching on the shower and beginning to undress.

'Gabriel...' I state, throwing my hands out into the air. 'I'm still here?'

He turns slowly, his T-shirt now in his hands.

'Why?' he asks with a sharp look of condescension.

'You want me to be open with you; I'm trying. I'm sorry if you feel like I'm being difficult about McGuire!' Tears of frustration swell in my eyes. I'm losing control of everything. I've been at the centre of so much destruction already. I can't bear to see anyone else dragged down with me. 'I just need you to understand.'

'Understand that you're dangerous, deceptive, manipulative, inconsiderate, irrational? Because you're talking, but that's all I'm hearing.'

'You have no idea what I'm capable of.' I spit, shouting over the repetitive spray of water on the ceramic floor. 'So, if you can't trust me, then trust this – If I were working for them, if I wanted revenge for Mario's death, I wouldn't bother carrying out this whole charade, living here with you. I wouldn't bother keeping you alive. I would have come here, got what I needed, killed you and left. That's how I'm trained. And you know that.'

He scoffs, disbelieving. 'Keep your fucking head down, stop making my life ten times more complicated than it already is, and when I ask for information, give it to me.' He appears unfazed as the thick fog from the shower slowly fills the bathroom. 'Go to bed; we'll talk in the morning,' he says, putting his hand on the door.

I step back, allowing him to shut it without another word and return to my room, my body shaking with anger. And then my mind freezes on something else, flitting to the moment we had before everything turned nuclear. Gabriel's long fingers around my wrist, his dark eyes studying my face. The moment before the switch flicked and he became an entirely unreachable human being. That requires a skill I've only seen in fellow soldiers. *What happened to him?* He has the potential to achieve anything he sets his mind to. At first, I saw the steel mask and no-bullshit persona as strength, but he's travelling at one hundred miles per hour on empty. Gabriel James has always been the fuel that can ignite any fire. I just pray that nobody lights the match.

GABRIEL

CHAPTER TWENTY-SIX

Alexandra has me entirely distracted, thinking about finding her in the warehouse: her sad fragility mixed with the chilling distance from her actions; her determination to keep McGuire safe; the way she destroyed my character, the heated glow in her eyes as she told me exactly what she thought. I don't know what I was thinking earlier. All I *do* know is that every bone in my body wanted her close. It was like a strike of electricity that neither of us could ignore, and the more she obliged, the more she leant into me, the more I couldn't stand the distance. Then amongst all of that, she sets me on edge more than anyone I've ever met, with each unpredictable confrontation, never knowing what she might do or say next. I'm always in control of every situation, influencing those around me to my will, but not Lex. She sees through it, refuses to engage. Her clever mind scrutinises every word, her eyes dissecting my thoughts as if she can see them etched on my face. She's a volcano; a looming, dormant presence with a future promise of destruction. And yet I find myself back there. Time and time again. I was so sure the fixation had ended. I sit against my headboard, close my eyes, and will my brain to grey over her, painting her unavailable with the clear objective of keeping a level head. *So much rests on me now; I won't screw this up.* My phone vibrates on the side table, jolting me back to reality.

'James.'

'It's Stanley.'

I sigh audibly. 'It's late.'

'You're going to want to hear what I have to say.'

After letting her stew for a few seconds, I take a breath to reply: 'Trying for another go?'

'God, you're annoying. I actually have something you'll want to hear.'

'Get on with it, then.'

'We got an anonymous tip that Samantha Kingley was being kept in a warehouse in Canning Town.'

'And?'

'She wasn't there.'

'Need me to come and take a look?'

'We've given everything we have to Collins; she wants a meeting tomorrow. We're pretty sure this is part of Paytak's trafficking ring. We found three deceased minors.'

'Right...'

'We also found two deceased police officers.'

'Jesus... Who?' I say, trying to lace just the right amount of concern in my voice.

'We're working on identification.'

'Were they undercover?'

'Not sure the extent of their involvement.'

'Are you sure you don't need me there?'

'I think it was her, Gabriel.'

'You think what was who?'

'Alexandra. All of this... it's her.'

My body tenses, and I take a breath to control the tone of my voice. 'Based on what evidence?'

'The coroner's report came back on Kristine. Her throat was slit exactly the same way as one of the men we found today.' She pauses, and I picture her flicking through the report. 'And there are markings on her neck. The coroner tells me the width and span are consistent with a female.'

I look down at the floor, trying to remember Lex's hands. *What size are her hands? How have I spent so much time with her without remembering that, at least*? Images of the dead bodies in the warehouse flash through my mind. I picture Lex doing the same with Kristine, slitting her throat without a moment of hesitation. I blink rapidly, urging the picture to disappear.

'If you have no DNA, then that is just one expert opinion. I could find a coroner tomorrow to tell me it was a midget.'

'Alexandra Christofi is the ex-Forces assassin Paytak hired… isn't she?'

I look up to the ceiling and sigh, zoning back into the middle of her rambling.

'…skin under her fingernails, so the CPS signed a warrant for us to search Alexandra's apartment.'

'Wait, what…? Repeat that.'

She huffs impatiently. 'The coroner found traces of Alexandra's skin under Kristine's fingernails. It's her, James. This is all her.'

I cover the mouthpiece and drop my head, miming *fuck* a few times as I recall Lex's words. *Paul had to pull her off me.* This just got a lot worse for us.

'Like I said… congratulations.' I finally respond, grateful I can't see her smug expression.

'Why aren't you taking this seriously?'

'What, do you want a gold star for doing your job? You got what you wanted. Thanks for keeping me in the loop. See you tomorrow.'

'James, I know that there's something you're not telling me.'

'Let me put it this way; you know everything I am cleared to tell you. Anything you don't know relates to the wider case, and it's confidential. There's a chain of command, Stanley. We all had to go through it.'

'She a good shag, was she?'

'Sorry?'

'We all know you went to the same Uni at the same time. And I can see it in your face, hear it in your voice whenever we talk about it, whenever we mention her. I can't think of another reason you'd be so adamant to protect her. You've fucked her.'

'Watch how you speak to me.'

'You don't seem like the type to get attached, so either she was an unbelievable fuck, or you're scared.'

I grit my teeth. 'Careful, or you might start to sound a little jealous.'

'Well, she is beautiful; looks a bit mad behind the eyes, but you can't blame her with a father like that.'

'I think you need to take a long, hard look at yourself first.'

'Is that how you like them? A bit messed up in the head?'

'Watch your fucking mouth.'

'Oh, am I offending you?'

'You don't want to push me, Stanley.'

'Or what? You'll have me sent away like you did Amelie Felton? Or will I disappear like Mario Christofi? Poor guy thought he'd found an ally in you.'

'What is it you want?' I bang my hand hard against the table. I am so fucking tired of this woman's sloppy attempts at trying to rattle me at every opportunity.

'You've shut me out since this started. There's information you're sitting on, and right now, Mummy is letting you do it because she thinks you all have a bigger fish to fry. But just wait until she learns what I'm about to bring to the table.'

'You know what, Theresa,' I glance nervously at the bedroom door, expecting to see Lex come running in. 'Please keep coming at me. Keep coming for this case, and I hope you get it. It's taken me years to learn how to survive in this world and if they hand it all over to you, I hope it fucking eats you alive.'

THE BURNT CHILD

I hang up the phone whilst she's mid-sentence. It's only a matter of time until this entire thing blows up in my face. And all I can think about is protecting the girl across the hall.

ALEXANDRA

CHAPTER TWENTY-SEVEN

I sit up and rub my sore head, desperate for water as I recall tossing and turning all night, trying to break haunting visions of sandstorms, forty-five-degree heat, and hiking through villages with no food or water. I used to think anything would be better than that, but at least there was a clear end in sight. I creep out of the bedroom, shielding my eyes from the bright winter sunlight. My entire body jolts as the morning's silence is abruptly interrupted by the grinding of the blender.

'Do you want a smoothie?'

I look up to see Gabriel staring down at me as I perch on the kitchen stool, his eyes appearing softer than the last time we were in each other's company.

'I guess… thanks,' I say, offering a polite smile in the hope I might get one back.

He stares at me for a few seconds, an unreadable wariness in his eyes as he rests his palms flat on the surface of the counter, his shoulders appearing tense. *No such luck.*

'Are you alright?'

'Yeah, I'm just not sleeping very well.'

'Is it the nightmares?'

I look up, a little surprised. 'Was I yelling in my sleep?'

He offers a small smile. 'A bit.'

'Oh…' I look down, feeling embarrassed.

'Is it things you've seen on tour? Or something else?'

'Partly that, partly family stuff,' I confess, thinking of all the times I've dreamt of finding my father's dead body. I take a breath, trying to move past the image. 'I finally get to a point where I believe all the therapy was worth it, that I'm healing. And then...' I stop, realising I'm oversharing. *He doesn't want to hear this.*

'And then?' he presses, intrigued.

I hesitate. *Maybe he does.* 'And months later, something triggers it. It's like the wound is opening up again.'

'I know the feeling,' he says, looking off into the distance.

'I was only in the Forces for a few years...' I confess. 'Some of the B Squad...' I shake my head, thinking back to McGuire and Gibbs. 'They'd been doing this for over half my life.'

'Perhaps they lost the capacity to feel.'

I nod, agreeing. 'I used to wish for that...'

He watches me intensely as if trying to see straight into my soul.

I take a deep breath and step off the stool, summoning the courage to draw a line under last night without causing another argument. 'Please can we put yesterday aside and agree to be honest with each other from now on. If I were working with them, you'd be dead already.'

'Encouraging...'

'It is... actually.' I roll my eyes at his victorious smile, and for a moment, all my composure dissolves. 'I don't want to yell at you anymore.'

'Well, there's a relief.' He grins, flashing his dimples.

I take another step in, my heart beating faster. 'I'm sorry for putting your life in danger, for nearly wrecking your career, for wasting your time when we should be working together.'

'It's fine,' he murmurs, fixated on my lips, neither of us really taking in what the other is saying. I squeeze my hand against his shoulder, acknowledging how comfortable it feels to be close, to show affection versus trying to keep our distance. The truth is, we don't know each other any other way. I allow my eyes to trail up to his, savouring this moment, the world around us becoming meaningless. The fear, the worry, the uncertainty - all of it dissipating. For these few lingering seconds, nothing else matters, nothing but each other. Gabriel turns his head away, the muscles in his jaw twitching as he looks at the floor.

'Can I ask you something?' I blurt out.

'I think you're going to anyway...' He murmurs, taking a step back from me.

'I thought you wanted to go into politics.'

'That wasn't a question.'

'What happened?'

'I guess I can ask you the same thing.'

'No, but what I mean is... Why did you go into law enforcement?'

He takes a sharp breath. 'Something happened that made me want to make a difference.'

I remain still, instantly regretting my decision to probe him so soon after last night. 'I'm sorry...' I offer quietly, trying to think about how to change the subject.

'No, it's fine.' He shakes his head, his shoulders shooting towards his ears.

'I joined the Army because I wanted to prove to my father that I could be more than just a gangster's daughter,' I utter, choosing to offer him something about me to ease the tension.

'What made you come back?'

'I guess I resigned to being a gangster's daughter.' I laugh.

'You've always been so much more than that.'

'I don't know what I'll be,' I confess, drawing slow circles on the marble counter.

'None of us do.'

'We'll get Paytak, Gabe…' I reach over and place my hand on his, wanting him to know he's not alone, willing him to understand I've got his back.

'I know, Lex,' he mumbles, his thoughts elsewhere.

'What is it?' I ask as he stays silent, staring down at the counter. 'Gabriel… what's wrong?'

'Someone on my taskforce…' he stops, hesitating. 'They found your DNA under Kristine's fingernails.'

'Who?'

'DI Stanley. She's leading the Kristine Kingley investigation.'

'I told you about the laundrette.'

'I know,' he says, holding his hand up. 'But Kristine was murdered in the same way as the guy in the warehouse. And Stanley… she's convinced they're both you.'

'You mean Kristine's throat was slit?'

He nods.

'Gabriel, if this person was in the Forces… we've all been trained the same way.'

He stares at me for a time, something battling behind his chestnut brown eyes. 'Look, Lex… I do need to speak to McGuire.'

'Fine.' I close my eyes and sigh.

'Today.'

'Oh…'

He rubs his hand over his face and closes his eyes. 'Contact him. Get him to meet us.'

'Right…' I respond, trying to push past the guilt for involving him. 'But I'm coming with you. McGuire could shoot you if you approach him unannounced.'

He studies me cautiously. 'I swear to God… if you try anything stupid, I will drive you straight to the station.'

I sigh a long, deflating sound.

'Get changed. We're leaving in five.' He turns to walk towards his bedroom.

'I'll be on best behaviour.'

GABRIEL

CHAPTER TWENTY-EIGHT

We pull into the carpark of an old repair shop set back from a country road in what appears to be the middle of nowhere. I notice a truck parked up in front of a garage door and turn to the backseat where Lex sits, shielded by the blacked-out windows of my Audi.

'Is this the place?'

She pulls up the crest of her black cap, her golden eyes squinting as she takes in the tiny building with its derelict surroundings. 'Yeah, this is where I stayed.' She swallows hard before leaning forward with her head in her hands.

'Are you alright?'

'I—I think I'm going to be sick,' she says, her face a sudden pale green.

'Shit.' I jump out of the car and rapidly move around the other side, pulling the door open. She clambers out, quickly rushing over to a patch of shrubbery. I turn away to give her some privacy, but there's no escaping the aggressive sound of hurling a few metres away. I take the opportunity to look around. McGuire has been camping out in a disused repair shop situated outside a village in Hertfordshire, surrounded by nothing but fields and an old dirt track. You can understand why this might be a good place to hide. I hear Lex groan behind me, and she slowly begins to stand up straight before wiping her mouth with the sleeve of her arm.

'Eugh… Sorry, that was really gross,' she gripes, shaking her head. I smirk, about to make a sarcastic comment, when I notice her eyes widen, her gaze drawn to something behind the truck. 'Someone else is here.' She mutters, still fixed on the same spot.

I immediately pull the pistol out of my holster and step carefully towards her, gesturing for her to get behind me. She scowls, attempting to march forward. I quickly pull her back as I tread quietly around the filthy pickup truck, instantly noticing a very clean, shiny motorbike parked near the door. I step forward and place a hand on the engine. It's warm. *Whoever it is hasn't been here long.*

I turn to Lex and gesture for her to get back in the car. She instantly sets her mouth in a firm line, crosses her arms, and shakes her head. *For fuck's sake.* I roll my eyes and point at the floor, signalling for her to stay where she is. She returns a glare but eventually nods, her eyes loaded with adrenaline. She's itching to be involved; staying put goes against every fibre of her being. Stepping in, I find myself at the edge of a dimly lit mechanic's workshop that smells distinctly of stale cigarettes and oil. The walls are lined with dusty shelves and workbenches; old car parts are scattered around the place, littered between disused machinery and metal scraps.

'Police!' I call out, treading around the mess. 'Come out with your hands above your head!'

Nothing.

'I need you to come out slowly!'

Still nothing.

'I won't ask again!' I yell, training my eyes around the room, braced for an onslaught. I start to edge around a beaten red Ford Fiesta sitting on a crank in the middle of the workshop, listening out for signs of motion, picturing an ambush by Paytak's assassin. As the thought hits, my eyes shift to movement on the other side of the shop, and I catch the image of a man's startled face through the driver's side window. Average height, blonde hair, and extremely muscular, his bright blue eyes widen, but my gun is already trained on him, my index finger sitting over the trigger, raring to go.

'Stay where you are!'

'Identify yourself!' the man replies in a clear-cut British accent. *This isn't McGuire.* The man disappears suddenly. I step back, my eyes darting to the floor, noticing his shadow looming closer, a dark sketch of him angling around the front of the vehicle. 'I'm a soldier. I came to check on Charlie.'

'I'm a police officer,' I reply bluntly.

He comes into view, holding a pistol out in front of him.

'Put the gun down.'

'Show me some identification!' he shouts, edging towards me.

'Stay where you are and put the gun down.'

'No can do.' He shakes his head. 'I find my friend dead, and you're the next person to show up.' He gestures behind him.

I squint past his body, making out a lifeless heap in the shadows. 'Move again, and I will shoot you!'

'Simon?!' Lex's puzzled voice travels through the walls.

'Alex?' he calls out, recognition swamping his face.

The side door scrapes open, followed by her approaching footsteps.

'Lex! Stay where you are!' I yell at her over my shoulder before instructing Simon to hand me his gun. His eyes flit behind me, his brain working hard to put the pieces together.

'Simon…' Lex's voice resounds from behind me. 'What are you doing here? Where's…' She stops as she registers his expression. 'Where's Charlie?'

So, this is the ex-boyfriend, the father of her child. Simon stares back at her with a mixture of adoration and regret, his Ken-doll eyes softening. It's almost as if he desperately wants to spare her from a truth that's all too set to come out, like a parent explaining death to their child for the first time. He doesn't answer. Instead, he looks back at me, imploring me not to say it. Pain needles Lex's face, her eyes hooked on the space behind Simon.

'Stay where you are, Lex,' I warn.

'Gabriel, he might need medical attention.'

'I'll do it.'

'Gabriel, plea—'

'I will do it, Alexandra.'

She takes an exasperated breath. 'Alright.'

'Come here.'

She offers a questioning look.

'I need you to switch with me.'

Simon starts shaking his head. 'Alex, you need to understand the situation here.'

'Lex, I know you think you can trust Simon but think of this logically. We arrived here, and Simon was alone with McGuire.'

'Alex. We served with Charlie. It's against the code. Look at me. Listen to what I'm saying,' Simon interrupts.

'We need to be smart here,' I warn, cutting him off.

'Alex, don't allow fear to cloud logic.'

'He's been trained just like you, Lex.'

'Alexandra, stand down,' he instructs in a clear, authoritative tone.

She snaps her head up, and in that second, I observe her overwhelming urge to obey, the tremendous need to do exactly as he says.

'I just need you to keep the gun on him, that's all.'

She starts to move towards me.

'Soldier!

'Lex!' I shout again, trying to take her attention away from him. 'If you want to help McGuire, you need to come here.'

She hesitates.

'I am going back there. I will help him.'

Simon frowns, looking between the two of us, clearly aware he's missing something as he attempts to assess the dynamic.

'I'm trying to protect you. Do you understand?' I fix my eyes to hers, willing her to hear what I'm saying. If McGuire is dead, I can't predict how she will react. And if Simon is responsible, I can't let her go down that road. She looks at Simon one last time, her obedient mind torn. Until finally, she turns to me and nods. Stepping forward, she takes the gun, cocks it, and points it at her former commander.

ALEXANDRA

CHAPTER TWENTY-NINE

Gabriel determinedly makes his way around the back of the broken Ford Fiesta and moves behind Simon. I grip the handle of his gun, braced for a twitch or a single movement out of the ordinary. I watch Simon's feet, knowing that he can easily take me down, gun or no gun, if he inches close enough. *Can I shoot the father of my child?*

Simon is elite, he's the best there is, and he led B Squad for five years. I would go as far as to say he's one of the most highly trained assassins in the world, which makes him a perfect candidate for Freeman Powell. But it's also why I'm ninety per cent certain that whatever happened to McGuire has nothing to do with him. When it comes to his duty, no matter who or why, Simon is committed with everything he's got. He's an expert at switching off emotion; he knows how to stamp away doubt, fear, pain. He taught us how to do exactly the same in the field; it was his responsibility to detach and desensitise us in the desert. He gets in, does the job, gets out. If he had to kill McGuire, for whatever reason, there is no way he would hang around afterwards. The minutes tick by and I wait for Gabriel to say something, to tell me it's ok, that I can lower my weapon. But nothing comes, and my heart hammers like a bird stuck in a cage, desperately seeking release.

'You know what happened the last time you pointed a gun at me.'

'You think this is the time?'

'Look how it goes the minute you leave me, Alex. The minute you step into the real world, chaos ensues.'

'Tell me why you're here,' I demand, ignoring his attempts at rattling me.

'You need structure, control. You can't expect to reshape your world without proper guidance.'

'I'll shoot you, Simon.'

'You see, you're over-emotional.'

'I swear to God, Si!' I yell, stepping back and moving the gun towards his knee cap. *I said I'd shoot him, but I won't kill him.*

'Charlie called me this morning. He said we needed to meet.'

'Why?'

'He had something to tell me but couldn't talk over the phone.'

I shake my head, puzzled.

'He was running an op.'

'He hadn't got a call-up.'

'This was different.'

'How?'

Simon swallows hard, his Adam's apple bobbing with frustration. He doesn't like being on the other end of the trigger. It doesn't matter who I am or what I was; he will do anything to retrieve the upper hand. *I have to be careful.*

'He'd been hired for an op, and it was connected to Beirut.'

'What about Beirut?'

He shakes his head; sadness etched on his face. 'He said he'd been tasked with bringing *her* in and got into some hot water.'

'Like what?'

'The line wasn't great; he was rushing, but he said things had gone sideways, and someone was after him.'

'Our Op in Beirut?'

'That was my first thought.'

'Who would be coming for him?'

'Well...' he shrugs. 'You were in Beirut, and what with everything on the news.'

'Yeah, a lot of people have made that assumption recently.'

'I came here as quick as I could.'

'Was he alive when you got here?'

Simon's eyes widen.

'Si is he alive?!'

Gabriel rounds the corner, his hands covered in blood, his face ashen. I know that look… *Dread.* I drop my head, my heart feeling as though it's fallen through my body.

'I'm sorry, Lex…'

I barely hear him as I realise that I exist in a world without my closest friend. *He's gone.* Hearing my mind spell out those words causes a prang of sharp acknowledgement, but I have to swallow back the ache of loss. Death is a part of the life we chose. McGuire knew that. He would expect me to battle the pain, channel it into action, and find whoever was responsible. But as I'm trying to steer the thought away, to lock it down and maintain control, I've begun to stutter something even I don't understand. My mind swims with memories of McGuire, his laugh, the way he took me under his wing on my first op, the things we'd talk about missing when we were on tour, his disappointment that I'd never seen *Goodfellas*, my promise to watch it with him for the first time. I will never do those things with him again; his thread in my life has been cut. I blink at the floor, acutely aware that Gabriel and Simon are observing my behaviour. Gabriel steps towards me, a worried expression on his face. I can hear my voice saying *no* repeatedly. But it doesn't sound like me. I feel Gabriel closer now, and I try to push him away. *I can't give in to this. I'm not weak. I don't need this. I'll be fine.* He pulls me into his arms. I start to yell, telling him I'm ok, demanding he gets away, trying to wrestle free. But he holds me tightly against his chest. *This isn't me. I don't fall apart.* Simon is watching this, all of it. But I can't make it go away. I can't make it stop, and I close my eyes, a wave of nauseating sadness hitting me, causing my body to feel like it's drowning under a

THE BURNT CHILD

weight of grief. And in that second, I finally concede, giving up the struggle against Gabriel's hold, stilling all movements save for my breath. I stare at the floor, surrendering to the will of emotion as tears cascade down my face and frantic sobs fall from my mouth. I close my eyes, accepting that pregnancy isn't just changing me physically. It's rewiring everything I thought I knew.

'What's wrong with her?' Simon asks, his tone telling me that this version of me is alien to him, too. *Get it together, Alexandra; this is embarrassing.* Shame creeps up my neck in red, anxious rashes, and I make to stand up straight. Then I feel the gun in my hand, and everything topples into frantic action.

'What have you done?'

Simon jerks his head back. 'Excuse me?'

I point the weapon at him, my finger poised over the trigger. 'Are you working with Paytak?'

'Lex...' Gabriel warns.

'Did they hire you through Freeman Powell?'

'Have you lost your ruddy mind?' Simon demands, his eyes sharp with disappointment.

'Lex... it wasn't him.'

I turn to Gabriel. *How is he defending Simon all of a sudden?* I look between the two of them.

'McGuire's throat was slit... If it were Simon, he'd have blood all over him.'

I flit my eyes over Simon's body, taking in his clothes, thinking about the warehouse and Gabriel's words when he found me. *Is that your blood?*

There's not a single mark out of place. *It can't have been him.* I lower the gun as I picture McGuire putting up one hell of a fight, refusing to go until the split second the slice of metal hit flesh and bone, the knife cutting into him with devastating effect.

'Do you know who did this?' I ask him, finally able to speak in a measured way.

He frowns, a spike of irritation on his face.

I inhale another long breath, ignoring Gabriel's protests, before rushing to the back of the workshop. Knocking odd bits of metal out of the way with my feet, I scramble to get to him. On reaching the dark corner, I stand motionless over McGuire's body. Memories regurgitate immediately: flashing images of our friendship flurrying down like dashes of salt into the wound of my subconscious. A haunting showreel of McGuire showing me around camp, introducing me to the *Elite of the Elite*: a silly term for the people he and Gibbs made friends with; that deep, infectious wheeze of a chuckle that made me laugh, even without knowing the joke; the sacrifices we both made to look out for each other; his hilarious impressions of Simon; his determination to defend me when I was asked to leave, the countless letters he wrote to the S.A.S recommending they let me stay. Tears roll down my face as I whisper tormented apologies for not being able to return the favour, for always relying on him but not being there when he needed me, for not having his back, for letting him die.

I look around the cluttered space, knowing he deserved so much more than all of this. But he couldn't get his head out of the conflict, opting to live a simple, isolated life. I lean over and gently close his eyes, unable to draw my gaze away from the sticky, congealed slice of flesh across his neck, and I make a single promise to him: I will find whoever did this, and I will make them pay.

CHAPTER THIRTY

We watch Simon leave on his bike. Anxiety taunts me as I realise another person who served their country is being put in this position: having to run for their lives, forced to hide with no explanation. And then there's the guilt: letting him leave without telling him about the baby, the regret at feeling nothing for him, and mostly, the relief that he's driving away. As Gabriel hurtles down the M11 back towards London, I rest my head against the cold glass, watching the flash of streetlights fly past. *Someone was after him.* I recall Simon's words, thinking back to Aldyn Wolfe's certainty that someone was coming for him too, the greeting I received in the warehouse, the markings on Kristine Kingley.

'Paytak's hired a female assassin….' I announce into the brooding silence between us. '…that everyone thinks is me.'

'Yeah…' Gabriel frowns, turning his head to me quickly before training his gaze back on the road. 'I know…'

'The men in the warehouse, it took them too long to realise I wasn't one of them. They were expecting a woman. You think Kristine was murdered by a woman. And McGuire told Simon he had been tasked with tracking *her* down.'

His eyes slide to the left, studying me. 'Yep.'

'McGuire also told Simon that all of this was connected to an op we ran in Beirut. And there were only five people in Beirut. Me, McGuire, Simon, and two others. Wayne Gibbs and Rhiannon Benson.'

'Ok…'

The facts line up in my mind. 'Rhiannon and Gibbs were captured. Gibbs is missing, presumed dead. His body was never recovered. But the Foreign Office managed to get Rhiannon back.'

'And where is she now?'

'I haven't seen her since the day she was taken. But if McGuire mentioned Beirut to Simon and something about tracking *her* down. It could only be her.'

'You sure Beirut isn't something else?' Gabriel responds unconvinced.

'Beirut means nothing else. If McGuire said that to Simon, he wanted him to know there was a connection.'

He narrows his dark eyes on the road, his jaw working as he thinks about this.

'We know Paytak is hiring ex-military through Freeman Powell. You said he hired a woman. How did you know that?'

'I heard it from a source....' He hesitates, clearly weighing up the risks of letting me in on the information. 'It's Nicky Black. We've been using him for intel.'

'Of course Nicky's involved.' I murmur, shaking my head. 'What did he say?'

'Just that Paytak had hired an ex S.A.S. female soldier to tie up loose ends.'

'Well then... McGuire was hired to track Rhiannon. Rhiannon Benson is Paytak's assassin.'

'But if McGuire knew that Rhiannon was dangerous, why didn't he warn you?'

'Perhaps he thought it was too risky to reach out, in case it led her to me. But I think he tried – I think that's why he called Simon.'

'Ok,' he concedes, his hands nervously shifting on the steering wheel.

'We know this Agent Roe approached McGuire, so maybe he was the one who hired him to find Rhiannon?'

'We need to find Roe.' Gabriel nods, abruptly beginning to fiddle with his hands-free, flitting his eyes to and from the road.

'What do you want to do?' I snap, batting his hand away from the screen. 'I'll do it. We can't go through all of this and then die on the North Circular.'

A slight smirk teases the corner of his lips. 'Call Amber for me...'

'You have a distinct lack of manners; you know that?'

'Call Amber for me, *please*.' His eyes flash with amusement.

'Better,' I comment before selecting her name on the touchscreen. Within seconds, a loud ringing echoes around the car.

'Guv? Everything ok?' A nervous, high-pitched voice asks.

'I need you to look into someone for me. Keep it between us,' he instructs, his voice layered with authority.

'Sure.'

'Can you find out who Agent Roe is? He's part of an agency, I think.'

There's a pause on the other end. Silence fills the line, save for her steady breathing.

'Amber?'

'Yeah, sorry, just writing it down.'

'And this is strictly confidential, ok?'

'Yes, Guv,' she replies quickly before hesitating slightly. 'We might not get anything.'

'Let's at least try,' he interjects before hanging up.

'You think Roe's dirty?'

'I think he knows who killed your friend.'

GABRIEL

CHAPTER THIRTY-ONE

'Jake Roe is an Interpol agent,' I announce, leaning against the door frame of the guest bedroom. Alexandra rests against the headboard, watching a few giggling stragglers exiting the pub through the window. She shifts on the bed, looking up at me, expectant energy replacing the grief.

'Do you know anything else about him?'

'I'm working on it.'

'How did Amber…' She starts the question with a suspicious tone and then stops. 'Amber didn't find this out for you, did she?' she stands up from the bed, closing the space between us. 'How Gabriel?'

'I know a few people.' I reply casually.

She twists her lips, her eyes penetrating mine. 'We need to find him.'

'We will.'

'Why would Roe hire McGuire? Hasn't he got enough resources at Interpol?'

I hold back my suspicions that Agent Roe isn't the person that hired Charles McGuire and move past the question. 'Let's just concentrate on finding Roe, but we have to be careful, Lex. He could be bent.' I warn, trying to lower her expectations. I don't want her on a pointless vendetta. 'Are you hungry?' I ask, changing the subject. 'You haven't eaten all day.' I turn towards the kitchen, heading for the fridge to check what might still be edible.

I hear the soft patter of Lex's footsteps following me out of her bedroom and into the living area. 'Don't you think it's all the same person?'

Jesus. I inhale a deep breath as I stare at a packet of peppers, mustering up the energy to engage with her on this. 'We need to focus on what we know and build evidence from there. These questions will be answered. We need to take it step by step.'

She nods, sitting at the counter, her focus welded to the floor, her brain motoring at one hundred miles an hour.

'I'm ordering in. We have no food.'

'Isn't that a bit risky?'

'You think The Singularity might have infiltrated Deliveroo?' I jibe, and she rolls her eyes. 'Sorry...' I say with an apologetic smile.

She breaks out into laughter. 'You would have got on with him, you know. He had your dark sense of humour.'

I move to stand across from her, noticing the smile isn't quite reaching her eyes.

'What do you think he would say to you? If he was here?'

She looks off into the distance. 'Chin up, Lex, get the bitch, and we'll call it even.'

'Really?' I ask, grinning.

'He didn't have much tolerance for grief or sadness.'

'We would have got on well, then.'

'I think so,' she replies, offering a beautiful but very surprising expression of warmth. I fixate on her for a beat too long before sliding my phone across the counter. 'Pick what you want. I'm not fussy.'

'Thank you.'

'It's nothing. I really will eat anything.'

'No, I mean, thank you for being there today. It wasn't... If it had just been Simon and me.' She stops. 'Just, thank you for understanding.' She trails off slightly, her eyes shifting from mine to the floor.

'Your friend died, you don't owe me anything.' She avoids my gaze as she looks back to the phone, swiping her finger across it a few times before handing it back to me. 'It's clearly been hard for Simon to let you go,' I add suddenly. *Where the hell did that come from?*

'You heard what he was saying?'

'Some of it. He's…intense.'

'I just ran… I didn't even tell him I was leaving.' She meets my eyes, both of us thinking exactly the same thing in that split second. 'Look, Gabriel... I never got to explain-'

'It's been years; it's not relevant.' I sigh. 'We were kids.'

'It was a family matter; I had to.'

'It's nothing.'

'Cambridge let me finish over the summer. I wanted to reach out.'

'Lex,' I snap. 'Don't make it a big deal.'

'I know, but-'

'We're both old enough to understand how the world works. It was a fling… It's in the past.' I cross my arms defensively, watching disappointment flicker across her face.

'I'm sorry, is all I wanted to say.' She adds, frowning as I laugh. 'What is it?'

I shake my head. 'Whenever we're in this kitchen, you're apologising.'

She smirks, rolling her eyes before taking a long, heavy breath. 'Simon doesn't know about the baby.'

'I gathered.'

'He's a complicated person.'

'He seems pretty straightforward to me. He likes power and control.'

'I knew the minute I told him he would feel like he owned a piece of me again.'

'Is it that bad?'

'I thought it would settle down when we left the military. It got worse, in fact. And as soon as I found out I was pregnant, I knew I didn't want that life for a child. If he knew...' She pauses, searching for the words. 'I'm worried he'd never let me go.'

'Did you come to London to get away from him?'

She nods slowly. 'Don't get me wrong, he's not a bad person, but he was controlling; his life is about discipline. It's what makes him the best. He lives and breathes structure.'

'Did you meet on tour?'

'It's sort of unexplainable, but I think I was in awe of him, really. I've always been attracted to power, I guess.' She shrugs, appearing uncomfortable suddenly. 'The way he trained us, he made us feel like we needed him to operate. And in that small, confined atmosphere, I became addicted to it... his abilities, his approval. He made us all what we are today; he moulded us, physically and emotionally. His approach to conditioning was unprecedented; people have written books about his methods. He used simulations and sound triggers; he'd set up game-like scenarios, all with one thing in mind.'

'Which was?'

'He taught us how to detach from ourselves, creating complete desensitisation. And it's how we operated, everywhere we went.'

'Did he ever teach you how to switch it off?'

'He didn't.' She shakes her head. 'But McGuire showed me. He taught me how to *leave it at the door.* That's how he'd put it. And when I got back to my everyday life, when I realised there was a whole world beyond the desert, I began to see how warped I'd become. And it was clear that Simon wanted to keep me that way.'

'Jesus,' I whisper under my breath, wondering what Toff would have made of Simon Haines. *I could venture a pretty good guess.*

'It was intense. And now with the baby…' She looks down. 'Everything Simon did to flatten down the edges; it's all growing back, everything I suppressed.'

'How do you mean?'

'Have you ever slept funny on your leg or your hand?' she sits up, her eyes brightening.

'I guess.'

'And you wake up in the middle of the night because something feels off; you realise you've gone numb. And as you try to move that limb, it's unreactive. In those few moments, it has no ability to feel. But then the sudden rush of blood creates a tingling sensation under your skin as your body puts its energy into reviving the piece of yourself that shut down, the part that became temporarily unresponsive.'

I nod, knowing exactly what she means.

'And then, all of a sudden, you're twitching from the overload of your nerve endings sparking together; it feels good to have it back again, but it's also incredibly uncomfortable, all at the same time.'

'I know the feeling.'

'It's that, but up here.' She taps her head. 'Simon thinks he wants me back… He wouldn't want this person.'

I think about the way he kept looking between Lex and me, studying us as I held her in my arms. *I think he will always want her.*

'Perhaps he doesn't deserve this person,' I confess, knowing all too well what it's like to desire an all-encompassing numbness to pain. 'But what do you want?'

'I just want to be happy.'

'Did you ever wonder if he suppressed your emotions because he was scared?'

'Scared of what?'

'You see a control freak; I see a man who's afraid.'

She appears confused.

'I think you need to consider the possibility that he suppressed you to keep you dependent on him. I think you should consider that he was frightened of how powerful you might be if you learnt to live with your instincts.' I think back to the warehouse, the woman who took down two fully grown men with a single weapon.

'He told me it was too dangerous to be myself, that women must learn to control their emotions. More so than men.'

What a prick. 'Dangerous for whom?'

She looks away.

'Can Simon be trusted?'

'Simon is many things, but he is loyal to the Army and dedicated to his country. He hasn't got the mental capacity to defect. It's not in his make-up. But I'm glad you were there today… You seem to understand, somehow. I know that I push you too far. I keep waiting for you to have had your fill of the madness and give me up…'

'I understand more than you realise.'

She tilts her head curiously.

'I know what it's like to want to shut down completely, to live a life of solitude as opposed to experiencing the pain of loss again. And I know what it's like when lucidity creeps in, and you begin to feel it all at once.'

She stares at me, taken aback.

'I don't mean us,' I clarify. 'I lost my sister… a few years ago. My younger sister… Janie, you didn't meet her.' *Why am I telling her this? I haven't brought up Janie in years. Not since my first stint in rehab.*

Her body stills, her large eyes glinting with sadness. 'I'm sorry, Gabriel… I had no idea.'

I nod, working hard to keep my expression neutral as I swallow past the constricting lump in my throat. Having said the words after keeping it shoved down for so long, it's kicking up every single heavy emotion.

'How did she die?'

I inhale, my hands clutching the edge of the kitchen counter. I know I have the choice to stop, to bring an end to the pain of remembering Janie, but something about being around Lex makes me want to open up, to share the truth of my grief. I've never spoken with anyone like this, not since her. 'She took her own life…'

'Oh…' she whispers, suddenly standing up from the stool and moving around to join me. 'I had no idea… I'm sorry.' She starts shaking her head. 'I can't believe… I'm sorry, I can't stop saying sorry.'

'It's alright, Lex.' I clear my throat, feeling my mind tensing up, shrivelling under the exposure of her gaze. Now I've started this; she won't let me brush past it. She's brilliant at stamping down her own problems but won't allow anyone else to suffer. Maybe it's what I need; for someone to tow the words out of me, piece by piece.

'How did it happen?'

I lean against the counter. 'She was very unhappy. And none of us paid enough attention to understand why.' I take another breath. 'But we've since learned that she was abused. It had been going on for a very long time.'

'Who?! Who would do that?' she exclaims, her hand reaching up to caress my shoulder with kind, soothing movements.

'A teacher from her school.' I close my eyes, picturing his face, the face that makes me want to commit a long list of crimes in a matter of seconds. I stand up from the counter and walk a few paces to the sink, needing to create space between us as the recurring fantasy of closing my hands around his neck flashes into my mind.

'The reason I'm telling you... it's why I understand. I know what it's like to fight the urge for revenge, to attempt to stop it from taking over, the need to make someone pay for their actions. It's all I feel when I think about Janie, with the children you found. It's all I see when I think about Diren Paytak.'

We stare at each other, saying nothing, our bodies having shifted at an angle towards one another. I want to reach out and touch her, pull her close to mask the ache of missing Janie.

'No child should ever learn that kind of evil, and no person should understand this hell.'

'Gabriel, I-'

'I would have murdered them too, the men in the warehouse. I should have told you that before.'

Her eyes brim with tears. 'We'll get them. No matter what happens, we'll stop it.'

'I hope so.'

'What about your parents?' she asks suddenly. 'How did they cope?'

'They chose to pretend it didn't happen and tried to pave over the cracks with money and pointless holidays.' I admit, shaking my head as I recall every failed attempt to get them to open up, so we could mourn Janie together as a family.

She steps towards me, the scrutiny of her wide, golden eyes causing my body to tense. 'I wish I could make it all go away,' she whispers, running the pad of her thumb gently over the frown sitting heavy on my brow. I close my eyes, allowing myself to relax into her touch. 'I wish I could make it disappear for both of us.'

This is why Alexandra Christofi will always compromise every relationship. *Nobody is her.* My eyes snap open suddenly. I'm in dangerous territory. I stand straight and place her hand by her side, resuming an unreadable expression. She looks taken aback but doesn't comment.

    She steps away and leans against the counter adjacent to me. 'Whatever happens, Gabriel, we can't go back. I want to find the people responsible for all of this, but I'm leaving the woman from the military behind.'

    'You don't have to go back, Lex,' I assure her, before reminding myself that in reality and for a number of unpredictable, uncontrollable factors, I shouldn't be making any promises.

ALEXANDRA

CHAPTER THIRTY-TWO

I wake to the shrill sound of Gabriel's apartment buzzer, its blaring noise cutting through my dreams. My eyes fly open. I sit up and look around, all of a sudden feeling tremendously hot and clammy. My arm is stuck against Gabriel's lean body, his chest rising and falling steadily as he lies beside me, stretched out across the massive L-shaped sofa. We must have fallen asleep here. We were talking and talking and then... I can't remember anything. The buzzer goes again, and I groan, clambering over impressively long limbs, grabbing the gun from the coffee table, and making my way to the intercom. Staring down at the security camera, I see a tall, attractive brunette. Her lips are pursed, waiting impatiently as she holds a large bag in her right hand. *Is this his girlfriend?*

I pad over to Gabriel, both surprised and impressed that he can sleep through the aggressive sound. 'Gabriel...' He stirs a little, his dark eyelashes fluttering before he turns over. 'Gabriel!' I raise my voice, shaking his shoulder. The buzzer resounds for the third time.

We both jump as he shoots up, nearly knocking me backwards; he quickly catches me before I topple over the coffee table. He eyes me warily, his handsome face dazed. 'Shit!' He breathes.

I frown, confused. 'What?! Who is it?'

'Can you buzz her in?' he calls out, running down the hallway to his bedroom. *Has he lost his mind?*

'What?' I yell. 'No! Gabriel, what's going on?'

'I completely forgot...' he says, returning to the room, his face flushed.

'Forgot what? Who is that?'

'My sister!'

'Pardon?!'

'I asked her to come to check on you.'

'Why?'

'She's a midwife, and I'm worried about you. You went days without eating.'

'OK, firstly, the fact you asked your sister to check over a pregnant woman at your apartment, and she came seemingly without question tells me a lot about you.' I point at him, raising my eyebrows. 'And secondly, as soon as she sees my face, she'll know who I am.'

'I trust her more than anyone.'

'We're implicating her, Gabriel.'

'Nobody will know she was here. She won't say anything, Lex,' he reassures me, stepping towards the front door. I turn away, wanting to run. *Why does he do things like this without asking me?* Even when he thinks he's helping me; he can't tell me all the information. It's exhausting.

'Gabriel, this will be awful for everyone involved if she tells anyone, you know that?'

'She won't.'

I sigh. 'Send her up.'

GABRIEL

CHAPTER THIRTY-THREE

Lily stands in the doorway, motionless, her almond eyes glaring at me. 'Are you going to bother explaining this?' she asks, storming past me and into the apartment, discarding her bag on the kitchen table. I catch movement over her shoulder. Lex emerges cautiously from the guest bedroom. Lily hesitates and follows my gaze, barely hiding her shock.

'I think it's pretty self-explanatory, don't you?'

Lex crosses her arms, her wide, golden eyes flitting between the two of us.

Lily's head tilts sideways. 'Are those my clothes?'

She looks down apologetically and shrugs, 'Oh yeah, I'm sorry…'

'She couldn't keep wearing mine,' I interject.

'Tell me what is going on,' Lily demands.

'Can you give us a minute, please?' I ask Lex.

She takes a breath to protest.

'We need a minute,' I assert, my voice raised.

Her eyes narrow before she turns on her heel, marching into her room and shutting the door with deliberation.

'Now, who does that remind me of?' Lily turns to me sarcastically.

After offering my sister the most basic, top-line explanation possible, I watch the information sink in.

'You could both go to prison for this.'

'I don't have a choice, Lily.'

'Of course, you have a choice,' she whispers. 'Get her to leave; this is not your battle.'

'She is part of this operation. I need her close by,' I say, keeping my voice down. 'You're telling me you'd walk away from those children? Put yourself in the parent's shoes. God forbid, what if it was one of yours?'

I watch tears fill her eyes, considering this. 'Then continue with the case but distance yourself from her.'

'If it were an option, Lily, I would have done it a long time ago.'

'I don't understand why you're so adamant she's innocent.'

'I know she didn't do it. I've seen the evidence.'

She sighs disapprovingly, beginning to pace. 'She's going to get you killed, Gabriel.'

'I can't walk away now.'

'When was the last time you went to a meeting?'

'That's irrelevant.'

'What did your therapist say about throwing yourself into situations to alleviate guilt?'

'This isn't about Janie.'

'It's always about Janie.'

I whip my head up, feeling an urge to tell her to fuck off and get out of my business. Lily has had the luxury of moving on because her grief isn't the same. She didn't find Janie. She wasn't the one who dismissed our little sister when she reached out, saying she needed to talk. She wasn't the one who mumbled a disinterested goodnight, the last words Janie James ever heard before she died. I know I'm haunted. I know I've made mistakes sprung from guilt. I don't need to be told over and over again.

'You're just one man...' she whispers, rubbing her hand over her forehead. 'God, you're the most selfish, selfless person I know.'

'I'm close to figuring this out.'

'Why did it have to be you? Tell her to find somewhere else.'

'Because it's my jo-'

'Your job is to stop criminals. Nowhere in the description does it say invite them into your home.'

'It's about doing what is right.'

Even as I say the words, I'm not convinced. *It is about her, one way or the other.* If it's not about helping her, it's about saving her, and my sister can see that plain as day.

She clamps her mouth shut, more tears of frustration threatening to spill out. 'What if you don't get the answer you're looking for?'

'It doesn't matter what I want. It's about the truth.'

She shakes her head, her shoulders slumping.

'Lily, please could you check her over? Then you can walk away and have nothing to do with any of this.'

'You're my little brother. You think I can leave here and forget what you're doing? Gabriel, it would break me if something happened to you. I can't lose you too.'

'I've got this under control.'

'I've heard that before.'

I swallow back the urge to disagree and think about all the times I asked her to trust me, to believe that rehab was working, that I was changed, that I wasn't an addict anymore. Until I fell back into my old habits. *She has heard it before. Too many times.*

'Please, Lily. I am more than capable of figuring this out.'

'I'm scared of what this will do. You can't go backwards.'

'If there's one thing I know about Alexandra, she won't let me.'

Concern marks my sister's classically beautiful features; she searches my eyes for any indication that I might need her more than I'm letting on. Of course, I need her. I always need her; she's looked out for me my whole life. But if I let her see that, if I give in to regret, if she senses even a speck of fear, I know she won't leave. I hold my breath, willing for her to believe what I'm saying.

    She looks up at the ceiling before suddenly exhaling. 'Fine… I'll do it.'

ALEXANDRA

CHAPTER THIRTY-FOUR

Lily glides the ultrasound over my skin with delicate precision. I squint at the monitor, trying my best to make sense of the out-of-focus blurred shapes.

She looks over at the screen. 'It's ok if you don't see it right away; it's not always clear...'

I look up at her, analysing her expression for any sign of concern or panic. I'm struck by the resemblance between them. Like Gabriel, Lily is tall, with long limbs and a slender figure. Her skin has the same deep tan as if she grew up in the sunshine. Her features are almost a mirror image of Gabriel's: the bone structure, the deep chestnut irises, the perfectly formed lips. Except, Lily is clearly more comfortable in her own skin. Her gorgeous eyes profess an endearing vulnerability that her brother can't allow. Perhaps it's because, in her line of work, kindness and care are traits that a person should value rather than ignore.

'Ah there!' She points at the screen, and I lift my head, following her finger. 'Do you see? That's the head, and they're the feet.'

'Oh, shit...' I whisper, finally making out the shape of a tiny little human. I place my hand over my mouth, involuntary tears springing from my eyes. I feel like I'm floating. A surge of warmth flows through my veins, circulating my entire body. Nothing else matters as I stare at my child with such a tremendous rush of happiness. And finally, I feel that motherly, protective instinct. The tears run down my face quickly now, my mouth stuck in the widest smile. I find I can't tear my eyes away from the little blur on the screen. *That is my child, my baby.*

'Everything seems fine. The baby appears healthy. There's a good strong heartbeat,' Lily states professionally, handing me some tissue to remove the gel from my skin.

'Lily, thank you for doing this. I'm really sorry about everything...' I trail off, watching her expression change. *I know that look. I've seen it many times before.*

'He'll go to prison. You know that, right? Or worse, end up dead. You'd have to be an idiot not to see it, Alexandra, because I can.' She meets my eyes. A rock forms in the pit of my stomach. 'You must know this isn't just...' she exhales slowly, stopping to regain composure. 'I've never seen him look at anyone the way he looks at you.'

The shock on my face is evident. It's not flattery. She meant it as an accusation.

'You walked in the room, and I saw it all over his face...In any other circumstance, I'd be overjoyed that he's finally found someone he loves more than himself. After what he's been through, he deserves happiness. But with you...' She stops. 'It broke him when you left the first time. He won't be able to handle it again.'

I take a deep breath, still recovering from the heightened state of my emotions but understanding her need to protect her family. 'I never meant to hurt him. I would never cause him harm.'

'Not intentionally,' she snaps.

I say nothing because she's right. I can't guarantee that. When I knocked on his door, I wasn't thinking about Gabriel, the person, the brother, the son; I was thinking merely of the capable, smart detective, the man my father respected. I didn't take a moment to wonder how this might affect him personally, only that I needed to divide the burden for someone else to carry.

Lily watches me closely, witnessing my mind fire into overdrive. 'Why did you come here? You must have known what you would do to him? How it might ruin his life…'

'I needed his help; I know that's selfish. I just… I wasn't thinking.'

'Did you know he would agree?'

'I hoped he would.' I pause, twiddling my fingers through the ends of my hair nervously. 'I don't want to hurt him. I care about him… I could find somewhere else to go. I could leave…'

'It's too late for that. I don't know if this is what you intended, but I know my brother.' She pauses, considering her words. 'He's an addict, Alexandra. Once he has you, he'll never let you go.' The warning sinks into the air, made more severe by the softness of her tone. It should sound like a good thing. But the edge in her voice, the low, careful way she tells me, it's more of a threat.

'I would make sure he couldn't find me. Nobody would.'

She pinches the bridge of her nose and looks down. 'You two…' She shakes her head. 'When an unstoppable force meets an immovable object.'

I reach out my hand. 'I want you to know that it's not one-sided. I would do anything to protect him.'

'You want to know why Gabriel is desperate to do the right thing all the time?' she asks, challenging me. 'He's riddled with guilt. And it wasn't his fault. But he blames himself, of course.' She hesitates before she looks down. 'Never mind.'

'I want to make this right for him.'

'That's what I'm afraid of.'

The earlier euphoria now having completely dissolved, I lie back on the bed and close my eyes, wishing for his sake and mine that I had never met Gabriel James.

GABRIEL

CHAPTER THIRTY-FIVE

After Lily left, I took a call from Collins, her assertive voice summoning me to the station. By her tone, I instantly knew something wasn't right. And that was made all the more evident by the curious eyes studying me as I marched through the department.

Having nothing to do but sit at my desk and wait to be beckoned, I browse the mass of files piled up over the last few days. There are folders upon folders of information about every member of the Christofi family, and I make a mental note to take it home with me on the way out.

A fast approach catches my attention, and I look up to see Collins standing above me, her arms folded. 'Why do you still have your coat on?'

'Well, from the look on your face, I'm not staying long, am I?'

She stares at me, unimpressed. 'In my office.'

I sigh and slowly rise from my chair, following her. As she closes the door, I sense another body in the room; turning my head to the right, I see a pristinely polished gentleman seated on the black leather sofa. I frown at Collins, who ignores me and walks to stand behind her desk, gesturing for me to take a seat opposite her.

'This is Agent Roe.' She nods over to the fair-haired stranger, who has a very precise, non-threatening air around him; his short hair is styled with skilled accuracy, and his grey eyes analyse me before he nods a curt greeting. I run my eyes over his face, unable to believe that he's sitting in front of me: Agent Roe, the man who flipped Aldyn Wolfe and perhaps the key to many answers.

'Detective.' He offers his hand. I crane my neck to meet his cool gaze; he's a few inches taller than me. *That makes him a very tall man.*

'Can you tell me what this is about?' I ask, shaking his hand.

Collins clears her throat. 'There's no easy way to start this conversation, Gabriel, so let's try and keep it civilised.'

I pull my head back, frowning across the desk. 'Right.'

'Agent Roe is from-'

'Interpol.' I interject.

A wry smile graces Roe's lips. 'I'm aware you've been looking for me, Detective, so I thought I'd make it easier for you.'

Collins dismisses the arrogant remark, 'Agent Roe and I have been working on something.'

'Ok...'

'I wanted to make you aware.'

'Thanks?'

She continues. 'A few months ago, we were asked to pull resources for an investigation into a global crime syndicate.'

'You mean The Singularity?' I ask, eager for them to cut to it, noticing the uncomfortable look in her eyes. 'You knew all along...'

She nods, a hint of an apology in her expression. 'I had my suspicions.'

Roe shifts. 'This organisation has been fast-growing all over Europe. They've infiltrated police forces, governments, intelligence agencies... the list goes on. We've been tracking their activity across the continent, trying to understand their patterns or gain concrete evidence. Everything we have is circumstantial; we know they're out there; we've seen what they're capable of.'

'Which is what?'

He ignores the question, continuing the monologue: 'According to our sources, everything is centred around a man named Higgs. He's recently been linked to several extremist groups in the Middle East.'

'Linked? *Linked* how?'

'Financing terrorists in Syria, Jordan, Iraq...'

I lean forward and rub my hands over my face, trying to piece this information together. 'You're telling me that The Singularity is a terrorist group?'

'They appear to be supporting multiple groups.'

'What has that got to do with Paytak's trafficking operation?' I turn to Collins. 'Do you know what they're doing with the children?'

'They've got their fingers in a lot of pies, Gabriel. This is just one piece.'

'It sounds like you've got quite a job on your hands.'

Collins takes a breath to speak.

'We're trying to put a stop to all of this,' Roe replies, cutting her off.

'The number of times I told you something was up with Toff's case.' I turn to Collins with disbelief. 'You could have told me when I first mentioned The Singularity.'

'This is highly confidential, Gabriel.' she replies calmly, her bird-like eyes regarding me with disapproval.

'So, you're aware they're using Diren Paytak and Kristine Kingley?' I ask Roe.

'I'm aware.'

'Because Aldyn Wolfe told you?' I snap. 'You're going to have to explain why your name keeps popping up...'

'We got wind of Higgs a few years back when I was put on a homicide case in Zurich. It was a dead Saudi national. A known associate of UBL. It looked like a professional hit. We soon realised this guy had been buying artillery from someone via an encrypted chat, and he'd been sending money to a Swiss bank account.'

'How do you know it was The Singularity?'

'Because we managed to hack into their chatroom – the only correspondence that referenced the money was between him and a contact who calls himself Higgs. Higgs has sold a lot of weapons on the black market. Since then, we have been trying to locate him. We've infiltrated other chat rooms, phone calls, but he's a ghost… nobody has met him.'

'And Counter-Terrorism knows about this?'

'They're aware,' Collins cuts in.

I think back to my father leaving here just a few days ago. 'So, you're here because we're hunting Paytak. And you need him to find Higgs. Is that it?'

Roe nods.

'What did you hire Charles McGuire for?'

Roe's sharp eyes drift to Collins and back to me.

'He was running an op for someone,' I clarify.

'Not for me.'

'Then why did you make contact with him?' I ask slowly.

'He worked some of the most high-profile operations in the Middle East. We wanted to know if he'd come across Higgs or The Singularity.'

'You know he's dead, right?' I exclaim, a little more harshly than intended. 'He was murdered by an assassin. Presumably, it has something to do with who he was working for. That's what I thought you wanted to discuss.'

'How could I possibly know that he's dead?'

'You're everywhere, it seems.'

'We didn't know he was dead, Gabriel…' Collins affirms.

'Then if I'm not here because of that, what is it you need?'

Collins looks at Roe with a worried expression.

'What is it?' I snap, becoming impatient.

Roe turns his whole body to face me. 'We know you're concealing Alexandra Christofi.'

My lungs freeze. I bite down hard, saying nothing.

'As soon as Alison told me you'd found Paytak's connection with The Singularity, I looked into your background. You failed to mention that you went to Cambridge with Mario Christofi's daughter.'

'Me, her, and most of MI6.'

'Alison also tells me you have an eyewitness who saw Kristine Kingley taken by two police officers on the day she was kidnapped. Seems convenient.'

I glare at Collins, who remains tight-lipped.

'Aldyn Wolfe told me she paid him a visit. She told him that she was working with a detective to find Paytak.'

'Paytak's a very popular man.'

'Aldyn claims Alexandra drove to a warehouse where Diren Paytak was keeping trafficked children.'

'DI Stanley told me about the situation in the warehouse.'

'I checked the cameras around Canning Town, Gabriel.' He sits forward, pulling a file from Collins' desk before opening it slowly, licking his finger and reading from a single sheet of paper. 'At eighteen forty-six, Aldyn Wolfe's Bentley is picked up here.' He holds up a printed image of the car driving down an A Road. At seven minutes past eight, a black AUDI S7 registered to Gabriel James is picked up travelling in the same direction.'

'I know it's not very scenic but driving around Canning Town isn't a crime.'

'Cut the shit, Gabriel,' Collins interjects. 'As the Director of this department, I should have your fucking head for this. You've perverted the course of justice, you lied to multiple police officers, and you deliberately misled DI Stanley and Major Investigations.'

'I'm not sure your father can get you out of this one,' Roe comments with thin-lipped superiority.

I blink across at him, regarding him with a cool disposition. 'I can't see how that's relevant?'

'He's the director of one of the largest Counter-Terrorism teams in the world, and his son is committing crime after crime on his doorstep. How do you think he'd react to that?'

'Edward James is a borderline sociopath; he doesn't react to much.'

'We've got a lot we could charge you with, James,' Collins comments. 'We know Alexandra Christofi murdered the two police officers in Canning Town, which makes you an accessory… Either you think you're invincible, or you're completely deranged.'

'Again…' I announce into the small space between us all, 'I'd like to see what evidence you have for any of those accusations.' I challenge her, fixing my glare on her furious eyes. 'Traffic cam footage proves nothing.'

'Gabriel, she's wanted in connection for the murder of Kristine Kingley, the disappearance of Paul Theo, and now she's a suspect in the killing of two of our own.'

'Two of our own.' I scoff.

Collins raises an eyebrow.

'Everyone in this room knows those officers were corrupt. Stanley might not have all the answers yet but I'm pretty certain neither of them was working a case that gave them a suitable reason for being in that warehouse.'

They both remain silent.

'Who were they? The officers. What did they do?'

Roe sighs. 'Border Enforcement.'

My lips twitch. 'There you have it.'

'Sounds like you're admitting culpability here, James.' Roe interjects.

'Merely providing you with the background, Agent.'

'We know she's with you.'

'If Counter-Terrorism is aware of the situation, and they're investigating Higgs, then why are you two still on the case?'

'We're not at liberty to discuss the details.' Collins explains.

I nod knowingly. 'Edward is ignoring all the terrible things The Singularity are doing in Europe because he believes Higgs' connections in the Middle East are the priority.'

'Correct,' she admits reluctantly.

'So, this taskforce…' I flit my hand between the two of them. 'It's now off the record, and you're trying to take the whole organisation down without the help of SO15?'

Collins' sallow, gaunt face tightens, her hair having sprung up wildly around the sides.

'We're under no illusion that we have to bring it all down.' Roe admits. 'That means Higgs, the corrupt police officers, the politicians, the gangsters… everyone.'

'We know Paytak is looking for Alexandra,' Collins adds.

'I don't know where she is.'

'Gabriel…' She tilts her head. 'No bullshit.'

I catch the desperation in their faces, my mind waning with uncertainty.

'James, we're trying to work together on this. If you help us, we can help you. Both of you.'

I exhale, a long deep sigh. 'You think I'd be sat here if she knew where Paytak was?'

'Well, perhaps it might be easier if she made herself known to him.' Collins suggests.

'You want to use her as bait?!'

'She is the best way to get to him.'

'You said yourself that nobody had met Higgs.'

'It's the only route we've had to him in years, Gabriel.'

'You think Paytak is going to flip on an organisation like that?' I shake my head. 'He'll kill her first.'

'She can get a message to him somehow.'

'You realise Paytak has hired an assassin to tie up loose ends on the instruction of The Singularity? Even if he did flip, Higgs would find out and kill him. Then come for all of us. You'd be risking her life for nothing.'

'It's the only lead we have,' Roe admits.

I stand, shaking my head vigorously. 'I can't help you.'

'Sit down, Detective,' Roe instructs, standing from his seat.

'I won't let you sacrifice someone on a whim.'

'You're awfully protective, James.'

'It's about doing what is right,' I step in.

'And what is right…' Roe narrows his eyes, 'is that she makes up for the fair amount of chaos she's caused. Which includes you too.'

'You can't expect us to overlook everything she's done. Everything you've done to protect her, Gabriel. If she helps, we can make everything go away; the charges against her and against you for hiding her. Think about it,' Collins suggests.

'Director Collins is offering you an out. I'd take it if I were you.'

'I don't need an out.'

'Daddy won't be able to get you out of this one.'

'You don't want to go up against me, Roe.'

'Gabriel!' Collins raises her voice from the other side of the room.

'We're done here.' I turn towards the door.

'If that is the case,' he calls after me, 'then SIO James, I'm afraid you're under arrest, and we'll be coming for her anyway. She's a criminal. You'll both get what you deserve.'

I'm ground to a halt as his words force me over the edge; a spike of enraged adrenaline crashes through me, and I pivot suddenly, throwing my weight against him, pinning him hard against the wall with my forearm.

'You don't want to go down this road, Gabriel,' he croaks, struggling under the weight of my body.

'Detective James, I will call security!' Collins yells, her voice shaking.

'If you go anywhere near her!' I spit into Roe's patronising face.

'Gabriel!' Collins shrieks, managing to get between us, gripping onto my arms, clawing through the material of my coat, begging me to stand down. 'Stop it! Do you hear me? I will have you arrested!'

I sigh, releasing Roe to the ground. He crumples, hanging over his knees, rubbing his throat.

I turn to leave for the second time, needing to get away from them and back to Lex.

'James...' he pants. 'I admire you... I really do. You're dedicated to your job, and you're very good at it.'

I refuse to turn around, afraid of what else I might do.

'I'll be honest with you, ok? Alexandra is a Christofi, which means at some point, she's dead. No matter what any of us do. So, you either work with me, and she draws Paytak in under your protection, or you refuse, and I expose you both, then use her as bait. So, you tell me... which is it?'

CHAPTER THIRTY-SIX

I walk urgently down Belgrave Street, fiddling with a key fob in my fingers, kicking through heaps of dry, burnt-orange leaves. Groups of tourists keep appearing from small hotels on the street, and I determinedly swerve to avoid them whilst trying to keep up the pace as they struggle with their luggage into black cabs. Roe's smug words replay in my head over and over. It kills me that I'm proving him right, but I don't have the luxury of caring. I need answers. Reaching the tranquillity of Warwick Square, I head towards the plush communal gardens, cordoned off by a bold, iron fence. Swiping the fob through the sturdy gate, I pass the tennis court and make towards the bench that sits under a tall oak tree.

I can't see that Edward has arrived, but it doesn't mean he's not there. The man is hugely paranoid and refuses to sit in one place for too long. No doubt he would have got here fifteen minutes earlier and started pacing out laps of the garden to kill time. I settle down on the bench, throwing my hands into my pockets as a cold breeze drifts past.

'You're late,' an obnoxious, deep voice announces from behind.
'I'm five minutes early,' I respond without turning around.
'What have I told you?'
'Edward, I don't have time for this.'
'The irony.' He dispels an incredulous breath before settling down on the bench, his long legs matching the size of mine in their perfectly tailored suit. 'I've got fifteen minutes.'
'This won't take long.' I turn, taking the opportunity to glance at him properly. He looks well. He's always made an effort with his appearance, even if it's to leave the house to grab a pint of milk. And despite being in his mid-seventies, my father continues to retain that

youthful resilience with every look and superior comment aimed in my direction.

'What do you need?'

'You hired Charles McGuire, didn't you?'

He twitches his head to the side.

'Did you hire him to find Rhiannon Benson?'

'Where is this coming from?'

'He's dead.'

'I see.' He crosses one leg over the other, looking down at the grass. 'How has this landed on your desk?'

'McGuire was looking for a woman. A woman who he claimed is connected to an op he ran in Beirut. Rhiannon Benson served with him there. It's where she disappeared.'

He says nothing.

I decide to push harder. 'I'm going to assume Rhiannon is connected to the operation you were leading with Roe and Collins. I'm also going to assume she's connected to Higgs and Diren Paytak, which is why you're so interested.'

'Ah…'

'Didn't fancy sharing that information?'

'There isn't much I can tell you, given our distinctly different responsibilities.'

I roll my eyes. 'On the instruction of Higgs, Diren Paytak has hired this woman to murder a lot of people.'

'I know what she's doing, Gabriel.'

'Did she work for you?'

'She didn't.' He replies quickly, looking away as if he needs to distance himself from the admission.

'You hired McGuire to find her because she'll lead you to Paytak, who can take you to Higgs. Am I hitting the mark?'

'I can't protect you if you go down this road.'

'Is Higgs funding terrorist groups?'

He sighs and closes his eyes.

'Listen to me… I know how you operate in SO15, and I know that you don't give a fuck what The Singularity is doing in Europe; you just want Higgs. As long as Islamic extremists aren't blowing anyone up, it's not your problem. But people are dying; children are being abused and murdered, police officers are being corrupted at the instruction of this organisation.'

'And now they're after your girlfriend, which is what this is all about, isn't it?'

I freeze for a second, and I know he's felt my body tense next to him.

'Alison Collins gave it away so you can save yourself the effort.'

'I don't know where you're going with this…'

'You know the apple doesn't fall far from the tree.' He smirks with a winning arrogance in his eyes. 'She is the only way you could have found McGuire and thus Rhiannon so quickly.'

I say nothing. *He's got me there.*

'Just be aware that we might need her at some point.'

'Not a chance.'

'Someone has to finish the job.'

'She's not the right person.'

'She's got experience of the criminal underworld and the Forces. I might go as far as to say she's the only person.'

'Forget it,' I assert, making to stand. 'You've seen what happened to McGuire.'

'This is a matter of national security, Gabriel. A lot more people will die if we don't find Higgs,' he warns.

'You don't even know who the man is. Meanwhile, you're sacrificing countless lives to find a ghost.'

'If the girl agrees to help us find Higgs, then you can have all the information you want.'

'Not happening.'

'We can work together on this, Gabriel.'

'I don't think you know how. Rhiannon's on the loose, McGuire is dead, now you want Lex to take his place.'

'She's *Lex* now, is she?' He shifts on his seat, his condescending gaze fixed on a point in the distance. 'Look, Son… You have a duty to this city. I applaud your tenacity, but my duty is to this country. Alexandra would understand.'

'You don't know her.'

'I know what she's capable of.' He pauses, and I sit on my hands in a bid to prevent from grabbing and shaking him senseless. 'If Alexandra agrees, we'll protect her.'

'Unless you're willing to do something about Paytak and The Singularity, this city and this country will be ruined.'

'We need to think of the bigger picture.' He sighs, seemingly bored as if stuck with a petulant toddler.

'Rhiannon Benson has murdered a politician and an ex-S.A.S operative, but you still haven't learnt.' I stand, ready to walk away, resigned to his insistence on being the world's biggest prick.

'Gabriel…' he calls from the bench, and I turn to see a flicker of concern in his eyes. 'You need to be careful. Higgs is nothing like you've ever encountered. The Singularity is very well-connected.'

'And you're the man willing to overlook everything, to fight a war that's been going on for centuries.'

'If you take things into your own hands, I can't protect you.'

'Don't I know it,' I turn my back to him, keen to get away from his laser-like stare and smug superiority.

With fury coursing through me, I jump into the car, throwing my foot down on the accelerator and pull out of Belgrave Road.

Concerned I'll end up in an accident if I continue, I stop and pull over, groaning as I hit my hazards on, banging my hands on the steering wheel before taking a deep, frustrated breath. If we worked with SO15, we'd have the resources we need to bring Paytak's trafficking operation to an end, along with the means to stop Rhiannon and Higgs, but not if it requires handing her over. Both Roe and my father have the same thing in mind, stating their intentions in such detached ways; both willing to use her to further their agendas without consideration for her wellbeing.

There has to be another way to get to Paytak. I won't let Lex die to further a pointless cause, all to find a man whose existence nobody can confirm. I start the engine, suddenly feeling panicked that she's on her own in the apartment. *Could Roe have sent people there already?* I know she can handle herself, but the potential fall-out if she harms one of his men is not worth it. Nothing else matters but getting home. I drive erratically through the busy city, trying to shake my head clear, irritated that I've become so good at tricking my mind into denying something so blatantly obvious. Every night over the last few weeks, I've fallen asleep to her, woken up to her, practically lived every waking minute in her presence. I should have seen this coming when I found myself drifting to thoughts of her as if they were the default setting. I thought rehab and therapy had done all they could, plastering over the cracks with self-help affirmations and twelve-step programs, but five minutes in her company lifts the heaviness somehow. Her smile alone changes everything in a single moment, and I know I would do anything she asked just to see it again. I spent years convincing myself she couldn't possibly mean anything, but the truth is she's always owned a piece of me, ever since she left. If this is going to be messy and complicated, then why deny myself the one thing that alleviates it, even if it's short-lived? *Why hold back?*

ALEXANDRA

CHAPTER THIRTY-SEVEN

I jump off the sofa, my mind screaming danger as a loud crashing resounds from the opposite side of the room. Still clutching the gun tucked into my waistband, I exhale with relief on eventually seeing Gabriel steam through the door; his eyes gripped with panic.

'What's happened?' I frown.

He throws his keys down and stalks towards me. 'Are you OK?' he asks, looking around again. 'Everything alright here?'

Before I can answer, he's reached out and pulled me into him. I'm unable to voice the many questions circling my mind as I lean in warily, noticing his heart rattling in his chest. After a few moments, I wrap my arms around his torso. His body relaxes into my embrace, his arms loosening a little. I crane my neck and look up, trailing my gaze over the strained muscles in his neck, the tense jawline, the torment in his eyes. His breathing slows as I move closer.

'Gabriel?'

'Hmm?'

'What's going on?'

'Nothing, I…' He trails off.

I step back, concern taking over.

He releases me but continues to linger his fingertips on mine, stroking my hand in the most vividly, distracting manner.

'Is everything alright?' I ask, my voice strained.

'I urm…' he breathes. 'No, it's…' He shakes his head. 'I can't focus, I can't sleep.'

I swallow past the lump in my throat. This is my fault. *I've caused this.*

'I'm sorry.' I say, looking at the floor. 'I've made your life complicated.'

'No.' He frowns, seemingly irritated. 'I can't sleep because I can't concentrate. I can't stop thinking about you. And when you're here on your own, it's all I think about...' He works to gather his thoughts. 'I want you to be safe. I want you to get Paytak, I want you to live your life. I want you to be happy. I want you.' He stops as if shocked by his own admission, running a hand through his hair and looking away. 'It's driving me to near fucking distraction. I'm doing all I can to hold back, to not go there and make this even messier. I thought it was better. I thought it was safer, but that...' He stops again before exhaling. 'I don't want to... I can't. I can't do it anymore.'

'Then don't...' I utter.

He pulls me inward, pressing his insatiably cool lips against mine, before he starts to kiss me with a feverish passion, the taste of him sending hot electricity down my spine. He slides his other hand down to my waist, moving my T-shirt upward so he can softly glide his fingers over my bare skin. The way he touches my body makes me feel like I'm simultaneously floating and on fire. I grab onto his arms to steady myself, relishing the feel of his strong muscular form against me, like a protective, possessive shell. He moves his tongue to my neck, and I mutter his name under my breath, my whole body shivering with anticipation as the weight of desire dances through my nervous system, an unfathomable hunger for him. He clutches me against him, every touch on my skin, every grip of my flesh with his hands, sending a pulsing sensation between my legs. I stare into his heated gaze, our chests heaving in tandem as our foreheads rest against each other. He brings his hand up to my face and tucks an unruly wave of hair behind my ear. 'Lex...' he murmurs against my skin, the sound of my name in his low, drawling voice sending electric currents through my body. He takes my hands, placing them by my side. 'I'm sorry.'

'For what?' I rush out, my body yearning for the return of his touch.

'You're not safe here.'

'Why?' I step back, anxiety standing in place of every emotion I felt mere seconds ago.

He grabs my hand, pulling me to the sofa. 'Roe…'

'Yes?' I nod, trying to ignore the flurried beating of my heart.

'I met him today.' He pauses, swallowing hard. 'We were right. He's investigating Paytak and The Singularity.'

'Ok…'

'Cut a long story short; he thinks Paytak is the key to locating Higgs, and he wants me to help.'

I blink a few times, trying to process the information, my brain still lagging from the switch of our passionate exchange to a more severe and complicated conversation.

'Help how?'

'He wants me to find Paytak.'

'Gabriel, what exactly is he asking you to do?'

'He wants to use you to find him. He knows you're here.'

'What does he want with me?'

'He thinks you can draw Paytak out. I told him no chance. I'm not going to let them use you.'

I pause at the fear in his eyes, the prospect wreaking havoc with his mind.

'Let him.'

Gabriel looks up suddenly.

'Let him use me…'

'No fucking way. You saw McGuire.'

'If it means we will get the job done quicker.'

'Alexandra, think about what you're saying. Think about what has happened to anyone that went head-to-head with these people.' He snaps, standing from the sofa.

'We both agree we need to find Paytak, Gabe.'

'And we will.'

'I think it's a good idea.'

'Roe won't make any effort to protect you. He doesn't give a fuck about you, Lex.'

'I can handle myself.'

'He will happily let you take a hit to get what he wants. He will sacrifice both of us to find Higgs. Everyone will! If we hand this off to someone else, then we will be collateral damage.'

'What do you mean everyone will?' I stare at him suspiciously.

He hesitates, his dark eyes circling the room, looking for a way out. 'It was Counter-Terrorism running the op with McGuire. They hired him to find Rhiannon Benson.'

A cold shiver slithers over my skin, making my shoulders jerk. 'She killed him. I was right… it was her.'

'It looks that way, yeah.'

'How do you know for sure?'

'I have contacts in CTC.'

'CTC being…' I ask, my mind feeling hazy.

'SO15. Counter-Terrorism,' he replies in a clipped, impatient tone. 'They're after Higgs. They know he's linked with extremist groups in the Middle East, and they want to use his intel.'

'Do they know about me too?'

He nods. 'They want you to take McGuire's place.'

'They want me to go after Rhiannon?'

'Either that or find Paytak.'

'If it appears to be the most logical, efficient way to stop The Singularity.'

'You're not hearing me. CTC isn't planning on stopping anything that you or I have seen. They'll take Paytak in, offer him immunity. He'll be free!'

'We can't do this all by ourselves, Gabe.'

'We'll find another way.'

'We won't win. Do you hear me? I've been part of countless operations, and I know what the odds are.'

'Why does it have to be you!' he bites back, beginning to pace.

I can't help but notice the true meaning of his words, remembering his sister's warning. I can't allow him to sacrifice everything for me. I can't continue to derail his life.

'Fine, forget Counter-Terrorism. But we need to consider working with Roe. I fought to keep this country safe, Gabriel. If we let them get away with this, it was all for nothing.'

'I'll work it out.'

'How?' I yell. 'How can you get around this one?' I fist my hands into the sofa frustratedly. 'You need to come up with something quickly, or they're going to use me anyway.'

'Just stop, Lex! Stop acting like you're expendable, like your life doesn't matter, with no regard to anyone around you, for the people that care.'

'I'm not-'

'Why am I surprised? This is how you've always been. You come back when you want, leave when you want. Now you want to get yourself killed working for people you don't understand.' He grinds his critical words to a halt as he glares down at me.

He's telling the truth, but he's tripped a wire, and I can't control what comes next. I stand from the sofa, overcome with the furious need to defend myself. 'Tell me then, what is the alternative!? You go in my place? Put yourself in the firing line! You're exactly the same way. You're going to break all kinds of rules so you can find Paytak or Rhiannon yourself, all so Roe doesn't have to bother with me. It's insulting. What makes you think I'm not capable?'

'I don't doubt you for a second, but selfishly, I can't allow it.' he asserts, striding past me towards his bedroom.

'Where are you going!?' I shout after him. 'We're not done talking!'

'Away from here.'

'Typical Gabriel…' I snap. 'Running from something you can't handle, pushing it to the back of your mind, refusing to deal with the problem, letting it fester.'

'Don't pretend you know what typical Gabriel is,' he turns viciously towards me. 'And if I recall, you're the one who runs away.'

I reach out, placing my hands on his face, waiting for his breathing to slow.

'You do not have to push everyone away when you're afraid.'

He scoffs, shaking his head.

'A minute ago, you told me you didn't want to be apart. Now you're desperate to leave.'

He swallows hard, his eyes filled with a heavy sadness.

'I know you, Gabriel. You shut down to avoid feeling vulnerable; you attack people to push them away, to deter from feeling the same pain you felt when you lost Janie. You don't have to constantly sacrifice yourself to alleviate your guilt.'

'You weren't there…' He pulls away.

'I've spent a lot of time with people who are too scared to feel anything at all.'

'You think I should be taking advice from you, Lex.'

I continue, ignoring his attempts at shutting me down. 'You can be happy. Letting go of your grief doesn't mean letting go of Janie. This isn't how she would want you to live.'

'And how the fuck do you know what Janie would want?' he bites, his face struck with a combination of rage and hurt.

Tears escape, rolling down my cheeks, and I close my eyes, instantly hit by exhaustion. 'Because I know the man you were. I see who you are now. And I know which one she would prefer.'

He stares at the floor, his eyes fixed to a point. *Is he going to ask me to leave once and for all?* I take another step towards him, trying not to feel intimidated by the sheer look of wrath on his face. 'Letting go doesn't mean Janie will disappear,' I tell him softly. 'It might make room for something more, something better.'

His eyes penetrate mine, his face possessing a gaze that unravels all my thoughts, burning a hole into my brain. I refuse to break eye contact. I want him to know that I'm not backing down, that I believe he deserves happiness, and that the person I knew all those years ago is still in there somewhere.

'We may have seen dark and terrible things, but it doesn't mean we get to be dark and terrible.'

His anger dissipates, and he reaches out, wrapping his fingers around my wrist before using his firm grip to draw me closer.

'Forgive yourself…'

I barely finish the words as his mouth takes mine. I press my palms against him, deepening the kiss before frantically pulling his T-Shirt up and over his head. He watches me closely, his pupils dilating, his breathing heavy as my hands trace his skin, my eyes lingering on his broad chest, marvelling at the gloriously sculpted muscles beneath my fingertips. Abruptly he grips my arm and pulls me with him to the sofa, the urgency in his movements staggering my heart into a fast, restless rhythm. He drops to his knees in front of me, his hand clutching my hips before possessively dragging me to the edge of my seat, seizing my lips with his. I moan into him, raising my arms in the air as his feverish hands pull my vest over my head. Throwing it on the floor, he returns to me, his teeth grazing my neck, pausing under my ear to offer slower, more sensual contact with his tongue. I grab a loop on his jeans, pulling him with me and move backwards, longing to feel the weight of his body on mine.

'I don't want to crush you.' He whispers against my mouth.

Snaking an arm around my hip, he flips us around, easing me closer. I straddle his lap, caging him between my legs and rock against him slowly, the coil of pleasure in my body tightening, clenched with a desperate, uncontrollable craving for more.

'Lex...' Gabriel groans, closing his eyes.

A hiss escapes his mouth as I trace the waistband of his boxers, caressing the hardening bulge of his jeans with slow torturous strokes.

'Take off your clothes.' He demands, stilling my hands.

He watches me with fascinated curiosity as I stand and strip to nothing but my underwear. He pulls me back the second my bra hits the floor; both of us frantic to return to each other, desperate to be skin on skin. He grips my hips, guiding my movements with controlled determination. His eyes flicker with pleasure, his jaw working hard to retain composure whilst he trails his long fingers along the top of my thigh. Hot panting breaths of anticipation fall from my mouth, and I almost whimper, feeling him slide into my pants. He watches me, revelling in the swell of pleasure on my face.

'Relax....' He breathes, caressing me lightly.

My head drops back, my shoulders releasing all tension. My hips roll in rhythm with the pad of his thumb, feeling misery and stress leave me with every tantalising touch. The pressure builds, clutching me harder, threatening to conquer everything with a thick, deep, richer purpose.

'Don't stop, Gabriel, please.' I breathe, losing all sense.

His arms tense at the sound of his name falling from my mouth. I continue pleading with him, hooked on his movements, held hostage by the insatiable contact of his soaking wet fingers.

'That's it…' he whispers, driving me to the edge, hovering me on the verge. 'Let go.'

His words are my undoing, launching me to the peak. I erupt around him, shaking as if I've come undone, falling apart completely. Every nerve screams with ecstasy, overflowing with the freedom of release. I grip his chest and melt away, calling his name over and over again. All whilst he watches, his stunning face captivated by my unravelling.

CHAPTER THIRTY-EIGHT

Blinking a few times, my mind attempts to focus on the strange room. Peering over my left shoulder, I try to make sense of the figure next to me. My pulse spikes as pictures of last night replay in my head with passionate ferocity – flashes of our bodies intertwined on the sofa, the counter, the bed. Gabriel James is the reason my relationship with Simon was never going to work. For years I craved this, the recurring twist of pleasure and pain we derive from each other's company. I smile at the sleepy sound of his breathing, stealing a few glances at the flex of muscles. He stirs, turning on his back before his eyes blink heavily, a drowsy smirk descending on his face.

'Are you being a creep?' he asks, turning over to me.
'Yes.'
'Good,' he moves closer, encasing me in his arms.

I laugh, rolling on top of him, pushing my palms down against his chest. He sits up, offering a sly grin, giving me the most amazing view of his dimples before our bare bodies melt into each other, nothing but white sheets covering our modesty.

'How's the wriggler?' he nods down to the tiny little bump and slowly glides his hand across my midriff with a heart-swelling tenderness. If he's bothered that all of this happened whilst I'm carrying another man's child, it doesn't show. For once, I'm grateful for that arrogant self-assurance. I stare at him for a time, enjoying this side of him, wanting to steal a piece of it away forever. I find myself wishing that this was our child, that this could be something that Gabriel and I share, taking Simon out of the picture completely. But that's not fair on either of them. Almost as if to remind me of the world outside these four walls, my stomach sinks, my mind travelling back to reality. I can't let myself get caught up like this. It's irresponsible to hope for a semblance of normality amidst the chaos we find ourselves in. Nothing about us is ordinary and may never be. That's the truth of it. The comforting, reassuring calm I felt mere seconds ago dissolves, and I look away, training my attention elsewhere before climbing away from him.

'Lex?' He asks with a confused tone, having just witnessed the change in my expression.

'I don't feel sick, so that's a good thing, I guess.' I release a long, tense breath, avoiding his gaze.

He stands from the bed and takes my wrist, one eyebrow raised.

I tilt my head, knowing I've been rumbled. 'How are we going to get to Paytak, Gabriel?'

He looks down at my hand in his, his face suddenly serious. 'I've got an idea.'

GABRIEL

CHAPTER THIRTY-NINE

Theresa Stanley twiddles her thumbs in the passenger seat of my car, reflecting on my theories about Diren Paytak. The bottles of wine over dinner have certainly helped soften her up, mixed with my apology for not seeing things her way. The minute I confessed that she was right, Alexandra is involved: her guard dropped, her eyes lit up, and she reached across the table, thanking me for my honesty. I'm not proud of my manipulation of her but it's necessary and what I need to do, to protect Lex.

'Do you want me to drive you to the entrance? You'll get soaked otherwise.'

'Are you sure?'

'Yeah.' I say, putting the key in the ignition.

'No...' She shakes her head, screwing her eyes shut. 'Are you sure Alexandra is working for Paytak?'

'Yes.' I drop my hand, looking ahead.

'And you're sure it was her... it was her who killed Kristine?'

'The source said she was hired to tie up loose ends.'

'There has to be someone in your department working with her, protecting her.'

I tense and bite my tongue. 'Mmhmm.'

'How are we going to get to Paytak? If he's responsible for all of this... we need evidence,' she ponders, watching the rain. 'Did your source mention anyone else?'

'No. But I got word from this Agent Roe bloke that Paytak hired Alexandra through a private security company called Freeman Powell Technologies. They've been supplying The Singularity with all kinds of resources.'

'Resources...' She ponders the thought. 'Like what exactly?'

'I don't know the details but in the absence of Alexandra - if we get the intel on Freeman Powell; location, accounts, employees... that's how we'll get closer to Higgs. The Singularity are using this company, a lot. There will be answers there.'

She nods enthusiastically. 'If we can prove that Paytak and The Singularity are using them, we might get a warrant for their account.'

'Exactly.'

'I just don't understand why this has to be off the books. We should be proud of this, Gabriel. We're the ones getting closer.' She turns her head excited. 'You and me.'

'We've got people watching our every move. Roe is with Interpol. Counter-Terrorism is after The Singularity. If I go in there and run a search on Freeman Powell, they'll get an alert, Theresa. And if either of them finds Paytak first, we've lost the power to stop him. This won't be our case anymore.'

'They want Paytak to snitch.'

'You know that's always the way.'

'Ok, so how do I get into the system?' she asks, her tone urgent. 'Are you sure they're not tracing me too?'

'Use your own details; run the search on Freeman Powell. Look for charges brought against people who have worked for them. Anyone that looks like they could have been a contractor, ex-military. Then look for any investment or endorsements to the company from politicians or people of influence.'

She nods, absorbing this.

'Remember to delete the history. They won't have flagged your credentials, so as long as you cover your tracks, you'll be fine.'

She apprehensively blinks at the space in front of her.

'Take this.' I put my key card into her hands.

'Gabriel.' She shakes her head, exhaling a nervous breath. 'This is a lot.'

I'm hit with an epiphany suddenly. I'm not proud of it, but I do know it's the only way. I remove my seatbelt and lean across the seat, keeping my eyes locked on hers, closing the space between us. 'Theresa...'

She looks at me warily.

'Please, I need you to do this. If we get everything we can on Freeman Powell, that's our way in. We can finally find him. This will be a huge win for us.' I reach my hand up to her face, forcing myself to picture Lex as I tuck a stray piece of peroxide hair behind Stanley's ear. She smells like cigarettes and musty perfume, and it takes all my willpower to stay close as I watch her shoulders relax. 'You can do this.'

She leans in, the wine in her system urging her brain to accept my show of affection before she closes the small gap between us, pressing her mouth to mine gently. I give into her, hating myself but getting it done, nonetheless.

'We need to work together, and I need you.'

She swallows before opening her eyes. 'Ok.'

'It's going to be ok.'

'We don't know that,' she utters, her worried eyes finding mine before she steps out of the car and begins to run through the rain.

I watch her quick, determined pace towards the door, noticing her look around before buzzing through. I sigh, drumming my fingers against the steering wheel, my eyes flitting to the entrance as the rain continues to beat down against the metal of the car, the repetitive sound only adding to my persistent anxiety, making me wish I smoked, just to give me something else to do with my hands.

After what feels like an hour, I see Stanley emerge. She nods before throwing an enthusiastic thumbs-up, smiling a winning grin. *Hell fucking yes, Theresa.* Finally, that relentless determination has been put to good use. I wait, watching her approach through the passenger-seat window, when something appears from my peripheral vision. The blur of a black SUV comes into view, hurtling down the road, forcibly breaking every speed limit in existence as it sprints towards us, bound for the oblivious, excited figure in the road.

I look to Stanley and jerk back, my hands flailing to get out of the car. I yell at her to run, warning her to move out of the way. Oblivious, she strides across the road, only detecting the imminent threat when she registers the look on my face. She turns her head towards the menacing rev of the car's engine, now seconds from impact. I throw the car door open, racing out onto the pavement, sprinting around the bonnet. We lock eyes. She opens her mouth, but she knows it's too late. An acceptance arrives on her face. I run into the road. She shakes her head. *She's telling me no.* It's the last thing I see before the front of the vehicle hammers into her. Her face twists, her eyes scrunching shut, her entire form distorting on impact. The sound of crunching metal and glass reverberates around us as it crushes against her bones, devastating her entire anatomy. I'm welded to the spot, watching first-hand the dire consequences of hundreds of pounds of metal slamming into a human being. Her back arches into an incomprehensible shape, her body thrown several feet into the air, her limbs swinging out at her sides. She flings over the bonnet, skewered across the roof, pummelling into the concrete with a dull thud as the vehicle continues speeding into the darkness. I yell her name at the top of my lungs, speeding towards her, but in the few seconds that pass, I already know she's dead.

ALEXANDRA

CHAPTER FORTY

I hear him come in around midnight, his boots thudding against the floorboards before he heads straight to his bedroom. I stare at the ceiling, fighting the urge to seek him out straight away. *But can I honestly wait until tomorrow? What if he knows where Paytak is?* The life of my unborn child depends on this information. *I'm not waiting anymore.* I throw the duvet back and march out of the bedroom, crossing the living room with heavy footsteps. I stop myself suddenly as something causes me to hesitate. My ears prick at the low, muffled sobs from Gabriel's room. Worried, I softly tap my knuckles on the door and wait, hearing shuffled movement before it swings open. There he stands, topless, his hair glistening, wet from the shower. He stares down at me blankly, his face void of emotion. Sometimes when I look at him, it's like I've been hit straight through the chest with a hammer. The enormity of my feelings complicates all words, and I find myself completely distracted from the bigger, more prominent issue at hand. I squint, taking a second to look into his dark eyes, noticing the red tinge framing them, the usual blazing irises now heavy and bloodshot.

'Not now, Lex.'

'Gabriel...'

'Can we speak in the morning?' he asks quietly, his voice low and gruff. His whole body appears heavy. He reaches up, gripping both hands on the door frame, exhausted from the task of merely having to hold himself up.

'What happened?' I reach out to him, looking around the room, searching for a sign, an explanation for his fractured appearance. He quickly turns away, leaving the door open and walking back into the room. Resigned to the fact I'm not leaving him alone, he sits on the edge of the bed, instantly burying his face in his hands, rubbing them restlessly over his head.

I join him, silence hanging thickly in the air as I rack my brains, wondering what could have happened. He sighs into his palms, his elbows resting on his knees. His shoulders sag wearily forward, his whole body heaving, his tears falling to the floor. I watch him fall apart in front of me, speechless at witnessing him breaking piece by piece before my very eyes. I try to put my hands around his torso, stroking his back to soothe him, moving in slow circles. He moves slightly, his hands wiping his face before he sits up straighter.

'Gabriel, look at me.' I instruct, placing one hand on his face. 'Tell me what happened.'

He takes a deep, shaking inhale. 'I killed her.'

I move my head closer, wanting to make sure I've heard him correctly. 'Killed... who?'

'Stanley.'

My chest restricts in a tight, unrelenting vice.

'Gabe...' I whisper, holding back the panic. 'What happened to Stanley?'

He slowly raises his head. The despair in his eyes nearly knocks the breath out of me. 'She's dead.'

'How?'

'I used her. I lied to her.' He shakes his head, screwing his eyes shut as if trying to forcibly burn the memory from his brain.

'Tell me what happened.'

We don't move from the edge of his bed for what feels like hours whilst he describes the entire evening, start to finish. I stay silent, letting him run through each detail: timings, the drinks they ordered, the food they ate, topics of discussion, then finally driving her to HQ, convincing her to go inside, right up until the very moment itself. I sit beside him, watching the torment flare up in his eyes, mixed with a flash of guilt and self-loathing. I've seen him angry, disappointed, unaffected, and distant, but this heart-crushing sadness is the most unbearable of them all. *I lost someone.* The memory of those words swims through my mind. I wonder if tonight's encounter has triggered thoughts of Janie. He reaches his right hand up to his bare chest, rubbing his palm over the centre as if trying to cure a soreness in his heart. *Whoever did this wanted him to bear witness. It was both a warning and a solution to a problem.*

'Did anyone see you at HQ?'

'Nobody.'

'What about CCTV?'

'I had to leave her.' He closes his eyes. 'I can't believe I just left her…'

'Gabe, there's nothing you could have done. She was gone.'

'I made her go in there. I said we'd close the case…I should have found another way.'

'But what other way was there?'

'I was being stubborn; I could have done it myself.'

I wait for him to elaborate.

'I made her go in there. I made her use her own details to search for background on Freeman Powell.'

'Right…'

'I made her think we could work together, that she'd get ahead. I told her I needed her. I manipulated her. I told her everything she wanted to hear, and then…' he hesitates, 'I kissed her.'

I can't help but shake my head; my face pinched with disappointment.

'Counter-Terrorism is watching my every move. They think they can back me into a corner, get me to hand you over. I know how he works. He'll have access to everything I do in the system. Stanley was the only one to get the information I needed, so we could do this without them.'

'Who is he, Gabriel?' I demand, thinking about the source that gave him Roe, the person who knew about McGuire.

'Edward...' He flits his eyes to mine for just a second before looking away. 'My father.'

My hand drifts to my mouth. He used Stanley to get the information to stop Counter-Terrorism from using me. To protect me as he always does. And in doing so, he's inadvertently murdered another. I take a breath to lie to him, to tell him that he didn't have a hand in her death. But I can't. In the military, no person's life means more than another. Death doesn't discriminate, and neither did we. But not here, not in the real world. The simple fact is Gabriel used Theresa Stanley because her life meant less to him than mine.

'You were protecting me like you always do.' I say finally, swallowing past the deep, nauseating sickness in the pit of my stomach. *Look at the collateral damage that rests between us.* 'She knew the risks.'

'I didn't know anything about her.'

'I'm sure the team will contact her family,' I say, almost wincing.

'We're no closer to getting Paytak.'

Clarity drops into my brain like a light bulb being switched on for the first time. 'Does Roe know who your father is?'

He looks up, nodding slowly.

'Gabriel, I don't think Roe was ever planning on using me, a civilian. It's reckless. Especially for an agency like Interpol.'

'So what then?'

'I think he knew that if he threatened to use me, you'd find every resource you could, every contact, every means of access. He goaded you into doing his work for him. He knows that with a father like Edward, you'd have a whole network at your fingertips.'

'Well, that hasn't worked, has it.'

'There has to be another way.'

'I know what you're thinking, and I won't let you do it.'

'It might be the only card we have left to play.'

'I can't, Lex. I can't put you in harm's way.'

'Here… sit with me.' I instruct, pulling him back towards the bed, and shuffling up to the headboard.

He obliges, his long body shifting backwards. His eyes stare up at the skylight. His head hits the pillow. I nestle into him, listening to the thrum of his heartbeat, sensing he can't help but replay the image of Stanley's body in his mind.

'Remember what I told you…' I whisper, matching the direction of my eyes with his, looking into the glow of darkness above us. 'Just because we've seen dark and terrible things doesn't mean we get to be dark and terrible.'

'God, I want a drink,' he whispers, almost as if he didn't mean to say it aloud.

I turn to him, sensing the anguish of his words. 'I'm sorry, it must be hard. Fighting that every day.'

He considers this, his body tensing as if reluctant to revisit the destruction of those years. 'It's a work-in-progress. It helps to go to meetings. I'm fortunate that my vices stop at drink. Others I was in rehab with, it was like a gateway to something more sinister.'

I nod, my mind drifting to my sister, who's endured years after years of rehab and psychiatric hospitals. 'Did you go just the once?'

'I've been in and out countless times, Lex. I'm not proud of it, but I'm trying.'

'What's it like?'

'Rehab?'

'Addiction...' I clarify softly, suddenly aware I could be pushing him too far.

'I guess it's like having the same song circling your brain with no end. It's like constantly trying to ignore an itch, knowing the consequences of scratching are worse than the itch itself.'

'I don't think Olivia has quite figured that last part out.'

'Part of me still hasn't. Part of me wakes up every morning questioning why I can't just down a litre of whiskey. The addict in me is incredibly persuasive. I tell myself I don't need a job, friends, or family, that the itch is the most pertinent, burning priority and that I am well within my rights to drink as much as I want. But then, thankfully, the recovering alcoholic has since learnt that although it might feel good for a day, maybe even two, to satisfy that urge, it's not worth the self-loathing. It's not worth the guilt. It's just...' He stops, trying to find the words, 'it's like your brain is choking on a perpetual loop, and alcohol is oxygen. But I know that when I'm on a binge, my mind will reach that stage where it becomes restless and yearns for more. Addiction is never satisfied. You always want more. I work at it every day to make sure the recovering alcoholic wins the battle.'

I sigh, astonished by his honesty. 'I'm sorry... for making you talk about this.'

'No, it's good. It's healthy for me to talk about it with someone who isn't being paid to listen.' He takes my hand in his, offering a shy smile.

'Do you still see someone?'

'Work makes me see a therapist, and I go to meetings when I can.'

He drops his head, his sudden vulnerability making my chest ache as his long eyelashes flutter with uncertainty. *He's worried that his honesty has unveiled too many of his flaws.*

I glance up at him, sad that his life has been so hard since we knew each other. 'You're still the most impressive man I know.'

His head rises with surprise.

'In your recovery, you've been surrounded by sober partners, sponsors, other recovering addicts - you think you're just one of a crowd. But not to me.' I reach out to caress his cheek tenderly. 'Never to me.'

I let the words hang in the air between us before leaning up to kiss him. He exhales slowly, relaxing into me before his mouth becomes more urgent, his cool tongue skirting mine with a sensual repetitive neediness. I take a breath, my body feeling hot, my skin itching for his touch. He moves his hand to my nape, and I moan at the way he grips my hair, holding me in place with assertive dominance.

'I never got over you,' he whispers suddenly, his striking face softening as he lets out a long breath, almost as if he's been waiting to say that for a long time. The admission makes me pause. It's in these moments that I see how he really feels, how desperate he is to keep me close.

'Me neither...' I smile, moving his hair out of his face. 'And I hope I never have to.'

We sit like this for a while, his arms wrapped around me, stroking our fingers in circles across each other. 'I uh...' he starts, his voice cracking. 'I really am sorry... for everything, Lex.'

'Shh, it's ok,' I soothe.

He turns on his side, pulling me into his bare chest as he nestles his head against mine, his face surrounded by my wild head of hair.

'Please don't leave again. There's nothing... nothing I wouldn't do for you.'

THE BURNT CHILD

I tense, the admission pulling on a deep-rooted thread of anxiety. Theresa Stanley's death is a testament to those words. I close my eyes, urging darkness to dissolve the guilt.

GABRIEL

CHAPTER FORTY-ONE

Dressed and ready to head to HQ, I make my way across the living room towards the guest bedroom in search of Lex. Sensing a presence behind me, I turn quickly, noticing that she's stood by the kitchen island, her hair pulled back, a single pen holding it up with a few loose strands falling delicately against the glow of her face. I do my best to halt my eyes from staring as she stands facing me, a knowing smirk playing on the corners of her lips.

'For a detective, you're not very observant, are you?'

'We don't all have S.A.S stealth.' I smile, moving towards her urgently, breathing in the euphoric scent of her hair, wanting to take her to bed for the rest of the day.

'I'll take that as a compliment.' She smiles.

I pull away, something pricking at the back of my mind.

'What's wrong?'

'How did Paytak find Stanley last night?'

'He's got eyes everywhere.'

'He has someone on the inside; we've always thought that.'

'Yeah…'

'That person must have been at the office. Otherwise, how else did he know?'

'Who?' she shakes her head. 'How?'

'Think about it; Stanley goes into HQ, using my key card. She starts searching for information on Freeman Powell. Ten minutes later, she's dead.'

'Right…'

'And if we find out who was there last night, we might be able to find Paytak…'

I slide out my phone and log in to the NCA portal, my thumb frantically scrolling through the digital log, noting the extensive list of names from every department until I reach mine.

'Fuck.' Realisation pinches at the front of my brain as everything finally falls into place.

CHAPTER FORTY-TWO

'How long have you been helping them?'

Dark circles hang heavily under her eyes, tainting her usually fresh face. This has all but nearly eaten her alive, and it sends a pang of sadness through me. Despite everything, I wish it wasn't her.

'Amber...' I press irritably.

She sighs, walking through to the small living room. Her trembling hands rake through her hair as she falls onto the couch.

I follow, standing opposite her, noticing the swell of tears threatening to spill over.

'One of Paytak's associates contacted me, he asked me to get rid of the CCTV.' She blurts into the air in a single breath. 'They knew it would look too suspicious if I didn't find something, so they gave me the footage from the shop across the road.'

'And they doctored the two police officers out of it?'

'The woman said they would help with Graham's clinical trial. She said they'd pay for everything.'

'What woman?'

She shrugs, wiping more tears from her face.

'Did this woman ask you to do anything else?'

'The deal was to help with the CCTV and then...' She hesitates, blowing air through her cheeks as if trying to dispel the nerves from her body. 'They knew you were getting close. They asked me to keep them updated. They wanted you out of the way.'

'They murdered an innocent woman, Amber.'

'I'm sorry, Guv,' she whispers. 'They threatened Graham.'

All this time, they were one step ahead.

'I'm so sorry...' she weeps into her hands. 'I had to.'

'Why Stanley, Amber? Why couldn't you just let her walk away.'

'It was meant to be you!' She throws the words out in the air, shame plaguing her face. 'I had an alert set up... the system said you were in the building. I saw the search, and I thought it was you.'

I close my eyes. 'What did Stanley know? What was on the search?'

She shrugs. 'She deleted her history.'

'You should have told him to stand down.'

Her face pales.

'Paytak knows it was a failed attempt?'

'Yes.'

'Fucking hell.'

'I'm sorry, Guv. I didn't want to... I didn't want to hurt you.'

'Where is Paytak now?'

'I don't know.'

'How do they contact you?'

'A burner.'

'I need the phone.'

She stares at me, panicked.

'I'll make sure they can't get to you, but you need to work with me.'

She nods slowly.

'How do they pay for Graham's treatment?'

'They send money from a Swiss bank account.'

'I need access to your bank statements. Did you ever speak to anyone called Higgs?'

'No, Guv... Just Paytak and the woman.'

'I need the phone now, Amber.'

She stands slowly and gestures to the kitchen. I follow her through as she opens the cupboard under the sink and leans in, searching around before pulling a small black burner phone from a white bin bag. I open my palm, and she places the phone in my hand.

'What now, Guv?' she wavers before staring up at me. 'If they can't contact me, everything with Graham...'

I sigh, knowing I can't allow myself to dive into the consequences of Amber's actions. I look away, freezing out every ounce of fondness towards her, keeping my brain trained on the professional task at hand. Deep down, I want to help her. I don't blame her for giving me up. I might have done the same, given her position. But there's a long list of people counting on me right now, and the best I can do for Amber is my job.

'There's an agent outside. He's part of an independent investigation. He is going to take all these details from you and send you somewhere safe.'

Her lip quivers, her fingers gripping her scalp. 'They'll get to me inside.' She sobs, her eyes darting around the room as if she's trying to memorise the space. 'And what about Graham?'

'Agent Roe will run surveillance on your house; he is going to select the officers himself. They'll look out for Graham, ok?'

'He's the love of my life,' she says suddenly, causing my head to rise from the floor. 'You understand, don't you? Wouldn't you do anything... anything to save that person?'

I stare back at her. The desperation I see before me is undeniably familiar.

'I wish you had come to me sooner. I would have helped you.'

'I didn't want to put you in that position.'

'I've been in worse.'

She crosses her arms. 'I know.'

My heart stops as her words empty into the air like bullets, pulling together my worst fears.

'I won't tell anyone, Guv. I want to make up for what I've done... I know you want to keep her safe.'

'How do you...?'

'When you said you had a witness, someone who saw the police officers in the laundrette with Kristine, I knew it had to be her.'

'Does Paytak know she's with me, Amber?'

'No,' she whispers. 'But I had to give them something. They wanted to know who saw the officers.'

'What did you do?'

'Nicky Black...I gave Nicky to Paytak.'

'So, he's dead?'

She nods solemnly.

'We good?' Roe asks from the passenger seat as we slide into the back of his unmarked car.

'Yep... let's go.' I say, offering Amber a reassuring nod.

'Officer Brooks, I'm Agent Roe.' Roe turns over his shoulder. 'I'm going to take you to a secure location for questioning.' He signals for the uniformed driver to start the engine. 'My officers have been informed to maintain surveillance on your house for the time being. Your husband will be safe.'

'Will I be back here soon?' Amber asks in a small voice.

'We'll have to see about that.' I lock eyes with Roe, silently imploring him to keep quiet.

'It's just my husband...he's not well. He needs me.'

'When we get to the safehouse, you can make a call. We'll arrange for someone to be with him.' I reassure her.

'I just wanted to save his life. I had to... I had to find a way.'

'You just concentrate on giving us what we need, then we can go from there.'

She nods solemnly.

Roe continues to run Amber through the details and precautions as we drive through Central London to an Interpol safehouse. Amber stares out of the window, her eyes glazed, her expression distant, numbness having replaced fear. I've seen that look before. I make a mental note to have Roe place her on suicide watch.

As we near Finsbury Park tube, I lean forward, gesturing towards the station. 'Drop me off here, please.'

Roe considers this for a second before nodding at the driver. 'We need to talk,' he winds down his window, calling out as I exit the vehicle. 'I'll text you a location.'

'Maybe…' I respond noncommittally, offering Amber a short nod. Her ghostly expression regards me for a second before the car pulls away.

Having spent hours with Collins discussing today's most pertinent breakthrough, it's a little after midnight when I finally get home. With Stanley's murder and Paytak still determined to end my existence, I agreed that the NCA could place armed officers on surveillance in the mews. I offer them a brief *hello* before letting myself in the building, wondering what my neighbours will think of the strange men sitting in a van all night. Despite their presence, Lex still isn't safe here, and the pressure to find Paytak and Rhiannon is now tenfold. Whilst it might be everyone else's priority to use them to get to Higgs, I will gladly end both their lives without a second thought, as long as it means she's safe.

Knowing I don't want to sleep without Lex tonight, I creep into her room, hoping the feel of her next to me will soothe the ache in my chest from the turbulence of events. I sink into the mattress, feeling my whole body relax at the sound of her steady breathing. Her face is tucked perfectly into the pillow, her hair falling messily around her shoulders in the most eccentric waves, her berry-red lips slightly parted whilst she takes calm, sleep-dazed breaths. I fight the urge to reach out and touch her before drifting into a restless sleep.

CHAPTER FORTY-THREE

'Gabriel…'

The repetition of my name in the darkness stirs me from sleep.

'Gabriel, wake up…'

I bolt upright. Lex is standing at the foot of the bed, her hands gripping the gun that was under my pillow just minutes ago.

'Someone is trying to get into the flat.'

I move towards her, catching a glimpse of her wide, anxious eyes. I grab the gun out of her hands and instinctively pull her behind me, motioning for her to sit on the bed.

'Let me come with you,' she insists,

I shake my head vigorously, placing my left index finger over my mouth, willing her to stay put before I gesture down to the baby, not having the time to elaborate. Thankfully, she gets the point and reluctantly nods in agreement.

'If I'm not back in five minutes, you have to climb out the window, do you hear me?' I ignore the struggle behind her eyes, knowing she wants to accompany me.

I silently step out into the living room, my head whipping up in response to someone shuffling in the hallway outside. I creep slowly towards the noise, pausing as the light shifts under the door, a shadow of a figure looming on the other side. Adrenaline jumpstarts my senses, knowing I have to successfully disarm said person as quickly as possible. I reach for the handle with all sorts of possibilities racing through my mind, convinced Paytak has come to finish the job.

I don't waste a second in swinging it open and seizing the culprit by the collar, my gun pointing directly at their head in one swift movement. They struggle beneath my grip, shouting for me to stop. With my survival instinct in full throttle, it takes me a while to allow context to fall into place. *I know that voice.*

'For fuck's sake.' I yell, letting go of Julian. 'Are you trying to kill me?'

'The irony that you're the one asking that question...' He pants, his voice strained.

I swiftly drop the pistol to my side.

He steps back, wiping sweat from his forehead and pulling his jacket down.

'Can I help you mate?'

'Amber...' He pants. 'I came to tell you. Collins called me. Amber is the mole.'

'I know.' I say, quickly twitching my head over my shoulder. I hope Lex can hear me chatting, giving her a clear indication that there's no further threat.

'I couldn't sleep. I had to make sure you knew.' He says, worry carved into his youthful face. 'Terrible, isn't it? All this time, she was the leak.'

'I know.' I repeat.

He raises his head. 'How?'

'Long story.'

'And poor Stanley...'

I realise I haven't seen Julian since she died. I'm losing chunks of time with all that's going on. *What else might I not be focusing on?*

'Collins told me you were with her.'

'Yeah, I was there.' I mumble, wincing at the memory of Stanley's lifeless body. *The way I used her in the last few moments of her life.*

'None of us are safe. I keep thinking we're missing something, Guv. No OCG has ever gone to this much trouble.'

'Look, we'll chat tomorrow. Collins knows what's at stake.'

He hesitates, and I can't help but notice the faltering look of concern. I'm practically holding my breath, waiting for him to turn and disappear down the stairs.

His lips part hesitantly, and I immediately know what he's about to say. 'She's in there, isn't she?'

I stare at him, no longer having the energy to lie.

He scoffs. 'I knew it.'

'It's complicated.'

'What the fuck are you thinking?'

'I'm doing my job.'

'Our job is to work with the system whilst we investigate this together!'

'How did you know she was here?'

'When you found out she was missing, you were hell-bent on finding her. We both were. Then one day, you have an eyewitness at the laundrette.' He hesitates before continuing. 'And then it struck me. You're no longer killing yourself to find her because you know exactly where she is.'

'We can't trust Witness Protection. Look what happened when we even discussed the prospect of putting Toff there.'

'I hope you know what the hell you're doing.'

'She needs help, Jules.'

'This is out of control.'

'I know it is, I know,' I admit, acknowledging I'm in way over my head. 'But I have to get her out of here, Jules. It's only a matter of time before Paytak comes here.'

He starts backing away. 'If this is about her, then I can't, Guv. I've got a family. I'm sorry.' He holds up his hands. 'I can't get involved.'

'I just need you to take her somewhere safe. Nobody needs to know where you've been. You can leave tonight.'

He continues to shake his head disparagingly. 'If you do not stop this, Gabriel, you'll end up dead.'

'I would take her, but it's too dangerous,' I plead. 'There are too many eyes on me.'

He sighs. 'Where would I even take her?'

'There's a safehouse. Please, just trust me, Jules.'

'All I ever do is fucking trust you. But look at where we are.' He looks around before transitioning to an angry whisper. 'Amber is corrupt, a police officer is dead, and you're hiding a fugitive!'

'She didn't kill Kristine Kingley.'

'Even if you get Paytak, The Singularity will send someone else to come at you again.'

'If we let someone else handle this, we will never know if it's over.'

'This is what the Christofis do. They suck you in and drag you down with them.'

I find myself battling the instinct not to jump down his throat to defend Lex. 'Jules, please.'

'Where? Where is the safehouse?'

'I'll give you the address if you agree to leave with her now.'

'Tell me where it is, Guv!'

My brain is itching to say it, finally to get it out in the open. Times up. The truth has to come out. I no longer care about my life, but the hesitation comes from the harm this will cause Lex. *It will be the end for us.* Deep down, I always knew. I always knew this moment would come. *All I want is for her to be happy.* She will never forgive me, that I'm certain. But I have to find a way to protect her. I have to make this right, even if she hates me for it. *That is the priority, and it must be done.* I picture the words clawing at my mind, desperate to break free.

'Guv, where-'

'To her father.'

Julian blinks at me, dumbfounded.

I clear my throat. 'I need you to take her to her father.'

'Mario Christofi?'

'Correct.'

'Mario Christofi is dead.'

I shake my head.

'What do you mean? What is he?' His face reddens.

'He's alive.' I respond flatly.

'Fucking hell. Fucking hell.' He bends over, his hands on his knees. 'You lied.'

'I had to.'

'He's alive. He's been alive this whole time…'

'It was the only way to keep him safe.'

'You lied to me.' He straightens, backing away again. 'Every single bloody day.'

'Look, you can hold this against me for the rest of my life, turn me in, have me arrested. I know you don't owe me anything, you never did. But I am telling you now if she stays here… she will be murdered, Julian.'

'You're harbouring one here and the other God knows where!'

I rub my hand over my head and look down at the floor. 'Jules, if this were Sarah, what would you do?'

His head rises, suddenly comprehending what I'm implying.

'She's pregnant. I have to protect her, Julian.'

His eyes dart left and right across the floor between us. 'Who else knows about him?'

'No one.'

'That's why you kept her here.'

'Partly the reason I didn't immediately turn her in, yeah.'

'You were the one who always warned me not to get attached. You should have let it go... Why couldn't you just be done with it?!'

I twist my mouth, unable to answer his questions. I don't know why. At every turn, I thought I was making the right choice.

Julian puts his hand over his forehead and inhales a long, tedious breath. 'You're a good man, Gabriel. And for whatever reason, you feel obliged to help this family, to save this woman, but they are going to get you killed. I can't... I'm sorry,' he whispers, beginning to descend the stairs.

I watch him leave, knowing I couldn't have expected much more. He has a family to think of. He's made the right choice. He's done what I should have from the start. I push my apartment door open and look around at the stillness, a stark contrast to the intense battle in my mind. *Wouldn't you do anything... anything to save that person's life?*

I would. A world without her is colourless and grey. My life's perspective has been fenced in by the routine of disaster and suffering, surviving the passing of time, never thriving, never really living. And then she came back. The remedy of hope amongst despair. The extraordinary light she emanates, the infectiousness of her laugh, her unique ability to penetrate the depths of my conscience, using her own darkness as an instrument to heal me, expecting nothing in return. I'm better for knowing her, better for seeing her again and better for loving her. *I've always loved her.*

I take a step towards her bedroom, eager to tell her how much she means to me before everything around us falls apart. She has to know. But as I make my way across the living room, movement from behind stops me in my tracks. Taken by surprise, I turn around quickly, my hand braced on the trigger of my weapon.

My stomach drops.

Lex's eyes are hostile and penetrative, seething with betrayal, her face gleaming from streams of tears that have rolled down her cheeks. Her face is set in a distant, cold expression. Her arms tightening her grip around the gun pointed at my head. 'He's alive?'

ALEXANDRA

CHAPTER FORTY-FOUR

We journey through narrow country roads, frequently having to slow to a stop to allow other cars to pass as drivers give a grateful wave of their hands. We continue through tight country tracks, winding around corners packed with thick grasses. Every so often, tiny villages come into view, hidden behind tall, wild verges that guard the boundaries to their untarnished, sanctimonious communities. I feel the knots in my shoulders begin to ease, tension dissolving with every mile Gabriel puts between us and the confined chaos of London.

My eyes feel heavy and sore. Another sleepless night, another devastating shift of the ground beneath my feet. My mind strains for rest, but I'm unable to tear my thoughts away.

You let me believe he was gone. My own father. This whole time you pretended to care. I trusted you. None of that meant anything.
I wanted to tell you so badly.
You're a coward and a liar.
I'm sorry, Lex. I'm so sorry.

I spring my eyes open, craving the distraction of something else beyond the realms of my subconscious, searching for something out of the window to take my mind away from Gabriel's devastating betrayal and my father's selfish actions. I rub my chest, staring out to the expanse of the Oxfordshire hills, trying to persuade my lungs to inhale a full breath.

'Are you alright?' Gabriel asks concerned.

I say nothing, unable to even look at him without wanting to put a thousand miles between us. He took everything away, the one person I counted on. And when he had the opportunity to give it back, to atone for his actions, he chose not to. I hate him. And I'm broken by that fact. I should feel delighted that Mario is alive. But how long for? This can't go on forever; none of us can continue like this. *How long until someone finds him? Until someone finds all of us.* The complicated tangle of lies and treachery has to end somewhere. *Maybe we should all allow ourselves to be eradicated. Put us out of our misery.*

'I have to drop you off and leave straight away,' Gabriel informs softly.

I pretend not to care about the where and the why, trying instead to concentrate on how striking the landscape looks, with bright emerald treetops standing out amidst the grey, gunmetal sky. *He can leave forever as far as I'm concerned.*

We pull into a driveway lined with a row of trees. I watch as they bluster uncontrollably against the wind, their leaves clinging onto their dying branches, unwittingly refusing to fall with an uncharacteristic stubbornness. The driveway eventually snakes down a small hill, and a large country house comes into view. An idyllic manor built with soft buttery Cotswold stone. It's covered with a wisteria that's weaved itself up the bricks, intertwining around some of the windows.

'We need to knock on the door,' Gabriel instructs, pulling up the handbrake. *Still incapable of looking at me, I see.*

I roll my eyes petulantly and pull myself out of the car, my body shaking from the combination of cold weather and trembling anxiety. Before Gabriel is even halfway to the house, I hear a light bell sound behind me, and the front door is swiftly pulled open. My mouth becomes dry, failing to move in time with my brain's commands. I forget to blink. My feet become anchored to the spot. The wind whips my hair around me, causing my eyes to screw shut.

There he is. Mario Christofi. The man I cried out for a thousand times through misery and grief. All those moments, I locked myself away from Simon, lying on the bathroom floor, broken by the loss of him. I recall the days I spent surrounded by an unrelenting fog, how the world had changed irrevocably, every day on the wheel of sorrow; no taste in any food, no joy from music, numb to everything. All of that wasted. My brain swirls with confusion, unable to understand how or why this happened to me, to us. The thoughts begin to multiply, and it starts happening again: the loss of control, the surge of emotional turmoil. The last thing I remember before the world turns, and my vision blurs is Gabriel racing towards me. Then everything goes dark.

CHAPTER FORTY-FIVE

Opening my eyes, I stare in a daze at the unfamiliar ceiling. I shift myself up a blue velvet sofa, my body becoming swallowed into a mountain of cushions. I take a small glance around the room, my brain struggling to understand my surroundings. *Whose house is this? Does my father live here?* I can hear his gruff voice in the hallway, his furious ranting travelling through the walls. I turn to follow the sound, noticing Gabriel sitting on an armchair in the corner of the room.

His eyes brighten as he looks up from his phone, leaping up to hand me a glass of water. 'Sit up slowly.'

I wince. *Did I hit the ground?* With a striking sense of alarm, I quickly place my hand on my stomach, begging that my body somehow protected the baby.

'I caught you,' Gabriel reveals, reading my thoughts.

I stay quiet, standing slowly, waiting for betraying signs of pain. Gabriel watches on uncomfortably whilst I glide my hands over my stomach. I finally take a breath as I feel a flurry of energetic fluttering, giving me the reassurance I needed. Sinking back into the sofa, I close my eyes, swallowing past the dull slab at the base of my throat. It's strange how the human body can become so attached to the concept of a child, my hormones working collectively to ensure I have a sealed connection to my offspring before I've even held my baby.

'You feeling alright?'

'I think so...' I murmur without looking up.

He turns and leaves the room, mumbling something about finding Mario. As soon as I watch him go, I instantly long for him to return. *I'll have to learn to let that go.*

'...fainted. Fainted on the driveway, Gabriel!'

I sigh, remembering what it's like to endure the wrath of Mario Christofi.

'She found out last night,' I hear him concede in a low drawl.

Would he ever have told me? Or would he have spent the rest of our lives keeping me in the dark? Listening to me talk about the loss of my father on multiple occasions, never once dropping the veil. Every promise, every feeling tainted with the lie. *I'm sorry for everything, Lex.* His words to me now make complete sense. My head begins to throb. *Was he acting on instruction from my father? Is he just as manipulative, deceitful, and vindictive as Mario Christofi?*

The front door slams suddenly, and I jump. Quickly moving to the window, I see Gabriel's car accelerate down the long driveway. Anguish takes hold, and my chest tightens. *What if I never see him again?*

CHAPTER FORTY-SIX

'Alexandra…'

I turn slowly, almost scared to lay my eyes on him, just in case he's ripped away from me again. But I find he actually appears healthier than ever, dressed more casually than I've ever seen him, in bleached jeans, a baggy T-shirt, and a zip-up hoody. I instantly smile, wondering if Gabriel picked out his clothes. He looks so incredibly well, his tanned skin reflecting a healthy glow, his body lean and fit, his eyes energised and expectant as they stare back at me.

'Dad…' The word gushes like a plea into the air. I never thought I'd get to say it ever again. 'What happened?'

He rushes over in an instant, cutting me off and hugging me tightly. I relax into his arms, the whole world feeling right again. I allow myself to breathe in the scent of Hugo Boss and cigarettes: a smell I didn't realise I'd miss so much until he was gone. 'You left us. My life was ruined… I lost everything.'

'I'm sorry, Lexy, I'm so sorry.'

I pull back, unable to control my anger as the swell of every moment of sadness I've felt over the last year reaches the surface. I thump against his chest with my arms. 'It broke me. It killed me to lose you. Why did you do it? Why would you leave me?'

'I'm sorry I had to go, darling. I didn't want to leave. I didn't have a choice.'

I take a step back, trying to gain my composure. 'It made it worse! Look at us now? We needed you.'

'It was a mistake, Lexy.'

'I can't believe you're here. You're really here.'

'I can't even begin to imagine the pain I caused you. You have every right to be angry.'

'We had a funeral; it was the worst day of my life.' My breath catches in my throat, the oppressive memory stirring a sharp prick of nausea in my stomach.

'You know I couldn't have put you through that if there was another way. I thought it would help.' He says, clearly convinced he was acting in our best interests.

My father will always be my weakness. No matter what he says or does, I will never give up on him. And often, to his detriment, I've never been able to hold him accountable for his destructive actions. 'Tell me what happened...'

He hesitates before taking me through the finite details of his dealings with the NCA, explaining what it was like to be targeted by one of the country's most tenacious Detectives. He tells me of the day he realised Gabriel was closing in, pushing him to make a deal: an agreement that allowed Gabriel to use my father's expert knowledge of the underworld to go after bigger, more lucrative fish. *Typical Mario. He surrendered on his terms.* My mind runs through all the decisions and vast collection of choices that lead us to this very moment.

'Where has Gabriel gone?'

'He's going to meet that Agent Roe.'

'It doesn't seem fair just to sit here whilst he takes all the risks.' My voice becomes high-pitched; 'We can't do that.'

'He has a plan.'

'But why should he always risk his life for us?'

'He knows what he's doing.'

'It's going to get him killed.'

A buzzing resounds in my father's pocket, and our attention immediately focuses on the phone.

'Yeah?' His hawk-like eyes dart around, listening to the information being reeled off by Gabriel's smooth voice. 'Ok, got it.'

'What is it?' I ask impatiently.

'Gabriel is meeting Roe tonight. Roe says he knows where to find Paytak.'

I can't hide the panic on my face, revealing my true feelings to both of us. 'So, they're going after Paytak together.'

'Seems that way.' My father shrugs.

I turn away and look at the floor, swallowing back the nauseating surge of fear. Paytak has eyes everywhere. Somehow, he will know they're coming. *He will know everything.*

CHAPTER FORTY-SEVEN

'Are you hungry?' My father asks from behind the world's largest oven, a sight I never thought I'd see.

'Whose house is this, Dad?' I ask, taking a seat at the counter.

'Long story, darling...' He mutters, walking towards a cupboard. He opens it with a casual ease, the way you might expect the owner of the property to navigate around their kitchen.

'What time is Gabriel checking in?' I ask anxiously as my thoughts drift back to him. *Like they always do.*

'After he's met with Roe. I'm making stir-fry. You need to eat, Lexy.'

'You two are the same person,' I mumble under my breath.

'What did you say, sweetheart?'

'Yeah, sure, I'll eat,' I call across the counter. 'You're not going to tell me whose house this is then?'

He sighs, switching down the cooker and turning to face me.

'Can you at least tell me if it's yours...?'

'It's Gabriel's.'

His eyes dance with amusement, watching my mouth drop before he turns back to the hob without another word.

'Gabriel James owns this property?'

'That's the one.' He holds a wooden spoon to his mouth, tasting something on the end of it.

'And that's all you know?'

'I didn't ask any questions apart from... Is it yours, and does anyone know about it?'

'He has so many secrets.'

'We all have secrets, Lexy,' he says, placing a bowl of steaming hot noodles in front of me.

'And Gabriel has more than most.'

'Can you explain something to me?'

'Sure...'

'At what point throughout all of this did he fall in love with you?' he enquires, his eyes full of gleaming speculation.

I blush. 'I'm beginning to doubt if he's capable of emotion.'

'And how do you feel?'

'Confused, betrayed,' I admit. 'For weeks he gave me such a hard time about earning his trust... and he was sitting on this.'

'He was acting on my instruction...' He shrugs, tucking into his food.

'So I never had his loyalty. You did.'

'I had to disappear as far as everyone was concerned. It was what was agreed. I wish it didn't have to be that way.'

'Over the last few weeks, I have never felt closer...' I pause, attempting to keep my voice level. 'I was just convinced that every line we crossed was to protect each other because... I guess because of the way we feel. But actually, every time he looked at me, every moment we spoke, he withheld the truth.' I shake my head. 'If there was no true loyalty, then how could any of it have been real?'

'And you think if it was all a lie, everything he felt. Then he wasn't crossing those lines to protect you, but merely because that's who he is.'

'I would have done anything to save his life, to keep him safe because...' I stop again, startled by the words that so nearly came out of my mouth.

'Because you love him?'

'Well, right now, I hate him.' I snap, trying to convince both of us. 'How can *anyone* love someone like that? It's a form of self-harm.'

He nods, placing both hands on my shoulders before looking down at me with that knowing, parental expression. 'He wanted to tell you. I know it was killing him. He's the most honourable, trustworthy person I know. I told him not to. He *was* being loyal, just not in the way you wanted or needed. He did a bad thing; he's not a bad person.'

'Seeing him again after all these years, it's dragged up so much. It's like opening my eyes after spending such a long time in the dark. The things I've seen in the forces and everything that happened with you, I shut down just to get through the day. But one look at Gabriel, and I know exactly who I am. He makes me feel everything, whether it's love, anger, sadness, or joy. It's like showering in colour. I'm the daughter of a gangster. I joined the S.A.S, but that's not all of me. And he sees that... at least I thought he did...' I trail off, suddenly feeling embarrassed and exposed about revealing something so personal.

'I always knew you were more. But with the experiences you've had, it's easy to forget.' He pauses for a beat. 'What do you mean after all these years?'

Oh fuck.

My father's phone vibrates on the counter, and we both narrow our gaze to the screen. I pick it up without thinking.

'Gabriel?'

'Isn't he with you?' a panicked voice asks.

'Who is this?'

'This is Julian, Julian Sleet. I work with him.' He pauses. 'Is Gabriel with you or your father, Alexandra?'

'He's gone to meet Roe.' I catch my father's eye as he starts gesticulating for me to give him the phone.

'Jules, it's Toff. Gabriel has gone to meet Agent Roe.'

There's silence on the phone, and we both look at each other.

Julian clears his throat. 'Collins and I are with Roe now. He's in hospital.'

'What happened?' I rush the words out.

'There was an accident. He's the only survivor.'

'Who else was in the car?'

He sighs a long, weary breath. 'Officer Amber Brookes and some bloke from Uniform. Roe was transporting Brookes to an Interpol safehouse.'

'That wasn't an accident.' I reply quickly.

'Wait...' my father interjects, his eyes wide. 'If Roe has been in the hospital, then who the fuck is meeting Gabriel?'

'I haven't been able to get hold of him.'

'Jules, listen to what I'm telling you... listen carefully. Someone has arranged a meeting with Gabriel. Do you have access to Roe's phone?'

Nerves shoot around my body as the line goes silent.

'It's not here...' Julian finally informs.

I hang up the phone, turning to my father. 'Is there a tracker? Can you get a tracker on Gabriel's phone?'

'Yeah...' He hesitates. 'We can call someone. I know a guy.'

I jump down from the stool. 'Give me his details.'

'Wait! Alexandra!'

'You keep this.' I press the phone into his chest. 'Give me a burner.'

'What are you doing?!'

'It's a setup! I have to go to him.'

'Alexandra, no!'

'Give me a burner.' I repeat, locking eyes with him. 'He would do it for us.'

'Hang on...' He sighs, jogging into the living room, rifling through draws before handing me a small mobile. 'You be careful. Do you hear me? You make sure you come back.'

GABRIEL

CHAPTER FORTY-EIGHT

The car rolls through the High Street and into the depths of Camden Town. I indicate, turning into a narrow, cobbled street next to the derelict church. Switching off the ignition, I rapidly grab my gun from the glove compartment and slip it into the holster fastened to my chest. I check the clock. Roe should be here in about five minutes. I step out of the car, surveying the street. There's nobody in my immediate vicinity, but there'll be a few homeless strays wandering around soon. This is exactly why I picked this location. A steady stream of activity works strongly in my favour. There's always someone around. And I don't trust Roe.

I check my surroundings once more before sliding through a damaged iron gate leading onto a forecourt at the back of the chapel. A tattered piece of tarpaulin slaps loudly against the metal in the wind, the repetitive sound contributing to my heightened state of awareness. Checking behind me, I shove my bodyweight against the fire exit door several times before the damp wood relents. Groaning against the floor, it slides open tentatively. Once a place of prayer and worship, the abandoned, derelict space now hosts a certain eeriness.

Moving determinedly with my pistol trained on the ground, I locate a set of stairs, deciding higher ground is the best vantage point. Hastily, I make to climb the first step when an aggressive grumbling of the door's hinges announces the presence of someone else. I step into the gloom of an alcove, pressing my back against the stone, listening to the approach of steady footsteps. My hand tightens around the weapon as the strides become louder and more prominent. I lean forward slightly, expecting to see the lanky fair-haired spook, assuming I'm going to be met with his cold, grey eyes surveying the premises. But the man I see instead is undoubtedly Diren Paytak. His big, broad body paces at the front of the church in a dark three-piece suit. A second figure shifts in the shadows, quickly climbing the stairs to the mezzanine, gaining higher ground. I look up and back to Paytak. He's blocking the exit. There's nowhere to go. No way out of this. I have to face it head-on, risking being shot in the process.

'Agent Roe, you look a little different today… Done something with your hair?'

If I startled him, it doesn't show. He flashes an insidious grin, his eyes suddenly shifting above me to his hired help. I point my pistol at his head despite sensing I won't get a clear shot before I'm taken out. *I've walked into an execution.* The realisation hits me too late. The crisp sound of a trigger cuts through the hollow air, and I forcibly drop to my knees, not yet knowing how or why before the excruciating, cataclysmic effects of the bullet burn through my nervous system. I cry out as it twists through flesh, mangling the muscle in my right leg. Paytak approaches, kicking my gun across the dust-ridden floor.

'Where is Jacob Roe?' I clench my fists, stopping my hands from trembling before attempting to still the gush of blood from the wound in my leg.

'I feel like I'm in the presence of a celebrity.' He laughs, his tone baleful. 'I've heard so much about you. It is brave, coming here alone.'

I grit my teeth as I heave myself to stand, refusing to let him stoop over me. Rhiannon's rifle follows me closely.

'It is a great burden to have to kill you. It causes a lot of problems.'

'I can only apologise…'

'Up until now, I left you alone because of your father. But you just keep digging and digging. It is not good to be so curious.' He raises his eyebrows as if we're conversing in an inconvenient business meeting.

'Cut the bullshit,' I snap, suddenly realising, with how I'm positioned, I can reach out and take his weapon whilst using him to shield myself before Rhiannon causes any more damage.

'What have you done with Roe?'

I ready my brain to instruct my body. But the loss of blood has created a delay, a lethargy that's slowing all reaction and mobility. My hand twitches towards Paytak, and another bullet is quickly fired in my direction, missing my ear by inches. I glare up, unable to see Rhiannon's face but certain there's a smug grin in the darkness. *Time to change tack.*

'How did you find Rhiannon Benson?' I call out. 'How has she gone from serving her country to the Head of the Turkish mafia?'

'Tell me where Alexandra is, and we'll leave you unharmed.'

'Save for my fucking leg...'

Paytak looks up the stairs. 'Well, yes, Rhiannon can be a little trigger-happy.' He pauses. 'I will only ask once more.' He flicks his index finger in the air. 'Where is she?'

'I honestly don't know what you're talking about.'

'You're protecting her!'

'You should leave here and make the most of the time you have left. You and your operation won't be going for much longer.'

He narrows his eyes. 'What gives you that impression, Detective?'

'Whilst we're having this delightful meeting, Amber Brookes is spilling her guts to everyone. You've got at least three intelligence agencies coming for you.'

He laughs; a huge guffawing sound that echoes around the looming stone walls. 'Amber is dead.'

I jerk my head back.

'Nothing you do will make a difference now.'

I swallow past the shock. 'And how long until you follow? You're just as expendable. How long until you're just another part of their collateral damage?'

He laughs. 'You want me to give up and join you, is that it? Help you take them all down? You need another snitch?!'

'Make no mistake, you're going down no matter what happens. I'm merely suggesting you might want the opportunity to negotiate your terms…. Be on the right side of this.'

'You have no idea what The Singularity are capable of.'

'Then tell me. Tell me who Higgs is.'

He slides his palms across one another, scraping non-existent dirt from his hands, absolving himself of the problem. 'It's none of your concern.'

'You think killing me will stop my colleagues coming for you?'

'It doesn't matter how many people try to stop them…they will always have the upper hand.'

'How many government agencies have they infiltrated?'

'Where is Alexandra?'

'How many?'

'Where is she!?'

'Why?' I bellow, frustrated with his games. 'If they're so powerful, then what does she matter?'

'You will tell me!' He lunges towards me, and I try to sidestep, but it's an action my leg won't allow. I end up travelling backwards, my back slamming against the wall.

'You seriously want to die for her?'

I catch the desperation in his eyes. 'You're afraid…'

He scoffs, turning away.

'You have to silence her because if you don't, The Singularity will punish you for allowing her to become a problem.'

'Tell me where she is, or Rhiannon will put another bullet in your body.'

'Fuck you.'

He swings forward with a closed fist. I block the attack, but he kicks my right leg out from under me. I grip the wall, trying to stay standing as another punch comes fast, knocking the wind out of me. I look up to see his gold ring incoming. A third blow strikes me back, my head rebounding off the brickwork; blood instantly rushes out of the wound above my right eye.

'That family would never protect you. What makes you so ready to die for her? They've been a burden to this city for a long time!'

'And what are you exactly? A leach, a fucking disgrace of a human being with no honour, no loyalty to anyone.' I pause, trying to fill my lungs with air, still wheezing.

Paytak's head jerks ever so slightly. The action is small but significant enough to trigger the third shot from Rhiannon's rifle. The sharp crack of her gun resounds in the chapel. My body grunts as the bullet rips through me. I swallow past a choking breath, my mouth working to find oxygen, fighting my throat as it constricts. My brain commands my body to shut down, surrendering capability to mere damage control. I slide down the wall, the burning, ruinous agony usurping all other senses. Adrenaline battles through, preventing me from hitting the ground, willing my muscles to hold me upright. I try to grip the stone behind me, sinking my fingers into the brickwork until a wet, sticky sensation causes me to look down. Blood gushes across my arm, dripping from my fingers and onto the floor.

'You seem a little defensive.' I croak, willing myself to stay conscious. 'Why does this matter so much to you?'

'It doesn't matter why, James.'

I muster a laugh. 'You knew The Christofi's would never step aside for a crime syndicate like The Singularity. That's why you did everything in your power to kill Mario.' I cough, trying to draw in a long breath. 'It's why you're after his daughter.'

'Enough!'

'You didn't expect she would come out of the woodwork, did you? The daughter who has what it takes to put you all down.'

'Shut up!' he yells.

'He has another, you know. What if you get rid of Alexandra, and Olivia decides it's her turn?' I sway slightly as my vision blurs, but I'm not stopping. Not until I've planted the seed of doubt in his mind. 'It was you who kidnapped her, after all. I'm surprised she's not already plotting her revenge.'

'Where is Alexandra!?' Veins in his neck bulge, betraying the riling effects of my comments.

Something nags at me as my mind slips in and out of focus; it's alerting me with a warning. I look up through trails of red pouring from the wound above my right eye. Shaking my head, I lose the thought, the slow approach of death replacing my mind's efficiency.

'I won't ask you again!' he shouts, stepping in, moving for his weapon.

I reach for the knife on my ankle, but I'm far too slow, and he gets there first, jabbing the end of his pistol into my chest and kicking me to the floor. 'You know you won't leave here alive, James.' He jabs his foot into my side, rolling me on my back. 'You know that we cannot let you go.' He spits, pressing his shoe into my sternum.

I think about fighting him, mustering my strength, and wrestling him away, but on glancing down at the pools of blood on either side of me, I acknowledge my reality. I hope that one day, at least Lex will learn that I tried. I tried to save her, every and any way I knew how. My mind desperately seeks unconsciousness, all awareness battling to drift away, when a sudden movement at the top of the stairs stirs my interest, and I manage to flit my gaze towards Rhiannon. Paytak glares up at the gallery, noticing the shift in my attention. I squint through my bloody right eye, my left aiming to focus on Rhiannon's outline. I know I'm suffering a concussion, but something seems off; either that or the blood loss has me imagining irregularities in the darkness. Using the distraction as an opportunity, I grab onto the wall. Inhaling shards of pain, I buck upwards and kick Paytak back, wincing as my body rises. *I'm not fucking dying on my knees.*

Paytak drops onto all fours, watching me sway. 'You want to die for her, Gabriel?' He sneers, clambering to his feet. 'Does she mean that much to you?'

'Get it over with.' I gesture to the weapon in his hand, knowing I have no energy left to fight the inevitable. It's taking all my strength to remain standing.

He raises his pistol, and I stare ahead, waiting for the finality of death. I'm not ready to go but more than willing to do what is necessary to keep Lex safe. I close my eyes, choosing another time, another day, settling on thoughts of her: the way she lies in bed next to me, drawing lazy circles up and down my arm as she patiently listens to whatever it is I might have to tell her at that moment. I smile, picturing that mane of beautiful blonde hair falling around her. The way she lays her head on my chest, whispering promises against my skin, planting kisses across my stomach. The sound of her smooth, velvet voice, even when she's shouting at me, standing on her tiptoes so her wildly gorgeous eyes can reach mine. All I will ever want is her happiness. She deserves to be free of her past, to live a joyful, wholesome life. The sound of the final trigger hits my ears, leaving me with one last thought. Someday, I hope she knows just how much I love her.

My eyes flash open. A metallic taste of blood commands all other senses. Looking down, I rapidly feel around my body, both hands running over my sternum. I trace myself for the inevitable wound. Focusing my eyes in front of me, the scene makes no sense. I look over at the crumpled heap, my brain glitching as Diren Paytak's lifeless expression stares back at me. I make to stand, grasping onto the wall with all my strength. Raising my head to the gallery, my mind itches to cling to a single thought and hold it there long enough to understand what has happened. I grip helplessly to the bricks, knowing I'm about to lose consciousness as Paytak's dead body swims ahead, a bullet having torn through the front of his skull. His splintered brains appear to be pulsing madly on the floor between us. I blink hard, stepping towards the altar, trying to focus on the exit. The sharpness of vision blurs into powerlessness, and I struggle to keep my eyes trained on a fixed point. Dragging myself forward, I carefully coach my legs to keep putting one foot in front of the other, using my left to carry most of my weight.

I stop as a figure appears by the doorway. My good arm searches for a weapon whilst my mind has begun to discard reactivity and awareness. I will my hand to move, but my head slumps backwards as I begin moving forwards. I fight gravity for as long as I can until the stone floor comes up to meet my body.

The figure approaches, and I peer up at the firearm trained out in front of them. My breath feels heavy and laboured as they crouch next to me, sliding the mask off in slow motion. The hair. The wild mane of hair. Perfect lips gasp my name, repeating words I can't compute. I smile with complete and utter gratitude, blissfully happy that she's the last thing I get to see before I go.

ALEXANDRA

CHAPTER FORTY-NINE

Paytak, the man who deserved to feel torture a thousand times over; one bullet to the head didn't even come close to the suffering I've wished on that man, but I did what I had to. And he's gone. Rhiannon never heard me coming, but she knows who beat her this time.

'Gabriel... it's me. It's Lex. I've got you. I'm taking you somewhere safe. Just stay awake for me?'

He closes his eyes, mumbling incoherent words. I drag him through the chapel and into the courtyard, having to pause a few times to catch my breath. Eventually, we reach his car, and I pat down his pockets to unlock the doors. *I can do this.* I heave him into the passenger seat. I've driven for hours in combat across the desert with wounded soldiers; I can do it across London. A sudden increase in the flow of blood from Gabriel's leg catches my attention, and I move to tighten the belt, trying to ignore the way he yelps in pain as I fix the buckle. I kiss his head, whispering reassurances against his pale temple before I race around to the driver's seat, hating every second in this dark cobbled alleyway, wishing it were safe enough to take him to a hospital.

'Forgive me...' He whispers weakly.

'Just concentrate on staying awake, Gabe.'

I slip my seat belt on and start the ignition, rapidly speeding out of the tiny street. I turn down Camden High Street, reminding myself to pay close attention to traffic cameras, police cars, and the sight of blacked-out SUVs.

'Paytak...' His head lolls, resting on the window.

Blood has begun to gush from his shoulder again, covering one side of the leather seat entirely crimson. I push the accelerator even harder, speeding around Regent's Park.

'It's ok. It's over now.'

I talk to him the entire journey to the Oxfordshire County line, I don't believe in God, but I find myself praying to somebody, begging anyone to keep him with me. The panic of losing him creeps up on me in intervals whilst I speed down the M40, but I refuse to let him hear it in my voice. I shake him conscious intermittently when his awareness dips, reassuring him over and over that he's going to be fine. He has to believe that there is hope. I won't let his final moments become flooded with fear. On speeding past Stokenchurch, I breathe a small sigh of relief, fiddling frantically with the handsfree.

'Guv?' Julian's alarmed tone fires through the speakers.

'It's Alexandra…'

'What!?'

'There's no time, Julian!' I shout, not preventing the hysteria in my voice. 'Gabriel is injured…badly! I'm on my way to the safe house.'

'Is he going to be ok? Shouldn't you bring him to a hospital?!'

'Listen to me! He's going to be ok, but I need you to focus.' I assert into the speaker. 'You need to get a unit down to Camden Chapel. Diren Paytak is dead, Rhiannon Benson is injured but alive.'

'Yes, yes. Ok.'

'Do it now.' I hang up and tap the screen again, scrolling for Gabriel's Oxfordshire landline.

'Gabe?'

'Gabriel is injured. He has two gunshot wounds and a few cracked ribs on his right side. Shoulder wound is a through and through. I can't take him to a hospital, Dad; we know what's happened to Roe. It's not safe.'

He swears quickly before gaining composure. 'Right, that's fine. We'll handle it. Tell me where the bullet wounds are exactly?'

'Urm...' I look down at Gabriel before training my eyes back on the road. 'One below his femoral artery and another just above his clavicle.'

'Drive safely but get here as quickly as you can. I'll be ready.'

I turn back to Gabriel just in time to see his head slump. 'Ok, he's lost consciousness.'

'If you get here, we can sort it, Lex, between us.'

'We'll be at the house in twenty-five minutes.' I gulp a breath; I cannot let fear win. *This isn't the day I lose him.*

CHAPTER FIFTY

I drift the car at high speed down the driveway, coming to an abrupt halt, the wheels skidding across the gravel. My father rushes to the passenger seat. We lift Gabriel out of the car, carrying him carefully into the kitchen and laying him on the counter. Streaks of red rapidly spread out from underneath his body. I freeze, gripped by terror, watching his face drain of life until the weak rasp of his voice pulls me back to the present.

'Shh, I'm here.' I take his hand, helping my father cut the clothes from his body. 'We're going to help you. Just hold on a little longer... please.'

I grab a wooden spoon from the drawer and slide it into Gabriel's mouth, holding it in place. My father looks at me for affirmation. I nod, watching him dip the end of a sharp knife into boiling water, our only source of sanitisation given we're in the house of a recovering alcoholic. Fear clutches his eyes, but that's good. He needs that. He needs to know how important this is to me. He brings the tip of the knife to Gabriel's leg wound. His hand suddenly clamps around mine, his jaw ferociously biting into the spoon with full force as my father digs through his flesh, searching for the bullet.

'I'm sorry, it will be over soon!' I shout, watching his eyes gnaw with pain, his body writhing on the cold slab of marble.

'Dad...' I call out, half urging him to hurry, half questioning his progress. Gabriel's chest begins to shoot upward, and I struggle to push the solid, lean mass of muscle back down to the table. Holding onto his hand as tightly as I can, my lips press to his temple, promising him it will end soon. My heart shatters to see him this way; his pain-fuelled eyes screwed tightly shut.

Finally, we hear the sound of metal hitting the empty bowl, and his body stills, his face clammy and pale. I rush over to the sink and retrieve a wet cloth, gently placing it over his head.

'That's done,' my father says, breathing heavily, the vein in his head throbbing. I notice that he, too, seems to have lost colour in his face. We look down at Gabriel, whose eyelids are now heavy, his lips paled to match the unusually pallid shade of his skin. I place my hands against his neck, checking the strength of his pulse, relief finding me when I realise it seems ok, thus far.

'Keep him still. I need to close his wound.' I shift to stand above the open bullet hole in Gabriel's lower thigh. My father hands me a sewing kit, and I get to work, pouring vodka on tissue paper. I dab the wound, cleaning it thoroughly before sterilising the needle and stitching him up. I loathe every second of threading the needle into his skin, but he's passed out now, it seems. *At least there's that.* After closing him up, I wrap a bandage tightly around the puncture and elevate his leg. 'Keep an eye on that. We might need to cauterise if the stitches don't hold.'

My father nods. 'How's his pulse?'

'Steady.' I respond, moving to disinfect the wound on his shoulder. 'It's better that he's unconscious for this.'

'Are you sure you're ok?' He studies me, noticing my slowed blinking.

I take a long breath as my mind signals a warning, my body shifting to a sense of unease. 'Can you come here, Dad? I…' I hesitate, trying to understand what's happening to me. I take a step back from Gabriel's body. 'I think…I need to sit down.'

The ground begins to tilt, the room bending slightly. I try to steady my focus but my vision swims, a cold sweat arriving in a flurry down my spine.

'What's wrong?'

'Just give me two seconds,' I say, swallowing past the lump at the base of my throat. 'I need you to stitch his shoulder. I need you to take over me from me.' I take a seat, feeling my stomach begin to cramp.

He stares at me with a questioning look.

'Don't worry about me; please just stitch him up.'

'What about his leg?'

'Is it bleeding still?'

He shakes his head.

'Leave it for a second. I'll keep an eye on it. Just focus on the shoulder, please.'

I wait for his attention to drop back to Gabriel before I recoil, my hands wanting to hold my insides.

My father looks back up, catching my eye. 'Lex…' He swallows before his next breath. 'You're bleeding.'

I squint at him, trying to make sense of the words when a splinter of pain clutches my abdomen. Agony pounds through me as if my organs are being mangled in a vice. My body shudders, and I follow my father's worried gaze, noticing my blood-stained legging. Lone drops of red collect around my feet. My head shakes. My mind begs for time to stop, to go back just a few minutes, hours, or even days. *No. Please don't. Please not now.* I need more time. I need to process what this meant to me, feel more thankful, more grateful. This was my hope. This was part of what defined me now. *I need this. I have to do well at this. I need more time. Please don't.*

But my body is expelling that future. The path ahead disappearing. Dissolving into nothing. My baby is leaving me, slipping through my fingers with no way of bringing them back. *Why does my body reject the course of nature? If this is what is intended, then why does it have to fail?* I blink down at more tinges of dark red, trying to breathe through the rupturing ache. I curl myself forward, my arms encasing my abdomen as if they might be able to keep my baby there. But the essence of emptiness is settling in. I wonder if I might start to pray, but nobody is there. This is on me. I am the chaos that prohibited new life. *I don't deserve the privilege.*

CHAPTER FIFTY-ONE

My eyes are swollen and dry from a constant stream of tears, tears for the loss of my baby, tears from the fear of losing someone else, and hours upon hours of sleeplessness, allowing anxiety to win another silent battle in my mind. I'm certain I did everything right, everything that needed to be done to save him. I've stitched infinitely worse injuries in the field under much worse conditions. And yet I sit upstairs, studying his every breath, thinking back to every stitch, every step, every ounce of effort I made to keep Gabriel alive. And the fallible nature of memory has invited uncertainty. It's bedded down, and I've lost all sense of rationale.

'Did Gabriel know?'

I turn to the sound of my father's voice, nodding slowly.

'I'm sorry, sweetheart.'

'It's ok.' I whisper reassuringly but my voice cracks, and I stop, swallowing down the swell of sadness and anger. *It is not ok. It will never, ever be ok.* 'Best to save a child from all of this… you know.' My lip quivers, my chest aching from a sudden wave of emptiness.

'You will be a brilliant mother one day, Alexandra. I'm your father, and I know that for a fact.'

I offer a small smile. 'Look at how we fucked up Olivia.'

'That was me and me alone.' A glimpse of regret flashes across his face before we shove our emotions down again, unused to feeling so exposed.

'He'll wake up, Lex.'

'I knew him.' I say, suddenly.

'Huh?'

'I knew Gabriel at University. I knew him, before you, before all of this.'

His head twitches to the side.

'I don't want any more secrets.'

'How?' He clears his throat. 'How well?'

'We dated…well, actually, it was more than that. And since that time, since him… I've never met anyone who made me feel those things. Nobody will ever.' My voice falters. 'So, he has to wake up… he has to.'

He nods as if he knows exactly what I mean. 'What happened… back then?'

I shrug. 'I left.'

'Why?'

'Because Olivia had one of her episodes, and we had to take her to that rehab in Thailand, remember?'

'Well yeah…' He shakes his head at the floor. 'But we came back.'

'He had his whole life ahead of him.' I grip the mug in my hands, pulling it close to my chest, drawing comfort from the warmth. 'He was the Cambridge golden boy with all these serious hopes and dreams. I wanted him to have a chance.' I exhale as the pain of walking away returns to me like muscle memory. 'And I just knew that if he stayed with me, I would ruin him. I wanted better for him. I knew he deserved more.' I grit my teeth, recalling the last time I saw him, long before all of this, long before the world sunk its claws into him.

My father closes his eyes, and we sit in silence for a time, both of us deep in thought. *What if I hadn't left? If I had stayed, would we have ended up together?*

'I just want him to be happy, Dad. I want him to live a peaceful life, one that doesn't include so much pain.'

'When he wakes up, tell him that.'

'But what if I caused it then, and I'm driving it now?'

'Why would you say that?'

'Look around us.'

'Alexandra, have you ever known Gabriel James to act under the command or demand of anyone? He's his own man. He's where he wants to be.'

'He deserves more.'

'He needs you. I saw it the second he walked in. Whether you turned up at his door or not, I sense this is still where he would be.'

'You know this won't end at Paytak. I have to stop them. For Gabriel, for McGuire, for you.'

'You can't do it all on your own. Learn to accept help… otherwise, it will be a lonely path.'

'I swore a duty to protect.'

'We'll get them, Lexy. Together.'

'Please, can you promise to be careful from now on? Losing you again would tear me apart,' I plead, tears filling my eyes. 'Please?'

'I'm not going anywhere, darling.'

'Thank you…' I hug him, gripping him tightly.

A creak of the floorboards whips my attention towards the ceiling. I pull out of my father's embrace.

He breaks into a wide grin. 'Go on…'

I sprint out of the kitchen and up the stairs. I try not to bound down the hallway, approaching carefully. My heart races, my pulse quickening. *I so desperately want this to be true.*

I nudge the door open, slowly edging into the room with every single emotion breaking to the surface the second I see him. He's trying to sit upright, repositioning himself gradually up the bed. He suddenly notices me in the doorway and stops, a spark of energy reaching his weary eyes. I rush forward and drop beside him, my hand finding his, clutching at his fingers. 'Thank you… Thank you for coming back.'

'Hi…' he whispers weakly.

I haven't the energy to hide my relief, looking up at him through blurry, tear-stained eyes, savouring the moment of being able to hear his voice.

He tilts my chin upwards, his eyes peering straight into my soul, as they always do. 'It's all going to be alright.' he croaks.

I smile, my skin itching for more, relishing his touch. 'Trust you to be the one reassuring me when you've got one eye, a cracked rib, and two holes in your body.' I shake my head. 'You fucking idiot…'

'Cool, though, huh?'

'Don't make jokes.'

He nods, looking down before taking a deep breath and whispering my name on the long, exhausted exhale as if saying it will alleviate him from the pain. '…will you forgive me?'

'Sleep…' I say softly, pressing my lips to the back of his hand. His eyelids close almost at once. Suddenly I'm overcome with the urge to put everything behind us as I realise how much effort he was making to stay awake, just so he could give me a little more hope.

GABRIEL

CHAPTER FIFTY-TWO

Fuck. The unforgiving damage to my body causes my eyes to water. I slowly bow my head, acknowledging the cuts, scrapes, and bruises scattered across my skin, combined with tight, fresh bandages woven neatly around my left shoulder and right thigh. Immediately my brain plays catch-up, connecting the state of my limbs to recent events, my nerve endings reliving the first and second bullets burrowing through my flesh. Images appear in nonsensical fragments, sequences of events rattling in and out. I manage to settle on a memory of Lex in the chapel before a blurred reminiscence of slipping in and out of consciousness. I recall her voice clearly, but the lasting visual is of Diren Paytak. His cold dead eyes glazed with lifelessness, his eyeballs gleaming up at me from the floor, his face stuck with the shock of the bullet's impact. I swallow hard, every muscle in my body working to move without my usual capable mobility. I stiffen, the pain of my injuries starkly reminding me of the reality. Sweat runs down my face, and I carefully shift my weight up the bed with tentative movements, using my stomach muscles to sit up against the headboard until finally, I rest my head back. My lungs expand and contract rapidly, my chest heaving from the minimal effort of changing position. After a few moments of lying still, waiting for my pulse to steady, I realise I need water. My mouth feels like I've had cotton wool stuffed onto the top of my tongue for hours on end. I reach for the glass on the bedside table; the sheer frustration of being so useless grinds at me until I catch a flash of long, golden waves and bright big eyes coming towards me. Instantly, everything suddenly feels lighter. Lex purses her lips, twisting them to one side, her glassy eyes regarding me like an animal she might have rescued from the wild.

'Come here...' I wrap my one good arm around her, holding her small frame tightly to my chest. I Inhale slowly, cherishing the moment of feeling her close, sensing her whole body relax, taking in the soft smell of lavender from her unruly mane of hair.

'I'm so happy you're getting better... I couldn't...' She stops, sitting up suddenly. 'The thought of losing you. It...'

'It's ok. I'm here... I'm still here.'

A solitary tear escapes her eyes, travelling down her cheek and resting on her top lip.

I reach out, tracing my thumb over the small wet droplet. 'I'm sorry I lied to you.'

Her gaze shifts, her eyes fixed with pain.

'I don't expect you to forgive me,' I continue. 'I kept your father from you. But please... please understand, I would never intentionally harm you or hurt you.'

She nods, looking down at the bed.

'I love you. I haven't ever stopped loving you.'

Her breath hitches, another tear breaks free, and her eyes brighten. *I will never get enough of those eyes*. There's more soul in that one look than a single person deserves.

'If you lie to me again...Rhiannon Benson will be the least of your worries.'

I wait, watching her for a few seconds, wondering if she has anything else to add. Nothing comes, and despite expecting the rejection, it doesn't make it any easier. 'I understand.'

'Nearly watching you die has put a lot in perspective...' She shakes her head slowly, deep in thought. 'Let's just get through the next few days. But don't ever try to die on me again,' she whispers in a rushed, vulnerable breath. And despite wanting more, I know it's all she can give me for now, so I'll take it.

ALEXANDRA

CHAPTER FIFTY-THREE

I leave Gabriel's room and amble down the long staircase, finally able to breathe a little easier now he's awake. The tightness in my chest is easing, the pounding in my head lessening somewhat. He's alive. *At least there's that.* I couldn't bring myself to explain what happened over the last few days. Within seconds of seeing him, the words caught in my throat, and I knew I had to swallow them down. The relief on his face, the tiny glint of hope in his eyes. I won't tear away that away from him. I can't. Not yet. He needs time to come to terms with what happened in Camden. He might have a long road to recovery, especially if his wounds become infected. He needs all the strength he can get.

'Hi,' I say, stopping short of the door to the kitchen, surprised to see Julian scrolling through his phone at the long dining table.

'How's he doing?' he looks up as my father approaches from the kitchen with two steaming mugs.

'He seems a lot better,' I reply, keeping my voice low, knowing Gabriel would hate to think he was being whispered about around the house.

Julian nods a little regretful, his brow buried under a troubled expression.

'Do you want to go up and see him?'

He looks nervously up at the ceiling and hesitates. 'No, it's alright. Collins told me to bring these files to him. She said he needs to get back on the case as soon as possible.'

'Does she know why he's here? And what happened?'

'She does.'

'And Paytak?'

He nods.

'Is Gabriel in trouble, Jules?' my father asks.

'She just said she wants him to get better, for now.'

Mario shrugs. 'She knows he's not going anywhere.'

'Gabriel's always been her favourite.' His lips twitch. 'She knows there'll be a good explanation.'

'Which there is.' I insist.

'There's more pressing matters anyway.' He continues. 'We're still looking for Rhiannon Benson.'

'What do you mean looking for her?!' I practically splutter out.

He inhales. 'She got away.'

'I handcuffed her there. She was unconscious?!'

'Someone on the inside,' my father says, shaking his head.

I think back to our phone call in the car. 'Julian, give me your phone.'

He frowns, taken aback.

'Give me your phone!' I demand, and he slides it out of his pocket quickly. I immediately pull off the back with frantic fingers, yank out the sim card and dunk it into my father's tea.

'What the—?'

'Someone is probably tapping this device,' I explain. 'Did you mention this address or anything about our whereabouts on here?'

'No, we would never do that anyway. Not on an open line.'

'Ok, good.'

'So Paytak is dead, Rhiannon is in the wind, and we're all still fucked,' my father calls over his shoulder as he pours his tea down the sink, turning on the food processor.

'Collins is working on it with Director James.'

'Gabriel's dad is involved again?'

'Yeah, he has a vested interest in protecting Gabriel, but what with Roe, Amber and Stanley, we need his resources.'

'Can you tell Collins to call us from a secure line? We can help. Whatever you both need.'

'I will do.' He stands, pulling his gloves out of his pockets and beginning to place each one on his hands.

'Are you sure you don't want to see him?'

He looks up the staircase before returning his nervous gaze to me, his eyes lingering across my stomach. 'It's fine…' He hesitates. 'He won't want me to see him like that.'

I sigh heavily, throwing daggers at my father. 'Really?!' I say, furious. 'You told Julian?' I lower my voice, 'You told Julian before I could tell Gabriel?'

'I'm sorry, Lexy. He asked how we were.' My father shrugs, his expression regretful. 'But Gabriel would want to know.'

'And I told you… I want to give him just a few hours before I hit him with something else. I don't know if I can even say it out lou…' I trail off, my voice cracking. 'I will tell him, but I just need more time.'

'He wouldn't want you to deal with this alone...' Julian adds softly.

'I'm not alone,' I say defiantly, suddenly feeling outnumbered. 'You know what I mean.'

I suddenly wish the two of them would stop staring at me. Sadness is creeping up my body. My neck and chest begin to turn red. *I'm not ready to talk about this openly.*

'Thank you, Julian, for helping us.' I change the subject, stepping in to hug him, mainly so I can hide my expression. Tears spike the corners of my eyes as I hold onto him. 'Keep safe, please.'

'Let me know if you need anything.' He says, finally stepping back. 'I'll ask Collins to reach out.'

'Keep us in the loop, Jules,' my father says, opening the front door.

'Look after yourselves.' He strolls out into the winter air, turning once more before waving and ducking into the car.

I watch his vehicle disappear up and around the verge, feeling guilty for endangering his life. The last thing he deserves is to be dragged into this with the rest of us. I stand transfixed on the tree on the front lawn, its supple branches bending and grappling in the wind with majestic fluidity. Each turbulent gust uncompromisingly wrestles each branch, goading them to surrender and crack in its wake. Still, it stands defiant as it has done for years and years, self-assured with its place in the world. And I wonder if we're at all capable of doing the same.

CHAPTER FIFTY-FOUR

Swinging the door open to Gabriel's bathroom, I find him standing as straight as he can manage at the sink. His eyes are focused, his brow furrowed with concentration, using his thumb to balance on the white porcelain whilst his other hand glides a razor over his face.

'You could have told me...' he murmurs with mock accusation.

I smirk, tilting my head, waiting for him to elaborate.

'I look like I've been stranded on a desert island.'

'So, vanity got the better of you,' I tease.

'I'd rather not *look* like I'm falling apart, at least.' He drops the razor, meeting my eyes, and I instantly break into a huge smile. More colour has returned to his face. Finally, it seems he's getting better. I step in, crouching down to check the wound above his knee. He flinches as I pull back the dressing.

'Does it hurt more than usual?' I ask, inspecting the scarred, angry red flesh.

'It's fine.' He shifts, trying to move away.

'It looks good.' I say, replacing the bandage. 'We'll change the dressing later.'

'No need to amputate then?'

I straighten and examine his shoulder. 'Not funny.'

'What's wrong, Lex?' He steps in. 'I can tell when something's wrong.'

'It's healing fast.' I stroke my fingers down his arm. 'Perhaps I should become a doctor.'

'Lex?' he steps in, aware that I'm holding something back.

I look down, suddenly wanting to disappear. *This is too soon. Am I ready to talk about this?* With the time that's passed since it happened, small twinges of resignation are settling in, as if having needles slowly sinking into the surface of your skin. I had something precious. Something that the world tells us is natural, simple to have, easy to keep. Part of nature's plan for women. Nobody talks about the near misses, the failures. You don't realise how extraordinary it is until it's not with you anymore. The process, the privilege of creating life. You don't understand until you long for it more than you've ever wanted for anything. And then your hormones take the reins, steer your every thought, every desire, guiding you into the fascination of being a mother. A role that never interested you before. Not once. *Will there ever be acceptance? Or just the surrender to a different future?* My mind doesn't know how to flick the off switch. *How do I revert back to the person I once was?* The woman who did not need this to feel whole. The woman whose currency was more than fertility. *Will my body continue to work against me in a detached, uncontrolled way? Are we justified in feeling grief over a child that we never meet?*

'Lex?' Gabriel repeats, concerned.

'I lost the baby…' I blurt out, suddenly.

His face tenses with shock. 'When?'

'A few days ago.'

He pulls me into him instantly. 'Fuck… I wasn't here.' The sentence is barely audible, but I hear the sadness in his voice. 'I'm sorry you had to go through this. No one should ever… I'm sorry.' He repeats, his hands stroking my back.

'It's fine…' I lie. 'I just…' I take a long deep breath. Now he knows it's become real. *I don't have a baby anymore. It's just me. All there is… is me.* 'I didn't know how to tell you. I didn't know if you would live or die. It didn't seem right… it didn't seem fair to add to your problems.'

'Listen…' He pulls back, placing his large hands on my face. 'Don't hold things back… I can help. I want to help.'

'I know this is a chaotic mess.' I pause, trying to steady my voice. 'Neither of us knows if we're getting out of this situation. But the baby…' I hesitate, terrified to say it out loud. 'We had hope.' I whisper, looking down. 'There was a small piece of hope.'

'I know,' he soothes softly.

'I have been responsible for so much loss, Gabriel.' My voice falters. He pulls me in again, and I bury my head into his chest. 'I finally felt privileged to create life… instead of taking it.' I grip his arms, beginning to sob.

'This will be over.' He states, stroking his hand through my hair. 'You will have a life filled with hope. I promise you.'

I wipe the tears from my face and take a long breath. 'What if I lose who I am again? I don't want to go all the way back. I just want to stop hurting.'

'The army made you cut pieces of yourself away. It won't happen again.' He straightens, his dark eyes finding mine. 'Alexandra, you're so full of chaos and heart; nobody will ever take that from you.'

'B Squad was a version of me I needed to be to survive. But it's not me, I want something different now.'

There's a long, weighted silence as his gaze fixes on the floor.

'You…' I say finally. 'I don't want to be without you.'

He smiles a quick breath of relief, his shoulders relaxing. 'Lex, I spent twelve years trying to ignore my feelings for you, crushing away every memory, trying to forget you with drink after drink. I won't go back either. And I will do everything in my power to ensure neither of us has to.'

'It hurt, Gabriel,' I admit quietly. 'It hurt to feel betrayed by you.'

'Never again.' He reassures me before leaning in, gliding his top lip against mine. 'Are you feeling ok?' he whispers warily. 'Don't hide your pain from me because you think I can't handle it.'

'We're more than what's happened to us.' I nod defiantly, urging myself to believe my own words. 'We have to be.'

CHAPTER FIFTY-FIVE

Gabriel hangs up the phone, and we sit in silence, all of us reeling from being on the receiving end of a verbal battering from Alison Collins. We had to repeat the admission three times and even put my father on the phone to prove Gabriel was telling the truth. After yelling incoherent sentences that included the words: *fired, dead man* and *fucking liberty*, she's insisting on coming here herself, determined to dictate our next steps in person. I also think she needs to see it with her own eyes. This reaction is based on a lie that Gabriel discovered my father was alive mere days ago. I can't even begin to imagine what she would do if she knew the truth. But Collins seems like a smart woman. She at least has an inkling.

I observe my father and Gabriel closely, both of them reminding me of two people working to diffuse a complicated bomb, their intelligent eyes flitting between wires, clippers shaking in their hands as they move from red to green, to blue to yellow and then back to red again. I tap my foot silently against the mahogany floor, speaking out when I see a red flag in a prospective course of action. Despite the inevitable danger that each plan entails, I still enjoy the assured way Gabriel drawls objections in sharp, considered words - the way he's not afraid to tell my father that he's wrong.

'Collins is going to suggest we stay out of bounds until they've got a handle on the Rhiannon situation,' Gabriel suggests. 'But Edward is after her, too. He thinks she can lead him to Higgs. There's going to be a battle at some point.'

I visibly sag into my chair at the sheer scale of complications.

'Did you serve with her, Lex?' my father asks.

'We were on an operation together in Beirut.'

'What was she like?'

'Quiet.' I pause, thinking back. 'We were there to do a job. You don't make friends.'

'What do you think happened to her?' Gabriel asks cautiously, sensing I'm not keen to open up.

'We'd been instructed to conduct surveillance on a meet between someone in the Lebanese government and a member of Hezbollah. Nobody could know the UK was interfering on foreign soil. Gibbs and Rhiannon got sloppy. Someone overheard the chatter on their radios. They were captured.'

'Captured by who?'

'We were told it was the Lebanese Secret Service. But there were rumours that it was the FSA.'

'The who?' Gabriel asks.

'The Free Syrian Army.'

'And your unit left them out there?'

I nod reluctantly. 'The instructions were clear: if we were caught, we acted alone.'

'Well…does Rhiannon want revenge?' my father asks. 'Did she seek out Paytak to teach you a lesson?'

'How would Rhiannon have known you'd one day interfere with Paytak's operation?' Gabriel interjects. 'She can't have guessed that he'd launch a manhunt for you. That wasn't within her control.'

'Then someone knows who she is to me….' I say as it falls into place. 'The Singularity. They must have brought her into Freeman Powell as soon as they realised I was a problem.'

'And then they gave her to Paytak…' Gabriel says suddenly. 'They hired her specifically to screw with you and McGuire because they know. The Singularity have someone on the inside who knew about the Beirut Op. Someone who also knew that McGuire was working for Edward.' He looks up, his eyes energised. 'Rhiannon was only hired after you found those kids, Lex.'

We sit in silence for a while, all three of us waiting for the lightbulb moment that will solve all our problems. Perhaps they're right; someone is messing with me, using my past to throw me off. Either way, I have to take responsibility for Rhiannon Benson, myself.

'That's enough for me for one evening.' My father stands from the table. 'We can scan through the rest of these tomorrow.' He gestures to the pile of files. 'Gabriel, get an early night. See you tomorrow, my darling.' He bends to kiss me on the forehead, something he's done ever since I was a little girl. I inhale the comforting scent of him before he trails off through the kitchen, halting in the doorway. 'Don't stay up too late.'

Gabriel grabs my hand and pulls me into his lap, foreseeing my anxiety. 'We'll be alright, Lex,' he reassures me, pressing his lips into my hair, his arm wrapping around my torso.

I shake my head. 'Collins is going to have you arrested.'

'Alexandra, listen to me,' he says, firmly taking my face between his hands. 'Alison Collins has bigger fish to fry.'

I take a deep breath. 'But they will want you out of the equation eventually.'

'Come with me,' he struggles to his feet, grabbing my hand and limping forward determinedly.

'What are we doing?' I ask, laughing at his insistence on dragging me along with just one working leg.

'Tonight, we're going to act like normal people,' he says, leading me to the sofa.

I sink into the cushions, staring up at him. 'Do you even know what normal means?' I tease.

'What do you want to watch?' he asks, ignoring me. 'We have the entire box set of *The Sopranos*... seems appropriate,' he mutters before craning his neck to look along the shelf. 'Or we can watch a film about green tomatoes that I've never heard of.'

'The film...'

'You don't even know what it's about.'

'Doesn't matter... normal people watch boring films.'

Grabbing the DVD from the shelf, he lowers himself level with the console, using an impressive amount of core strength to bend on one leg.

'I should really have done that myself.'

'No, you just relax,' he says sarcastically as he rises back up, looking tired.

I laugh, settling back on the armrest before he joins me, stretching his long body out on the sofa and putting an arm around my shoulders. I bury my face in the crook of his neck, feeling the steady rise and fall of his chest, relishing this moment of peace. After a while, I look up to check if he's fallen asleep. His dark eyes slide down to meet mine.

'Are you following this?' I ask, amused.

'Slightly distracted, if I'm being honest.' He smirks suggestively, looking down at my vest top.

'You know you were only in bed for like two days, right?' I offer him a sly grin. 'Anyone would think you'd been celibate for two years.'

He sits up slightly. 'I did well for the best part of the four weeks you were in the flat.'

'You hardly spoke for a lot of it.'

'Doesn't mean I didn't want to fuck you.'

'Charming.'

'You know me.'

I yawn, and his eyes widen with the overbearing urge to tell me what to do. 'Yes, alright.' I cut him off as he opens his mouth, 'I need to sleep, I know.'

'I was actually going to ask you to turn off the TV.'

He stands from the sofa, waiting for me to turn off the lights before we make our way upstairs. I smile as I follow him, secretly loving this semblance of routine and the comfort of simply switching off the downstairs lights, heading up the stairs to bed together like this is our everyday life – settling down for the night as a couple.

'Which one is our room?' he asks casually.

'I don't know! It's your house?' I whisper, amused. 'Have you never stayed here before?'

'Nope.'

'Well, this one...' I suggest. 'This looks nice.'

I turn the light on and inhale, revelling in the comfort, enjoying the soft, inviting energy of the room, admiring the king-size bed dressed entirely in crisp white linen.

Gabriel leans in the doorway, his broad shoulders filling the space. His unusually long hair falls around his face, a small smile playing on the corners of his lips.

'What?' I stand and move towards him, wrapping my hands around his torso, careful not to hold him too tightly.

'Nothing,' He rests his chin on my head. 'It's just... this is nice, isn't it?'

'Yes...' I say, closing my eyes. 'Yes, it is.'

He kisses me before turning to empty his pockets, placing his belongings on the tall, ornate chest of drawers. He limps across the room towards the ensuite, throwing off his t-shirt, mumbling something about setting the alarm and who should get which side of the bed. I look around once more, feeling a sudden surge of hope. One day, this could be our home; this could be the life we have together. And I silently plead an impassioned wish to whoever might be listening that everything does go according to plan. I want the routine, I want the mumblings about alarms, the conversations about who locked the back door, the scribbled reminders of anniversaries, the bickering of whose turn it is to take the bins out. I want the mundane, the boring, the day-to-day; *I want it all*. But the catch is that I want it with him, and I can't help but wonder if I'm asking just a little too much of the world.

GABRIEL

CHAPTER FIFTY-SIX

I'm slumped in the passenger seat. Blood pours into the footwell. Litres upon litres leaving my body. Alexandra's panicked hands grip the wheel. The car speeds on in quick unintelligible flashes. I look down at the wounds. It doesn't hurt anymore. Paytak is here. His sneering grin turns towards me. That family will never protect you. Always leaving other people to clean up their mess. The bullet sits in his skull, lodged at the front of his face. Do you really want to die for her Gabriel?

I jerk upwards, breaking free from the nightmare and reach out to Lex's side of the bed, my hands eager to touch her; a comfort to dissolve the fragments of trauma left behind. The bed is empty. Looking around the room, I search for signs of her, listening out for a tap being turned on or a remote shuffling.

With as much strength as my beaten body can muster, I swing out of the oversized bed and dress quickly. Gathering my T-shirt in my hands, I limp towards the landing when the low persistent buzzing of my phone resounds from behind. I turn towards the vibration, begrudgingly making my way to the dresser. Looking down at the long list of missed calls and texts, it's clear Julian has been trying to get hold of me since the early hours - either he's had a breakthrough, or Collins is on her way. I swipe Julian's contact and wait for the dial tone.

'Guv,' he snaps.
'What's up? What's going on?'
'Did you listen to the message I sent you?'
'No, I haven't seen anything—'

'I haven't got much time—'

'Jules, get on with it.'

He begins rushing out words, taking me through facts and details of evidence that ticks various boxes of complicated questions, finally making sense of the missing fragments of information. And piece by piece, all the unanswered issues begin to align. I think back to all those moments something pulled at me, nagging me to pay attention, yanking my thoughts to stay awhile longer, to look harder. Wondering how two ex-soldiers allowed Lex to get so close before they attacked, how Paytak knew to use Rhiannon Benson. My mind wanders back to Diren Paytak, the sudden loss of control, the look of pure unadulterated fear. I know the look because I suffer the same twisted anxiety.

'I'll call you back.' I hang up the phone in a bid to find Lex, regretting the choice to conceal my suspicions over the last few days. I wish I'd at least broached the subject or even hinted that somewhere in the dark depths of my mind, there was a consideration, a tiny, nagging thread. I hurtle down the stairs, gritting my teeth past the pain needling through my body. On finally reaching the kitchen, the floor begins to swim below, and I'm visibly out of breath. Lex and Toff look up, their faces dropping when they register my expression.

'What is it, Gabe?' Toff asks.

Lex climbs off the kitchen stool, stepping towards me, concerned.

'There's something...' I pant, 'Something you need to know.'

CHAPTER FIFTY-SEVEN

Mario throws his hands over his head, looking up to the ceiling.
'I know it's not what you want to hear, Toff...'
'Play it again,' Lex interrupts.
'What?'
'Play it again... the voicemail. I need to hear it again.'
I sigh, reluctantly placing the phone on the table, cranking up the volume.

'Look, Collins doesn't know I'm in touch, but I couldn't keep this from you. After we saw Olivia, something you said about her not being afraid had me thinking. So, I thought I should run my own background check on her, see what came up. I ended up ringing to have a chat with one of the psychiatrists that used to treat her, Dr Thompson. Nice lady. I've got the report one sec... Despite ongoing treatment, this patient exhibits persistent anti-social behaviour, continuing to show impaired empathy. Ms Christofi has a delusional grandiose sense of importance with concerning egotistical traits that refrain her from understanding the moral differences between right and wrong. It is my recommendation she continues treatment under careful observation, attending daily sessions with myself and Dr Harling... There's loads more, but the important part is that Dr Thompson said Olivia had a boyfriend who regularly visited her. Apparently, he was there when she discharged herself only last year. She never mentioned a boyfriend to us. So, after I'd finished speaking to the doctor, I checked out the visitor logs for The Priory and I've since checked logs of every rehab Olivia has ever been to. They were all the same. Each log had one name scribbled down every week without fail. Eren Malas. I asked Amber to run checks on him because I knew it rang a bell. She said she couldn't find anything. At the time,

I didn't push it. I thought it was a dead-end and left it there. But since we found out about her, I wanted to go back over everything. That's when it clicked. The name is familiar because we looked into it when we started Sandbank. If we'd just got hold of this earlier… shit. Sorry, I fucked up, Guv, I really fucked up. I'm sending everything over now, and you'll see for yourself. But Eren Malas was an alias used by the Turkish Mafia in the early days. More specifically, Paytak. Paytak was the one visiting Olivia, Guv. Has been for years.'

Toff rubs his hand over his face with an impatient lethargy, his eyes screwing shut. The wrinkled creases of his forehead matching that of his crumpled, white T-shirt.

'When we started Sandbank, we put together a list of bank accounts linked to the Turkish Mafia. The name Eren Malas kept coming up, and after a lot of digging, we linked it to Paytak. He was using it to move money.' I pull out the page of The Priory's visitor logs. 'It's not a common name, Toff.'

He says nothing.

'You already knew…' Lex whispers, taking a disbelieving step back.

Thoughts of conspiracy dart rapidly across my mind, the shock now edging towards irritation. 'How long have you known?'

He shifts uncomfortably, perching on the edge of his seat, continuing to stare at the floor.

'How long, Toff?' I yell into the room, my right hand gripping the frame of the doorway, my fists clamping onto the wood, taking my frustration out on the nearest inanimate object.

His left index finger rubs the top of his left eye. 'I knew she'd been seeing someone, but she was in and out of rehab, and I just assumed it was some other fucked-up junkie.'

'When did you find out?'

'About four years ago, Olivia overdosed…' he waves a dismissive hand at me like it's nothing. 'It happened all the time. Anyway, this specific time, I saw Paytak in the waiting room of the hospital. The man was pale… sheet white almost.'

'Did he see you?'

'No, I kept my distance, but it kick-started something in my head. It made me look into the possibility.'

'And then…'

'I had her phone tapped…'

Lex throws her head into her hands.

'I couldn't hear her conversations, but I knew who she was calling. So, I thought I'd keep tabs, you know… Get a tracker installed.'

'In her phone?'

'In a watch I bought for her twenty-first birthday.'

Lex's head snaps up. 'This whole fucking time, you knew…'

He stands from the chair, his eyes firing between the two of us. 'Businesswise, it was useful to keep my knowledge in my back pocket. It helped me stay ahead, to have her around him.'

Lex laughs, unconvinced. 'People have died to find him, Dad. Two government agencies wanted to use me to find him. What if Gabriel had died a few nights ago? Do you think I would have forgiven you?!' she shouts hysterically. 'This is on you. All of this!'

She flings herself towards him in a fit of rage. I lunge forward to catch her as she grapples between my arms, trying to break free. Part of me wants to let her go, so he can get what he deserves, but I know it will solve nothing. I need to calm her down. She thinks he is the match that lit the all-consuming fire, responsible for everything: for abandoning them, for allowing Paytak to take over, his manipulation of Olivia, for allowing him to infiltrate their family, for all the sacrifices we made when the answer was there all along. I don't blame her for feeling this way. *I feel it too.*

'I had no idea she was still with him!' Toff protests.

'You know what I'm grateful for right now?' Lex says, finally calming down. I relax my arms as she pulls away from me. 'All of this has made me realise that there is zero point in trusting anyone. Least of all the two of you!'

'Toff, what you're saying is…' I interject, trying to move past the sting of her words. 'You used the situation to your tactical advantage.'

'It was a business decision.' He throws both hands out, his shoulders twitching casually. My eyes narrow, trying to wrap my brain around his decisions. There are still so many dangerous, unpredictable levels of Mario Christofi I haven't even seen.

'She's your daughter!' Lex yells. 'You used her as a Trojan horse,' she adds with a judgmental tone. 'You must have been aware he was grooming her? Turning her against us?'

'In my mind, the damage had been done. She already had such a dark mind. It kept her occupied.'

'It kept her from being your problem, you mean.'

'That's not fair!'

'A man of your intelligence didn't think it was dangerous for her to be in a relationship with the person that kidnapped her when she was fourteen?' I ask, disbelieving. 'Or had you lost your fucking mind at that stage?'

'Don't fucking speak to me like that, Gabriel.'

Ignoring him, I continue, erupting with fury. 'The shit you gave me… pushing me to find who was responsible for Lex, and all the while you were sitting on this.'

Toff slumps into the brown, vintage armchair tucked in the corner of the room. With absent-minded movements, he picks at the tassels hanging from the throw tossed across the scuffed armrest. 'I was trying to figure out the best course of action. I was sure Olivia couldn't possibly know the extent of Paytak's crimes… I didn't think she'd ever be with him if she knew.'

'Not only did she know the full spectrum of his glowing personality Mario, but she's clearly been his spy for years.' I pause, letting that sink in. 'He was using your own daughter against you, and you let him because the advance to your business was far more important.'

'It was an affair!'

'Wake up, Dad!' Lex shouts, her voice booming against the walls of the house. 'Listen to what the evidence is telling you.'

'She's not capable—'

'Oh, isn't she?! I'm a trained killer, and you actually tried with me.'

'Lex is on the right side of this, but your girls are more than capable of committing acts that serve their greater purpose,' I confess, unable to look at her.

'Olivia wouldn't truly do anything to hurt this family.' His grey hair flops forward: crazed, wayward strands standing on end.

'Last night when we were talking about Rhiannon…' Lex starts. 'You must have thought of the possibility. Olivia could have known about Beirut… all she had to do was read one of my journals in the flat. Olivia is the reason Rhiannon Benson is involved.'

His mouth opens and closes like a fish, his mind stumped and stuttering at the implication.

'Paytak has brainwashed Olivia, Dad. And he did it right under your nose.'

'That is just one theory.'

'Accept it.' Lex snaps. 'It's true.'

He closes his eyes as his face twists with torment.

'Look, Mario, I don't blame you for wanting to believe better of your own flesh and blood, but we don't have time to stand here and persuade you. We need to find Olivia.'

'I don't believe this is right. She's not with him now. It wasn't serious!'

'Alright.' I nod with resignation, slipping my phone out of my pocket, taking a few steps forward until I'm standing above him. 'I didn't want you to see this, but if it's the only way you'll listen to me...'

Toff grabs the phone, his head continuing to stubbornly shake as if battery operated until his dark eyes focus on the screen. 'What the fuck is this?' he breathes with impatience. 'Who is that?'

'This was taken recently. And I didn't see it either at first, but in the context of what we now know, look at the woman hugging Paytak. She's been with him this entire time, Mario. Paytak is gone, but Olivia could know who is pulling the strings. The Turks will continue to work with The Singularity if we don't find her.'

'Fine.' His eyes drop, his face surrendering. 'Call Collins. Call them all.'

ALEXANDRA

CHAPTER FIFTY-EIGHT

We sit around the table as Collins takes the group through an impromptu team briefing. I look around the room, my eyes scanning from Simon to my father, lingering on Julian's apprehensive expression before resting finally on Gabriel. He stares ahead, his mouth set in a firm, irritated line. He wasn't happy about drafting in a second ex-B Squad operative, foreseeing a whole list of complications on the horizon. But the truth is we need Simon Haines more than I'm willing to admit. With Roe in the hospital, Amber and Stanley dead and Edward James refusing to come to our aid on account of having his own agenda: this group are now the only people in the world capable of stopping The Singularity.

Simon's judgemental glare creeps across the table every so often. His piercing eyes analysing the pieces of me he doesn't recognise. When we served together, he would tell me that hope is efficiency's worst enemy. Although I knew he was right, part of me wanted to believe a soldier needed something to hold onto, something more than commands and duty. But never Simon. The words *I told you so* are etched into his face. He's so desperate to tell me that my insistence on attachments has made me sloppy and weak. He's wondering what happened to *his* Alexandra; the focused, determined, well-trained operative with no fucks given, the woman who saw everything, the person that was always ten steps ahead. He's telling himself that I'm worse off since leaving him. That I'm lost without him. But somehow, along this devastating path, I've retrieved the person I once was. It might not make me the most efficient soldier, and it certainly makes me a liability, but it also makes me human—a flawed, fallible human.

Simon nods obediently as Collins runs through the agenda, but his fingers twitch now and again. He's desperate to take charge and lead this operation. It's in his nature to be the alpha. Unfortunately for him, this room is full of them. For the most part, Gabriel ignores him, acting bored the minute he opens his mouth to speak. In fact, Gabriel appears totally disinterested in this entire meeting, but it's an act that no longer fools me. I see the concern in his eyes as they frequently drift to mine. It's like he has to check up on me, in case I crack right here at the dinner table. *He knows me so well.* I do want to crack. I want to scream. I want to tear the whole bloody room apart.

'Lex?' Gabriel's soft drawl cuts through my thoughts.

I look up to see the entire room staring at me expectantly. 'Hmm?'

'I said...' Collins starts impatiently. 'If you contacted Olivia, do you think she would agree to meet you?'

I absorb the question, wondering myself... *What is the truth?* 'Only if she thought I was handing myself over.'

'Out of the question,' Gabriel jumps in.

'She can handle herself, Detective.' Simon interjects.

My father's eyebrows shoot towards his hairline. Gabriel's dark, intimidating stare pincers Simon to the spot. If looks could kill, Simon would have fallen off his chair instantly.

'She might be able to handle herself, but I believe, and I'm sure Mario would agree, that she shouldn't have to in this instance.'

'She is sitting at the table and can also speak for herself,' I interrupt them, irritated.

Collins clears her throat. 'I am going to suggest that Alexandra speaks to her sister on the phone and arranges a meet. I don't intend on her going anywhere. It's my professional duty not to put civilian lives at risk, whether they can handle themselves or not. Julian, Gabriel, and I will be at the location to bring Olivia in.'

'What about Simon?' Julian speaks up, sizing up his bulky shoulders and muscular arms.

'Simon is a civilian.'

'With all due respect, Alison.' Simon looks to Collins. 'If Rhiannon is there, you need me.'

'I need you like a hole in the head, Mr Haines.' She drops her head and sighs. 'But as we're running this off the books and CTC want nothing to do with us,' she mumbles. 'I'm inclined to allow it.'

'Simon can go instead of Gabriel,' I blurt out.

Five heads turn towards me simultaneously.

Gabriel's eyes soften; he recognises the look in my eyes; he knows I'm afraid for his life.

'He can barely get out of that chair. He'll just slow you down.'

'Thanks Lex…' Gabriel murmurs sarcastically.

'I'm happy to go in Gabriel's place,' Mario announces.

Collins rolls her eyes. 'Can everyone shut up unless I ask them a direct question?' She waits for a moment, making sure she's got everyone's attention. 'Mario, you're not going anywhere. Alexandra stays here, as does Gabriel.' She looks to Gabriel as he begins to protest. 'She's right; you'll slow us down.' She looks to Julian. 'I need you to speak to Roe. He can pull in a favour, get a TAC team.'

'He's still in the hospital, Ma'am.'

'Is he conscious?'

'Yes…'

'Well, then he's capable of making a phone call,' she says decidedly. 'Once that's done….' She announces to the group, 'Simon, Julian and I will head to the meeting point. This is an extraction. We get in quickly and take Olivia to a secure location.'

'Jules, can you give us the intel on the safehouse?' Gabriel asks.

'Yep, we've got an NCA safehouse in Torrington Park. The house has been secured. I'll tell the TAC team to take her there.'

'The NCA will give you a safehouse but no backup,' my father gathers under his breath.

'The safehouse is easier to keep under the radar. Requesting an entire firearms unit attracts more attention,' Gabriel responds without looking up from the table.

'What if Rhiannon is there?' Simon asks, frowning.

'If she's there, then you have to secure her first. She's the most dangerous; if she slipped away, you'd never find her again. Olivia isn't trained the same way; she'll be easier to extract.'

'I'll brief the TAC team.' Collins assures.

'It makes no sense to keep Alex here.' Simon interjects. 'We need all resources. She's a trained S.A.S operative, a very bloody good one.' He turns to me. 'If Rhiannon is there, then we need you.'

'Not in her current condi—' Julian starts.

I cut him off quickly. 'This is my sister Simon…'

Gabriel shifts in his seat, tension rising from him.

Simon studies me with cold ferocity, his expression entirely unimpressed as he holds back the urge to berate me for being soft.

'Olivia won't tell you anything, you know that don't you?' my father utters, looking directly at Collins. 'If you take her in, you can never let her go again. You'll have to offer her a deal. Go in hard – a few years won't scare her; she's done worse stints in psychiatric hospitals.'

'Use the psychiatric hospital,' I interject. 'When you're speaking to her, tell her that's where she's going. It'll be easier to get the information you need.' I notice my father close his weary eyes. 'When are you leaving?'

'As soon as Julian speaks to Roe,' Collins replies flatly.

'You want me to go now?' Julian says, taken aback.

'Now is as good as any.'

We stand with him, and he nods, almost psyching himself up.

'Let us know when it's done. We'll contact Olivia soon after.'

I look at him, my eyes betraying my hesitation. 'Where should I suggest meeting her?'

'It needs to be a public space, not too busy, not too quiet but with accessible entrances and exits.' Simon instructs.

'The German Hospital.' Gabriel suggests, his eyes spiked with adrenaline. 'Let's go back to where it all began.'

CHAPTER FIFTY-NINE

On my father's instruction, I head towards the garage in search of Gabriel's comprehensive weapons stash, keen to provide Simon, Collins, and Julian with sufficient artillery before they embark on the task ahead. Crossing the driveway, I slow on my approach, picking up the sound of muffled voices. I frown at the tense back and forth, the sharp words being exchanged between two people.

'That isn't the woman I served with.' Simon's low, insistent tone hisses into the air.

'What is it you want me to say?'

I recognise the drawl of indifference at once.

'This is because of you… You're coddling her. She's gone up against drug dealers, war lords, every extremist group you can imagine, and you're treating her like a child.'

'You need to respect her decision.'

'She's never turned down a mission before.'

'This is her sister.'

'That shouldn't make a blind bit of difference. She's one of the best. The Alexandra I know executes everything with killer instinct, no matter what.'

'You might want to consider that you don't know her very well.'

'She's diluting her abilities, dampening herself down for you.'

'Simon, you're going to want to let this go,' Gabriel warns, the threat in his tone undeniable.

'I knew it. Ever since I saw her that day with you. To tell you the truth, I thought she was manipulating you. She's done it before…pretends to be fragile to get what she wants.'

'My earlier comment still stands.'

'My Alex doesn't know how to be vulnerable, so you might not want to get too attached.'

'She's her own person. Let her live her life.'

'Let her be with you, you mean.'

I hear Gabriel huff; he's trying to remain calm. He's doing his best. If this were any other person, they'd have been forcibly silenced by now, but he knows what it means to keep Simon on side.

'She's been through a lot. Her father died, then came back to life; she's being hunted by her own sister, not to mention the Turkish mafia and a soldier she served with.'

'It's more than that.'

'Can I go now?'

I hear movement and step back from the door, frantically searching for somewhere to hide.

'I don't think you're good for her, Detective,' Simon calls out, and the footsteps stop. 'She needs discipline, guidance, structure. Six weeks in your company, and she's a bleeding car crash.'

'I can remove you from this team just as easily as we got you down here,' Gabriel warns. I picture his face as I hear the words ejected into the air through gritted teeth.

'You won't be able to control her, Gabriel.'

'We're done here.'

'The Alex I knew was ruthless, cunning, powerful, formidable. That woman in there is a stranger. She's over-emotional, unreliable.'

'*That* woman saved my life.'

'And shot the Head of the Turkish mafia in the process. This is why I taught her to take emotion out of it.'

There's a long, drawn-out silence, and I wonder if Gabriel is covertly strangling him. After a few moments, I finally hear his confident, authoritative voice. 'Alexandra is the bravest, strongest, most brilliant woman I've ever met. Who she was and who she is now is no business of yours or mine. But I'll tell you one thing,' Gabriel's voice lowers, 'whatever she wants or decides for her life, I won't let you dehumanise her again... never again.'

Simon offers a sarcastic laugh as angry footsteps storm towards the door. *No doubt it's Gabriel. All six-foot-three of him about to barge through the only exit and find me eavesdropping.* I quickly hop back some steps and casually walk towards the garage as if I've only just ventured outside. The door swings open, and he emerges, a face like thunder. I smile at him, and he softens immediately, a tiny smirk on his lips. *He knows.* I roll my eyes and brush past him, my fingertips touching his for a brief second.

'Are you alright?' he asks, moving his hands up to my face.

'I'll see you inside,' I whisper.

He nods knowingly, walking back to the house.

Listening to the distant crunch of Gabriel's shoes against the gravel, I brace myself for the difficult conversation ahead. Closing my eyes, I take a deep breath before stepping inside and leaning in the doorway. Simon is propped against the bonnet of a car I've never seen before. *Likely another of Gabriel's possessions I know nothing about.* He's cleaning the butt of a rifle, his eyes fixed on the weapon, deliberately refusing to look up.

'Can we talk?' I ask in a polite, professional tone and immediately regret it. Not only is he not my boyfriend anymore, he's also not in charge of me. He lost that power when we left the Forces. I have no reason to hold back. I have no reason to cower in his presence. 'I'm sorry I left without saying anything.'

'Not now, Alex.'

'There appears to be a lot you want to say.'

'We're in the middle of an operation.'

'I was pregnant,' I blurt out.

His head snaps up, and he stares through me, his mind struggling between accepting his instinctive reaction or stamping it down.

'But I... urm....' I take a breath, continuing. 'I lost the baby.'

'You had a miscarriage?'

'Yes, that's what...I just... I thought you should know.'

'Well.' he replies quickly. 'Thank you for telling me. We said we didn't want children so...' He nods repeatedly, his eyes attached to mine.

'I really am sorry, Simon.'

'It's part of living: loss, grief, disappointment. We acknowledge it. We move on.'

My chest tightens. He thinks I'm apologising for my body's uninhabitable womb. *What did I ever see in this man?* 'I meant...' I start, exasperated. 'I'm sorry for leaving. The military was a large part of my life-'

'Would you have stayed if I'd asked?'

'I didn't have a choice; you know they found out about my father.'

'No, Alexandra. If I had asked you to stay with me...in our relationship. Suppose I had asked you to come back after you ran away from us. Would you?'

I stand rooted to the spot, trying to gauge the reason for his question. *He's always been so hard to read.* 'No.'

'Then it's for the best, isn't it?' He instantly looks down, busying himself with the rifle once more.

I swallow the shock of his callous reaction. Quickly turning away, I forget all reason for being in the garage in the first place as the overwhelming urge to get away from him takes hold.

'Why aren't you coming with us?' he calls out after me. 'You might enjoy Gabriel's role of protector now, but I know you, it'll bore you eventually.'

'This isn't about that, Simon.'

'You need to get a grip, soldier.' His authoritative words cut through the air like a knife. 'Take yourself on a run; think about it. We need you in the field.'

'We both know what happened in Beirut. It's an unpredictable situation. Not to mention, she killed our best friend.'

'We were following orders.'

'We left two soldiers behind.'

'And you're leaving me to deal with the fallout alone.'

'We're not in the Forces anymore.'

'So, the rules don't apply? The very foundations of your discipline, the moral code you swore to uphold.'

'The world is not black and white, Simon; it never has been. The notion might have helped you pull the trigger in Bosnia, Iran, Beirut… and God knows where. But there's a huge grey area.'

'And where did you get the impression that you deserve the luxury of the grey? You follow orders.'

'Islamabad. That's where,' I snap, recalling the faces of three innocent, brainwashed boys.

'You're weak, and you're attributing that weakness to one incident.'

'Tell yourself what you need to make you sleep at night.'

'They were terrorists.'

'They were children!' I yell, my blood boiling from the indignation on his face.

'It's a good thing you aren't coming because you're totally lost. I can see that now.'

'For the first time in years, I know exactly who I am.' I turn towards the door, desperate to get away from him.

'You can't just cut away that part of you!' He shouts after me. 'The trained killer… it doesn't go away.'

'I know.' I scoff, shaking my head. 'You made sure of it.'

CHAPTER SIXTY

Abeer holds the vest, looking up at me. I calmly tell him to place it down; slowly, gently. He carefully rests it on the floor, his eyes so full of fear, his arms shaking as he sets it down. I hold my hand out, telling him it's alright, he can come with me now. He's safe. Nobody will hurt you anymore. He takes my hand, and we turn towards the door. I take a step, but he drags his feet. I look back. Abeer has gone. In his place is another child... my child. A little boy, staring up at me with wide, frightened eyes, eyes that are pleading with me to save him. I crouch down, desperate to pick him up and hug him tight. I wrap my arms around him, but he begins to fade. I hold on, pulling him into me, trying to keep him there. I yell, crying his name, begging him to stay. But his existence withers until I'm sitting in the compound alone with nothing left.

I wake, quickly reaching down to my stomach before I'm reminded of the harsh reality. Hairs on my skin raise, alerting me to the impending sadness. I sigh, willing myself to get out of bed, moving past the misery with a stern determination. Gabriel is absent. *Can't he stay put and not have me frantically searching for him at any given moment?* Putting everything else aside, I move out of the room and descend the stairs, sensing something in the air.

'Stay there Lex...' Gabriel's low voice demands from the sofa. He's sat in nothing but joggers and a Kevlar vest, barely looking up from assembling the pistol in his right hand.

'What's going on?'

'Something's off.'

'What do you mean?' I ask, my eyes frantically searching the living room.

'Stay where you are.'

'Tell me what is going on.'

He grabs a second pistol from the table, throwing it at me. I catch it quickly and switch the safety off. 'Collins and the TAC team have gone dark.'

'Right...'

'It's been 2 hours. There's been no call. No text. I can't reach Simon or Julian.' He exhales. 'Something happened. I know it.'

'Maybe your father intercepted them...'

'I've left Edward a message...Step away from the window.' He jumps up and pulls me towards him.

'What's going on?' Mario appears from the staircase.

I look up at him, not knowing the answer, as all three of us register the footsteps on the gravel outside.

My father's bemused eyes dart from me to Gabriel and back to me. I signal for him to stay low, creeping backwards against the wall. My hand grips the pistol, my body's braced for action. Abruptly the footsteps stop, depositing an uncomfortable weight of silence in the air. Gabriel turns, the fear in his eyes converting to realisation as a violent blistering of bullets tears through the front door. Rattling through the air, they penetrate the walls, splintering the furniture, shattering glass everywhere.

'Gabriel! Get her out!' my father yells with brittle panic.

Having assessed our slim chances of escaping, Gabriel turns, abruptly slamming his hand into my chest, throwing me over the sofa with full force. He only narrowly misses the second round of bullets himself as he dives after me, pulling the sofa with him to shield us from another inevitable assault. I throw him a look of concern, hearing the front door abruptly kicked open.

He locks his eyes to mine, mouthing. 'You ok?'

I look down at my body and nod before quickly scanning him for bullet holes, relieved when I see that, for now, he appears unscathed. He reaches around to unstrap his vest, pausing when I frantically shake my head. He raises his eyebrows, his dark eyes disapproving before removing it completely and hurriedly shoving it in my direction. I throw it on, noticing my father peering around the corner from the top of the stairs. He's clutching a shotgun in both hands. Aware that we're completely exposed from behind, I gesture for Gabriel to stay put, signalling my plan to crawl into the kitchen and secure the back of the house. He starts to protest, but he knows one of us has to do it. And he's not exactly mobile. He eventually nods, ready to cover me. I begin to army crawl towards the doorway when a sudden crunching from the kitchen brings me to an abrupt halt. I've heard that noise countless times before. *Heavy-duty boots on broken glass.*

'I'll cover you...' Gabriel mouths.

I quickly stand, checking the silent space around us. *Nothing.* Gabriel follows before looking at me, confused. The room has gone from being under siege to an unsettling nothingness in a matter of seconds. It's empty. I turn and train my eyes ahead, heading towards the kitchen and flattening my back against the wall. I look to Gabriel to tell me I'm clear. He offers a reassuring nod. I take a step forward, instantly colliding with Levi Nabilla, Diren Paytak's right-hand man, who steams around the corner, his gun trained in front of him, the sawn-off end swinging between his hands as his body slams into mine. For a second, he yells in a coarse Turkish accent, his small, black eyes regarding me with shock. A look that only lasts a few seconds before the gun twitches in his hand. I quickly flick the muzzle of my own weapon to his temple and instantly pull the trigger. Bone and brains spurt outward across my face and shoulders before his body falls to the floor.

'Gabriel!' I shout, spotting another gunman at the front door.

Gabriel dives for cover, throwing himself up the stairs as a stream of deadly bullets is ejected into the air. I drop to the floor, ducking behind furniture, determined to get as close as possible to the perpetrator before they close in on him. I wait for the bullets to stop, count to three and spring up, taking full advantage of my Kevlar protection. Cold, black eyes regard me with surprise from behind the black balaclava. With very little time to react, I yank my finger against the trigger, over and over, firing rounds with an unrelenting stubbornness; my brain set on one clear objective. The man drops to the floor, and I race to the front door, needing to know for sure that the threat has been eliminated.

Without warning, a final shot resounds from behind me, the waves of its existence ricocheting around the room. I turn back quickly, my gun braced for a reaction, only to see Gabriel standing above a third, now deceased, shooter by Levi Nabilla's corpse.

'Everyone alright?' my father calls out.

'We need to get out of here,' Gabriel says, moving towards me, his eyes neurotically searching my body. 'You good?'

I stare back, unable to respond, my mind racing. There are so many unsecured areas of this house. We need to get to the weapons in the garage. *How did they get here? How did they know? Where are the others?*

'Lex?' Gabriel says forcefully.

'Let's get to the garage, pick up what we can. Then we need to leave.' I offer a small smile that doesn't reach my eyes.

'Oh, but I was so looking forward to a reunion.' A familiar voice cuts through the air.

I turn to see a pistol pressed into my father's skull. My sister stands ahead with Rhiannon Benson. They look between us, their expressions fixed with sadistic grins, enjoying the pain of realisation on our faces.

GABRIEL

CHAPTER SIXTY-ONE

'Olivia... you need to stop this.' Toff shouts, attempting to discipline his daughter.

She ignores him before nodding at Rhiannon, who quickly registers the insinuation and throws Toff into a chair, slamming the butt of her gun into the base of his skull. A crack of metal against bone resounds around the room. His head lolls forward, unconscious.

'This is what's going to happen,' Olivia directs with a clear, calm inflection. 'Both of you are going to lower your guns to the floor and kick them to me, or Rhiannon is going to decorate the walls with Daddy's brains.'

I try to form my thoughts into working order, assessing the distance between us, running through the possibilities of rattling off two shots in quick succession before Rhiannon has a chance to think. But as I listen to the panicked breath of the person next to me, I realise the risk is just too great. *I can't lose her.* I nod at Lex, instructing her to lower the gun as I do the same, both of us kicking our weapons away.

'Olivia... is this who you want to be?' Lex says before glancing at me from the corner of her eye. *She's stalling for time.*

'Oh, this is me, Alexandra. This is exactly me.'

She's high. Her pupils are practically saucers. Her eyes dart erratically between Lex and Toff, then back to Lex, her tongue repeatedly darting out to lick the corner of her mouth as she does so. *So that's how Diren Paytak inspired her loyalty, keeping her hooked with drugs.*

'Why?' Lex asks before turning to Rhiannon. 'You should have kept this between us.'

'There will be time for that,' Rhiannon replies coldly.

Olivia tuts. 'Don't bully poor Rhiannon. She's just the hired help.'

'This is madness. Do you understand what you've got yourself into? Do you understand what these people do?' Lex yells.

'It's just business, Alexandra.'

'Did Diren do this to you? Did he make you this way?' '

'Don't you say his fucking name!' Olivia fires the words out, her composure dropping like an iron curtain.

'I know everything-'

'Stop fucking talking.'

'Does it seem right to turn against your own family?'

'What did I just say?'

'Is that why you're here? To avenge him…'

'Say it out loud. Say what you did!'

'I had no choice.'

'You murdered him!' Olivia bellows. 'You took away the one…' She stops, regaining composure. 'He was my person!' She takes another step forward.

My breath catches in my throat, unable to bear the sight of Olivia's weapon drawing closer to Lex's body. Rhiannon clocks my sudden movements and takes a step forward, shifting her pistol to aim it at my head, warning me with robotic blue eyes. Her face appears pinched by the hard, brown ponytail pulling the skin-tight across her forehead, giving her a more severe, intimidating look. She cocks her head slightly, working out a better vantage point for her aim.

'Wait!' Lex shouts. 'Wait, let's talk about this. Let's figure this out.'

'We know you love the sound of your own voice, Alexandra, but please, give us a fucking break.' Olivia quips.

'Just please explain to me why you're doing this. I need to understand.'

'Because like him...' She throws the weapon in Toff's direction. 'I'm running a business, and that comes first.'

'A business that harms innocent children. A business that involves working with an organisation funding terrorism?'

'The world is a disappointing place... It's survival of the fittest. I learnt that real early on. When you both insisted on sending me away, locking me up in one hospital after the other, he helped me. He visited me.'

'You were sick, Olivia. We just wanted you to get better.'

'He was there when you rejected my pleas to come home. He was the one who took me in!'

'It was for your own good!'

'How the fuck did you know what was good for me? You ignored me your whole life. Diren gave me meaning. He gave me the attention I deserved. He made me a part of something special. And then you took him away. It's what you do, Alexandra. You take, and you take.' She cocks the gun, pressing it against Lex's head.

My body lurches with fear. *I have to distract her.* 'The truth is Olivia...' I start, needing her focus pulled away from her sister. 'No matter what happened to you as a child, there's always a choice. You could have risen from the shadow of your sister, but instead, you chose to sink into darkness. You chose to be resentful because that's so much easier. Trust me, I've been there.'

Olivia scoffs, shaking her head.

I continue, eager for her attention to be focused solely on me. 'But you're not free. All you've done is jump from one man's approval to the next.'

'Someone's been in therapy before.' She raises her eyebrows.

'Help me out here... as I think I'm shaping up quite the story. Diren needed to pay off his debts to the cartels, so you both agreed to work for The Singularity. They paid you a large sum of money to traffic children across the continent. You have access to all of their resources. And with Aldyn Wolfe's warehouses, it's been working very well for you, hasn't it? You had Kristine Kingley. You had Amber on speed dial. But your father was an issue; he might have turned a blind eye to the Hellbanianz, but this is different. This is children, and you knew he wouldn't allow it, so you thought you'd use your position as Mario's daughter to get rid of him. The Turks could traffic for Higgs without Toff's interference, and it cleared the way for you to be with your twisted boyfriend, living out all your weird Stockholm Syndrome shit.'

There's an unexplainable twinkle in her eye. *She's enjoying this.* I'd go as far as to say that she's proud.

I continue... 'You thought Toff was gone, The Singularity was paying you, everything was good. But then your sister decides to come back to London, and you hadn't expected that, did you? She's always been away, travelling the world. You didn't think she had any interest in being here, and it scared you. Because you know what she's capable of. You've read all her journals; you know what she's done in the past. And it made you panic. So, you and Diren went back to The Singularity to access Freeman Powell. You hired someone that could rival your sister's skillset.'

'Detective, this is a family matter; I'll ask you to keep out of it.'

'British Intelligence is after your little pet, Olivia. They hired Charles McGuire to find her. And they won't stop. Not until they have you both.'

'Rhiannon... shoot him.'

'No!' Lex shouts.

'Rhiannon!' Olivia yells again.

Rhiannon steps forward.

'No!' Lex sobs. 'You're here for me! Take me!' She insists, beating her palms against her chest. 'You want me, please just take me.'

'Rhiannon!' Olivia screams.

I turn to Lex for what I deem to be the last time, but there is no resignation there. Her body is braced, she's not giving up that easily. She lurches forward, diving across the room. I duck, shielding myself from the reactionary bullets being discharged in our direction until suddenly, they cease. Lex has Rhiannon, pulling her backwards in a chokehold, using her as a shield. Olivia grips her gun hesitantly, aware she won't be able to get a clear shot without taking Rhiannon down too.

'Beirut or no Beirut. I should kill you for McGuire,' Lex snarls, holding a knife to Rhiannon's neck, the exact knife that was strapped to my ankle mere seconds ago. 'For Kristine and Samantha... for nearly murdering Gabriel.'

'Now Alexandra...' Olivia warns.

'Drop the fucking gun, Olivia.'

'You really are just wasting time.' Olivia comments with a casual impassivity. 'You're all going to die here either way.'

'Drop the gun, or I'll do to her what she did to McGuire.'

Olivia's body tenses with frustration before she lowers the gun to the floor, her eyes scorching daggers into her sisters.

'Kick it to Gabriel.'

She turns her thunderous expression to me, shifting her foot forward before her boot slides the weapon across the floor.

I bend to retrieve it, placing it carefully in my holster.

'Tell me what's happening to the children.' Lex demands, her forearm tightening around Rhiannon's neck, the knife's edge pressing into her skin.

'How's that any different to the things Mario did for his business?'

Mario's deep, throaty chuckle vibrates from across the room. 'All these years, I thought I taught you better.'

'If you had just paid the ransom, then none of us would be here!' Olivia snaps sharply.

I jerk my head back, surprised by the revelation.

'It's not like you were short on cash!' she yells.

'Calm down, Olivia.' Lex warns as Rhiannon continues to struggle.

'He left me for four months, Alexandra. Four months!'

'That's not true!' Lex protests. 'Is that what Paytak told you?'

Olivia's expression stills, her drugged-up, harrowing gaze resting on her sister with a chilling serenity. 'And that is why you have to die, Lexy. You will never see how evil he is. You'll always fight back.'

She reaches behind her, her fingers enclosing around a second, smaller pistol with every intention of pulling the trigger, suddenly willing to sacrifice her own henchman in the process. *I won't watch this happen.* Drawing a sharp breath, I throw myself forward, flying towards Olivia. Ramming her into the wall, I catch the butt of her gun in my right hand and angle it away from my head. It goes off with resounding explosivity. I drag her down to the floor, straddling her writhing torso, holding her wrists in a tight grip above her head. Her eyes take on a crazed gleam as she turns, cutting daggers into Lex's face. I throw the pistol to Lex. She skilfully switches the knife for the gun, training the butt of the weapon into the small of Rhiannon's back before shoving her down on the sofa.

'Now...' Toff walks over to Rhiannon. 'You're going to tell us everything you know about The Singularity, or I'll put so many bullet holes in your body, you'll look like a fucking sieve.'

I throw Olivia down next to Rhiannon. 'Who is Higgs?'

She grins, a wide sneering expression.

'How could you work with him?' Lex asks accusingly. 'Where's your code?'

'I have a code,' Rhiannon snaps, leaning forward. 'I have a code!' she repeats with the same distant look in her eyes, a reflection of the way I found Lex in the warehouse. 'Do you know what we were doing on those ops? Of course not. You were too busy fucking the team commander. You didn't care what you were shooting as long as you had a gun in your hand. What I'm doing now is no different to what you've done your whole life! B Squad were manipulating history, re-writing, and re-framing everything, causing wars, covering up for corrupt politicians, ruining lives. We were just expensive housekeepers, changing the course of the world in an unnatural way.'

'Is this what Higgs has brainwashed you with?'

'I saw your file,' she sneers. 'I know what happened in Islamabad.'

'She's riling you up on purpose, don't buy into it.' I warn.

Rhiannon continues. 'That is why I'm so surprised that you can't see things their way. You saw what happened. You've learnt how the world truly works.'

'You weren't there.'

'Poor Abeer, forced to make bombs for his uncle, enduring injury after injury, burnt to shit, too afraid to say no. Rumour has it... he was unarmed and surrendering to you. That's why it didn't surprise me when you left us to die. I knew what Haines was capable of. I saw the pictures of those boys.'

'Shut up...' Lex whispers, closing her eyes.

Rhiannon watches on, enjoying the show with sick distortion. 'Gibbs told me everything. I can't remember – which one of you shot him and his little brothers?'

Lex's eyes spring open, her face set with vengeful purpose as she flicks the knife out, driving it straight into Rhiannon's leg. 'That is for what you did to Gabriel.' She yells amidst agonising howls. 'And that…' She says as she pulls it out, '…is for McGuire!' She drives the knife in again, this time opting for Rhiannon's other leg. Rhiannon wails, her eyes bulging as her chest begins to heave. Lex moves in closer, her voice low. 'You work for an organisation that murders innocent people and traffics children. This is the very least of what you deserve.'

'At least I'm part of something bigger now,' Rhiannon manages to say, sweat dripping down her face.

'What happens to the children!?' Lex demands, holding the knife up again. 'What does Higgs do with them?'

'What makes you think Rhiannon has all the answers?!'

'You're high, Olivia,' I interject, 'Your addiction drives everything you're doing here.'

Olivia looks up at her sister, her wide, black pupils bulging with rage. 'I told them to leave you until last, Lexy. Just so you know what it's like to lose everything.'

'Told who?' Lex shouts, her attention shifting. 'Told who, Olivia?!'

'If my contacts don't hear from me in the next five minutes, they're sending people here. They're coming for you.'

I grasp the weapon in my holster as my eyes dart to the front door and out to the driveway. The vision of what's to come bleeds into my brain. An image of Lex standing here with our lifeless bodies taunts me with a nauseating realisation. And in the brief second my mind is elsewhere, Rhiannon lurches up from the sofa, punching the knife out of Lex's hand, pulling her across the room. I try to take aim, unable to get a clear view of Rhiannon whilst Lex struggles against her.

'Don't shoot, Gabriel, please!' Toff begs, restraining Olivia.

Lex throws her head back into Rhiannon's face. A crack of bone resounds, causing her nose to start bleeding instantly, but Rhiannon barely flinches. Instead, she uses the little strength she has left to drag Lex into a stranglehold, forcing her grip tighter with every passing second.

Olivia seizes the opportunity, elbowing Toff in the face before splitting free and scrambling for Lex's discarded gun. 'Step away from Rhiannon, Gabriel!' I turn, eyeing the pistol trained against her father. 'Put your gun down.'

Lex's face is drained of colour, her complexion matching the sheet-white strain of her knuckles as she grips Rhiannon's arm, fighting against her. I look down at the gun in my hand, listening to Olivia's raging demands for me to drop it, her impatience increasing by the second. Knowing I have to act fast, I glance at Toff. He nods, with acceptance in his eyes. There is one priority between us. He trusts that I would rather die than let anything happen to his daughter. As would he. His eyes implore me to act, encouraging me to do what's right, saving the person we both love more than anything. Olivia continues to yell at me over and over, her finger nestled determinedly against the trigger, more than willing to murder her own flesh and blood to regain control. I throw all existence of her to the back of my mind and tighten my grip.

'Are you listening to me, Gabriel!?' Olivia bellows. 'If you take another step towards Rhiannon, I will kill him!'

I draw my next breath, barely registering her words, before swinging the pistol to Rhiannon and pulling the trigger, watching the bullet enter the space between her eyes. Another shot cracks around the room, the echoes of its release thrown into the air. I close my eyes, bracing for impact, expecting darkness to prevail. My ears ring. My head pounds, blocking me from obtaining any insight into what's happening. Finally, the high-pitched chiming of my eardrums subsides, and I hear a pained cry of alarm; the harrowing sound instantly narrows my brain into focus. I process the scene, my consciousness stepping into sixth gear. Rhiannon is dead. Olivia is gone. Lex is crouched over an unresponsive figure, her shaking hands covered in blood. She mutters and pleads over the body. Mario's body. The man who just took a bullet to save everyone's life.

CHAPTER SIXTY-TWO

I tear Toff's shirt open to get a look at the wound at the base of his neck.

'It's not working. It's not fucking working! We need an ambulance!' Lex yells with persistent gushes of blood pouring over her fingers. 'Call an ambulance…please, Gabriel!'

I pull out my phone and dial for emergency services, quickly reeling off information to an operator. Lex stutters reassuring words to a fading Mario, her hands trembling as they try to plug the gaping hole.

'They should be here soon…' I say, crouching down to her level. 'Prop him up. Try and stop the blood flow.'

'I can't!'

'Switch with me.' I give her my gun. 'Keep this trained at the door.' I lean beside her father, carefully shifting him to rest against the wall. 'Toff? Mario… can you hear me?' I repeat, noticing the dark circles under his eyes, standing bold against his paling complexion.

'It's ok, Daddy. Gabriel's going to help you.' Lex reassures, her lip quivering for less than a second before she turns away.

Toff reaches out for her before drifting out of consciousness, the rise and fall of his chest slowing. I remove my shirt, pressing it into the wound, trying to stem the bleeding. 'Help me lay him down flat.'

Lex hands me a cushion, and we prop it beneath his head before I move to start CPR. She stands back, whimpering and pacing frantically, her words flitting between positive reassurances and despairing pleas. I work as hard as I can, exerting pressure on his chest. *Press and release. Mouth to mouth. Press and release. Down and up.* My pulse kicks into action, sweat gathers on my forehead, my arms straining from the constant repetition, throwing all my energy into keeping Mario with us. Part of me knows this is futile; I can feel his body surrendering. My stomach drops as I glance down. His body is limp, only moving under the weight of my efforts. The looseness of his pale lips and the stillness of his face tells me everything I wish I didn't know. I release my hands and press my bloodied fingers to his palm. *Nothing.* I sit back and close my eyes, unable to look at Alexandra.

'What are you doing?' she asks in a clipped tone. 'You have to help,' she demands, her hands tightening around the gun. 'An ambulance is coming. You have to help!'

I stare down at Mario, my chest aching for her. *I'd rather go endless rounds in a chapel with Diren Paytak compared to this.*

'Please help me, Gabriel,' she pleads, dropping to her knees, her fingers clawing at my hands. 'Please don't… don't stop.' Tears eject sharply from her eyes, rapidly running down her face.

Unable to see her fall apart, I nod and resume compressions, knowing it's in vain because just seconds ago, I watched him die.

ALEXANDRA

CHAPTER SIXTY-THREE

I sit staring at the grey wall with an alarming sense of tranquillity. I keep looking down at my hands. Despite the fact I've washed them repeatedly at every opportunity, I can still see my father's blood etched into the fine lines of my skin. I wonder how long it would take to erase all traces of his DNA.

An alarm suddenly reverberates around the room, and a tall, handsome older gentleman walks through the heavy door with a confident air of authority. I scan my eyes over him, trying to piece together his place in all of this. His long body is expertly dressed in a tailored three-piece suit, and his slightly aged, tanned skin glows against the harsh lights of the interrogation room. He undoes the button on his jacket before sitting down. The second those arrogant eyes meet mine, I know exactly who he is.

'Alexandra, I'm the Director of Investigations for SO15. London's Counter-Terrorism Command.'

'Edward James.'

He regards me with controlled curiosity. 'We want to discuss a few things.'

His mannerisms aren't quite like Gabriel's; something about the immaculate curve of his lips pronounces a sense of cruelty. Both men are striking, but where Gabriel's presence is commanding, inspiring even: Edward appears to suck all the life from a room as if joy were a privilege and not a right.

'My condolences for what happened to your father.'

I close my eyes, unwilling to acknowledge his hollow commiserations as a blurred, agonising showreel of my father's body flashes across my mind.

'We need to discuss where we go from here.'
'Tell me if the others are ok… please.'
'They are recovering.'
'What happened?'
'Someone told your sister that they were coming.'
'Are they going to be alright?'
'I have to say I find this very odd.'

I look off to the side, trying to determine the meaning of his words.

'Why didn't you accompany them to extract your sister?'
'Why didn't you?' I raise my eyebrows.
'Answer the question, please, Ms Christofi.'

I shrug. 'Someone with my skill set needed to stay back.' I frown. 'Are you suggesting that I planned to meet my psychotic sister, then called her back, told her all the details, and gave her my address?'

'Gabriel thinks that's highly unlikely.'
'Am I under arrest?'
'As I said, we have a few things to discuss.'
'And they are?'
'You know, many believe you're the cause of all of this.'
'So I'm told.'
'Some think all of this mess began when you came back.'
'And you?'

He sighs, crossing his legs. 'We think they're over-estimating your capabilities.'

'We?'
'My team.'
'SO15.'
'You understand you're being held responsible for a lot of the chaos we see around us?'

'Are you offering me a way out?'

'Perhaps.'

'What is the alternative?'

'Who do you hold responsible? Who is at fault for your father's death?'

His words sink in like a toxin, and I bite my tongue to stop the tears from escaping. 'The Singularity.'

'Let us talk about my son.' He suggests, appearing bored.

'Leave him out of this.'

'Did you know that Gabriel was one of the best investigators in the country? He was going to make director level before his thirty-fifth birthday.'

He slides a folder across the table. I hold his gaze before looking down, fully aware of what he's doing. A mug shot of Gabriel's injured yet devastatingly handsome face stares up at me. I tense to hide my reaction, ironically showing his father how much he means to me. *It's obvious.* He can see it all. I sit on my hands to prevent them from moving. Edward neatly closes the folder and pulls it back. I watch Gabriel disappear across the table again.

He clears his throat. 'An accessory to organised crime, perverting the course of justice, concealing a fugitive, accessory to murder, grievous bodily harm. His life has taken quite the turn since he met you.'

'What is the point of this? I raise my voice this time, unable to prevent his words from lighting the rage inside me. 'What is the point of using him to manipulate me?'

'We both want the same thing here, Lex.'

'Don't call me that.'

'We have to find The Singularity.'

'*We* do not have to do anything. I've lost everything, everyone. *I* will find them because that is what *I* need to do...' I trail off, not knowing where I'm going, but I believe what I'm saying. *I don't have the energy to fight someone else's battles. Not anymore.*

'This is a matter of necessity.'

'You need them for information,' I snap. 'If I found them, I'd kill them all.'

He hesitates, looking across at the dark glass before continuing. 'We think we might be better aligned if we take a different approach.'

'Did you come up with that all by yourself?'

'We'd like to discuss opening a contract.' He sits back in his chair as if he's already got what he came for. 'If you agree, you'll be released today. We'll give you a list of instructions. You'll have a new place to live, a new identity.'

'This is ludicrous,' I laugh.

'Don't you want to bring justice to the people responsible for this? For the children you saw, for McGuire, for your father?'

'This isn't about justice.' I shake my head. 'You realised that Higgs isn't just the man with all the contacts. He's at the centre. This means your agenda has now aligned with the Roe's with Alison Collins,' with Gabriel's. You need to find him because he's the head of the snake.'

'As more details come to light, we will share them with you.'

'You want me to take McGuire's place.'

'Something like that.'

'I'm not an assassin.'

'You will never be expected to act without the full details,' he replies confidently.

'Then tell me what you know.'

'The Singularity is a network made up of high-net-worth, high-powered people who have always used their influence and financial means to further their personal and political interests. But over the past few years, there's been a shift. They've started funding terrorism, sex-trafficking rings, dealt weapons to extremists. They've been behind some of the most controversial political decisions and assassinations in the world.'

I swallow past the dry, anxious lump in my throat as he continues.

'They manipulate governments from the shadows, anything you can think of, they've facilitated it.'

'Why? To what end?'

'That isn't clear.'

'So, you've been aware that they're killing and abusing innocent children?'

'Alexandra, if we infiltrate one spike of the crown, we might risk losing the whole piece.'

'What you're saying is, up until this point, it's suited you to let them sell innocent children into sex rings?'

'We don't think that is the point of their activities.'

'What else is there?'

'Put it this way; we have no evidence these children have been sold on.'

'Then, where are they?'

'We think they are being smuggled across borders. In and out of the Middle East - Pakistan, Libya, Syria.'

I think back to Abeer, the memory of him sewn into my brain. 'How long have you been sitting on this?'

'We've never had a strong enough thread…' He pauses, staring at me intensely. 'Until you.'

'Listen…I stumbled across those children by accident, but I vowed to put an end to their suffering. Some of them won't even remember a time before pain and fear.'

'Right…'

'If I help you, we start with the trafficking. We put a stop to Paytak's tradeline.'

'We can see about that.'

'It's the only way, Edward.'

'As long as you collect the intel we need, turn everyone in, no compromises to the operation.'

I stare at him, wondering how he finds this so easy. 'I presume I'll have access to necessary intelligence, weapons, safehouses?'

He looks at the dark glass before sighing, 'We have a safehouse in Eton Square. You will have everything you need.' My eyes suddenly feel heavy as the reality of the choice dawns on me. *But is this a choice?*

'And Gabriel?' I blurt out, needing to know that his father will help him too. *I can't let him suffer for my actions.*

'He will be fine.'

'When can I see him?'

'Alexandra...' Edward sighs. 'To work with us, you must cut ties. I'm not just saying this because he is my son, but you can't have attachments. It's not safe for you or for...' He stops suddenly, his mind working. 'I will focus on protecting Gabriel. You have my word that he will be safe; how about that?'

I blink a few times, registering this, trying to order my thoughts, absorbing the true meaning of his words.

'You work with us, and everyone remains safe.'

'So, it's blackmail. If I don't comply, then the person I love... your own son, suffers?'

'However you might decide to view it, it is what it is.'

'You didn't say—'

'Alexandra, from the second you appeared, Gabriel's life has fallen apart. He's done things he never imagined. What do you think that means? Think what might happen if you stick around... What will be waiting for him at the end of it? Doesn't that frighten you?'

'How can I trust that you'll keep him safe? How do I know you'll protect him?'

'You asked me to save him... He is my son. It's taken care of.'

I glare up at him. 'If anything happens to him, the deal is off. I will come for you.' I whisper, my chest constricting before dropping my head. 'How am I meant to just leave him?'

He inhales a long sharp breath. 'Let me put it simply, you join us, and he gets to return to his life. You can back out, of course, but naturally, it will become more difficult to overlook your crimes. Both of you.' He exhales exasperated as if explaining to a child. 'If you want to save his life, you must let him go.'

I stare ahead at the wall, fighting despair, the sharp blow of his words crushing my lungs. I grit my teeth, willing my emotions to pull together, desperate to be alone so I can fall apart.

'Think about it.' Edward stands, gesturing for me to leave the room.

He escorts me back to my cell, and I count the steps one at a time, my jaw aching from restraining the rising sadness. Deep down, I knew. I knew I would lose him. Somewhere within me, I envisaged this day, knowing it was coming with every kiss, every look, every smile. Every time I traced his lips with mine, every moment he held me, smiling until my cheeks were on fire. Every second I listened to the addictive sound of his steady breaths, the way he made love to me like he might never get over us. I knew the pain was coming. I knew the way I felt for him was too rich, too pure, too real to survive the world around us. Inevitably he would be torn away, just as every other wonderful thing in my life has been.

I take a deep breath as the door closes, aptly leaving me in the darkness. I begin to lock away every single feeling I've ever had for

THE BURNT CHILD

Gabriel James, packing it tightly away, and pushing it into a dark box. I close my eyes, waiting for detachment, praying that soon, I'll feel nothing.

GABRIEL

CHAPTER SIXTY-FOUR

I count along to the beeping of hospital machinery from somewhere down the harshly lit corridor.

'Are you listening to me?'

I slide my eyes over to Collins. 'Not really.'

Her eyes search my face, properly taking in the mix of green and purple patches of bruising. She turns her head to the door and gestures outside to the nurse's station. 'Are they looking after you in here?'

'It's the NHS... They're understaffed.'

She sits down on the edge of the bed, rubbing her fingers over her eyes. 'All charges against you are being dropped.' She leans over and hands me a clear plastic bag. 'Here's your phone, badge, and various other belongings. Your father's set up a meeting with another agency... You know the one.'

I frown at her. 'Right...'

'You've got a new phone, a new number. There's a safe house you can use until this all dies down.'

'I don't need a safe house.'

'You didn't think you could just go back to your old life, surely?'

'Slow down a second...'

'Gabriel, these are the terms.'

'The terms of what? The charges are dropped, but I have to disappear?' Dread washes over me. *Truthfully, all I care about is one person.* 'What about Lex?'

'We just need you to keep a low profile until this blows over. We have a few things to iron out with internal affairs. Edward is handling.'

'Where is Lex?'

She sighs. 'She'll be fine, Gabriel.'

'When can I see her?'

'Look, don't contact anyone at the NCA for a while. Like I said, we're trying to work things out-'

'Tell me where she is.'

Her eyes twitch knowingly.

'What has she done, Alison?'

'We can't talk about this, Gabriel.'

Logic whirs like an engine, cutting through the fog from the pain meds. Knowing Alexandra as I do, she's sacrificed all semblance of a life to pursue a vendetta.

'I need to see her.'

'Alexandra made her own decisions. Decisions that have enabled you to move on with your life safely. Take the opportunity she's provided.'

'It's him…She's working for him, isn't she!?' I sit up, furious. 'He can't keep me away from her.'

Collins leans in. 'He doesn't need to keep you away from her, Gabriel… She's gone. She knows what is best for you. Listen to what I'm saying and move on.'

'She wouldn't just leave.'

'I offered her the chance to say goodbye, but she didn't show.'

'You expect me to start a new life and forget everything that's happened?'

'Your father will be in touch.'

I lay my head back on the pillow and close my eyes. *She wouldn't leave. This isn't right.* 'And what if I want to find her?'

'Edward has been very clear; you can either be without her as a free man or with her in prison. We've done more than our fair share to help you. More than you deserve, frankly. This is for the best.'

I look down at the clear bag of belongings. 'What about Lily?'

'This isn't Witness Protection. If you want her to know where you are, then it's up to you.' She stands and begins to straighten out the collar on her coat.

'Collins…'

She turns to me, her ice-cold eyes regarding me with something that resembles pity.

'All I ever wanted was to do what was right.'

'There is no right or wrong, Gabriel. We're all stuck in the perpetual grey area.'

She lets the words hang in the stale air of the hospital room before turning on her heel and striding out. Her departure permits the questions to start aggressively flooding in. I need to get back to the apartment; perhaps Lex will be there. I rip the IV cord out of my arm and swing out of bed in search of my clothes.

CHAPTER SIXTY-FIVE

TWO WEEKS LATER

It's the kind of cold you feel in your bones, and the weather reflects the atmosphere. Lily is with me; she thinks she has to come for support. I know Lex won't allow me to see her, but she will be here, no doubt. Whilst she's not at all religious, she will need to say goodbye, then she can get back to whatever mission she's on. Revenge is her anaesthetic, and I know it's helping her get out of bed in the morning.

We sit close to the back. Lily squeezes my arm and gives me a reassuring smile. I am grateful she's here, but I'm irked that she feels the need to babysit me. *Does she think I'm going to drop to my knees and dissolve into a million pieces in front of all these people?* Mario's mother is sitting at the front, between two elderly Greek women. I can only see the back of her head, but I sense her sadness; her shoulders are slumped, her body quietly shaking. One of the women comforts her, rubbing her tiny back. Watching her hand make repetitive, infinite circles sets me on edge, and I start to look around again. I find it hard to believe Lex would leave her grandmother to grieve alone today. The woman just lost her son for the second time; plucked cruelly from her twice. I guess grief ruins your moral compass and makes you behave in strange ways.

As the ceremony begins, my mind wanders. *How life can fuck you so quickly.* This once successful, thriving family ruined by the city that created them. I find myself unable to deter the flashbacks of Mario proudly showing me pictures of his girls. Little did he know, I already loved his eldest daughter.

A family friend struggles through her reading, battling tears, her sadness causing my own eyes to sting, and my hands turn white from gripping the wooden bench in front of me. Suddenly she stops, her mouth gulping, leaving significant gaps of silence. I narrow my eyes, catching her staring over my head. The space around me instantly feels cold; *She's here.* I've stood up before my mind makes the decision. I'm causing havoc, trying to get to her before she disappears. I'm running down the aisle, my boots pounding the stone floor. I throw the doors open and look around the graveyard, my breath creating mists of disappearing fog in the winter air. I finally see her silhouette hunched by a large tree. One arm grips the trunk, the other clutches her chest as she heaves for breath.

    I run towards her, finally able to drink her in. She will always be unbelievably beautiful, but the usual spark of light has vanished. Her complexion is ghostly, her rounded cheeks gaunt, her once maddening curves have faded into sharp angles.

    'Are you ok?' I know the question is futile, but I need to say something, anything.

    She starts shivering, and I hurriedly take my jacket off, covering her shoulders. Reaching out, I try to stroke her hollow cheek, but she flinches away.

    'I'm sorry, I just needed a minute.' She turns, her tone distant.

    'Where have you been? I nearly lost my mind looking for you, Lex.'

    She hugs my jacket tighter and looks away. 'You need to stop doing that, Gabriel.'

    'Do you really expect that you're in any state to take them on? Look at you…you can barely stand up, Alexandra.'

    'It's not your concern.'

    'It is my fucking concern.' I raise my voice before remembering our surroundings, stepping in to lower my tone. 'You are my concern.'

'Well, it's not like you can arrest me...' she challenges, raising her eyebrows.

'You know that all I want to do is take you home with me.'

'Look how well it turned out the last time.'

Her harsh words twist into my gut, and I search her face for signs of hesitation, an indication that this is all a front. I take a heavy breath, deciding to take a different approach, attempting to break through all the walls she built before they're impenetrable. 'We said we would figure it out together, remember?'

'That was before.' Tears give her away, escaping her determined eyes – She's beginning to crack.

I reach out to grab her arm, pulling her into me quickly, desperate to satisfy the longing ache for her. She fights me for a while, but I don't concede, and eventually, our bodies mould to each other. I will for her to surrender, to remember this feeling, the connection I can't and will never shake. I want to cure her the way she once cured me, to glue all her shattered pieces back together, however long it takes. I'd do it for the rest of my life, just to be with her. I keep her like this, wrapped in my arms, breathing in the floral scent of her hair, wishing this could last forever as she succumbs herself to me. I tilt her chin up to look at me, savouring the brilliant specks of gold in her eyes.

'Gabriel?'

'Yes?'

She swallows hard. 'Please...'

She begins to pull away; despite her fingers still being interlinked with mine. She slowly steps back, placing my arms by my sides and takes off my coat, holding it out in the space between us, defiance having replaced vulnerability.

I hesitate, my throat drying as if I've already heard the words. 'Please what?'

'Forget me. Forget this.' She gestures between the two of us. 'I don't want you to look for me because all I see is what happened to him. So please…just let me go.'

She delivers that final blow, and I fight harder than ever to keep my expression neutral. Since speaking to Collins, I would not accept that she would disappear without saying goodbye. But seeing her now provides the explanation I need. *Lex is gone.* I have lost her to the vendetta that will allow her to cope with reality's constant agony. Against every part of my being, I accept what she's asking of me because this will help her carry on living. So, I do nothing. Nothing but watch as she walks away.

GABRIEL

EPILOGUE

The car travels smoothly around the corners of the endlessly winding hills before crossing the border into Monaco. I had hoped there would be more traffic, merely to give me more time, and I draw a deep breath, trying to still the dangerous thoughts threatening my concentration.

I lower the window, craving the warm air after leaving London's unsurprisingly glum and disappointing summer. My parents used to bring us here when we were younger, every May and August Bank Holiday. They said it was a tradition, a family outing so we could spend quality time together, but truthfully, it was so my father could meet up with his mistress under my mother's sanction, like a parent giving a child their fix of sugar to keep them quiet for just a while longer. Being so young, we enjoyed the simple things Monaco had to offer, the wide promenades where we could ride our scooters, the never-ending ice-cream trucks, the kids' clubs, and the sea. I squint behind my dark glasses, steering the car through the Monegasque streets nearly twenty-four years later, acknowledging a new perspective. Somewhere, in and amongst the swell of activity, is the one person I've sought to actively erase from memory over the last eighteen months, and she has no idea I've come all this way, just for her.

The Sat Nav indicates that I'm nearing my destination, and I exhale. I don't know what Lex will do when she sees me, but I'm not expecting a warm welcome. I turn right before the tunnel and immediately recognise the Hotel, slowing the car to a halt. I switch off the engine, look through the reception and straight out to sea, noticing a large glass window on the other side of the building. I take another long breath. *I'm here to do a job. I've got forty-eight hours to get her back to the UK with me.* On paper, it looks straightforward, and if you remove her from the equation, then obviously remove me, it's entirely uncomplicated. I shake my head, loosening the doubt before telling myself to get a fucking grip. I lean back to grab the duffel bag from the back seat before stepping out of the car. I nod to the doorman, who looks more like a catwalk model than staff. He greets me warmly, asking me about my journey amongst all the usual questions. A second doorman, seeming to appear from nowhere, holds the door open before smiling and offering out a gloved hand. I hesitate, wondering how he expects a tip when I'm more than capable of opening a door myself until I quickly realise he's asking for my car keys. I swiftly drop the frown from my face and slide the keys out of my pocket, politely smiling before handing them to him.

Feeling on edge from the unusually attentive service, I practically stumble to the reception desk. A very pretty French girl with warm eyes welcomes me, offering a brief background of the hotel, with details about dining options, dress codes, and spa treatments. I nod along. *If only.* Having been in a rush to get out of the country, I relied on my sister to organise the details. Knowing Lily, I should have guessed that her suggestion of lodgings would be entirely inappropriate. I'm sure I could have found something that was a step up from an MI6 safehouse that didn't draw so much attention. I politely thank the girl I now know as Marie, for her excellent welcome. Pretending not to notice her blushing, I swiftly grab the key card and stride to the lift.

I barely take in the fineries of my huge room before I throw my bags down and grab my workout gear, knowing I need to pace out a few miles on the treadmill to clear my head. In the last few months, exercise is the only commitment I've managed to uphold, not only does it keep me in shape, especially now I've taken up drinking again, but running is the Valium for my scattered mind. And over the past few months, it's become more necessary to replace unwanted thoughts with the dry scorch of bursting lungs, burning limbs, and exhausted joints. Physical exertion is the closest I can get to feeling something without having to feel anything at all.

A few hours later, having showered and changed into jeans, a stiff white shirt, and worn brown boat shoes that almost match the colour of my skin, I sit at the member's bar, watching a French sommelier polish crystal tumblers with a crisp white napkin. I raise my glass and ask the barman for the bill, looking out through the sliding doors, noticing the sea has darkened, suddenly becoming rough beyond the wharf. I stand, leaving my jacket on the stool and head towards the deck of the large open terrace. Placing my drink down, I roll up the sleeves of my shirt and peer over the side, noticing kids have begun to climb onto small sailing boats that bob eagerly on the water. All of them are dressed in matching life vests with the Sailing School crest etched proudly into the breast. I watch as they chat excitedly. *What I'd give to be out on the water.*

A flicker of movement causes me to swivel my gaze beneath my sunglasses, and I almost crush the glass in my hand. Just a few small paces away and completely oblivious to my presence is Alexandra, climbing onto one of the stools on the terrace, her long, blonde hair falling in delicate waves down her tanned back as she talks animatedly to the man opposite her. Every nerve in my body has woken with a hot jolt. And I realise, suddenly, that amongst all the pain I've felt since losing her, none of it has ever come close to this particular twist in my gut. There has been no healing. *None whatsoever.*

Music that inspired The Burnt Child

Daddy Lessons
Beyoncé

Monster vs Angel
WDL, Mawe

When the Night is Over
Lord Huron

Vide Noir
Lord Huron

Ancient Names (Part 1)
Lord Huron

Short Change Hero
The Heavy

Monster
Jacob Banks, Avelino

Midnight Mischief
Jordan Rakei, Tom Misch

Running Up That Hill (A Deal With God)
Kate Bush

Unholy War
Jacob Banks

THE BURNT CHILD

What You Do
James Gillespie

i love you
Billie Eilish

Way down We Go
KALEO

Six Feet Under
Billie Eilish

Us
James Bay

Eye for an Eye
UNKLE

when the party's over
Billie Eilish

Worthy
Jacob Banks

Black Flies
Ben Howard

Acknowledgements

To Henry, thank you for encouraging me to strive for greatness every single day. Also, thank you for supporting me even when I go into *'book zombie mode.'*

To my brilliant Dad, thank you for giving me the gift of stories. You have no idea how precious this is to me.

To my Mum, the most determined, driven woman I know. You are the reason I never stopped.

To John, thank you for all the times you sat with me when my imagination ran wild. Learning to control it has been more valuable than you'll ever know.

To my Grandma. Thank you for always believing in me. Thank you for being my best friend. This book wouldn't exist if it weren't for you.

To my brothers, my sister, my best friends, and family - you know who you are - Thank you for always being there, no matter what. You have given me the confidence and the courage to put this story out into the world. I can't wait for you to read it.

Printed in Great Britain
by Amazon